THE
AUTHORIZED
ENDER
COMPANION

By Orson Scott Card from Tom Doherty Associates

Empire
The Folk of the Fringe
Future on Fire (editor)
Future on Ice (editor)
Invasive Procedures (with Aaron Johnston)
Keeper of Dreams
Lovelock (with Kathryn Kidd)
Maps in a Mirror: The Short Fiction
 of Orson Scott Card
Orson Scott Card's InterGalactic
 Medicine Show
Pastwatch: The Redemption of
 Christopher Columbus
Saints
Songmaster
Treason
A War of Gifts
The Worthing Saga
Wyrms

THE TALES OF ALVIN MAKER

Seventh Son
Red Prophet
Prentice Alvin
Alvin Journeyman
Heartfire
The Crystal City

ENDER

Ender's Game
Ender's Shadow
Shadow of the
 Hegemon
Shadow Puppets
Shadow of the Giant
Speaker for the Dead
Xenocide
Children of the Mind
First Meetings
Ender in Exile

HOMECOMING

The Memory of
 Earth
The Call of Earth
The Ships of Earth
Earthfall
Earthborn

WOMEN OF GENESIS

Sarah
Rebekah
Rachel & Leah

From Other Publishers

Enchantment
Homebody
Lost Boys
Magic Street
Stonefather
Stone Tables
Treasure Box
How to Write Science Fiction and Fantasy
Characters and Viewpoint

THE
AUTHORIZED
ENDER
COMPANION

WRITTEN BY

JAKE BLACK

TOR®

A TOM DOHERTY ASSOCIATES BOOK

NEW YORK

THE AUTHORIZED ENDER COMPANION

Copyright © 2009 by Hatrack River Enterprises

A Tor Book
Published by Tom Doherty Associates, LLC
175 Fifth Avenue
New York, NY 10010

www.tor-forge.com

Tor® is a registered trademark of Tom Doherty Associates, LLC.

The Library of Congress has cataloged the hardcover edition as follows:

Card, Orson Scott.
    The authorized Ender companion / Orson Scott Card and Jake Black. — 1st ed.
        p. cm.
    ISBN 978-0-7653-2062-9
    1. Card, Orson Scott—Handbooks, manuals, etc. 2. Wiggin, Ender (Fictitious character)—
Miscellanea. 3. Wiggin, Peter (Fictitious character)—Miscellanea. I. Black, Jake. II. Title.
    PS3553.A655Z74 2009
    813'.54—dc22

                                                                    2009031592

ISBN 978-0-7653-2063-6 (trade paperback)

First Edition: November 2009
First Trade Paperback Edition: December 2011

Printed in the United States of America

0 9 8 7 6 5 4 3 2 1

To
Michelle and Jonas—my companions forever
and
Ian and Cathy—my parents

—J.B.

CONTENTS

INTRODUCTION

I needed this book to exist, for my own selfish purposes. It's just a bonus that Tor is publishing it so you can have it, too.

I need it because the Ender books are a series I never intended. When I first wrote the novelette *Ender's Game* back in 1974, I had no thought of its ever becoming a series. I felt lucky that I had managed to turn it into a story.

All I had was the battle room, the orbiting Battle School, the ansible (borrowed from Ursula K. Le Guin's word for a faster-than-light communications device), and the fact that kids were using a "simulator" to control distant fleets of starships.

Ten years later, when I set out to write the novel version of *Ender's Game*, I was primarily using it to set up *Speaker for the Dead*. It's not that I was careless or lazy with *Ender's Game*; I was simply paying most attention to the elements of the novel that I needed for *Speaker*.

If I had known how often I'd come back to the world of *Ender's Game*—and, most specifically, Battle School and the war—I would have taken more care to jot down all the choices that I made, so I could refer back to them later.

Instead, I invented things on the fly and forged ahead. I remembered the choices I had made long enough not to contradict them within *Ender's Game*, but not for a single moment longer. (I long ago discovered that, having filled my brain with excessive reading as a child, I had no room for new information. I certainly wasn't going to give up any of my memories of those early books!)

The sequels to *Speaker*—*Xenocide* and *Children of the Mind*—did not refer back to the events in *Ender's Game* very often, and when they did, I relied on memory alone. I take no pleasure in rereading my own fiction—I keep rewriting it in my head, conforming it to the skills and concerns of my present self instead of trusting in that younger self who wrote the original. So when I can avoid rereading, I do.

As I wrote these books, however, time passed and the world changed. The Internet (with the World Wide Web) was not available to the general public when I had Peter and Valentine change the world by writing anonymously on "the nets." But there were services like Delphi and CompuServe.

I got on Prodigy when it appeared, because its graphical user interface (GUI) made it friendly enough for my family to use, and there I first began to talk to readers of my books. Prodigy was a nightmare, however, because they policed the forums so rigidly that I could not answer questions about "Orson Scott Card" in first person!

So I quickly migrated to America Online, where I formed a user group called "Hatrack River" and began to discover how much better some of my readers knew my books than I did! America Online eventually jettisoned us—they wanted higher numbers than I could attract—and we migrated to the Web, where we still are (all my websites can be found by going to http://www.OrsonScottCard.com).

One thing remained consistent in all our websites: When I couldn't remember some detail when writing in any of my series, I could post a question to my readers and somebody would come up with the answer so quickly that there is no way I could have found the same information myself!

While my other series—The Tales of Alvin Maker, Homecoming, Empire, Women of Genesis—were intended to stretch across several books, the Ender books are an accidental series. (The Shadow books, within the overall Ender series, were planned as one long story.) I had no overarching plan. I did not systematically develop the universe in which all the stories take place.

As a result, the Ender universe was not consistent. At the end of one book, thinking I was wrapping everything up, I would send one character off on a voyage; then in a later book, forgetting I had done so, I would have him conveniently hanging around on Earth.

I would give some obscure character a family, and then later forget that I had done so and give him a different family or make him childless. Then that minor character would become important, and I had to decide which set of facts I was going to go with.

When I set out to write *Mazer in Prison*, I couldn't remember if, in all the mentions of him in all the books and stories, I had ever bestowed on him a wife and children. My readers soldiered through my books and got me the information I needed—but how much easier it would have been if the information had already been collected into a single database, where I could look up "Mazer Rackham" and find out every speck of information that I needed.

This book is the fulfillment of that wish. I met Jake Black through other unrelated projects, and he became both a friend and a reliable resource. When I talked to Beth Meacham at Tor and got the go-ahead to bring this book into being, Black was the obvious first choice to take the lead in researching and writing the book. But we continued to use and rely on information we got from the participants in our online community. (They have been credited in each book they helped me with.)

On a purely volunteer basis, the kids at Philotic Web (http://www .philoticweb.com) created a time line that I often used as a resource when writing Ender stories. That time line has now been added to this book.

Stephen Sywak long ago analyzed the Battle School as I had described it and determined a possible shape for the thing. While the artists creating the Marvel version of *Ender's Game* and *Ender's Shadow* have a pretty free hand in what they design, I have referred to Sywak's work when thinking about story possibilities. Naturally, I asked for his permission to include his ideas here.

For many years we had a "Virtual Battle School." It was not a game; rather it was a kind of on-the-fly collaborative fiction, where characters of the participants' own invention would interact in a large ongoing story.

It happened that some of these fanfiction writers had their characters break into the ventilation system of Battle School and start wandering through the ducts. Such a thing had never crossed my mind, but the idea was too good to ignore, so in a kind of homage to my readers, I sent Bean into the ducts in the book *Ender's Shadow.*

This back-and-forth between author and readers is not really all that new. Writers and readers have long corresponded, and it's a foolish writer who does not listen to the fans of his books. I don't always do what my readers wish, but I never reenter a series now without taking into account the story threads they care about and wish to see resolved.

That's because in my mind I do not write in isolation. In fact, I do not "write" at all. I conceive of myself as telling my stories orally to an (imaginary) audience that has gathered around the fire after the day's work is done. I type fast enough that my writing really does come out at the speed of speech, and scientists now assure us that written language is still processed through the aural speech centers of the brain, being perceived as sound rather than as visual images. (We might imagine visual images from the "sounds" we "hear," but they do not come from and are not related to the marks on the page, which merely cause us to know which sounds to "hear.")

When I am actually telling a story or making a speech to a live audience,

I interpret the audience's responses continuously. If I can sense (through movement, coughing, etc.) that they are bored, I move on to a more interesting topic; if I can sense hostility or doubt, I make my statements more clear—or soften them, if that is appropriate; and when they are paying close attention, then I know I am providing something they're enjoying, and I keep on doing it. All good speakers do this; and when my readers write to me or post their responses or concerns online, it's the next best thing to having them there listening as I tell the story.

All of this explains why I have relied on my conversations with readers on my websites, and why I asked Jake Black to write and assemble this book, and how I intend to use it.

But what in the world will *you* do with it? There will be stories in the Ender universe written by people other than myself—Black's script for a one-shot Marvel comic about Valentine was just authorized, and there will be others—but that hardly applies to most readers.

As I write this, I'm in the midst of a semester of teaching at Southern Virginia University; one of the courses I'm teaching is on the fiction of J. R. R. Tolkien and C. S. Lewis. In this course, we have found it useful to consult books *about* the books we're studying. Annotations, critiques, studies of particular issues or subject matters from the books, all are useful.

A growing number of schools are using *Ender's Game* and other books from the series in their coursework. While this book certainly offers no critique, it will be a valuable resource to teachers and, perhaps, students in these courses.

But what if you're not a teacher—or a writer who has received authorization to write within the Ender universe?

I don't know about you, but when I got to the end of *The Lord of the Rings*, I was reluctant to leave the world in which such powerful stories had been told. So I went straight on and read the appendices. They did not give me the story again, but they gave me more of the world of the story, and I was happy.

So if you read *Ender's Game*—or another book or story in the Ender saga—and cared about the people in it, perhaps consulting this book will return you to that world and shed further light on events that took place in the future or past. If that is your goal in picking up this book, I believe Jake Black has done a fine job of providing a book that you will enjoy.

Since I've already had the manuscript of this book for some time, I have consulted it in writing the latest *Ender's Game/Ender's Shadow* screenplay, and in developing the stories for the pre–*Ender's Game* series of comics and short stories and novels about *The Formic Wars*. I consulted this book as I was writing *Ender in Exile*.

I hope that you, too, will plunge into these pages and find much to enjoy, enlighten, or inform you about matters you came to care about in my fiction. Be assured that as you read, you are looking into the very same resource I work with. You can't look over my shoulder as I'm writing—but you are certainly looking at the notes *I* look at while I write!

—Orson Scott Card

HOW TO USE THIS BOOK

This book is an encyclopedic reference to the events, characters, locations, and technology found within Orson Scott Card's *Ender Universe*. While every effort has been taken to be as thorough as possible, this book is not meant to replace the actual reading of any of the novels, short stories, or comic books in the Ender series. It is designed as a resource for fans of the series to augment their understanding of all Ender-related material.

The entries are listed alphabetically, with additional synopses of the novels and short stories included at the end of the encyclopedia portion of the book. Additional essays, charts, and time lines are also included to help readers further appreciate the universe of the Ender books. It is hoped that readers will refer to this book while reading the novels and short stories.

THE
ENDER ENCYCLOPEDIA

Key to Book Title Appearances (listed roughly chronologically):

"Polish Boy"—PL
"Teacher's Pest"—TP
"Mazer in Prison"—MP
"Pretty Boy"—PB
"Cheater"—CH
"Ender's Game" (Short Story)—EGS
Ender's Game (Novel)—EG
War of Gifts—WG
"Ender's Stocking"—NS
Ender's Shadow—ES
"Ender's Homecoming"—EH

"Gold Bug"—GB
"Young Man with Prospects"—YM
Ender in Exile—EE
Shadow of the Hegemon—SH
Shadow Puppets—SP
Shadow of the Giant—SG
"Investment Counselor"—IC
Speaker for the Dead—SD
Xenocide—XN
Children of the Mind—CM

Note: Titles with [ ] refer to character referenced, but not appearing in the book.

^Graff (ES)

^Graff was the screen name used by Bean Delphiki to break into the Battle School computer.

4gang (XN)

4gang was a computer password used by Han Qing-jao to access the Lusitania Fleet project. It refers to the allies of the wife of the first Communist Chinese leader.

Abo University (CM)

Abo University was a school on the planet Outback that supported the Lusitanian rebellion and the preservation of the sentient computer Jane, contrary to orders from Starways Congress.

Abyssian Hunter (IC)

Ender and Valentine Wiggin sought a room to rent on the planet Sorelledolce. They found a place owned by a man described as the Abyssian hunter. He was both their landlord and roommate.

Adornai, Brother (SD)

Brother Adornai was a teacher at the Catholic School in the monastery called Children of the Mind of Christ on the planet Lusitania. He worked with Grego Ribeira, and was once physically injured by the little boy.

Afraima (EE)

Afraima was an assistant xenobiologist in Shakespeare, the first human colony on a former Formic world. She was married to a man named Evenezer, but wanted to carry the child of her boss, Sel Menach, who was heralded as the smartest man in the colony. She felt that his genes would be the best for her potential child to have. Sel refused her advances, and even left his position as her superior to avoid the temptation.

Ahmed (WG)

Ahmed, a Pakistani, led a group of his fellow Muslim students at Battle School in daily prayer, violating Battle School rules of no religious observance. Ahmed had been put up to the rule-breaking by Christian zealot Zeck Morgan, who was offended that a secret celebration of Christmas and Santa Claus had gone unpunished. Ahmed and his fellow Muslims were arrested and taken away in handcuffs for praying.

Akbar, Ensign (EE)

Ensign Akbar was a crewman aboard Ender's first colony ship. He showed Ender and Valentine Wiggin to their quarters aboard the ship. When the ship arrived at the colony, Ensign Akbar tried to mediate a conflict between colonists Dorabella Toscano and her daughter Alessandra. Since Dorabella was married to the commanding officer of the ship, Admiral Morgan, she threatened Akbar with disciplinary action for his interference in a family matter. Ender Wiggin, the governor of the colony, encouraged Akbar to resign his fleet commission and to stay in the colony. Akbar chose to do just that.

Alai (EG, ES, SH, SP, SG)

Alai was Bernard's best friend at Battle School and a member of Ender Wiggin's launch group. Although initially a member of Bernard's gang, Alai teamed up with Ender in the group's first practice in the Battle Room. Together they joined with Shen and Bernard and froze the rest of their group in that first practice.

Alai and Ender became close friends, and both felt a great sadness when Ender was promoted to Salamander Army more than a year before the rest of his launch group. Alai had a tender good-bye with Ender, quietly sharing a sacred expression of friendship as he left.

Ender, not allowed to practice with Salamander Army, put together a group of friends to practice together during Free Play, including Alai. Alai was committed to these extra practices even when rumors of blacklisting for those participating circulated around Battle School.

Ultimately, though, when Ender was promoted again to commander of Dragon Army, Alai believed the lies and rumors disseminated from the Battle School officers that Ender considered himself too good to practice with the "little guys" anymore. Consequently, Alai felt a bit more motivation to defeat Ender in battle. He promised to whip Ender's ass, stating that the wish of peace they'd shared was not to be.

Alai was one of Ender's squadron leaders at Command School (after being at Tactical School for one week), commanding fleets of ships that he thought were simulated, but which were actually real. After Ender's victory over the Formic home world, it was Alai who told Ender about the war on Earth, and the conflicts that arose from it.

He was among those of Ender's colleagues who were kidnapped and taken to an undisclosed location in Russia where he was forced to play war games with his friends. He hoped that they would be able to contact Peter Wiggin who, he thought, held the key to their freedom.

When it was revealed the former Battle School student and serial killer Achilles Flandres was their captor, Alai and his friends were moved to separate locations throughout Russia. They continued their war games and were only allowed to communicate with each other via e-mail.

Along with his fellow prisoners (minus Petra Arkanian), Alai was rescued by Russian operatives. The mission was unimpeded by Achilles who focused his energies only on Petra.

Alai used his tremendous intelligence to achieve a position of great influence in the Muslim world. He led the powerful Muslim League. Bean knew that he needed Alai's help, and thereby the Muslim world's, to defeat Achilles as he continued his plans of world domination. Bean sent their mutual friend, Ambul, to Alai to seek audience for Bean and Petra, who were in hiding. The Muslim world, under Alai's direction, had become very isolated. Getting an audience with Alai would be very difficult, but Bean believed Ambul could accomplish the challenging task.

Ambul was successful, and Alai dispatched several Indonesian soldiers to rescue Bean and Petra, who were to be kidnapped from the Rotterdam women's clinic where they'd undergone an embryonic implantation. Alai promised safety in Damascus. It was revealed that Alai was not only the leader of the Muslim League, but was the Caliph who led all Muslims.

Upon Petra's arrival in Damascus, Alai treated her with somber respect. They were friends from Battle School, of course, but there was an emotional distance between them that they had not felt in their relationship before. Alai promised that while the Muslim world no longer made war on the West, and did not plan to attack China or any other nation, he viewed Achilles as an enemy, and vowed to help find Petra's stolen frozen embryos.

For months, Alai worked with Bean to plan a military invasion of China, freeing the captured Muslim peoples of Asia. Though Alai didn't trust Bean as much as he did the rest of his inner circle, they worked well together. Bean encouraged Alai to contact Vlad in Russia and Virlomi in India and to coordinate their attack with the soldiers at the others' disposal. Alai disagreed, but went forward with the attack anyway.

The invasion of China went very well. The Chinese government ignored the Muslim advances, discounting them as an insurgency. It made Alai a little nervous that it was too good to be true. Petra and Bean reassured him all was well and that it was time for him to make his first live speech as the new Caliph. He would update his people on the progress of the invasion and unify the Muslim world more so than he already had.

Fireworks preceded the speech in Damascus. Many people rushed into the streets to hear Alai address them. Petra and Bean left Alai's compound and watched the speech from a restaurant.

Alai was hailed as a great leader and a divinely appointed ruler. His soldiers were successful in freeing Asia from the Chinese military, and his influence was felt all over the world.

A few weeks after the victory over China, Alai met with Peter Wiggin and Petra. Peter had hoped to find an ally in Alai. They revealed to the Caliph that his people were murdering innocents in India, and that his position was one of figurehead, without true power. Alai, realizing this was true, took greater control over his inner circle and exercised real influence in the Muslim world. While he did not promise an alliance with the Hegemon Peter Wiggin, he reassured the leader that he would prevent further murders by Muslims in Asia and would take greater control as the leader of his people.

To accomplish this, he left the compound in Damascus and headed for the battlefields of India. There he would kill the rebellious general who led his armies in the killing of innocents that had been broadcast across the news nets. Along the way he met with Peter Wiggin, who asked that Alai name a successor who would be loyal to the Hegemony if Alai were killed in India.

Alai made such a statement on a vid, but it was unnecessary. His execution of the rebel general went perfectly, and the soldiers renewed their commitment to follow Alai.

Alai was certain that it would be he, not Peter, who would unify the world. He set up a new compound in India. Virlomi lived in a small hut just outside the compound. Her presence kept the Muslim and Indian people in check as neither side wanted to provoke the other.

Virlomi convinced Alai to marry her, unifying the Hindu and Muslim worlds. But Virlomi's ambition was too much for Alai, and he quickly fell out of love with her. She wanted to overthrow Peter Wiggin and rule the world; Alai had only wanted peace and unity between the peoples. Trapped in his marriage by threat of war against his people by Virlomi, Alai didn't know what to do. All he was sure of was that Virlomi had believed she was the goddess of India and was not an equal as he'd thought she'd be.

He was shocked to realize that many of his followers hated him, joining Virlomi's side because of her expansionist policies. He survived an assassination attempt made by those who were loyal to Virlomi over him. He escaped from India and returned to Damascus where he released a video statement calling for all true Muslims to embrace the religion of peace and to stop attacking others.

He called for revolution, and the result was the breakup of the Muslim world. Eventually, the various Islamic factions would join the Free People of Earth, Peter Wiggin's world government organization of peace. Alai, still believing himself Caliph, nonetheless left Earth to join a colony in space. It is unknown to what colony he went, though it is believed it was Mecca.

Alamander (SG)

Alamander was an adviser to Alai when the latter became the Caliphate of the Muslim world. Alamander was against the expansionist policies of the Free People of Earth, but for those of Alai and the Muslims.

When it became clear to Alamander that Alai was not a true expansionist, he joined a conspiracy to kill the Caliph. Alai killed Alamander during the attempted assassination, escaping to continue his reign.

Albion (*See* Hundred Worlds)

Alvarez, Joao Figueira "Pipo" (SD)

Pipo was the xenobiologist on the planet Lusitania. He worked closely with his son Libo, and studied the native Lusitania life—the pequeninos (or "piggies"). He built relationships with the piggies, gaining their trust, but was forbidden from sharing elements of human culture with them.

He was married to a woman named Conceição, and with her had six children. They were, like most of the population at Lusitania, actively Catholic.

When the leaders of the Children of the Mind of Christ on Lusitania came to him, asking him to see if a thirteen-year-old girl named Novinha was ready to take the xenobiologist certification test, he agreed to let her, though it was early.

Sadly, Pipo's friend among the piggies, Rooter, was killed by decree of the females of his race. In Rooter's heart was planted a tree, which the other piggies would later worship. Pipo and Libo were concerned but fascinated by this development.

A few years later, Pipo and Novinha unlocked the secret of the Descolada. The virus unraveled DNA and inserted proteins inside. Pipo recognized something previously hidden from him and raced to speak with the piggies to confirm his findings. He was killed by the small creatures, but unlike Rooter, a tree was not planted in his chest. Libo and Novinha discovered his body.

Andrew Wiggin was first called by Novinha to Speak Pipo's death. Though the call was rescinded shortly afterward, Andrew was already on his way to Lusitania.

Amaauka, Keikoa (XN)

As a young girl, Keikoa Amaauka fell in love with Han Fei-tzu on the Chinese planet Path. She left Fei-tzu when her family was exiled by the Starways Congress for discovering that the people of Path, who were thought to be godspoken—the chosen vessels for the will of the gods—actually suffered from a genetic mutation that resulted in the symptoms of obsessive-compulsive disorder. They did not suffer the actual disorder. The godspoken were not controlled by the gods, but by their own perceived compulsion.

In order to manipulate the people of Path, though, the Starways Congress didn't allow this information to be disseminated among the people. To keep it quiet, the Amaauka family was exiled.

Years later, the sentient computer program, Jane, appeared to Han Fei-tzu as Keikoa, revealing the research to him.

Amado (SD)

Amado was a child of Gusto and Cida, early xenobiologists on the planet Lusitania, and was killed by the Descolada virus.

Amaranth (SD, XN, CM)

Amaranth was a grain invented by the xenobiologists on the planet Lusitania.

Amato ([EE])

Amato was a citizen in the first human colony on a former Formic world, Shakespeare. He divorced his wife.

Ambul (ES, SP, SG)

Ambul was a soldier and toon leader from Thailand in Bean's first command, Rabbit Army, at Battle School. He was a good, reliable soldier, though he had been known to act insubordinately to commanders whose orders he disagreed with. He was toon leader to Bean's one-time enemy, Achilles Flandres, who had been assigned to Rabbit Army as a test of Bean's command ability.

Years later, after Ender defeated the Formics and Battle School was shut down, Ambul returned to his native Thailand. Unlike the many other Thai students from Battle School, Ambul was not considered to be an asset to the government or the military. As such, he returned to normal school.

When Thailand fell at the hands of the Achilles-led Chinese, Ambul escaped with his family to London. He was able to remain hidden in the United Kingdom for months, surfacing only after Bean, who was running underground from Achilles, contacted him.

Bean sent Ambul to visit Alai in Damascus. Alai, one of their Battle School colleagues, had ascended to a position of great influence within the Muslim world. Ambul was to solicit the Muslim world's support against Achilles and his plans for world domination. Ambul agreed to go on the mission, but was certain it was futile, given the segregated nature of the Muslim League and its general unwillingness to aid non-Muslims.

In setting up the meeting with Alai for Petra and Bean, Ambul made one request: that he fight alongside the Muslim soldiers as they liberate Asia, including Ambul's home of Thailand. Alai approved the request, and Ambul fought nobly and with full commitment alongside his fellow soldiers. He was assigned to a Muslim army from Indonesia, so he would not look too different from his fellow soldiers.

Once the liberation of Asia was completed, Ambul became the Minister of Defense in Thailand. Peter Wiggin, hoping to find in him an ally, contacted Ambul and assured him that the Hegemony—and Suriyawong specifically—were loyal to Thailand. Eventually, Thailand became loyal to the Hegemony, too, and joined the Free People of Earth.

Ancestor-of-the-heart (XN, CM)

The term "ancestor-of-the-heart" refers to the person for whom a citizen of the planet Path was named. The individual so named is to strive to be equal in honor and nobility to their ancestor-of-the-heart, and seems to share personality traits. An ancestor-of-the-heart is believed to watch over their namesake.

Anderson, Lieutenant/Major/Colonel (EGS, EG, ES)

A teacher at Battle School, Anderson held the most confidence in Ender. He was known to pick his nose when no one was looking, a fact that entertained the Battle School students. It was Anderson who put Ender and his army into battles every day, and was the first to tell his superior, Captain Hyrum Graff, that Ender was the "one" they'd been looking for. He was stern and formal in his approach to the children at Battle School, training them to be model soldiers. He first saw Ender when the boy traveled into space toward Battle School.

One of Anderson's primary duties was the issuing of orders. He was also responsible for troop assignments. When Ender was promoted to commander of Dragon Army, it was Anderson who spread the rumor that Ender considered himself too good to practice with his launch group friends. Furthermore, Anderson denied Ender's request for more experienced troops, telling Ender to work with what he had. Anderson also scolded Bean for a rabble-rousing speech in the mess hall, when Ender's life was threatened by Bonzo Madrid. It was he who gave Ender his new assignment to Command School.

When Ender left Battle School, Anderson was promoted to colonel and given command of the Battle School, succeeding Colonel Graff. Following Ender's victory and the end of the war, Anderson was assigned to the International Fleet's Training Division in Biggock County on Earth. He and Graff remained friends.

Andhra (See Hundred Worlds)

Ansible (MP, EGS, EG, GB, EE, SH, SP, SG, SD, XN, CM)

A device that allows instantaneous communication across any distance. Officially called Philotic Parallax Instantaneous Communicator. Originally used only for text information, later version allowed users to appear as holographic images, speaking with one another.

The fundamental principle of the ansible is based on philotic connections: two philotes (having no mass or inertia, but only position) that are connected within a meson are split and carried within the ansible, suspended in a magnetic field. The two philotes remain connected no matter the distance from each other, and when vibration is induced on one end, it is felt instantly at the other.

Antidote Patch (CM)

A medical device, the antidote patch is a transdermal patch that counteracts the effects of similar patches.

Anton (ES, [SH], SP, SG)

Anton was an old man, a former Russian scientist who developed a way to unlock accelerated human development—physical and mental—through manipulation of a single gene within an embryo. His research was meant to be confidential, and to protect it as such, an implant was placed in his brain to cause anxiety to the level of panic if he spoke of it.

When he met Sister Carlotta and she asked questions about the gene, he spoke in code, which initially prevented the implant from activating. He eventually reached his panic point and fainted, having given Carlotta as much information as he could.

Though still suffering from the internal implant, Anton was released from government custody following Ender's victory over the Formics. Petra Arkanian sought him out, hoping to learn all she could about Bean's genetic situation. She wanted to have Bean's children and needed to discover the truth about his origin, and if it could be undone.

Anton spoke plainly to Bean and Petra, trying to convince Bean to marry Petra and have children with her, if only to stave off the loneliness and sorrow that would otherwise accompany his life. Bean agreed, and admitted to himself that he loved Petra. Their children could be, perhaps, free of Bean's genetic mutation. Anton told them that Volescu, who had turned the key and created Bean, could unturn it in the embryos where it might exist.

Anton's life work was complete, and he was settling down with a family of his own. He was engaged to marry a woman younger than he, who had some children of her own. Anton planned to father some children with her and adopt her other kids.

Nearly a year later, Anton was reunited with Bean and Petra in Rwanda where they'd found Volescu working on a biological weapon that would have turned Anton's Key in all future generations of humanity. His wife was pregnant in the natural way, and Anton was excited to be a father.

He helped a team of scientists examine what Volescu had been doing and tried tracking down the surrogates for Bean and Petra's stolen embryos. When Bean and Petra's first child was born, two months premature, Anton examined the baby and learned that it had, in fact, been born with the genetic manipulation he'd discovered.

Anton's Fiancée/Wife (SP, [SG])

Anton's fiancée was a woman who lived in Romania and had several children of her own. She was marrying the older Anton, a Russian scientist exiled in Romania, and was going to try to have children with him, too.

She was pregnant with their first natural child less than a year later.

Anton's Key (ES, EE, SH, SP, SG)

Anton's Key is the name of the genetic code discovered by a Russian scientist known only as Anton. The research discovered a way to unlock accelerated human development—physical and emotional—within an embryo. The person created from the embryo would have higher mental function early in life but have a smaller body. The body's growth would speed up in adolescence, and result in a premature death. Bean was genetically altered to have Anton's Key.

Anwar ([EG], ES)

Anwar was a contemporary of Ender Wiggin's at Battle School. He was born in Ecuador to parents of Egyptian descent. He was assigned to Dragon Army when Ender took command. On the first day in the army, he complained about being naked.

Aparecida (SP)

Aparecida was the maid in the home of John Paul and Theresa Wiggin when they lived in the Brazil-based Hegemon compound. She was dutiful and loyal to the Wiggins.

Aquila, Cardinal (SD)

Cardinal Aquila was a colleague of a man named San Angelo on the planet Moctezuma. When Ender Wiggin Spoke San Angelo's death, he mentioned that San Angelo enjoyed provoking Aquila.

Aradora (SD)

Portuguese for "plowman," Aradora was the term used by the members of the Children of the Mind of Christ, a religious order on the planet Lusitania, to refer to their school principal.

Arbiter (SD)

The Arbiter was the top legal official on the planet Lusitania. He was actively involved in the investigation of the murder of Pipo, the planet's xenologist.

Arkanian, David (SG)

David Arkanian was the youngest sibling in the Arkanian family. He was conceived before the population restrictions were eased by the world government after the Formic War, but was born afterward.

When the world map was redrawn in the era of the new Hegemony, David moved with his parents to Brazil, where they were promised protection from the threats against their lives. When Achilles Flandres was brought to the Hegemon compound a short time later, the Arkanians were sent into hiding by the Hegemony's military leaders.

Once Achilles was killed, David and his family returned to Armenia. They welcomed Petra, her then-husband Bean, and their three babies to their home. David was growing quickly, fluent in Common, and preparing to attend the university near the family home in Armenia.

Arkanian, Mama (SH, SG)

Mama Arkanian was Petra's mom. A housewife, she loved Petra dearly, and missed her terribly during the nine years she was at Battle School. She was scared of the crowds and the press when Petra came home from the school, and didn't go to meet her.

She and her husband had conceived their third child before the laws preventing such were relaxed. He was born after the laws were loosened, however.

Her life was threatened when Petra was kidnapped along with the rest of Ender's team from Battle School. After Petra was rescued and the new Hegemony was established in Brazil, the Arkanian family moved there, where they were promised protection. The protection required the Arkanian family to leave the compound and go into hiding, safe from Achilles Flandres.

A few years later, she was present when Petra gave birth, two months premature, to her first child with Bean Delphiki. Mama insisted that though they were naming the child Andrew after Ender, it was actually after Saint Andrew since children were named for saints, not soldiers.

She and her family returned to their native Armenia and greeted Petra, Bean, and their children when the small family came to Armenia to negotiate a treaty between the Armenian government and the Free People of Earth. Mama reminisced with Petra and gave her advice on being a mother.

Weeks later, while Petra and Bean were involved in military matters, Mama babysat the children. Mazer Rackham arrived and took the babies, warning Mama not to speak about it to anyone but Petra. She called Petra immediately, who raced to the airport to meet with Mazer. Petra telephoned her mother again a few hours later, telling her everything was okay—she'd retrieved the babies and all was well.

Mama and Papa Arkanian cared for the babies, with Elena Delphiki's and Peter Wiggin's help for a year while Petra conducted military operations. *Elena* happily turned the responsibilities over to her *daughter* when Petra returned home from war.

Arkanian, Papa (SH, SG)

Papa Arkanian was Petra Arkanian's father. He picked her up when she returned from the Formic War and offered to get her some candy. They had a bit of an awkward relationship since it had been nine years since they'd seen each other.

He and his wife had conceived their third child before the laws preventing such had been relaxed.

The Arkanian family moved to Brazil following the establishment of the new Hegemony. There they were promised safety from world leaders who would seek to manipulate Petra. This promise required they soon go into hiding, to be hidden from Achilles Flandres.

Once Achilles was dead, the Arkanian family, minus Petra, returned to Armenia. Papa was happy to see his daughter, her husband Bean, and their children during a brief visit they made to Armenia, staying at the Arkanian home.

As Petra conducted military operations, her father informed her that Bean had been killed in combat. Papa wept for Bean and helped care for the grand-children Petra and Bean's responsibilities had left behind.

Once Petra returned a year later from Moscow and her army assignments, Papa greeted her at the airport in Armenia and told her to go home to her children and be their mother. She was still his daughter, and he wanted her to have the joy of being with her children as he'd had in his own life.

Arkanian, Petra (EG, ES, EE, SH, SP, SG)

Petra Arkanian was a couple of years older than Ender Wiggin, and one of the few female students at Battle School. At a very young age, she was taken to Ground School on Earth and was found to be so aggressive that the teachers and administrators there had her DNA tested to ensure she was actually female.

At Battle School, years later, she was a member of Salamander Army when Ender was assigned there. She was an outcast, primarily because of her gender, but nonetheless befriended Ender when he came to Salamander. She slept at the front of the barracks because their commanding officer, Bonzo Madrid, didn't trust her. Bonzo further alienated Petra from the male soldiers by not allowing any of the male soldiers to be naked around her.

She and Ender became friends. Petra took Ender to the Battle Room on his first day for additional practice, though she used much of her Free Play time to practice in the game room. The practices ended when Ender defied Bonzo's orders, participated in a battle against Leopard Army, and was traded to Rat Army.

She was promoted to command Phoenix Army, the second army Ender's new Dragon Army faced and soundly defeated. She was angry at the loss, but still tried to warn Ender that some of the other commanders sought to kill him. She did this because she knew she could fight alongside Ender, helping to protect him. She was extremely talented in hand-to-hand combat.

Petra was promoted to Tactical School, and a week later to Command School where she was one of the squadron leaders under Ender's command in the "exams." She suffered from exhaustion, which clouded her thinking during a battle on one exam. Because of this, she lost Ender's trust to a degree and was not used for a few exams. Though she eventually regained it, she carried great guilt about letting Ender down in the battles and was never as confident or in control as she'd been prior to the exhaustion.

At Command School, Petra became friends with Bean. Although their relationship was rocky in the first few weeks, they became close, confiding in each other, sharing a deep, mutual respect for one another.

Following Ender's victory in the "final exam," Petra joined her fellow squadron leaders and shared time with Ender as he recovered from the tremendous physical, mental, emotional stress he'd endured. She gave him some of the details of the war that had broken out on Earth immediately following his victory, and jokingly said that despite their saving the world, she and her friends would probably have to go back to school on Earth.

Petra and Ender shared a sorrowful good-bye as Petra left space to return to Earth. Ender told her that he loved her like his sister and that he would miss her terribly. She was worried about his apparent obsession with the Formics, stemming from his guilt of killing the entire species, and tried to convince him to let it go. Like siblings, the two shared parting banter, sad that they'd never see each other again.

Petra was greeted on Earth by her father and spoke awkwardly with him as they returned to her childhood home. She had a hard time understanding Armenian, and was nervous to see the rest of her family. Their reunion was joyous, but a bit awkward. She met her newborn youngest brother, David, and remet Stefan, who had been two when she'd left for Battle School.

Petra returned to school, and though she was initially accepted as one of the popular girls because of her heroic efforts in the war, she was relegated to being one of the outcasts/rebels.

She was soon kidnapped by a group of apparent Russian soldiers. She knew it was because of her role as one of Ender's closest allies. After nearly six weeks in solitary confinement, she was moved to another place where she was greeted by several others of Ender's allies. They were forced to play war games, as their kidnapper had apparent designs on world domination.

Most of her fellow captives thought that reaching out to Ender's brother Peter was the key to their escape, but Petra had another idea: Bean. She secretly sent him coded messages in pictures on the nets, but not directly to him. She just hoped he would find them and figure out the message.

She and her fellow captives met their kidnapper—Achilles Flandres, a former Battle School student who had been sent home to Earth to be locked up in a psychiatric hospital. He was a mass murderer, who had his eyes set on taking over the world.

Petra tried desperately to keep her friends with whom she'd been kidnapped unified in front of Achilles. But Achilles had other plans. Despite Petra's best efforts, the group was split up, each prisoner taken somewhere alone. They would be allowed to remain in contact with each other, but not in physical presence.

After several months in this undisclosed, solitary confinement, Petra longed for human contact. She knew that was her captor's goal, but nonetheless felt that she would believe the lies and consent to the demands of the first person who came to her.

That first person was Vlad, one of her fellow prisoners. He had decided to join Achilles and work with him in his plans and had come to ask her to do the same. She was surprised that she didn't give in right away, and Vlad left, rejected. She knew in her heart that if he had come back immediately and asked her again, she would have accepted. But that was not to be.

The next morning, a group of soldiers, led by a psychiatrist, took her from her cell. Her message had gotten through to Bean, and Petra and the others were being rescued. But it was a poorly planned rescue mission.

They took her to a van where she frustratingly bantered with the psychiatrist about the mistakes he'd obviously made in planning her rescue. Achilles revealed himself a moment later and killed the psychiatrist and the rest of Petra's rescuers.

Achilles made it clear that he knew about Petra's coded message, though he had been unable to figure it out. He assumed it had been sent to Bean, and was determined to understand what it meant. He also revealed that he was allowing the other prisoners to be rescued, but not Petra; she was too valuable to him. She had, after all, gotten the message out. In so doing, she proved she was the smartest and best of the ten prisoners.

Petra was taken from the van to an airplane where Achilles almost caused her to be sucked out and killed. But he helped her save her own life, and she resisted the urge to kill him. They traveled to New Delhi. Achilles hoped she'd help him rule the world; Petra had other plans in mind.

In India, she was forced to create strategies for the Indian army, which Achilles was planning to use to take over Asia, and then the world. Petra came up with tactics that were different than the other strategists' plans. She planned to divide the army up so its supply lines would not be a burden. Achilles ignored the plans, though.

Bean had been posting coded messages to Petra throughout the forums on the nets. He used historic code names. Petra read the messages and wanted to respond but was not allowed to.

She accompanied Achilles to Pakistan where he met with that nation's prime minister. Acting as a representative of India's prime minister, Achilles convinced the Pakistani leader to follow India's lead by pulling their military forces away from the Indian/Pakistani border. It was Achilles's plan to convince Pakistan to work with India in their takeover of the world. Pakistan would become the leader of the Islamic world while India maintained its hold on the Hindu population. They would not reunify, but only work together to achieve worldwide greatness.

Petra was shocked that Achilles had so masterfully manipulated the leader of Pakistan. Her appearance with Achilles was made known to Hyrum Graff who told Bean that Petra was alive. They thought she was working with Achilles, however.

It was clear to Petra that she was not in Achilles's camp, though. One day, after a failed assassination attempt on Bean and his Thai colleague Suriyawong that had been orchestrated by Achilles, Petra made an offhanded comment to Virlomi, a female Battle School graduate who had recognized Petra in the Indian military compound. Petra subtly told Virlomi that she was Bresis—the subject of Bean's secret computer messages.

Virlomi took it upon herself to answer the messages, and posted a not-very-well-coded reply to Bean's message that said Petra was alive and not responding to Achilles's demands.

Achilles called Petra to his office and told her that he would kill Virlomi for her seditious message. Petra insulted Achilles, and it turned into a physical confrontation between the two of them.

Knowing that Achilles would kill her for seeing him helpless, Petra used her own skills in manipulation to make Achilles believe she was actually on his side. She kissed him, trying to cover her feelings for Bean, which Achilles had also tried to prey upon.

That night, Petra hoped desperately that Achilles would not kill Virlomi for her message. The next morning at breakfast, she learned that Virlomi had disappeared. She was possibly dead, but it was also possible she had escaped from the compound and was still alive.

Virlomi had escaped and provided Bean and Suriyawong with intelligence to mount a rescue operation for Petra. In the meantime, Petra led a rebellion among the war planners who posted a strategy for removal of India's forces from Burma on the nets. Achilles killed all the rebels and took Petra hostage, knowing that Bean wanted to rescue her.

Bean arrived at the headquarters and used Achilles's Chinese soldiers to make a deal that would allow them to obey their orders by returning Achilles to China, but also to let Petra free. Petra was livid. She wanted Achilles to die. But the deal was made and enforced by the Chinese soldiers, and Petra was safe.

Though still angry with Bean for not killing Achilles, Petra realized that she loved him.

In the aftermath of Achilles's actions, China controlled Asia and aligned itself with Russia, which controlled Europe. Peter Wiggin became the new Hegemon, and Petra moved with her family to Brazil—the new home of the Hegemony. She told Bean that she wanted to marry him and have his children.

Although the Hegemon, Peter Wiggin, had promised to keep Petra safe, she was forced to leave the Hegemony compound a short time after arriving there. Peter had made the decision to bring Achilles from China to Brazil. Bean resigned from his position in the Hegemony, knowing that Achilles would want to kill him. He went into hiding, taking Petra with him.

Petra knew that if she was in hiding with Bean, she would be the safest she could possibly be. She was madly in love with him and continuously made overtures to him for marriage and parenthood.

Their hiding took them around the world. Bean had Petra use the IDs that had once been created for Bean's mother figure, Sister Carlotta. They traveled to Poland, where they met with another Battle School alum, Ambul. They sought the help of the Muslim League and called upon Ambul to help them get it.

Petra and Bean kissed for the first time in a park in Poland. Though Bean swore he'd never have children, he had tender feelings for Petra. Petra, for her part, decided to visit Anton, the scientist who had manipulated Bean's genetics. She wanted to learn all there was to learn about Bean's condition, particularly if it could be reversed in future generations.

Anton told Petra and Bean that Volescu, the scientist who had created Bean in the first place, could unturn the genetic key if it was active in Bean's children. The scientist also tried to convince Bean to marry Petra and have a family with her, stating that reproduction was the greatest human desire.

Bean consented to marry Petra and have children, but only if Volescu could ensure that the next generation would be free of his mutation. Petra was elated. She loved Bean, of course, and he finally admitted he loved her, too.

They were married in Spain, and bounced around the islands of the Mediterranean for a week as a honeymoon. Soon they arrived in Rotterdam, Bean's hometown, where Volescu had set up a fertility clinic.

In meeting with Volescu, Petra realized that he did not have a test to determine which embryos would have Bean's mutation. So, she changed their plans midconversation. Volescu and his staff would create the embryos from Petra's eggs and Bean's sperm, but they would take them to a neutral women's clinic for implantation.

It was hard for Petra to watch as Volescu and Bean disposed of the embryos that Volescu said tested positive for Bean's mutation, knowing that there was really no way he could actually know that. But, he gave the couple several embryos for implantation.

They went to the women's clinic and had the first embryo implanted, and agreed to part ways for safety reasons. They were to meet again in a week. As they walked out of the women's clinic, Petra was put in a cab driven by an Indonesian driver. Bean felt that the taxis that had Dutch drivers were too dangerous. It proved to be a smart move, as the Dutch drivers were supposed to kidnap Petra, and kill Bean. The embryos were also stolen.

The Indonesian driver was working for Alai, and took Petra to the airport where she flew to Damascus. There she would be protected by the Muslim League. Upon her arrival in Damascus, she met with Alai who, she realized, led not only the Muslim League, but the entire Muslim world as Caliph.

Alai promised her safety and that his people would find her stolen embryos. Petra found little comfort in Alai's promises and retired to her room. A short time later, Bean arrived and tried to comfort her as well. It was futile, as Petra had fallen into hopelessness regarding her embryos and Bean himself. She was convinced that Achilles had won, and there was nothing to live for.

Over the next few months, Petra grew sicker and sicker with her pregnancy. She and Bean had remained at Alai's underground compound, and both occasionally advised Alai and his military leaders on how to proceed with their plans to attack China and free the Muslim nations of Asia. She grew more optimistic about life, and consistently reassured Bean that her morning sickness was not his fault.

As Alai's armies fought their way into China, Petra reassured the Caliph that all was going well. She and Bean witnessed his first speech as Caliph via a newsnet vid at a restaurant in Damascus. They had given all they could to Alai's cause and had left his compound to resume their own lives and to search for their stolen embryos.

The search appeared to be short-lived. Achilles baited a trap for Bean, claiming that he had the embryos in his possession. Petra sent Bean to Brazil to regain their children. He joined with Peter Wiggin in storming the Hegemony compound. Petra didn't know all the details, but received an e-mail message from Bean a few days later saying that he had killed Achilles, who did not have the embryos.

Petra joined her husband in Brazil, and they moved in to a small house where they would raise their baby once it was born. And they began scouring the Earth, once again searching for their embryos.

Once again, the search was interrupted as Peter asked Petra to accompany him to Damascus where she would introduce him to Caliph Alai. They posed as bickering spouses, which was an easy act for Petra. She loathed Peter; she resented him for making Bean risk his life on Peter's behalf and for taking her precious time with Bean away from her.

In Damascus, the two met with Alai and informed him of Muslim-committed murders occurring in India. They revealed that many Muslims viewed him as a figurehead without true authority. When his own soldiers confirmed this by their actions, Alai was motivated to assume greater control over the Muslim world. He expressed his appreciation to Petra, who only wanted to get back to Bean.

She and Peter returned to Brazil and with Bean watched as Virlomi spoke out in a televised statement against the Muslim occupiers in India. Petra recognized that Virlomi was rallying her people for war against either the Muslims in India or China. She would marry the leader of one of the two, and fight with him against the other.

Petra and Bean counseled with Peter on the strategy to bring peace out of the impending war. Though Peter was hesitant to listen, they eventually helped him create a plan of action. This plan included Petra writing essays about Hegemony policy under the name "Martel," as Valentine Wiggin had done years before as Demosthenes.

The couple traveled to Rwanda where Volescu was hiding, creating a weapon that would turn Anton's Key in future generations of humanity. Bean nearly killed Volescu, but Petra stopped him. They called in Anton to study what Volescu had been doing and then searched via the nets for the location of all the surrogates of their babies.

Petra gave birth to their first child—a boy—two months premature. It was discovered that he had the genetic shift of his father. Nonetheless, they christened the boy Andrew Arkanian Delphiki, planning to call him Ender. They were surrounded by family and friends in the ceremony.

Bean told Petra that the International Fleet had offered him a starship to travel at relativistic speed, keeping him alive for decades while the people on Earth searched for a cure to his genetic manipulation. Petra insisted on going with him and their children. Bean agreed in the moment, but had second thoughts later.

They would be together in the immediate future, though. Peter assigned Bean to lead the armies of Rwanda. That nation's leader, Felix Starman, had requested Bean in exchange for ratifying Peter's Hegemony Constitution.

Petra did not stay in Rwanda for long. She learned that Graff had found one of the embryos. It had been born a girl, named Bella, and was carrying Bean's genetic mutation. She traveled to Lisbon, Portugal, where her daughter lived with the surrogate who'd birthed her.

It was heartbreaking for Petra to take this child from the family who'd had her for such a short time. Mazer Rackham, who had escorted Petra to Portugal, informed her that the father had lied to his wife. He was sterile, and the eggs they'd tried to fertilize hadn't worked.

Petra returned to Rwanda with her daughter, promising to find the rest of the embryos.

She was sent with Bean and the babies to her home country of Armenia to negotiate the Armenian joining of the Free People of Earth. She and Bean did a good job convincing the Armenian leaders that they would be protected from invasion if they joined.

While staying at her family home, Petra and her parents spoke about parenthood and shared memories of their past. Petra revealed her plan to go to space with Bean and the children, which was hard for her parents to hear, but they understood. They would just miss them very much.

While on assignment with Bean, Petra received a phone call from her upset mother: Mazer Rackham had come to the Arkanian home and taken the babies. Petra and Bean raced to the airport where they got on an airplane with Mazer. He had found five of the missing embryos, leaving only one unaccounted for. Four of the new babies did not have Bean's mutation, one did.

Airborne, Bean revealed to Petra that he had divorced her and was taking the three babies that had the mutation into space immediately. The world would think he was killed in combat, while Petra would know that he was in space. She was not to accompany him.

Petra was crushed. She was angry with Bean and Mazer for negotiating this plan without her involvement. She did not plan to remarry, but knew that she would need support to raise her five babies—and perhaps the sixth missing one, if it was ever found.

Of the new babies that were found, two of the normal ones were named Andrew and Bella to replace the two mutant children who would accompany Bean into space.

Heartbroken, Petra threw herself into her work with the Free People of Earth (FPE) military. She conducted operations in Moscow for a year, avoiding her children because seeing them would be too hard.

When she finally finished her work, she returned to her home in Brazil where Elena Delphiki and Peter Wiggin had been taking care of the babies. She was scared to see her children, and was angry that Peter had been caring for them. But they loved Peter.

Bean had left Petra a short note saying good-bye to her. She was too emotional to read it, learning it existed only after her year away. Peter read it to her, and in the process professed his love for her.

Petra married Peter, and together they raised the five children she'd had with Bean, and the five they had themselves. Though forever loving Bean, Petra loved Peter, too. She stood by his side as the entire world, save the United States, joined the FPE. When Peter died, at his grave, Petra read the book Ender had written from space about his brother's life.

Petra rejoiced, a couple of years later, when she learned that the final missing embryo had been found. Ender and Graff had located the boy on a planet called Ganges. He'd believed he was Achilles's son, but when he learned of his true parentage, he changed his name to Arkanian Delphiki. Petra's last child, found!

She never felt that she was the best, but everyone she'd ever known believed it.

Arkanian, Stefan (SH, SG)

Stefan was the middle child of the Arkanian family—Petra's younger brother. He was two years old when she left for Battle School, and was eleven when she returned.

He moved to Brazil with his family during the rise of the new Hegemony. There they'd been promised protection. They had to go into hiding a short time after arriving in Brazil, though, to be safe from Achilles Flandres.

Armed Soldier (CH)

The armed soldier arrested Han Tzu's father for helping his son cheat on the Battle School Entrance Exam.

Armenia (*See* Hundred Worlds)

Armenian President (SG)

The Armenian president met with Bean Delphiki and Petra Arkanian to negotiate Armenia's entrance to the Free People of Earth, the worldwide government led by Peter Wiggin. He wanted his people to join, but was worried about outside invasion by the surrounding Muslim nations. Petra reassured him that the armies of the Free People of Earth would protect his nation.

Arrow (SD)

One of the pequeninos on the planet Lusitania, Arrow was handy with creating weapons—like arrows—out of sticks and bones. He was one of the pequeninos to speak with Ender Wiggin, the original Speaker for the Dead, hoping that Ender would bring the pequeninos the Hive Queen, so they could learn the secrets of space travel.

When Miro Ribeira climbed over the fence that surrounded the piggies, Arrow was one of those who saw him and wanted to plant him into a fathertree.

As Fábricas (*See* **Hundred Worlds**)

Associated Planet (*See* **Hundred Worlds**)

Ata Atua (*See* **Hundred Worlds**)

Auía (XN, CM)

An "Auía" was a term that could perhaps best be described as a "soul." It represents the life force that binds all living things. An Auía exists in everything. That the computer Jane had one settled the debate about whether or not she was alive.

Baía (*See* **Hundred Worlds**)

Bairro das Fabricadoras (*See* **Hundred Worlds**)

Ballcaller (EG)

The Ballcaller was a device used to retrieve target balls from the Battle Room in Battle School during Ender Wiggin's time there.

Bark (SD)

Bark was a pequenino, the native species of the planet Lusitania. He met human xenologist Pipo and learned that Pipo was a father. Bark was confused that Pipo could be a father without dying, as death preceded fatherhood among the pequeninos.

Barkdancer (SD)

Barkdancer was a pequenino, the native life of the planet Lusitania.

Battle of the Belt (EG)

The Battle of the Belt was an historic battle in the wars between humans and the Formics. It occurred during the so-called First Invasion of the Formics (where the Formics destroyed China), and was in "the belt" region orbiting Earth. Human spaceships were inadequately armed to fight the Formics and the battle was a disaster for the human forces.

Battle Room (EGS, EG, ES)

The primary section of Battle School, the nine Battle Rooms were the zero-gravity training facilities where Battle School students practiced combat in anticipation of their fights with Formics.

Armies fought against each other, using Flashers to freeze their opponents. Victories earned armies higher rankings in the standings, motivating each leader to better prepare his army for real war against the Formics.

Battle School ([PL], [TP], [PB], [CH], EGS, EG, WG, ES)

Orbiting Earth, Battle School was a space station–like facility where children from Earth were trained to fight in the Formic Wars. Students were chosen because of their excellence on screening tests. It was considered by many families to be a great honor to have children selected to go to Battle School.

Students were assigned to armies, and lived with their armies while at school. They trained in combat together, and competed against other armies.

If students did well at Battle School, they were promoted to Tactical School and then to Command School. Ender Wiggin and Bean Delphiki were the school's top two students of all time. The primary feature of Battle School was the Battle Rooms, where students practiced combat and implemented strategy in anticipation of the Formic Wars.

Hyrum Graff was in charge of Battle School, working with several other officers such as Major Anderson and Admiral Chamrajnagar. Sponsored by the International Fleet, the school was turned into the base of operations for the Ministry of Colonization once the wars with the Formics were over.

Battle School Armies (EGS, EG, WG, ES)

The armies at Battle School were made up of forty-one soldiers—a commander and several platoons. They competed against each other in combat locations called Battle Rooms. Scores of the matches were posted in common areas throughout Battle School. The known armies are as follows:

Asp

Badger—Army commanded by Pol Slattery and defeated by Ender Wiggin's Dragon Army.

Bee—Army where Pakistani student Ahmed was assigned when he led the Muslim religious rebellion at the Battle School.

Centipede—Army against which Ender faced off in his first battle as a member of Rat Army.

Condor—Army that shared a bathroom with Salamander. Condor was the army Ender faced in his first battle as a member of Salamander Army.

Dragon—An army of poor repute. Dissolved until it was recreated for Ender to command. Their color code was Grey-Orange-Grey.

Ferret—This was the seventh army defeated by Ender's Dragon Army.

Flame—An army on the list Ender saw soon after arriving at Battle School.

Griffin—An army defeated by Ender's Dragon Army. Bean used his new rope strategy with his newly assigned toon to help defeat the Griffins. William Bee was their commander.

Hound—One of the surprised armies that Salamander beat as part of Bonzo Madrid's quest to increase Salamander reputation.

Leopard—Leopard Army faced Salamander Army while Ender was a member of that army. The eighth army in seven days Ender faced and defeated, Leopard Army was commanded by Pol Slattery.

Lion—A symbol on a door Bean saw early in his explorations of Battle School.

Manticore

Phoenix—Ender was a toon leader in this army at the age of nine. It was commanded by Petra Arkanian.

Rabbit—The first army Ender's Dragon Army faced, and beat. Rabbit was commanded by Carn Carby. Once Ender's army had proven dominant, Bean (a former member of Ender's team) had been assigned Rabbit. Achilles Flandres was assigned to Rabbit as a test of Bean's true leadership abilities. Nikolai Delphiki replaced Bean in command of Rabbit Army.

Rat—Army that shared a bathroom with Salamander and was commanded by Rosen. Bonzo Madrid bragged about beating Rat Army, using it as a step toward increasing Salamander's profile. Rat Army became Ender's second assignment, as Bonzo Madrid had him traded there from Salamander.

Salamander—The first army to which Ender was assigned. It was commanded by Bonzo Madrid, and had the color code Green-Green-Brown.

Scorpion—Bonzo Madrid bragged about beating this army in an upset while commanding Salamander.

Spider

Squirrel—Army that shared a bathroom with Salamander.

Tide—Ender saw this army listed in his earliest days at Battle School.

Tiger—Fought by Ender's Dragon Army and teamed in a two-on-one fight with Griffin Army. Commanded by Talo Momoe.

Battle School Counselor (WG)

The Battle School counselor unsuccessfully tried to calm Zeck Morgan down when the religious zealot took offense that Dink Meeker was allowed to give gifts celebrating a holiday while all other religious practices were forbidden and punished.

BATTLE SCHOOL SLANG (EGS, EG, WG, ES)

As with most communities, Battle School had its own jargon or slang that was used among the community members. Orson Scott Card created the slang used by the kids at Battle School from the following list (note, not all terms on slang list appear in Ender's books/stories):

Aboon: Father; i.e., godfather (Arabic: Abun, "father")

Asliha: Arms dealer (Arabic for "weapon")

Barred: Dead (Arabic: Bard)

Binoon: Especially close friend (Arabic: Ibnun, "son")

Bunduck: A gunman or hired thug (Swahili: Bunduki, "gun")

Chisel: To have sex (transl. Russian expression)

Dayboo: Fatso (Japanese: Debu)

Dakira: Stash, supplies (Arabic)

Dakwa: An invitation you dare not refuse (Arabic: Da'wa)

Doll back: A screwup, can't do anything right (Russian: Dolbak)

Dow: Weapon (Vietnamese: Dao, "knife")

Dull Bob: Idiot (Russian: Dolbaeb)

Eemo: Hick, person who's "out of it" (Japanese: Imo, "potato," derisive term for a country hick)

Emossin': Half-baked, lousy, fifth-rate (Japanese slang: Imasen, literally "a thousand things are missing")

Fedda: Money (Swahili: Fedha)

Fold: Kill; usually "get folded," for "get killed."

Forthwith: A command to appear in person immediately (police bureaucratese)

Gacha: A cop. Sounds like American slang for "got you" which perhaps encouraged Americans to pick up the Japanese criminal slang term "gacha" for "badge."

Git: Jerk (British slang)

Goffno: Excrement (Russian: Govno)

Greek: Disappeared, presumed murdered, as in "He went Greek" (from Arabic: Gariqa, to sink or plunge)

Greeyaz: Worthless trash, said of people or things (Russian)

Grim: Truly ugly woman (Russian: Grimza)

Habba: Death (Arabic)

Hafla: Clandestine meeting (Arabic)

Hakeeba: A bagman, a thieves' bank (Arabic)

Hareess: Watchman, lookout (Arabic)

Jeesh: Troops, army (Arabic: Jaish)

Kala: Fort or stronghold (Arabic)

Kalb: Dog (Arabic insult)

Kay-quop: Thief, crook (Vietnamese: Ke cuop, "robber")

Kintama: Testicle (Japanese)

Koncho: Traitor (Japanese: Kancho, "enema")

Krozh: Loot, winnings (Russian: Kurazh)

Kumo: Electronic thief. (Kumo is Japanese for "spider," and in Japanese criminal slang it means "cat burglar," but it has come to mean "electronic thief.")

Kuso: Excrement (Japanese)

Liss: Thief (Arabic)

Marubo: A violent, dangerous punk. Japanese slang, it means literally "B label," which may have meant "a second-rater" or (more likely) the B stood for boryoku, or "violence," the idea being that as a kid in school, this guy was stamped "B for boryoku."

Messed: Arrested (from Russian: Myesty, "to arrest")

Mintaka: A criminal's area of control, his turf (Arabic)

Myent, Myentura: A cop, the police (Russian)

Moose: A pushover; someone you can jerk around (trans. Russian for "cuckold")

Neeshka: Low-class woman (Russian)

Nessoon: Thief who steals high-tech items from factories and warehouses (Russian)

Nizodd: Struggle for power within an organization (Arabic: niza')

Nuzhnik: Toilet (Russian)

Oomay: A jerk or worse (Swahili: Uume, "male generative organ")

Piff: Screw up (Portuguese: Pifar, "to fall apart")

Puddle: Kill. Presumably from the idea of the victim lying in a puddle of blood.

Rabeeta: Connection, alliance (Arabic: Rabita)

Sabeek: Top guy, big boss (Arabic: Sabiq)

Shirty: Cop (Arabic: Shurti)

Shtuka: Thing (Russian)

Slither: Dangerous guy, snakelike, quick, sneaky.

Soak a noky: Get out of the way (Japanese: soko noke)

Stukotch: Informer (Russian)

Suroff: Accountant for a criminal organization (Arabic)

Toguro: A thing that's really cool (lit. a huge coiled turd)

Tude: Attitude.

Twiss: Freelance legal officer. A Japanese criminal slang term for "kill" is mageru, which means "twist." In America, the term was translated and mispronounced as "twiss," and "twiss boy" was "killer." This became a derogatory term for a cop, and then for somebody only pretending to be a cop—for instance, a bounty hunter, a security guard, a bouncer, or a private eye. The "boy" was eventually dropped so that "twiss" alone came to mean "boastful fake cop."

White rabbit: A small-time crook; literal translation of Japanese "shiro usagi," with the same slang meaning.

Vang: Electronic money, virtual money (Vietnamese for "gold")

Yelda: Male generative organ (Russian)

Zhopa: Buttocks (Russian)

Bebei, Sister (SD)

Sister Bebei was a teacher at the school portion of the monastery, the Children of the Mind of Christ, on the planet Lusitania. She taught Quara Ribeira.

Bee, William (EGS, EG, ES)

Commander of Griffin Army, William Bee was a contemporary of Ender Wiggin's at Battle School, and on the losing end of one of Ender's Dragon Army's victories. He was promoted to Tactical School, but was not thought to be compatible enough with Ender to go on to Command School.

Bella's Birth Father (*See also* Delphiki, Bella) (SG)

Bella was one of the embryos created by Petra Arkanian and Bean Delphiki, stolen by Achilles Flandres, and implanted in a Portuguese woman. The husband of this woman was sterile but he lied, telling her that their attempts at in vitro fertilization had worked. A rich man, he bought the embryo from Achilles, but had to surrender the child it became to her real parents, Petra and Bean.

Bella's Birth Mother (*See* also Delphiki, Bella) (SG)

Desperate for a child, the woman who carried the girl "Bella" thought she was giving birth to her own daughter, conceived in vitro with her husband. Her husband was sterile, though, and the embryo that had been implanted into her womb actually belonged to Bean Delphiki and his wife Petra Arkanian. Bella was born, and Petra discovered her existence, taking back the child that was actually hers and Bean's, and thus breaking the heart of Bella's birth mother.

Bellini, Radaghasye (SG)

Radaghasye Bellini was the president of Brazil when Peter Wiggin ascended to the position of Hegemon. He was one of the first to ratify Peter's worldwide constitution, and was given the top position of authority in South America, governing the continent as more and more of its nations joined the Hegemony, which Peter called the "Free People of Earth."

Belt, the (EG)

The Belt is a region of space not far from Earth's orbit where Battle School, a space station, was located.

Benedetto (IC, SD)

Benedetto had a rich Italian heritage. He worked as a tax collector on the starport at the planet Sorelledolce, and insisted on speaking Italian there, even though he was fluent in Starcommon. He doubted the veracity of Ender Wiggin's identification when Ender presented it to him in an effort to gain access to Ender's pension. Benedetto would not allow Ender access to his trust fund to pay his taxes because Ender had never paid taxes. However, once Ender's assets were revealed on Benedetto's computer, the accountant warmed up to the young man, and was more helpful. Once Ender left the bank, Benedetto tried to use an illegal Predator program to spy on Ender's finances, but discovered the programs he used for such matters were gone. Unbeknownst to Benedetto, they had been erased by Ender's financial program, Jane.

Benedetto figured out Ender's true identity and tried to have Ender incarcerated. However, Jane had restored the files, and Ender was free. Jane confronted Benedetto later, warning him to erase all his research and to forget everything he'd learned about Ender or confess everything about him. Benedetto chose to reveal to the world the identity of Ender Wiggin on Sorelledolce, but Jane intercepted the message, exposing Benedetto's corrupt accounting practices in the process.

Some of his past victims killed Benedetto for stealing from them. Ender Spoke Benedetto's death. Feeling bad for the tax man's death, Ender gave Benedetto's family an annuity.

Bernard (EG, ES)

A contemporary of Ender Wiggin's at Battle School, Bernard was the boy whose arm Ender broke on their first journey into space. Bernard held a particular enmity toward Ender and put together a gang of fellow students at Battle School. His gang shoved Ender around, and was generally mean to him. However, Ender hacked into the Battle School computer system and sent private messages to Bernard and their classmates calling Bernard a "butt watcher." When Bernard complained to Dap, his launch group's supervisor, Dap accused Bernard of questioning authority. Bernard and his gang picked on Ender more, in an effort to reassert their own power.

Bernard's best friend was Alai, who said that Bernard used to torture cats for fun. Alai and Ender invited Bernard to join their team in the group's first Battle Room practice. With his teammates, Bernard froze the rest of the group in that first practice.

Bernard joined Ender's Free Play practices in the Battle Room that were set up after Ender's promotion to Salamander Army. He grew disenchanted with Ender, however, when Ender was promoted to command Dragon Army. He accompanied Bonzo Madrid into the bathroom when Bonzo had decided to kill Ender there.

Bimba (SG)

Bimba was a child to Pipo and Conceição, born on the planet Lusitania.

Bloom, Klaus (SG)

Klaus Bloom was a world leader who helped ratify Peter Wiggin's constitution for the Free People of Earth, the Hegemony. He was given a position of authority in the growing world government in Europe.

Boatman (CM)

The boatman was a large Polynesian man who lived on the planet Pacifica. He was protective of the sacred island of his people and refused to have Peter Wiggin II and Si Wang-mu there.

Bob (SG)

Bob was married to Randi and ran a grocery store. He did not know that Randi had been in love with Achilles Flandres and had been implanted with an embryo she thought Achilles had fathered. Randi left Bob to have her baby in secret, per Achilles's premortem instructions.

Bosque, Mayor/Governor Faria Lima Maria do "Bosquinha" (SD)

The female political leader of the human colony on the planet Lusitania, Bosquinha was known for being a strong-willed Catholic woman. The position of mayor and governor were combined, and as such she held both. A solid leader, she governed the planet's colony fairly. She also became the legal guardian of a girl named Novinha, whose parents had died finding a cure for the dreaded, deadly virus known as the Descolada.

Bosquinha greeted Ender Wiggin when his ship arrived at Lusitania. The mayor/governor was opposed to the idea of "Speakers of the Dead," of which Ender was one. Her religion fought against the funerary right of Speaking, seeing it as pagan. Lusitania was a staunchly Catholic planet, and to maintain order with her colonists, she adhered to Catholic dogma.

Shortly after the Speaker's arrival, Bosquinha noticed that Starways Congress had begun absorbing all of the computer files on the planet. They had the right to do so, she knew, because something had gone wrong with the human interaction with the planet's native species, the pequeninos. She advised the religious leaders to do as the government had and transfer their most important files into Ender's well-hidden computer storage.

She attended the Speaking Ender performed for the late Marcão Ribeira, and afterward told the Speaker what they'd done with his computer storage. He said it was a good idea. She also told him that she had been demoted from her gubernatorial role, and was now merely chief of police, facilitating the evacuation of the planet.

Lusitania had lost its charter because of Miro and Ouanda's interaction with the pequeninos and was to be evacuated by the Starways Congress. Ender convinced her to forestall the evacuation and meet with him and the religious leaders to plan a rebellion against the Congress. She reluctantly agreed, hoping to save the planet she'd governed for decades.

In that meeting, it was discovered that the Descolada, the disease that had virtually wiped out the planet a generation before, was still active. All who lived on Lusitania were carriers. As a result, Bosquinha and the others decided that they should rebel, in order to prevent exposing other planets to the deadly virus, and to protect themselves. They made it appear as if they'd shut down the ansible, and they deactivated the wall protecting the pequeninos. In so doing, they symbolically left the Starways Congress.

A day later, when Ender Wiggin had negotiated a treaty between humans and the piggies, Bosquinha went into the forest with Bishop Peregrino. There she learned of the treaty and signed it as the political leader of the human colonists on the planet.

Bosquinha (*See* Bosque, Mayor/Governor Faria Lima Maria do "Bosquinha")

Boulanger, Nero (ES)

Nero Boulanger was a contemporary of Ender Wiggin's at Battle School. He was approximately the same age as Ender; however, he did not arrive at the school until a couple of years after Ender. Nero was in Bean's launch group, and argued with the commanding officer of their flight into space over who had the highest test scores in the launch group. The officer, Captain Dimak, mocked Nero's arrogance and ignorance, making an example out of him. Nero had been humiliated before ever reaching Battle School.

Braun, Helga (ES)

Helga Braun, or "Hazie" as she preferred to be known, ran a soup kitchen in Rotterdam, Netherlands. She hated the violence that went on in the streets around her kitchen, but was pleased that Achilles and other bullies like him had taken to civilizing the children. She contacted her friend, Sister Carlotta, a nun who helped recruit for the International Fleet, alerting her that something was going on: that civilization had come to the children of Rotterdam. She gave Achilles his name because of his gimp leg. She also named Ulysses because he wandered from kitchen to kitchen.

Brian (EGS)

A member of Ender's Dragon Army, Brian was promoted to commander three years ahead of schedule along with several members of their army.

Bridegan, Captain (WG)

Captain Bridegan was the International Fleet officer who tested Zeck Morgan, finding him fit for Battle School. He had used threats of arresting Zeck's parents to get him to consent to going to the school.

Brother Language (SD, XN)

The Brother Language was the language the male pequeninos spoke in their "second life."

Brown, Hinckley (TP)

Hinckley Brown was thought to be the top military mind of his generation, and yet left the army to be with his family, a Mormon brood noncompliant with the Hegemony's population rules. He was an outspoken critic of the population laws. As a result of his departure, the Hegemony pulled funding from his daughter Theresa's graduate research. Theresa and Hinckley did not get along, despite Hinckley's attempts at reconciliation. He had missed much with his family because of his military obligations.

As Theresa Brown's father, he was also the grandfather to Andrew "Ender" Wiggin.

Brown, Theresa (*See* Wiggin, Theresa)

Bruxinha (SD)

Bruxinha was a colonist on the planet Lusitania. She was married to Libo and together they had four children. She did not know that Libo had also fathered children with his childhood sweetheart, Novinha, until she heard it at the Speaking ceremony for Novinha's husband, Marcão Ribeira. She was crushed, but Ender, in Speaking, tried to ease her pain by making it clear that her husband's adultery was not her fault.

Buggers (*See* Formics)

Cabra (SD)

Cabra was a less-developed grass-eating animal on the planet Lusitania. They were all female and had somehow evolved to avoid extinction from the Descolada plague. How they reproduced was a scientific mystery to the planet's xenobiologists.

Calendar (SD)

Calendar was a pequenino—the native life on Lusitania—who interacted with the human scientists, Miro and Ouanda. He witnessed Miro's climb over the fence that surrounded them.

Calicut (*See* Hundred Worlds)

Canadian Kid (WG)

The Canadian Kid was a member of Rat Army who participated in Dink Meeker's Christmas celebration of secretly giving gifts in other soldiers' socks.

Capim (SD, NX, CM)

Capim was a plant native to the planet Lusitania. Grasslike, it was studied by Ender Wiggin's scientist stepchildren. When chewed, capim had anesthetic properties for the pequeninos.

Captain (EE)

The Captain was an officer in the International Fleet who showed Ender around the spaceship that would take the hero of the Formic War to his new colony. The Captain had a family on Earth, and was not going to the new colony. On their tour of the ship, the Captain showed Ender how Formic technology made faster-than-light travel possible, as well as the weapon that Ender had deployed to destroy the Formics.

Carby, Carn (EGS, EG, ES, SH, SG)

Carn Carby was a contemporary of Ender Wiggin's in Battle School. A little older than Ender, Carn commanded Rabbit Army, which was the first army to lose to Ender's unbeatable Dragon Army. Carby took the loss graciously in the Battle Room, but was embarrassed and angry in the public areas of Battle School.

He eventually came to respect Ender, and even sought to help protect him when his life was in jeopardy from Bonzo Madrid. Carn was graduated from Battle School approximately a month later and replaced as commander of Rabbit Army by Bean, Ender's closest confidant and best soldier. He was promoted to Tactical School and, two weeks later, to Command School.

Carn was promoted to become one of Ender's unseen squadron leaders at Command School, leading soldiers into battle during the simulated "exams" that were actually real conflicts.

After the Formic War ended with Ender's victory, Carn was one of the former soldiers who were kidnapped by Achilles Flandres and taken to Russia. There, he and his fellow prisoners were forced to play war games against each other, preparing Achilles's armies for strikes against the rest of the world.

The captives were eventually separated, and put into solitary confinement without face-to-face contact with each other from then on. After several months, thanks to the efforts of Peter Wiggin and from a distance, Bean, Carn and his colleagues, except Petra Arkanian, were rescued by Russian operatives.

Over the next year, Carn was made a leader in the Australian military, though that assignment did not have significant worldwide influence. He was approached by both Hyrum Graff and Peter Wiggin and was offered a ship to go into space as part of the colonization program, freeing him from the heavy responsibilities of Earth and its political instability.

As Peter built the Hegemony into the Free People of Earth, Graff again offered Ender's colleagues the opportunity to leave Earth and govern a planet. It was his fear that Ender's army would be used in the worldwide conflict, manipulated by whatever political power rose to prominence, and he wanted to prevent that. Every member who received the offer, which did not include Han Tzu, Petra Arkanian, or Alai, said no. The others were already too involved in matters on Earth to leave.

Carlotta, Sister (ES, SH, [SP], [SG])

Sister Carlotta was a nun who joined the International Fleet's recruitment program, searching for the next leader of the Fleet who would defeat the Formic armies. She believed that doing so would ultimately protect the children of the world, despite being ostracized from her order. Carlotta heard from her friend, Helga Braun, a soup kitchen owner, that a boy named Achilles had been civilizing the homeless children of Rotterdam. Thinking that this Achilles could be the leader the Fleet was looking for, Carlotta went to Rotterdam.

There she found that Achilles was not the person she was looking for, but instead discovered Bean, the smallest child she'd ever seen. She set up a school to teach Achilles, Bean, and the rest of their "family" of children to read. When Bean was revealed to already know how to read, Carlotta knew for certain that he was the miracle child she'd sought.

When Bean's friend and former crew leader Poke was found dead and her death blamed on a bully named Ulysses, Sister Carlotta helped him through his mourning process. In so doing, she discovered that Bean had witnessed the murder, and that it was actually Achilles who perpetrated it. Bean was scared for his own life, so Carlotta chose to test him for Battle School. It was her hope that by getting him into Battle School, he would be safe from Achilles.

She administered the Battle School screening tests, and Bean earned a nearly perfect score. Sister Carlotta tested him again, and he scored well again—unheard of in a four-year-old boy. She made the decision to recommend him for Battle School, even though he was very much underage.

While waiting for Battle School to decide whether to accept Bean or not, Carlotta took him in. She taught him lessons in reading, arithmetic, art, and fed him until he was fat. She listened to his memories of escaping the mysterious "clean place" by hiding in a toilet. When he snuck out to find the man who found him in the toilet three and a half years earlier, she followed him.

Sister Carlotta told Bean that she had protected him from thugs and sex offenders. She'd also learned that Bean had escaped from an illegal organ-harvesting plant. She never shared this knowledge with Bean, which created some emotional distance between them. A few months later, when Bean was five, she shed a few tears for him as he left for Battle School. Like a parent,

Sister Carlotta loved Bean and hoped he'd be okay at the space-bound military training facility.

Only a day after Bean left, Sister Carlotta continued her investigation into who he was. She visited the clean place/organ farm, and studied the toilet in which he'd hidden, but was no further ahead into learning more about him.

Colonel Graff, the commander of Battle School, contacted Sister Carlotta, seeking an interpretation of Bean's activities at Battle School. She told Graff that Bean was smart, and he knew that the Battle School officials were watching him. She was certain that Bean was intentionally deceiving Graff and his colleagues to gain control of his own situation. However, because Graff asked specifically about Achilles, Sister Carlotta grew concerned and was determined she had to find him before the Fleet did to keep him away from Bean.

In exchange for her information on Bean, Carlotta asked for information on any studies of the human genome that the Fleet had conducted in the last ten years. Graff reluctantly promised to get summaries to her.

These summaries led Carlotta to Sophia, Russia, where she met a retired scientist named Anton, who had discovered a way to genetically accelerate mental and physical human development in embryos. Anton spoke in code to Carlotta, telling her about his research before the implant in his brain (designed to stop him from discussing his findings) caused a panic attack. Carlotta was able to determine that Bean had been genetically altered by Anton's research, and because of that would not live to an old age.

As thanks for additional information exchanges with Graff, Carlotta was able to locate Doctor Volescu, the scientist who took Anton's research and put it into practice. She met with Volescu, who confirmed that he had illegally performed the procedure of turning Anton's Key in twenty-four fertilized embryos. Twenty-three of these embryos had been destroyed, leaving one to grow and mature—Bean.

Although Volescu provided Sister Carlotta with this information, he was arrogant and defiant in his attitudes toward her. This angered Carlotta, and she stated that he didn't deserve to have a son like Bean.

Carlotta discovered that Volescu was not the DNA donor, however. That honor belonged to Volescu's half-brother Julian Delphiki. Sister Carlotta told Julian and his wife Elena about Volescu's tests. She gave them hope that they might have another son—Bean, who had coincidentally befriended the Delphiki's firstborn, Nikolai, at Battle School.

Achilles was sent to Battle School. Sister Carlotta located Graff, on Earth with Ender at the time, and told him of all the murders Achilles had committed since killing Poke. Graff realized the extreme threat to Bean and contacted his colleagues at Battle School, desperately trying to get Achilles taken out of the school, per Sister Carlotta's warnings.

Sister Carlotta tried to stay in touch with Hyrum Graff after the Formic War was over, but she went into hiding following the war. She resurfaced with Graff a short time later, though, to come to Bean's aid.

Bean and the rest of the Delphiki family had been the target of an assassination attempt by Achilles Flandres, who had also kidnapped the rest of Ender's army from Command School. The Greek Army had been protecting the family, but Carlotta and Graff, with permission and help from the International Fleet, arrived and split up the family for their own protection.

Bean traveled with Carlotta again, while the rest of his new family went with Graff. They hid in Brazil and communicated via the nets, passing e-mail through enough servers that their location remained hidden.

Among these e-mail messages that went back and forth was a dragon image that had become popular among net users. Carlotta showed it to Bean, who figured out it was a message from Petra giving her location, and the relative location of her fellow hostages.

She was consistently amazed at Bean's brilliance. He knew, and assumed she did, too, that his training at Battle School and streetwise childhood meant that he was protecting her as much, if not more, than she was looking after him.

Bean used Petra's message to spur a rescue mission by Russian operatives. They successfully freed nine of the ten kidnapped soldiers, leaving only Petra in Achilles's hands. Sister Carlotta knew that they had to leave Brazil. Their timing was good, as Peter Wiggin sought communication with Bean and Carlotta. Carlotta decided to go to Peter's hometown of Greensboro, North Carolina.

In Greensboro, Sister Carlotta used her age and wisdom to fool a university administrator into helping her set up a meeting with Peter Wiggin at a restaurant near the school where he was a student. Bean and Carlotta met Peter there and discussed the Achilles problem.

Later that night, Sister Carlotta joined Peter and his parents for dinner at another restaurant in town. She and Bean conspired with Peter to join them as they went into hiding. As they discussed it further in private after dinner, Carlotta helped Peter understand that his identity as the political columnist Locke was sure to be exposed. With Bean, she and Peter crafted a plan that would allow him to reveal his true identity and begin his secret campaign for the office of Hegemon.

Carlotta promised the support of the Vatican. Peter joined their little group, though a tenuous trust existed between the three of them. However, he did not travel with them. Carlotta and Bean traveled to Thailand and were placed in a military compound.

Since Bean was not granted the military access he'd been promised on his arrival in Thailand, he began to test the patience and limits of the Thai government. In order to protect Sister Carlotta, he sent her away.

She went to Madrid. But as she left, she and Bean had a small argument. Peter had said in an earlier conversation that Sister Carlotta had written some memos about Bean prior to his time at Battle School. She never shared with him their content. Bean wanted to know, but Sister Carlotta didn't want him to learn what they contained. They were a touchy subject between the two people.

After six months in Madrid, and an apparent attempt on Bean's life in Thailand, Sister Carlotta boarded a plane to return. She made arrangements with Graff to forward an e-mail to Bean if he did not hear from her again. It was an ominous sign of what was to come.

Carlotta's plane was blown up over China. Achilles had orchestrated it, but no government officials would believe it. The e-mail she'd had Graff forward contained the content of her memos on Bean. They told the story of his genetic manipulation and warned him that he would die.

Bean was heartbroken over Carlotta's death, but did not seek vengeance; she had asked him not to. Ever faithful to Christ, she used the e-mail to remind Bean that she loved him deeply, and any vengeance was God's to take, not his.

The Vatican placed a memorial to her in its city, while Bean, living in Brazil, created his own marker to her life.

Catalog of the Voices of the Gods (XN)

The *Catalog of the Voices of the Gods* was a book on the planet Path, where the OCD-like manifestations of the "godspoken" were recorded.

Catalonian Exchange Bank (IC)

Bank on the planet Sorelledolce where Ender Wiggin tried to gain access to his finances centuries after his victory over the Formics.

Catholic Priest I (SG)

The Catholic Priest I presided over the christening of Andrew Delphiki, the first child born to Bean and Petra Delphiki.

Catholic Priest II (CM)

This Catholic Priest II performed the marriages of Si Wang-mu to Peter Wiggin II, and of Jane to Miro Ribeira von Hesse II.

Causo (CM)

Causo was the executive officer of the flagship in the fleet that was sent by the Starways Congress to destroy the planet Lusitania. He knew that Congress had changed the order as the fleet neared the planet, but was incapacitated by his superior, Admiral Lands, who went ahead and launched the devastating Molecular Detachment Device at the planet.

He was revived and learned that the Molecular Detachment Device had mysteriously reappeared in the ship's cargo hold. There, he met Peter Wiggin II and Si Wang-mu, who warned Causo he might want to disarm and dismantle the weapon. He did so, and overheard Peter tell Admiral Lands the content of the message he should send back to Congress, explaining his actions.

Ceifeir (SD, XN, CM)

"Ceifeir" was the term used by the members of the planet Lusitania's religious order, the Children of the Mind of Christ, for their abbotts.

Center Nation (CM)

"Center Nation" is a term used to describe a nation with a culture so strong that new citizens choose to assimilate themselves to that culture over maintaining their own cultural identity.

Chamrajnagar, Captain/Admiral/Polemarch (PL, EG, EE, SH, SP)

Chamrajnagar was among the high-level officials in the International Fleet that first reviewed six-year-old John Paul Wieczorek's screening test results. At that time he was an official representative of the Polemarch. From India, Chamrajnagar was optimistic about John Paul's test results, feeling that he may be the commander the Fleet was searching for. He was concerned, however, that Colonel Sillian, who had helped test John Paul, was not suited to make the final determination on John Paul's readiness for Battle School. Consequently, Chamrajnagar insisted, with the support of the Russian General, that Captain Hyrum Graff visit John Paul.

Chamrajnagar was promoted to admiral and given the assignment of overseeing Command School. Though they had met years earlier, Chamrajnagar stated that he thought he and Graff would be friends when Graff arrived at Command School with Ender Wiggin.

Following Ender's victory over the Formics, Chamrajnagar helped train newly promoted Admiral Ender Wiggin in the duties of his new rank. He watched Ender until the boy was sent into space on a colony ship. It was Chamrajnagar who assigned the commanders of the colony ships, including Admiral Quincy Morgan with whom Ender had several conflicts.

Chamrajnagar was present when the colony ship departed, using the event as a photo op to reiterate his influence in world matters.

A short time later, Peter Wiggin tried to convince Chamrajnagar to support his desires for world power, but the admiral refused. He even tried to cut off contact with Peter, threatening to expose him as the anonymous political pundit, Locke. Chamrajnagar agreed to help Peter, though, after speaking with Graff. He even withdrew the threat of exposure.

However, though a high-ranking member of the world leadership, Chamrajnagar had made a tentative alliance with Achilles Flandres, the serial killer who had his sights set on world domination. Locke had derailed one of Achilles's plans, and Achilles wanted revenge.

Achilles had begun working with the government in India, and it was feared that he would be able to learn Locke's true identity from Chamrajnagar. From an assignment in space, Chamrajnagar promised that upon his return to Earth, he would resign his position as Polemarch in the Hegemony, and return to India where he was given a high position in the Indian military. Achilles had made moves that would ultimately bring down India into Chinese rule, though, and Peter Wiggin advised Chamrajnagar to stay in space for the duration of the conflict.

When Peter reached the office of Hegemon following the Chinese takeover of Asia, he reinstalled Chamrajnagar as Polemarch, stating that doing so gave credibility to his office. He was loyal to Peter.

Years later, Achilles Flandres made an effort to overthrow Peter as Hegemon. Chamrajnagar would not heed Achilles's demands, and forcefully stated that Peter was still the Hegemon.

Chamrajnagar's loyalty to Peter and the Hegemony was further manifested as he provided shuttles to use when Peter and his family were hiding on the orbiting satellite home of the Ministry of Colonization. It was a ruse to expose a mole, but they needed the shuttles Chamrajnagar could give them.

Achilles shot down one of the shuttles, thinking it would kill Peter. However, the shuttle was empty, and exposed Achilles's plans against the Hegemony and the International Fleet. Chamrajnagar and Graff helped authorize an Earth-bound attack against Achilles, which would be led by Peter Wiggin and Bean.

Chapekar, Prime Minister Tikal ([SH], SG)

Prime Minister Tikal Chapekar was the leader of India following Ender's victory over the Formics. He worked closely with the master manipulator, Achilles Flandres, a former Battle School dropout and serial killer, who was set on world domination. Achilles had convinced Chapekar that India would become the most powerful nation in the world and the greatest force in Asia. Chapekar authorized Achilles to represent him in Pakistan where Achilles convinced the Pakistani government to join India, not in reunification but in military conquest.

It was all a plan by Achilles to turn Asia over to China. Chapekar was unaware of this, however, until it was too late. As the Chinese took over his nation, he reached out to Pakistan again hoping for that nation's support. He was taken prisoner by China, but released over a year later when Virlomi, a Battle School graduate who had come into great power in India, called for the release of all of the prisoners held by China.

He tried to regain his position of power in India, but no one wanted him. Virlomi called for Tikal to be ignored, and the people of India did so. He had to leave India for the Netherlands in disgrace. Exiled, he received a bit of government aid from the Dutch while he looked for new employment.

Chupaceu (SD)

Chupaceu, or Sky-sucker, was a pequenino, one of the native species on the planet Lusitania.

Cida (*See* von Hesse-Gussman, Ekaterina Maria Aparecida do Norte "Cida")

Cifi Unit (SD, XN, CM)

The cifi unit was the small jewel through which the sentient computer named Jane communicated directly with Ender Wiggin and Miro Ribeira von Hesse. Worn in the ear, it allowed the wearer to hear Jane, but also granted Jane access to its wearer.

City of the Jade Mountain in the West (XN, CM)

The City of the Jade Mountain in the West is the supposed home of the gods of the planet Path.

Colador (SD)

Colador was the cure for the Descolada, which was distributed to the settlers of Lusitania through their water.

College Chairman (TP)

The chairman of Theresa Brown's dissertation committee.

College Dean (TP)

The College Dean was Theresa Brown's superior while she was a graduate student. He called her in for a meeting where he, alongside his colleagues, informed her that the funding for her research had been withdrawn. It had been a political tactic made by the Hegemony to attack Theresa's father.

Colony IX (*See* Hundred Worlds)

Combat School (EGS, EG, ES)

Combat School is where graduates of Battle School go if they are not qualified for Command School or Tactical School.

Command School (*See also* Eros Asteroid) (EGS, EG, ES, [GB])

A large complex made up of tunnels that burrowed into the surface of the minor planet Eros, Command School was where Ender was trained on the "simulators." He took "exams," all of which were actually battles in the Formic War. He remotely commanded real armies by these simulators.

It was here that Ender met Mazer Rackham and destroyed the Formic home world.

Command School Observers/"Test Proctors" (EG, ES)

During Ender's "final exam" at Command School, several observers or proctors watched him take the test. They were officers in the International Fleet, and cheered Ender's victory against the Formic home world. Hyrum Graff was among them, as was Mazer Rackham, who revealed that the officers were observing because the exams had been real battles, and this "final exam" had been the defining battle against humanity's enemy.

Command School Technician (EG, ES)

The Command School Technician helped Command School students like Bean and Ender settle into their training "simulators."

Computer Voice (MP)

On board Mazer Rackham's private courier ship, the Computer Voice relayed messages and provided quasihuman companionship for the Admiral as he traveled what to him was a five-year journey, but to the people of Earth was decades. The Computer Voice had both male and female voices with which to read messages from the International Fleet and speak to Mazer. It was not sentient, however, and Mazer described it as "bland."

The Computer Voice would record Mazer's responses to messages from IF-COM, and send them via ansible. The computer also tracked Mazer's emotional responses and reported them to the Fleet. It also reported that Mazer had reprogrammed the ship to give himself complete navigational control.

Conceição (SD)

Conceição was a human colonist on the planet Lusitania. She was the librarian of the planetary archives, and was married to the planet's xenologist, Pipo. She was the mother of Libo, and a devout Catholic. She was devastated by the murder of her husband by the planet's native life-forms, the pequeninos.

Years later, at a very old age and still the archivist of Lusitania, Conceição learned of her son Libo's adulterous relationship with Novinha von Hesse.

Condor, The (ES)

The Condor was the name of the spaceship that Bean took to Battle School.

Copper Bugs ([GB])

Copper Bugs were large insectoids, bred by the Formics to mine for precious metals on one of their worlds. When that world was colonized by humans after Ender's victory against the Formics, the Copper Bugs were thought to exist because of the discovery of Gold Bugs by xenobiologist Sel Menach and his assistant, Po Tolo.

Their exoskeleton was seemingly made of the precious metal they mined, making the bugs themselves precious natural resources.

Córdoba (*See* Hundred Worlds)

Crazy Tom (EG, ES, WG, SH, SG)

Crazy Tom was a contemporary of Ender's in Battle School, and was one of the few veterans assigned to Ender's Dragon Army. He was the toon leader of C toon in Dragon Army. He had also developed a reputation for throwing tantrums if his superiors did things that bothered him.

He and his toon helped lead Dragon Army to victory over Rabbit Army in their first battle. They also helped protect Ender from Bonzo Madrid and Salamander Army, when Ender's life was threatened. In the army's eighth battle, Tom was frozen and used as a shield by Bean to defeat Salamander Army.

Crazy Tom was promoted to Tactical School and a week later was given command of one of Ender's unseen squadrons during the exams (that were truthfully real battles) at Command School.

After returning home, Tom, along with the rest of Ender's final army, was kidnapped by former Battle School student and serial killer Achilles Flandres. He was taken to Russia and forced to participate in war games with his fellow prisoners. He was soon separated from his colleagues and taken to a secret location elsewhere in Russia. There he continued to participate in the war games, which were used as training for Achilles's ever-growing army.

None of the captives was allowed to have physical interaction with the others. They could write and communicate via e-mail, but nothing else was permitted. Achilles allowed him, and the rest of the prisoners except Petra, to be rescued.

Over the next couple of years, Crazy Tom became a military teacher in Sandhurst, teaching strategy to future soldiers. He was approached by both Hyrum Graff and Peter Wiggin, and invited to leave Earth and its political instability and travel to space where he could begin a new life at a human colony.

As Peter built the Hegemony into the Free People of Earth, Graff again offered Ender's colleagues the opportunity to leave Earth and govern a planet. It was his fear that Ender's army would be used in the worldwide conflict, manipulated by whatever political power rose to prominence, and he wanted to prevent that. Every member who received the offer, which did not include Han Tzu, Petra Arkanian, or Alai, said no. The others were already too involved in matters on Earth to leave.

Christao/Cristã, Dona Detesai o Pecado o Fazelo Direito (SD)

Dona Christao was a member of the Catholic Church's order called Children of the Mind of Christ on the planet Lusitania. She taught at the local school and helped place children in their careers. She was on friendly terms with Pipo, and used that relationship to determine if a prized female student named Novinha could take the xenobiologist certification test earlier than the usual age.

Dona Christao was also married to Dom Cristão, and together they led the Catholic order the Children of the Mind of Christ. She, with her husband, helped Ender Wiggin learn about the people of Lusitania so he could better Speak about their deaths.

She was one who attended the meeting with the governor to discuss the Starways Congress's absorption of the planetary computer files. She also attended Ender's Speaking ceremony, learning of Novinha von Hesse's adulterous relationship with Libo Figueira.

As with the other important meetings, she was present when it was decided that, to protect Miro Ribeira from prosecution, and to protect other planets from the Descolada virus, Lusitania would rebel against the Starways Congress.

Cristão, Dom Amai a Tudomundo Para Que Dues vos Ame (SD)

Dom Cristão was the one of the chief religious leaders on the planet Lusitania. He was the Abbot of the Catholic monastery, which housed an order of the Church known as Children of the Mind of Christ. He was married to Dona Cristão.

He brought comfort to Libo and his family when Libo's father, Pipo, was killed by the native Lusitanian creatures, known as the piggies.

The Bishop, who was a semirival, asked Dom Cristão for his help in ridding Lusitania of the scourge of a Speaker for the Dead, Ender Wiggin. However, Dom Cristão saw value in what Speakers did, and instead helped Ender prepare to Speak.

When the Starways Congress began absorbing Lusitania's files, Dom Cristão noticed and began printing out on paper their most important files. With the governor's aid, he then transferred the bulk of the files into Ender's open computer storage, trusting Ender to return the files later.

He attended the Speaking for the Dead that Ender performed on behalf of Marcão Ribeira, and was surprised to learn of the adulterous relationship between Novinha von Hesse and Libo Figueira.

He was also present at the meeting where it was discovered that the planet's charter had been revoked, and the leaders of Lusitania elected to defy Starways Congress's orders and rebel. They did so to protect Miro Ribeira and Ouanda Figueira. Dom Cristão and the other leaders hoped the rebellion would open the door to taking their religion to the pequeninos—the native species of Lusitania.

Cups (SD)

Cups was a pequenino, the native species of the planet Lusitania, also called "piggies." He saw Miro Ribeira climb the protective, electrified fence that surrounded the piggies' land, and wanted to plant him as a tree—the highest honor in their race.

Custer (SH)

Custer was a military man who communicated with Demosthenes regarding the apparent Russian imprisonment of Ender's former colleagues.

Cyrillia (*See* Hundred Worlds)

Dag (ES)

Dag was a soldier in Ender Wiggin's Dragon Army in Battle School.

Dap (EG, ES)

An adult on Battle School, Dap was the supervisor for new recruits when they arrived at Battle School. He referred to himself as the new students' "Mom," and instructed them in where they were and were not allowed to go in the school.

When Ender hacked into the school computer system to send messages to his fellow students under others' names, Dap turned a blind eye. Student Bernard complained about the messages being sent in his name, to which Dap replied that Bernard must be sending them, though he knew it was Ender. Dap did not expose Ender to the other students. He chastised Bernard for yelling at him, a superior.

Ender, Shen, Bernard, and Alai teamed up and froze the rest of their launch group during their first practice at Battle School. It was Dap who unfroze the group, and chastised them for not being as ready as Ender and company had been in the same amount of time.

He was very paternal about the launch groups, and filed a report expressing concern for Ender's welfare. The report garnered the attention of the International Fleet, who sent General Pace to investigate.

Dap had a rivalry with Captain Dimak, another officer who oversaw a different launch group. Dimak had chosen Bean as the top student, and both he and Dap felt their students were best. They argued often, looking to better their own protégé's circumstances.

das Lagrimas, Commodore Vlad (EE)

Commodore Vlad das Lagrimas was the executive officer on the first spaceship transporting colonists to former Formic worlds. He served under Admiral Quincy Morgan.

Daymaker, Father (XN)

Father Daymaker was a pequenino, the native animallike sentient species of the planet Lusitania. He was a son of Human, the pequenino who was made into a fathertree at Ender Wiggin's hands, and trained to be a Catholic priest among his species by Quim Ribeira.

He was plainspoken when he talked with Quim, revealing that the Formic Hive Queen was building the pequeninos a ship to take them off Lusitania, where they would spread the Descolada to other planets.

Deadline (EG)

Deadline is a thin twine used during construction in space. Bean used it as a tool in the Battle Room to connect himself to the wall and rappel around the room in combat.

Deaf (XN)

Deaf was a pequenino, or piggie, the native sentient life on the planet Lusitania. Despite his name, Deaf was not hard of hearing. He was a close friend of Quara Ribeira von Hesse, Ender's stepdaughter and an up-and-coming piggie scientist.

Dean of the Cathedral (SD)

The Dean of the Cathedral was a high-up religious leader on the planet Lusitania. He contacted the abbot of the planet's other monastery, the Children of the Mind of Christ, ordering him to meet with the bishop to discuss the arrival of a Speaker for the Dead on the planet.

Debarkation Chamber (IC)

A debarkation chamber is a portion of a spaceship where a traveler lives. Similar to quarters or barracks.

Deedee, Nurse (EG)

Nurse Deedee assisted a doctor in removing Ender's monitor from the back of his neck. She said she was too weak to hold the struggling Ender as he squirmed during the removal procedure.

Dekanos, Colonel (SH)

Colonel Dekanos was a soldier in the Greek Army. He was in command of a group of soldiers who rescued the Delphiki family when their lives were in jeopardy during a vacation they took together after the Formic War. He told Bean that ten of his fellow members of Ender's team in Command School had been kidnapped.

Delamar, Dr. Vivian (ES)

Dr. Vivian Delamar was a surgeon. She fixed the damaged leg of Achilles Flandres, and was killed by him for it. Achilles used a hypodermic to simulate a heart attack. She'd been a close friend of Sister Carlotta, who attended Vivian's funeral in Cairo.

Delphiki, Andrew ("normal" child) (SG, EE)

Andrew Delphiki, the "normal" child, was one of the embryos created by Bean Delphiki and Petra Arkanian who was implanted into an unknown surrogate. He was born without Bean's genetic mutation, and given the same name as one of his brothers who had the mutation to prevent suspicion when the mutated brother was taken into space to await a cure with his father. This Andrew was raised on Earth by his mother, Petra.

As an adult, Andrew married a woman named Lani and had several children with her. He was frequently visited by his mother, Petra.

Delphiki, Andrew "Ender" Arkanian (SG)

Andrew Arkanian Delphiki, or "Ender" as he was known, was the first child born to Petra Arkanian and Bean Delphiki. He was born two months premature, a result of his accelerated mental and physical development courtesy of the genetic manipulation he'd received at the hands of Dr. Volescu, who had performed the in vitro fertilization that had created him.

He was loved by his parents, and they worried for his future. Would he grow giant like his father, who also carried the genetic switch? Would he die young?

He accompanied his father into space where they traveled at relativistic speed to forestall death, waiting for scientists on Earth to develop a cure for their mutation.

Delphiki, Arkanian (*See also* Flandres, Achilles II) (EE)

Arkanian Delphiki was the name chosen by Achilles Flandres II once he learned that he was actually the son of Bean Delphiki and Petra Arkanian.

Delphiki, Cincinnatus (mutant child) ([EE], SG)

Cincinnatus Delphiki, mutant, was the third of the embryos Bean Delphiki and Petra Arkanian created that suffered from the genetic mutation of his father. He traveled into space with his father and two siblings, awaiting a cure for their mutation.

Delphiki, Bella ("normal" child) (SG)

Bella Delphiki, the "normal" child, was one of the embryos created by Bean Delphiki and Petra Arkanian who was implanted into an unknown surrogate. She was born without Bean's genetic mutation, and given the same name as one of her sisters who had the mutation to prevent suspicion when the mutated sister was taken into space to await a cure with her father. This Bella was raised on Earth by her mother, Petra.

Delphiki, Bella Loyrinha "Carlotta" ([EE], SG)

Bella Delphiki was the second child born to Petra and Bean, though she was actually birthed by a woman in Portugal. Bella had begun as an embryo made of Bean and Petra's DNA, but stolen by Achilles Flandres. She was implanted into the surrogate in Portugal and birthed there. Petra retrieved the girl, who carried the genetic mutation called Anton's Key that had made her father brilliant but grow to be gigantic, and kept her to be raised with Bean. She had been named Bella by her surrogate parents.

She was taken into space with her brother "Ender," her father, and another sibling. One of her sisters, who did not have the mutation, stayed behind on Earth and was also named Bella to avoid suspicion when this Bella disappeared. To differentiate between the two, Bean called her Carlotta, for the nun who had cared for him as a child.

Delphiki, Elena (ES, SH, SP)

Elena Delphiki and her husband, Julian I, desperately wanted a child. When they finally conceived one, thanks to in vitro fertilization and surgery, they all but worshipped him. Their son Nikolai was the world to them, which made it so hard when he chose to go to Battle School.

While Nikolai was in Battle School, Elena and her husband met with Sister Carlotta, who brought saddening news. The remaining embryos that the

Delphikis had tried to conceive with, were stolen and destroyed by Julian's half-brother, a scientist named Volescu. There was hope, though Elena didn't know it at the time. One of the fertilized embryos had successfully developed into a child—a boy named Bean. Elena's husband told her of their unknown son, giving hope for the future.

She took her newly reunited family on a vacation after they returned from the war. But the vacation ended up being more dramatic than relaxing, as their house was bombed, and their lives threatened. They were rescued by a group of Greek soldiers and informed that several of Bean's colleagues from Command School had been kidnapped.

After being watched under guard in a small apartment, the Delphiki family was taken by Hyrum Graff and Sister Carlotta to another undisclosed location. Elena was uptight, wanting to know what was going on and what the real plans were. Carlotta and Graff split the family up for their own safety. Bean went with Carlotta, while Graff oversaw the rest of the family's protection and journey deeper into hiding.

The Delphiki family came out of hiding to join Bean in Brazil, where he was given a position in the new Hegemony that was centered in the South American country. They were promised protection from future kidnappings by living there. They had to return to hiding, though, a short time after arriving in Brazil. Achilles was on his way to the Hegemony compound and was a threat to the Delphiki family.

Achilles was killed months later, and the Delphikis were allowed to return to Brazil. They worked in the government for a time, but soon retired. Elena felt too old to be out working all the time.

Bean married Petra Arkanian, and they had several children through in vitro fertilization. Achilles had stolen and implanted the embryos, leading Bean and Petra on a worldwide hunt for their children. They eventually found them all, but Bean left Earth for space, where he and three of his babies would wait for a cure for the genetic mutation that cursed him and his children.

Elena cared for the babies while Petra mourned the loss of Bean and worked in the military. When Petra finally returned to Brazil more than a year later, Elena turned the care of her grandchildren over to her.

She was proud of her life's work, and wanted to see Petra live life fully with her family.

Delphiki, Julian I (ES, SH)
Julian and Elena Delphiki tried hard to have children, resorting to test-tube in vitro conception and surgery. Finally they got their son Nikolai and

treated him like he was to be the king of the world until the International Fleet came calling, wanting to take him to Battle School. At Nikolai's suggestion that he may be the next Mazer Rackham, they let him go.

Several months later, during a visit from Sister Carlotta, Julian learned that the fertilized embryos he and his wife had given to have a child had been stolen and destroyed. They were, in actuality, the same embryos that the evil scientist Volescu had grown illegally. *From them had been created Bean,* a wunderkind at Battle School.

Volescu was Julian's half-brother, and it broke his heart that the son of his father's mistress would steal the embryos that were to be his children. However, he held out hope that Bean, his unknown son, would return to them someday.

Bean and Nikolai both returned home after Ender's victory over the Formic home world. Julian took his boys and his wife on a vacation but quickly learned that it was dangerous to be related to Bean. Their home was bombed, and they were saved by Greek soldiers. They learned that ten of Bean's colleagues from Command School had been kidnapped, and Bean's life was in jeopardy.

After a few weeks under the Greek army's protection, the Delphiki family was moved again to an undisclosed location. They were to be split up, with Julian and Elena taking Nikolai with Hyrum Graff and going into hiding, while the nun who'd helped raise him, Sister Carlotta, took Bean.

They came out of hiding at the end of the conflict and joined Bean in Brazil, the new home of the Hegemony. Bean had been given a position in the new government, and his family was promised protection if they moved there. The promise was short-lived, and the family had to go back into hiding to avoid Achilles who was on his way to the compound.

Once Achilles was killed, Julian and Elena returned to Brazil and watched the events of the world unfold. They were proud of their family, and grateful for the grandchildren both Bean and Nikolai brought them.

Delphiki, Julian II "Bean" (EGS, EG, ES, [EE], SH, SP, SG)

He was without a name, but the boy who would one day become Julian Delphiki II, and be given the nickname Bean, was born precocious. At *under* a year old, Bean knew that his home, which he described as "the clean place," was dangerous. He heard adults fighting and hid in a toilet tank. He was found by a janitor named Pablo de Noches, and taken into his home. It is unclear how long Bean stayed with Pablo, though it was thought to be a very short time. He escaped from Pablo's house, and went into the streets.

At age four, Bean was tiny. He looked like he was two, and had barely any clothing to speak of. He lived on the streets of Rotterdam, in the Netherlands, watching how the different groups of homeless children worked together. These "crews" of kids were the key to survival, and soon Bean aligned himself with a crew led by a nine-year-old girl named Poke.

Poke was not a particularly smart crew leader, so Bean (who had been given his name by Poke and her crew member Sergeant) advised her to find a bully to protect the crew from other bullies. Poke found Achilles, who Bean knew would eventually kill Poke. However, Achilles was a smart, charismatic leader, and the crew fell in line behind him.

Bean was never truly accepted by Achilles. He knew that Achilles sought to kill him. In spite of this, Bean tried to help Achilles and the "family" gain food. He knew that his small stature would elicit compassion from the woman who ran the soup kitchen, and it did, granting Achilles's family access to the front of the food line.

Since Achilles would not accept Bean, Bean convinced another bully to protect small children, which led to more food being available at the kitchen because supporters wanted to care for the children. This made Achilles angrier, so Bean hid in the city. In hiding, Bean overheard talk by a group of bullies who was planning to kill Achilles, so he raced to warn Achilles.

Achilles supposedly went into hiding. When Poke left the family late one night to find Achilles, Bean followed her. He witnessed Poke and Achilles kissing each other and discussing a promise Achilles had made to Poke. Bean ran away from them, but realized that the promise they'd been talking about was Achilles's agreement not to kill Bean. Bean realized that Achilles would kill Poke instead.

He raced back to save Poke, but he was too late. Achilles had beaten her to death. Bean was devastated. Poke had given her life to save his. It was an act that would haunt Bean for the rest of his life.

Sister Carlotta told Bean about Battle School, and asked if he'd like to go. Bean said yes, warning that it was him or Achilles, but both could not go. He took the tests, and scored nearly perfect on them. Sister Carlotta tested him again, and the four-year-old Bean proved he was the most qualified Battle School student she'd ever seen.

Bean lived with Sister Carlotta, taking lessons in math, reading, and art from her. He shared with her his memories of hiding in the toilet at the "clean place." He snuck out one night to find Pablo de Noches, and was unknowingly followed by Carlotta. Carlotta protected him from sex offenders and thugs, and when Bean found Pablo, she was there to take him back home but also to learn more about Bean's past from Pablo. Pablo was not helpful, however, and Bean's past remained shrouded in mystery.

It was time for Bean to go to Battle School. He was five years old and told himself that Sister Carlotta was untrustworthy. She had kept any information she'd learned from Pablo away from Bean, and he didn't like that. He distanced himself from her, so that when he finally left, he would not miss her.

On his flight to space, Captain Dimak, the commander of the flight and a teacher at Battle School, exposed Bean's remarkably high scores on all of the tests to the other children in his launch group. The children resented him, and Bean realized that he was out of place in this group just as he'd been with Achilles's "family."

Bean was annoyed at the mockery launchies endured, but was grateful that he was being picked on as it helped make him more a part of his launch group than he'd been on the journey into space.

He figured out that the school officials monitored the students through their clothes, and that food portions were exceptionally larger than he was used to. He decided to explore the school, finding himself on a deck he was not supposed to be on, and meeting other students like Dink Meeker and Petra Arkanian. Bean was annoyed with Petra's apparent condescension at first, but soon became intrigued by her.

He also discovered the school's duct system, and learned that he could fit inside it and be able to travel anywhere in the school unseen. Curious about constant comparisons to Ender Wiggin, Bean decided to learn more about Ender by speaking with Ender's former commander, Bonzo Madrid. Bonzo spoke terribly of Ender, giving Bean a clear picture of Battle School politics. The games played at school, he realized, were designed to train soldiers in combat, but also to give them experience with incompetent commanders like Bonzo. Bean recognized that Battle School was just like living on the street with a crew. He knew how to play that game.

Bean knew that the teachers and administrators were always watching. In order to deceive them, to take control of his own situation, he set up an additional false identity, named for Poke, and wrote false diary entries that proclaimed love and respect for Achilles.

After several months at Battle School, Bean had begun the practice of hacking into fellow students' computers. He was caught when a member of his launch group, Nikolai, informed the school administrators that his computer had been hacked. This led to a discussion between Bean and their group administrator, Dimak.

They discussed space battle strategy as well as Bean's antisocial behavior. Bean pointed out many challenges of fighting battles in space. He expressed a theory that humanity had already sent a fleet into space to attack the Formic home world. Dimak denied it, but his profuse sweating confirmed the theory's accuracy to Bean.

From the conversation with Dimak, Bean resolved to become more social. He befriended Nikolai, sharing with him the things he learned about Battle School from hacking into the computers and seeing the school's maps. It made for a quick bond.

Bean continued his journeys through the ductwork, spying on Battle School faculty. He stole one teacher's computer password and used it to obtain confidential information. He also witnessed a conversation between his supervisor Dimak and school commandant Hyrum Graff. Graff informed Dimak that Sister Carlotta feared that Bean's intelligence and strange growth patterns had been the result of genetic manipulation in embryo. The fear Graff, Dimak, and apparently Sister Carlotta shared of a new species represented by Bean hurt the boy. But it also motivated him to become better than the best student at Battle School—better than Ender.

Using the stolen password, Bean studied the teacher's evaluations of other students, focusing on Ender's. Ender Wiggin became Bean's obsession for several months. He watched and studied what Ender did. He met with Ender's friends to learn about who he truly was. He learned from one of these friends, Shen, that Ender altruistically cared about others before himself. It was a concept foreign to him. He still couldn't understand how Poke had given her life for him, or how Ender could care about others first.

One thing he learned from studying Ender and from the teacher's evaluations was that there were several talented students who were being overlooked for promotion. They were a group of apparently average students. Bean knew that given the opportunity this group of students could excel above and beyond those students thought to be exceptional. All they needed was the perfect commander, who again was Ender.

Dimak and Graff recognized Bean's talent as well as his obsession with Ender, and assigned him to make up a theoretical army for Ender to command, made up of launchies and students listed on other commanders' transfer lists. Bean knew it was a real army, and assigned the students he'd studied through their profiles. He included himself on the list, as well as his only real friend, Nikolai.

When he assigned himself to Ender Wiggin's Dragon Army, Bean was confident to the point of arrogance. He was quickly bored by Ender's instructions regarding the enemy's gate and using frozen legs in zero-gravity combat situations. Bean knew he was Ender's best soldier, and made it clear on their first day together. Bean requested command of a toon, which Ender was hesitant to assign. Bean was loyal to Ender, even getting in a fistfight with toon leader Fly Molo over respect he felt Fly owed Ender.

Meanwhile, back on Earth, Sister Carlotta discovered that the people who donated the fertilized embryo that grew to become Bean were named Julian and Elena Delphiki—Nikolai's parents.

Bean was a very important part of Ender's army, and the rest of Battle School recognized it. This was why Bonzo Madrid confronted Bean and warned him that he was going to kill Ender. Bean antagonized Bonzo further, but afterward felt guilty. He was sure he'd signed Ender's death warrant and felt that he was reliving his past with Poke. He felt responsible for Achilles killing her, and felt responsible for Bonzo's threat.

Four weeks after Dragon Army had been created, after Bean had proven his value to the army by not getting frozen in battle and freezing nearly four dozen enemy soldiers, Ender gave Bean command of a toon. It was a special squadron of five soldiers—one from each toon in Dragon Army. Bean was ordered to hold special practices with them and teach them as many unique formations and attacks as he could.

Ender relied on Bean and confided in him that he was near his breaking point. Bean knew the officers could destroy Ender's spirit, but nonetheless comforted Ender, reassuring him that he would come out on top.

Bean's special squadron utilized a long ropelike supply used in space construction. It had been difficult for Bean to obtain it, arguing with Graff, Dimak, and another teacher, Dap, that he needed access to the storage closet. With that access eventually granted, Bean trained his special squad in using the rope as a tool in the null-gravity environment. He was disappointed that Nikolai refused to be in the squadron, but found a suitable replacement.

Bean also organized members of Dragon Army to be bodyguards for Ender when his life was threatened by Bonzo Madrid. Despite Bean's best efforts to protect Ender, Bonzo found him alone, but Ender protected himself, killing Bonzo. Bean was glad Ender lived through the attack, but was angry he could not protect Ender himself. Bean made the decision to kill someone; that someone would have to be Achilles.

He showed such skill as a toon leader that he was assigned command of Rabbit Army. Although he was four years younger than the usual age of a commander, Bean's army accepted him. The first soldier to embrace him as a leader was Itú. However, one of his soldiers was a new launchy—Achilles Flandres from Rotterdam.

Bean was certain that Achilles had a renewed desire to kill him. Yet, after his experience following Ender in Dragon Army, he knew how to command respect and utilize authority. He gave Achilles specific orders, refusing to tolerate Achilles's stories of their time in Rotterdam. Bean assigned Achilles to Ambul's toon, making clear the level of obedience he expected from his new soldier and renewed enemy.

Determined to make Achilles pay for Poke's murder, he, with the help of some of his toon leaders, laid a trap for Achilles. They lured Achilles into the duct system, and tied him up with deadline—Bean's chosen tool in the Battle Room. There Achilles would suffer from the heat in the ductwork and dehydrate to death. Unless he confessed on a recorder that he'd killed Poke and six others. Achilles confessed and was kicked out of Battle School for it. But he swore a new murderous vengeance against Bean.

After a week in command of Rabbit Army, and five losses in the battles, Bean was promoted to go to Tactical School. He was replaced in his army by Nikolai. As he traveled to Tactical School, Bean wrote letters to political analysts Locke and Demosthenes, telling them that Battle School should be shut down. The children at Battle School, he knew, would end up fighting in the world conflict that developed between the Russians, Muslim nations, China, and North America after the Formic War.

He studied at Tactical School for a week when another unexpected and perhaps premature promotion came. Bean was sent to Command School, where he served as one of Ender's squadron leaders in the simulator/exams, later revealed to be real battles. They communicated by radio.

During his time at Command School, Bean figured out that the simulators were real battles, and that the International Fleet had the ability to communicate ship to ship at light speed. He forced himself to disbelieve this, however, so as to allow himself to emotionally disconnect from the deaths that occurred in the simulators.

Also at Command School, Bean became friends with Petra Arkanian. They distrusted each other at first, but soon built a deep mutual respect between them. Around this same time, during a conversation with Graff (who had been reassigned to Command School), Bean learned his true parentage and true name. He was Julian Delphiki II, son of Julian and Elena Delphiki of Greece. And his brother was Nikolai—the truest friend he'd ever had.

Bean had been told that he was the backup plan if Ender snapped and was unable to complete his final simulator. He was ready to fulfill that obligation if need be.

When the final Command School simulation was played, Ender had been struggling with severe emotional trauma. It was Bean who eased his nerves by reminding Ender "The enemy's gate is down," a command Ender had impressed on Bean and the others in Dragon Army at Battle School. However, Bean realized he didn't have a strategy if Ender snapped. The point was moot, however, as Ender led the fleet to victory.

Following Ender's victory, war did break out on Earth. Graff protected Bean from being captured and used by either of Earth's factions. The conflict did not last long, though, and Bean was one of Ender's friends who told him that the war had ended thanks to something called the "Locke Proposal."

Bean returned to Earth and was adopted by his biological parents, the Delphikis. The new family went on a vacation together, but were attacked. Their holiday house was bombed, and it was clear that their lives were in jeopardy.

They were rescued by Greek soldiers, and from them Bean learned that ten of his friends, including Petra, were kidnapped. He thought that Achilles was mounting a war against the world, but couldn't be sure.

After a few weeks of living with his family in a small apartment under the protective guard of the Greek Army, Bean was ready to move on. He wanted to leave his family for their own protection and search for Petra and the others. When Graff and Sister Carlotta showed up at their hiding place and took the family to another undisclosed locale, it appeared that he might get his chance to do just that.

However, it was not exactly to be. Graff planned to take the rest of the Delphiki family further into hiding, while Bean would travel with Sister Carlotta. He didn't know what she had in mind, but he went along with the plan, if only to protect his new family. He wanted to find his friends and beat Achilles.

They traveled to Brazil where they kept on top of world matters through the nets and e-mail. They used a series of servers to hide their location and were successful in remaining hidden.

Bean loved to get out of their hiding place and go outside. With his training from Battle School and experience as a streetwise child in Rotterdam, he was safe. He knew that he was protecting Sister Carlotta just as much as she was watching over him.

One day, in looking at their e-mail messages, Bean and Carlotta came across a picture of a dragon. Bean thought it might be a signal from his captive colleagues. He stayed up all night decoding it and determined that it had been secretly sent by Petra Arkanian, disclosing her location in Russia.

Knowing Peter Wiggin could arrange for military rescue operations for Petra and company, Bean sent the information to him. Peter acted swiftly in his secret identity, Locke, and set in motion a rescue mission. The mission was successful, for the most part, though Petra remained in Achilles's custody.

Bean realized, in the course of this discovery, that he had deep feelings of affection and friendship for Petra. He promised himself he would do whatever he had to in order to protect and save her. She would not, he swore, become another Poke.

In response to Bean's aid in freeing the kidnapped soldiers, Peter Wiggin contacted Sister Carlotta and Bean, hoping for a meeting with them. They did not respond via e-mail, but rather together left for Peter's hometown of Greensboro, North Carolina.

It was Bean's first visit to America, and he was awestruck by the nation's apparent wealth and the unnecessary waste and extravagance that he witnessed there. With Carlotta, he went to Peter's university, and met the young man at a nearby restaurant. There Bean and Peter snipped at each other, verbally sparring to prove their own superiority.

Bean left his "grandmother" Carlotta and Peter and looked around Greensboro. He wanted to see Ender's family's house, and there he met Ender's mother Theresa. She knew who he was, and she took him into her home.

The two spoke frankly with one another, and Bean learned much about Theresa and her husband's goals for their children. They missed Ender and Valentine, who had gone into space never to return, but also were secretly proud of Peter. They knew that he was Locke, but pretended not to. Though Theresa at times felt that Bean was condescendingly judging or condemning her, she shared some of the most intimate details of her life with him. Particularly, she told him how much she loved her children and longed for Peter to have kids of his own. Bean was struck by that, believing that he himself would never have children, either.

As they concluded their conversation, Sister Carlotta and Peter arrived at the house. Peter introduced Carlotta as a traveler, but Theresa revealed that Bean had exposed his true identity to her already. Nonetheless, Theresa invited Bean and Carlotta to join her family for dinner, and they went to a nearby restaurant.

At dinner, Bean and Sister Carlotta planted a seed in Peter, hoping that he would join them in their travels-in-hiding. As they discussed it more later in private, Bean helped the trio come up with a plan that would set Peter on his path of political dominance, as well as prevent Achilles from exposing Peter's identity as Locke.

Bean simply wanted to find and rescue Petra, but knew that to do that he had to align himself with Peter. It was why he visited Theresa—to learn if Peter was trustworthy. In the process, he determined that he knew he had to trust Peter regardless and be his best general as he launched his rise to power in the world.

As Peter revealed his true identity to the world, Bean and Sister Carlotta traveled to Thailand. There they'd been promised a group of soldiers to command, and access to all intelligence related to Achilles and Petra. They got none. Bean spent much of his time posting secret notes to Petra on the computer forums, but she never replied. He was unsure if she was even alive.

He was also growing. It seemed that every day he was another centimeter taller. He outgrew clothing almost faster than he could replace it. Bean was rapidly becoming a giant, and it was a strange sensation. He'd been the smaller-than-average kid at Battle School; now he was growing larger and faster than normal.

After weeks of not getting anything he'd been promised, Bean tried to test the patience of the Thai military leadership. To protect Sister Carlotta, he sent her away. She left for Madrid. But before she left, she and Bean had a little fight. Peter had told Bean that Carlotta had written some memos about Bean before he went to Battle School. She'd never told him about the memos and refused to share their content with him. It was a touchy subject between the two of them.

When Carlotta left, Bean sent a message to the leader of the Thai military speaking about strategic matters. The message was intercepted by the military leader assigned to take care of Bean, a young man named Suriyawong, who was a Battle School graduate and a smart soldier. He met with Bean, and though he didn't trust him at first, saw that Bean was not a threat to his position in the Thai military.

Suriyawong gave Bean a group of soldiers to train, and maps. He did not share much intelligence, though. This was not a huge problem for Bean, however, as Graff and Sister Carlotta kept him up to speed on world affairs.

After six months of training his troops, Graff told him that the Indian and Pakistani armies had pulled their troops back from their shared border and appeared to be working together.

Graff also told him that Achilles and Petra had orchestrated the withdrawals. Bean refused to believe that Petra had sided with Achilles and determined that she was giving him solid military advice that Achilles was ignoring.

It was clear to Bean that the troop withdrawals were the preliminary steps to an Achilles-led Indian invasion of Asia. He was proven correct days later as India invaded Burma. With this knowledge in hand, Bean approached the leader of the Thai military, the Chakri, and learned that the Thai military would not act until they were directly threatened.

With Suriyawong, Bean returned to his barracks. It suddenly hit him that the Chakri was in cahoots with Achilles, and there was an imminent threat on his life and Suriyawong's. The two Battle Schoolers escaped from the barracks just as it was bombed.

Bean and Suriyawong called upon the soldiers Bean had been training to protect them. The Chakri had represented that Indian spies had killed Bean and Suriyawong, and their deaths would not go unavenged. Bean got a message to Graff, Peter, and Carlotta that explained what really had happened. The Chakri resigned from his post, caught in his nefarious scheme, and the Thai Prime Minister took Bean into protective custody.

It was time to find Achilles and rescue Petra. And Sister Carlotta was on her way back.

Bean went with Suriyawong first to dinner and then to the airport to greet Sister Carlotta. They learned there that her plane had been shot down over China, and there were no survivors. It had been Achilles who ordered the plane brought down. Bean was crushed to learn that Sister Carlotta was dead. He cried, and returned to the prime minister's home where he was allowed to grieve in private.

He soon received an e-mail that Sister Carlotta had asked Hyrum Graff and Peter Wiggin to forward to Bean if they'd lost contact somehow. It contained the content of the memos that had been such a touchy issue in their relationship.

The memos and this e-mail told Bean about his genetic manipulation and the turning of Anton's Key. This manipulation had made Bean brilliant, but also accelerated his physical growth. As a result, Carlotta said, Bean would die young.

Bean took the message as fact, particularly in light of his continual growth. He mourned privately, quietly for his beloved Sister Carlotta. She had been a mother to him, and he already missed her terribly. He would not seek vengeance for Sister Carlotta, as she asked him not to in the e-mail. But he would ensure that Achilles was stopped, no matter the cost.

He learned that the missile that shot down Carlotta's plane had been fired from China, and that Achilles was actually working with the Chinese to take over Asia. His actions in India were a cover to subvert that nation and Pakistan, preparing them for Chinese rule. Bean tried to tell the Thai government this, but they doubted him.

With his small squadron and the support of a lone Thai general, Bean went to India on the offensive. It was his goal to rescue Petra. He found Virlomi, an Indian Battle School grad who replied to Bean's forum posting looking for Petra. She gave Bean the intelligence he needed to mount a rescue operation for his friend.

They began the mission, and gave orders to kill Achilles as well. He rescinded the order to kill Achilles, though, upon confronting him. Achilles held Petra hostage, and Bean used Achilles's Chinese military allies against him. The Chinese had orders to return Achilles to China and brokered a deal with Bean that allowed Petra to go free and let them still obey their orders. The deal was kept, and Bean rescued Petra, though Achilles lived.

Bean was given the high-ranking position of Strategos in the new Hegemony led by Peter Wiggin. Though Bean and Peter still didn't see eye to eye, they agreed that they could work together. The Delphiki family moved to Brazil to be at the center of the Hegemony.

In memory of Poke and Sister Carlotta, Bean set up memorials to them outside of the Hegemony's compound. It was there that he and Petra spoke about the future. Petra told Bean that she wanted to have his children, while Bean, concerned that his children would suffer the same genetic manipulation he had, said he would never have children.

He was growing still and was nearly a fully grown adult, in size anyway, though he was barely a teenager. The disease he'd been given genetically continued to prey upon him, and it frightened and angered him.

Over the next several months, Bean grew very tall and large in stature. He towered over the small army Peter Wiggin had assigned him in the Hegemony. He trained the soldiers well and was preparing to take them on a mission to free a prisoner in China from a convoy.

The prisoner was Achilles, and Peter wisely took Bean off the mission, assigning it to Suriyawong instead. Achilles was to come to the Hegemony compound. The move infuriated Bean, who resigned from his position in the Hegemony. With Petra, he went back into hiding underground, using fake IDs to travel the world.

Petra continuously made overtures to Bean to marry him or to be the mother of his children. Bean adamantly refused her advances. She was able to at least convince him to kiss her. He did have tender feelings for her, but was not willing to bring more lives into the world that would suffer the same fate he did.

They traveled to Poland where Bean contacted one of his former Battle School soldiers, Ambul. Bean asked Ambul to go to Damascus and seek the help of another former Battle Schooler, Alai, who had ascended to a high position within the powerful Muslim League. Bean knew that if he could get Alai's help, he could finally defeat Achilles. It would be tricky to convince Alai, but Bean knew Ambul would be up to the task.

As they waited for word from Damascus, Petra convinced Bean to visit Anton, the scientist who had developed the gene manipulation that controlled Bean. He reluctantly agreed.

Anton spent much of their time together trying to convince Bean to settle down with Petra and have a family with her. It was the key to not dying lonely or depressed. Bean refused to believe this and tried arguing that he needed to stop Achilles. Having a family would interfere with that.

His arguments were in vain, however. As he spoke with Anton and Petra, Bean realized that he loved Petra and agreed to marry her and give her the children she wanted. But, he had a condition: he would only do so if the children could be born without the genetic mutation that had caused his growth and intelligence. Anton said that Volescu, the doctor who had created Bean in the first place, could ensure the request. Bean and Petra began efforts to find Volescu. They become engaged and were happy that they were in love.

They were married in Spain and honeymooned for a week in the islands of the Mediterranean. They made their way to Rotterdam, Bean's hometown, to meet with Volescu. Volescu agreed to determine if any of their embryos had Bean's mutation, but Petra was suspicious. She realized that there was no test for that. She changed their plans with Volescu, stating that he would test the embryos, but they would go elsewhere for implantation. Bean arranged for security to watch over Petra and the embryos every step of the way.

Bean and Volescu destroyed the "tainted" embryos together. The newlyweds took the remaining embryos to the nearby women's clinic for implantation. Along the way, Bean showed Petra many of the important landmarks from his Rotterdam childhood. It was an emotional experience, particularly when he returned to the site of Poke's murder.

As they prepared for implantation, Bean received a message from his Battle School colleague Han Tzu, informing him that Achilles had arranged for his own release from China, and that Peter Wiggin was playing right into his hands. Bean passed the message on to Peter's parents in Brazil.

Petra and Bean decided that once the implantation had taken place, they would need to leave Rotterdam separately. They made plans to reconnect a week later. Before they could part, though, the plans changed once again.

Walking out of the women's clinic, Bean placed Petra in a cab driven by an Indonesian driver. He did not trust the Dutch taxi drivers. It was a smart move, as the Dutch drivers were working with Volescu and Achilles to steal all of the embryos, and possibly kill Bean.

Bean escaped from his Dutch cab with the aid of some other Indonesian soldiers. From them he learned that Alai had sent them to rescue Petra and Bean. Petra was safely on the road to Damascus.

Through this conversation, Bean also realized that Volescu didn't know which embryos had the mutation and which didn't. He realized that as many as eight of their embryos were stolen, and could potentially grow to be humans like him—with the intelligence and size that resulted from his genetic mutation.

Traveling to Damascus, Bean realized that he loved Achilles, and had since they were children on the streets of Rotterdam. He felt that he had gone about defeating Achilles the wrong way—he'd been too reactionary, and tried too hard to avoid him. What he needed to do was directly confront him.

He arrived at Damascus, and met briefly with Alai, who had become the Caliph for the entire Muslim world. He was reunited with Petra and tried to comfort her in her hopelessness at the loss of the embryos. Bean promised his wife that he would find the embryos in time for Petra to give birth to the child she carried from the implantation.

Over the next several months, Bean and Petra stayed with Alai in his compound. They both acted as advisers to Alai and his Muslim military leaders. They helped plan a Muslim invasion of China, hoping to free the captive Muslim peoples of Asia. Alai trusted Bean, though he accused Bean of leaking information about the military's movements and plans to Peter Wiggin, or worse, Achilles. Bean was able to convince Alai that he was not the source of the leak, however, and their mutual trust resumed.

Bean and Alai consulted with each other frequently during the first stages of Alai's Asian liberation. Alai was worried things were going too well, since the Chinese hadn't acknowledged any kind of invasion or strike. Bean and Petra told him everything was good and helped him find the confidence to lead his people.

Having done all they could for Alai, Bean and Petra left his compound to resume their search for their embryos. They went to a restaurant where they saw Alai make his first televised speech as Caliph. They were pleased for him and were certain that his armies would be successful.

Both Bean and Alai hoped they would never be on opposite sides in a war, as they had sadly been with their Battle School colleague Han Tzu, who was a leader in China.

The search for the embryos appeared potentially short-lived as Achilles posted an online auction for them to bait Bean to face him in Brazil. Bean took the bait, but not unprepared. He traveled to the Hegemony compound in Brazil with Peter Wiggin and several bodyguards. There he confronted Achilles.

Achilles pretended that he had the embryos. He tried to blow up Bean. When that didn't work, he tried preying on Bean's emotions about the embryos, which he still did not have, but had implanted in other surrogates. Bean remained cool and calm. He killed Achilles with a bullet to the brain. He didn't feel satisfaction through the kill, but had a sense of justice for Poke and Sister Carlotta, who had died at Achilles's hands.

Petra rejoined him in Brazil a short time later, and they moved into a small house where they would raise their child once it was born. They also began scouring the Earth searching for the embryos and their surrogates.

A few weeks after Achilles's death, Bean was confronted by Mazer Rackham, the soldier who had trained Ender. Mazer was secretly working with Graff in the Ministry of Colonization and had an offer for Bean: take a newly designed starship and go into space with his children, traveling at light speed. This would allow him to exist at relativistic time, while years passed on Earth, and a cure for his manipulation could be found.

Bean considered this, knowing that the International Fleet would not make such an offer altruistically. He was right. In exchange for the ship, they expected him to aid Peter Wiggin in his assertion of world dominance. Bean believed that Peter wouldn't listen to him, but Rackham promised the ship if Bean at least tried. To preserve his family, and perhaps his own life, Bean agreed.

Rackham also promised to provide Bean with the intelligence the International Fleet had on Volescu's whereabouts. Bean would be able to ask the doctor himself about the location of his embryos.

Before heading out to find Volescu, Bean and Petra watched a televised statement made by Virlomi, who had become a virtual goddess among the Indian people. She declared war on the Muslim occupiers under the direction of Alai. It was her plan, Bean told Peter Wiggin, to marry either Alai or Han Tzu, the Emperor of China, and declare war on the other. Bean helped Peter develop a strategy for this impending war.

He and Petra traveled to Rwanda where Volescu was hiding. The doctor had developed a weapon that would pass on Bean's genetic mutation to all future generations of humanity. Bean nearly killed Volescu, but Petra stopped him. They called in Anton to study what Volescu had done.

He was by Petra's side when their first son, Andrew Arkanian Delphiki (whom they would call Ender), was born two months early. Bean told Petra of the ship and the relativistic travel that would allow him to live while a cure was searched for the genetic mutation. Little Ender also had the mutation, and so Petra insisted that she travel to space with Bean and their children. Bean agreed, but had second thoughts later.

While thinking about his future, Bean realized that Peter was embezzling Ender Wiggin's pension for his own purposes. After speaking with Theresa Wiggin and Hyrum Graff, Bean convinced the Ministry of Colonization to use the Mind Game (aka, the Giant's Drink) from Battle School as an investment counselor for Ender's money. This computer program had a level of sentience, and could use the money extremely well. Bean never knew that this decision led to the creation of Jane, who would become Ender's dearest companion during his journeys in space.

He also asked that the program be used to help find his embryos. In the midst of this, Peter assigned Bean to Rwanda to lead that nation's armies. The Rwandan leader, Felix Starman, requested Bean in exchange for ratifying the constitution Peter had written to unify the countries that followed him as Hegemon.

Bean and Petra, with son Ender, would go to Rwanda together. But Petra was not there long. She left for Portugal to retrieve one of the embryos Graff had tracked as being their daughter, named Bella.

Meanwhile, Bean trained the Rwandan army, and led the troops in combat against nations that were attacking people who had ratified Peter Wiggin's constitution. He had created a confederation of nations—made up of people, not governments—called the "Free People of Earth." With Bean's brilliant use of the militaries within the Hegemony, the Free People of Earth was continually expanding.

Bean traveled to the Philippines where another of his embryos had been born. This one, a boy named Ramón, was free of the genetic mutation. While there, looking for his son, Bean was invited to attend a meeting with the rest of Ender's Command School mates.

Graff again offered Ender's colleagues the opportunity to leave Earth and govern a planet. It was his fear that Ender's army would be used in the worldwide conflict, manipulated by whatever political power rose to prominence, and he wanted to prevent that. Every member who received the offer, which did not include Han Tzu, Petra Arkanian, or Alai, said no. The others were already too involved in matters on Earth to leave.

Petra and Bean traveled to her home country of Armenia, staying with Petra's parents, to negotiate Armenian entry into the Free People of Earth. Though the Armenians wanted to join the world government, they were concerned about invasion from their neighbors. Bean reassured them they'd be protected by the Free People of Earth (FPE) military.

Bean cared for his babies. He was a tender father despite his massive size. It was apparent to Petra's parents that he loved the children and Petra very much.

As the wars between China, India, and Russia began, Bean organized strikes with the armies of the FPE. His involvement with these armies was cut short, however, as a deal was made with Peter Wiggin and Mazer Rackham to allow Bean to take his mutated babies into space. Mazer tracked down the remaining embryos, save one, and delivered them to Petra and Bean. Three of their children had the mutation, while five did not. One was still missing.

Bean divorced Petra immediately upon finding these children, and put a plan in motion where he would fake his death in Iran and leave for space. He wanted Petra, who was furious with him for divorcing her and leaving her with five babies to raise, to remarry.

Though deeply saddened at having to leave Earth and never see Petra again, Bean knew it was for the best. He made sure his pension would be given to her to raise their children and asked that he and the three babies he was taking with him not be called back to Earth until after Petra died so she would not have to face him again.

He left for space with his three children, writing a good-bye note to Petra. He kept in contact with Hyrum Graff for a short while, thanking him for all the support Graff had given him over the years.

Bean was not optimistic that a cure for his mutation would ever be found, but allowed the sliver of hope—that it might be in time for his children—to carry him through his travels.

He loved Petra and missed her. He knew that he had done all he could for the people he loved throughout his life. Though the deaths of Poke and Sister Carlotta would forever remind him of his great failures, he saw his children, his wife, and the success of his friend Ender Wiggin and knew that he had truly done all he could.

Throughout Earth, Bean's life story became legendary: the Legend of the Giant. And indeed he was a giant—physically and figuratively.

Delphiki, Julian III ("normal" child) (SG)

Julian Delphiki III was one of the embryos created by Bean Delphiki and Petra Arkanian and implanted into an unknown surrogate. He did not have the genetic mutation of his father and remained on Earth when Bean left for space, to be raised by his mother.

Delphiki, Lani (EE)

Lani Delphiki was married to Andrew Delphiki, one of Petra Arkanian and Bean Delphiki's children.

Delphiki, Nikolai (ES, SH, SP)

Nikolai Delphiki was a contemporary of Ender Wiggin's at Battle School. A couple of years younger than Ender, Nikolai was a member of Bean's launch group. Bean had hacked into Nikolai's computer, which Nikolai reported to Battle School officials. He befriended Bean, however, after the computer hacking incident, becoming very close.

When Bean hacked into the teacher's evaluations of the other students, he saw that Nikolai was listed as "a place-holder." This news was hard on Nikolai, but he tried to turn that perception around through harder work and practice.

Bean was ordered to make up a list of soldiers for a hypothetical army, which Bean knew Ender would command. He had to use launchies and soldiers from transfer lists only. He included Nikolai on the list, which meant that Nikolai would be transferred with Bean to Dragon Army, commanded by Ender Wiggin.

Nikolai was insecure with his abilities, but stayed close to Bean. He helped protect Bean during a fistfight he had with Fly Molo. When teachers like Anderson and Dimak asked why Nikolai was so close to Bean, Nikolai said they were brothers. Though he meant it metaphorically, it was literally true. Nikolai and Bean were brothers, grown in vitro from embryos belonging to the same people—Julian and Elena Delphiki.

He refused to be a part of Bean's special squadron in Dragon Army, and the decision placed a brief wall between the two brothers. They quickly reconciled, and Nikolai was able to support Bean when he was upset about not being able to protect Ender from Bonzo Madrid's death threats.

After Ender's army was dissolved, Nikolai was assigned to Rabbit Army with Bean as his commander. He helped Bean capture Achilles Flandres and get him to confess his murderous ways. A week later, Nikolai was promoted to commander of Rabbit Army.

After Ender's victory at the Formic home world, Nikolai returned home to Greece. He was joined by his brother, Bean, whom his parents adopted as their own son. While vacationing as a family, though, the Delphikis realized their lives were in danger.

A mysterious group of soldiers bombed their vacation home. Nikolai and his family were rescued by the Greek Army. They were placed in a small, guarded apartment until Hyrum Graff and Sister Carlotta took them further into hiding.

Nikolai went with his parents and Graff to an undisclosed location, while Bean left with Sister Carlotta. He resurfaced after the crisis in Brazil, joining Bean there in the protective Hegemony compound. Nikolai and his family had to leave the compound soon after arriving, though, as Achilles had resurfaced, and it was clear he was coming to Brazil. They went back underground.

They resurfaced once Achilles was killed. Nikolai got married a couple of years later; and according to his mother, lived a happy life.

Delphiki, Petra "Poke" ([EE], SG)

Petra Delphiki, or "Poke" as she was called, was one of the embryos created by Bean Delphiki and Petra Arkanian. She did not have the genetic mutation of her father and remained on Earth when Bean and three of her siblings left for space. She was raised on Earth by her mother and nicknamed for the first person Bean ever loved—a little girl in Rotterdam named Poke.

Delphiki, Ramón (SG)

Ramón was one of Petra Arkanian and Bean Delphiki's stolen embryos. Born in the Philippines by his surrogate parents, he did not have the genetic mutation his father and siblings did. He was the first of Bean's children to be born without it. Bean went to the Philippines to find him. He remained on Earth to be raised by his mother, Petra, when Bean and three of Ramón's siblings were taken into space.

Demosthenes (EG, ES, EE, SH, SP, SG, IC, SD, XN, CM)

The pseudonym for ten-year-old Valentine Wiggin, used when she wrote political and military commentaries on the computer nets. Her columns, and those of her brother Peter written under the name "Locke," became popular throughout the world. John Paul Wiggin, Peter and Valentine's father, even quoted passages of the columns to his family. The International Fleet determined Demosthenes's true identity while Ender was in Battle School; however they maintained a laissez-faire attitude toward both Demosthenes and Locke.

Talented Battle School student Bean wrote Demosthenes and Locke a letter giving reasons that Battle School should be shut down and predicting a worldwide conflict between Russia, Asia, the Middle East, and North America in the aftermath of the war in space. Demosthenes took up this charge in essays.

Demosthenes and Locke effected change in much of the international community in the aftermath of Ender's victory in the Formic War. Demosthenes argued for Ender's return home, but soon gave up the campaign and disappeared from the nets. However, the mysterious essayist began a career of writing books.

Valentine went into space with Ender to colonize worlds with other human settlers. It was on these journeys that she wrote the many books she did. During this time on Earth, though, Peter took over writing the political essays of Demosthenes, writing both him and Locke.

One of Valentine's books was a work on the planet Helvetica, which had fallen into disarray. Many fans wrote letters to Demosthenes, believing the author to be an old historian. This fact entertained young Valentine greatly.

One important book written by Demosthenes was *History of Wutan in Trondheim*. This book, the history of the planet Trondheim, created the scale of defining life, using Icelandic terms like "utlanning," "framling," "raman," and "varelse," which became common among scientists on the different human colonies.

Two decades later, Demosthenes exposed the Starways Congress's plan to use the Molecular Detachment Device on Lusitania, causing public outrage against a potential second xenocide. The essays caused revolution among the different colonies and planets of the Congress.

On the planet Path, a young girl named Han Qing-jao undertook an assignment to uncover the truths about the fleet, in defense of the Starways Congress. She began a galaxy-wide search for Demosthenes, hoping to uncover the essayist's true identity. A few months later, she did, and used the discovery to expose Demosthenes's true identity as Valentine Wiggin to the Starways Congress.

The Starways Congress was pleased to know that Demosthenes was on Lusitania, knowing that she soon would be killed. The political pundit who had caused so much anti-Congress feeling would soon be dead.

She survived, thanks to the combined efforts of nearly everyone on Lusitania, and wrote yet another book—the history of Lusitania. This book, potentially her final, featured much about Ender, but was not a book about him.

Descolada (SD, XN, CM)

The Descolada was a virus that destroyed all living things with which it came in contact, except the native life of the planet Lusitania. Fatal to humans, the Descolada helped provide the life transition for the pequeninos, and even inhabited other fauna and flora on the planet. It ravaged the ecology of Lusitania, leaving only a few species as survivors.

The virus destroyed humans inside out, killing them slowly and painfully. Removing the virus had the same effect on the pequeninos. Created on the planet Descoladore, the virus appeared to be a chemical form of communication intended to be used to expand its creator's influence throughout the universe.

A team of scientists on Lusitania, led by Ender Wiggin's stepchildren, were able to isolate and eradicate the virus on the planet without killing the pequeninos. Some of the scientists believed the virus was itself a living organism, but no definitive answer has been reached in determining its life status. Research continues into its origins and evolution.

Descoladore (CM)

The descoladore was the name given by Miro Ribeira von Hesse and his sisters, Quara and Ela, to the race of beings that created the Descolada. The descoladore communicated with the virus by sending messages that the virus translated into molecules. The communication was reciprocated likewise.

They'd sent out probes into space, carrying the virus to distant worlds. They had tried to terriform different planets to make them suitable for their own habitation. After decoding the message of human DNA that Miro and company had broadcast to them, the descoladore launched several spaceships against the humans. Miro and his comrades escaped the attack by using their faster-than-light instantaneous travel methods.

Quara, Miro, and the rest felt that the planet needed to be destroyed and the threat of the descoladore wiped out. It wasn't until Peter Wiggin II, who carried the soul of Ender, appeared on their ship that they were talked out of rashly committing xenocide. Humans would continue to visit the descoladore world, hoping to build understanding over generations of time, allowing all life to live in the galaxy.

Desk (EGS, EG, ES, EE)

A desk was a personal computer used by children at normal schools on Earth as well as at Battle School.

Dimak, Captain (ES, SP)

Captain Dimak was the commanding officer of Bean's flight to Battle School. He was a no-nonsense officer who mocked the ignorance of the children on Bean's flight. He also exposed Bean as scoring the highest of the launch group on the screening tests, though lowest on the physical tests. This revelation alienated Bean from the rest of his launch group.

Dimak oversaw the launch group at Battle School, training them on their lockers, schedules, and other aspects of school life. He grew concerned about Bean's social development with the other members of his launch group and confronted him about it. In the process of the conversation, Bean revealed his thoughts on space-war strategy, telling Dimak that he was certain humanity had already launched an attack fleet against the Formic home world. Dimak denied it, but was sweating profusely. His reaction confirmed to Bean that the fleet had been created.

Dimak grew more concerned about Bean when he and Colonel Graff spoke about findings a nun named Sister Carlotta had made that implied Bean had been genetically engineered. Dimak also discovered that Bean had hacked into a teacher's computer, and was even moving through Battle School's ductwork to spy on the officers. He made the decision to ignore these rule violations in an effort to continue studying Bean.

Graff ordered Dimak to have Bean put together a hypothetical army for Ender Wiggin to command. Bean knew the hypothetical was real, but followed the order. Dimak had been frustrated with Bean in this process as Bean seemed arrogant. But Dimak and Graff took the list Bean created and made the transfers to assemble the army just as Bean suggested.

Dimak had a rivalry with Captain Dap, another Battle School officer. Both he and Dap felt that their protégé was the one to lead the armies of Earth against the Buggers. They argued on behalf of Bean and Ender often with Hyrum Graff, with neither man getting the upper hand.

Once Graff left Battle School, Dimak continued to be an advocate for Bean, but quickly stopped when Graff's replacement, Colonel Anderson, made it clear such advocacy would not be tolerated and would be considered insubordinate.

Years later, after Ender's defeat of the Formics, Battle School was transformed into the Ministry of Colonization. Graff was the minister, and Dimak was the Underminister. He greeted colonists and helped them find their quarters on the station as they awaited transfer to a starship that would take them to their new homes on a human colony.

He was charged with protecting the Wiggin family when they stayed briefly on the station while Achilles Flandres made an attempt to subvert Peter Wiggin's position as Hegemon on Earth. He aided in a plot Graff and Peter developed to protect the Wiggins and to expose a potential mole on the station.

Dispersal Project (YM)

Official title of the International Fleet's colonization project, sending humans to former Formic worlds. Generally looked for responsible, high-profile members of society; however, in some cases exceptions were made.

Divine Wind (*See* Hundred Worlds)

Djur (*See* Hierarchy of Alienness)

Docility patch (CM)

The docility patch was a medical device worn on the skin and used as a type of anesthetic.

Doctor (EG)

This doctor removed Ender's monitor device from the back of his neck. He was assisted by a nurse named Deedee and complained that leaving the monitor devices in children's necks for three years was too long.

Doctor on Ganges (EE)

The doctor on Ganges helped patch up Ender Wiggin following a beating he took at the hands of Achilles Flandres II.

Donnabella (IC)

The capital city of the planet Sorelledolce, Donnabella was home to a million colonists.

Drinker, Grace/Teu 'Ona (CM)

Grace Drinker, or Teu 'Ona as she was known in her native Samoan, was a large religious instructor on the planet Pacifica. She was a teacher in the Ua Lava religion, and taught her good friend Aimaina Hikari on the planet Divine Wind the philosophies of her faith.

Her personality was so dominant that the rest of her family was known as "Grace's husband" or "Grace's son." They were seemingly insignificant next to her. But Grace clearly loved her family, and they loved her.

When Peter Wiggin II and Si Wang-mu traveled to Pacifica as part of their mission to bring down the Starways Congress, Jane led them to Grace. She had heard from Hikari that they had visited him impossibly a day earlier, and confronted Peter II and Wang-mu with their lies and false identities. After finding out the truth about them, she set them up to meet with the revered chief teacher of the Ua Lava believers, Malu.

She acted as translator for Malu, who spoke the ancient, revered language of the gods.

After Malu spoke with Wang-mu and Peter II, it was apparent that Jane had been forced from the computers, yet still lived. Grace invited her guests to watch her and her son restart their new non-Jane compatible computer networks. The reboot came off perfectly, but Grace and her son had another surprise: Jane had helped the people of Pacifica use their old computers (which were instructed by Starways Congress to be discarded save for student use at the university) to re-create a network wherein she could place her consciousness.

Grace revealed that the network of old computers spanned several planets, but Congress didn't know about it. Moments later, Jane used it to relearn how to do faster-than-light travel. Grace and Malu cheered, for their god lived despite the government's best attempts to kill it.

Ducheval "Shovel" ([EG], ES)

A soldier in Ender's dominant Dragon Army, Ducheval was chosen by Bean to be in the special squadron Ender created and assigned to Bean. He was the second choice, being invited to the squadron only after Nikolai Delphiki said no. He was French and hated his nickname, Shovel.

Dvorak (GB)

Dvorak was a Czech composer whose music Sel Menach played to keep sane during his battles with Formics.

Ecstatic Shield (EG)

The Ecstatic Shield was a force field that was used by the nations of Earth and in spaceships for protection from nuclear devices during the Second Formic Invasion.

Edge Nation (CM)

"Edge Nation" was a term used to describe a nation, near another, that lived in the shadow of its neighbor. Canada can be considered an Edge Nation to the United States.

Eiichi (CM)

Eiichi was a wise philosopher among the Japanese colonists on the Hundred Worlds. He was impressed by the efforts of Yasujiro Tsutsumi to sway Congress from destroying Lusitania, and invited the young man to join him on his home planet twenty light-years away where he would be made Eiichi's protégé.

Ekumbo, Gobawa (SD)

Gobawa Ekumbo was the chairman of the Xenological Oversight Committee of the Starways Congress. She was responsible for revoking the charter of the planet Lusitania after the sentient computer program named Jane sent a memo throughout the computer networks stating that the planet's xenologists had taught the native life-forms agriculture—a violation of interstellar law.

Ekumbo learned that the Descolada, a virus on the planet Lusitania, had the potential to spread throughout the Hundred Worlds. He authorized the use of the Molecular Detachment Device to destroy Lusitania and all of its inhabitants.

He compared himself to Peter Wiggin as a political leader, complaining that he had more responsibility and less brilliance. He also wanted to expose Demosthenes, who made public his plans for a second xenocide. (Note: Ekumbo's name is also spelled Ekimbo.)

Ela (*See* Ribeira von Hesse, Ekaterina Elanora "Ela")

Encaixarse (CM)

Lusitanian term for the instant starflight the sentient computer Jane discovered, accomplished by traveling through Outspace. The term translates to "to encase."

English Kid (WG)

The English kid was a member of Rat Army that participated in Dink Meeker's Christmas celebration of secretly giving gifts in other soldier's socks.

Englishman (SP)

The Englishman learned of Alai's ascension to the position of Caliph in the Muslim world while eating at a restaurant in Damascus. He said that he was worried that it symbolized a return to misogyny and the murder of foreigners by Muslim extremists.

Ensign (EE)

The ensign, a young man of about twenty, was the assistant to Admiral Quincy Morgan, the commanding officer of the first transport ship of human settlers. Admiral Morgan yelled at the ensign a lot.

Eros Asteroid (*See also* Command School) (EGS, EG, ES, [GB])

Location of Command School. Although technically a moon, Eros is considered a minor planet. It had once been a Formic base for their initial assault on Earth. The Formics had carved great tunnels into the moon's surface, which were later used by the International Fleet as the foundation for its Command School.

Esquecimento, Sister ([SD])

Sister Esquecimento was a nun who taught at the Catholic school on the planet Lusitania. She was said to have menacing fingernails. Ender Wiggin's stepson Grego held a lifelong disdain for her.

Etruia (SD)

Etruia was an Italian-settled planet of the Hundred Worlds. It was home to the University of Sicily, Milano Campus.

Evenezer ([EE])

Evenezer was married to Afraima, the assistant xenobiologist in Shakespeare, the first human colony on a former Formic world. Evenezer loved his wife deeply, and didn't know that she wanted to cheat on him with Sel Menach, the head xenobiologist.

Exams/Real Battles (EGS, EG, ES, GB, [EE])

In Command School, Ender was put in charge of battle games, called "exams," that required him to command fleets of ships in combat against Formic ships. The exams were later revealed to be actual space battles, not games.

Fairyland (EG)

Fairyland was the seemingly impossible destination of the computer game Giant's Drink, played in Battle school.

Falstaff (*See* Hundred Worlds)

Fan-liu (XN)

Fan-liu was a young teenage girl on the planet Path. Of Chinese descent, she was put into service for a high-ranking family at a young age. She was friends with Si Wang-mu, and prepared her for the life of a servant by telling her that the pretty servants work less than the less-attractive ones.

Father Tongue (SD, XN)

Father Tongue was the means of communication between the pequeninos who had entered the third life known as fathertrees, and their "sons," the living pequeninos. It required rhythmic drumming by the pequeninos and the fathertrees.

Fathertrees (SD, XN, CM)

The fathertrees were the next evolution of the pequenino male on the planet Lusitania. The most revered pequeninos, when they died, had a tree grow from their chest. The pequeninos' wisdom and experience lived on in the tree. The fathertrees could communicate with one another and the pequeninos by way of the Father Tongue. Fathertrees were the only male pequeninos that could reproduce. If a male piggie wasn't made into a fathertree, he would have no progeny.

Female Student (TP)

A young female student was the first to answer Theresa Brown's questions during a college class called Human Community. She was a classmate of John Paul Wiggin and asked their teacher if she was teaching based on science or religion. Theresa expelled the student from her class for the question, stating that the student had asked a bigoted, troublemaking question.

Ferreira (SP, SG)

Ferreira was the computer expert in the Hegemony compound in Brazil. He had a very close relationship to the Hegemon, Peter Wiggin, and created the computer security protocols that were meant to track Achilles Flandres while the serial killer was in the compound.

Although he seemed loyal to Peter, he was actually working with Achilles. When Achilles attempted to discredit Peter as an embezzler, Ferreira fabricated the evidence to support Achilles's claims.

Once Achilles was defeated, Ferreira returned to Peter's side. Peter forgave the earlier disloyalty, and Ferreira continued his position as the head of electronic security in the Hegemony.

He helped Bean and Petra track down their stolen, implanted embryos, even traveling to Rwanda to study the continued illegal work of Dr. Volescu. Ferreira and a group of scientists were able to discover that Volescu had intended to spread the genetic mutation known as Anton's Key to all humanity through a virus. It was Ferreira's research that jump-started Peter Wiggin's campaign to combat Volescu's virus.

Ferreira also helped Bean and Petra search for their stolen embryos by using the Ministry of Colonization's semisentient computer program, the Mind Game or Giant's Drink, to track the information in the birth databases from around the world. He didn't feel this was a good use of his time, but had said he would and was a man of his word.

Ferreria, Mrs. (PB)

Mrs. Ferreria is an older Portuguese woman Bonzo Madrid and his mother met in the marketplace. She was upset with her daughter's life choices, but Mother Madrid helped her see the positive things Mrs. Ferreria's daughter was doing.

Figueira, China (SD)

China was the second child born to Libo Figueira and his wife Bruxinha on the planet Lusitania. She was best friends with Ela Ribeira von Hesse, before Novinha Ribeira forbade her children from having Libo's children over.

Figueira, Prega (SD)

Prega was the third child born to Libo Figueira and his wife Bruxinha on the planet Lusitania.

Figueira, Zinha (SD)

Zinha was the fourth and final child born to Libo Figueira and his wife Bruxinha on the planet Lusitania.

Figueira de Medici, Liberdade Graças a Deus "Libo" (SD)

Libo was the middle child in the Figueira family, and like his father, Pipo, became a xenologer on the planet Lusitania. At age thirteen, he was still an apprentice xenologer, but was known for his talent and maturity despite his age.

In his earlier years, he had known a girl named Novinha at school, and was not glad to learn that she would be taking the xenobiologist certification test earlier than the usual age since he was still an apprentice and liked working with his father. Like the rest of his family, Libo was devoutly Catholic growing up.

Libo and Novinha developed a deep friendship that turned to romantic feelings. They spent so much time together that it was a natural outgrowth of their experience working together.

One day, Libo met with Rooter, one of the planet's native creatures known as the pequeninos or "piggies," and they discussed male/female relations in their two societies. Rooter called human women weak for not killing Libo or his father once they learned they were wise. Libo and his father, Pipo, thought that Rooter was killed by the other piggies for the conversation, which brought great guilt to Libo.

Libo and Novinha were the two who, a while later, found Pipo's dead body. It was a crushing discovery for both. However, with his father's death, Libo became the xenologist for the planet. He wanted access to the research Novinha had gathered, but Novinha refused to give it to him, since she didn't want him to die like his father had.

Although Libo married a woman named Bruxinha, and had four children with her, he had always hoped to marry Novinha. They had a sexual relationship outside of their respective marriages, however, and Libo fathered all six of Novinha's children. Novinha had refused to marry Libo despite loving him, because of her fear that he'd die like Pipo.

Years later, Libo was killed by the piggies in the same fashion his father had been.

Filhos de Mente de Cristo (*See* Children of the Mind of Christ)

Fiorelli, Mil (CM)

Mil Fiorelli was a human colonist and scholar who lived among the Hundred Worlds after Ender's victory over the Formics. His most famous book was *Observations of Distant Worlds with the Naked Eye,* which became a philosophical resource among the human settlers on the different worlds.

Firenzette (IC)

Firenzette was the local currency of the planet Sorelledolce and was used throughout the Hundred Worlds. Worth 1/674 of a Starcount. Ender Wiggin discusses the currency while searching for his finances on Sorelledolce.

Firequencher (CM)

Firequencher was a pequenino scientist on the planet Lusitania. He joined Miro II, Valentine II, Ela and Quara on a mission to study the home planet of the Descolada virus. He was present when the aliens on Descoladore launched an attack against them and helped decipher the insidious message they'd sent, designed to kill all humans.

First Secretary of Starfleet Admiralty (CM)

The First Secretary of the Starfleet Admiralty was a high-ranking officer who first issued the order to destroy the planet Lusitania, but repealed that same order. The fleet was instead instructed to quarantine the planet.

First Speaker of Starways Congress (CM)

The First Speaker of Starways Congress worked with the Starfleet Admiralty to repeal an order that had been given to destroy the planet Lusitania.

Firth, Nichelle (*See* Randi) (SG)

Nichelle Firth was the alias of a woman named Randi, used to hide her identity to sign up for a colony ship and to protect her son, Achilles Flandres II, from capture by Peter Wiggin and the Free People of Earth.

Firth, Randall (*See* Flandres, Achilles II) (SG, EE)

Randall Firth was an alias given to Achilles Flandres II by his mother, a woman named Randi, to protect him from being taken from her by the Free People of Earth led by Peter Wiggin.

Flandres, Achilles I (ES, [EE], SH, SP)

Achilles (pronounced ah-SHEEL) Flandres was a bully on the streets of Rotterdam in the Netherlands. He was smaller in stature compared to the other bullies who stole food from the smaller kids in groups called "crews." Achilles's status as a dominant bully was also challenged because of his bad leg. He walked with a limp that portrayed weakness to the other, stronger bullies.

When nine-year-old female crew leader Poke was advised by Bean to find a bully to protect her crew, she chose Achilles. It was a poor decision on Poke's part, however, as Achilles's charisma and intelligence quickly manipulated the crew into following him more closely than Poke. He called the crew his "family," filling a need the kids didn't know they had—love. Bean admonished Poke to kill Achilles, but it was too late. Achilles was the new unofficial leader of the crew and promised to take care of them like family.

Achilles arranged for Sarge, his right-hand man, to pick a fight with another bully named Ulysses in line at the local soup kitchen. The fight, which Achilles won by seriously hurting Ulysses, led to the family being in the front of the line and the first to get food. Achilles never accepted Bean or Poke, though. In fact, he was determined to kill them. This murderous desire grew when Bean convinced other bullies to protect small children, taking away the family's exclusive rights to the front of the soup kitchen line.

It was Bean who warned Achilles that the other bullies were looking to kill him in retaliation for hurting Ulysses. Achilles went into hiding, running from the bullies, or so it seemed to his family. In actuality, it was a plot to kill Poke.

Poke knew where Achilles went and sought him out the night he left. They kissed, and Poke reminded him of a promise he'd made her: not to kill Bean. Instead, Achilles killed Poke. He beat her to death and left her body in the river. He returned to his family, blaming Ulysses for the murder. He swore revenge against Ulysses, never revealing it was he who killed Poke.

Over the next several months, Achilles underwent several surgeries on his gimp leg, performed by Dr. Vivian Delamar, whom he killed. The goal was to get him physically up to par to send him to Battle School, where he would be a test for Bean. Sister Carlotta warned against assigning him to Battle School, but the warnings fell on deaf ears.

Achilles arrived at Battle School around a year after Bean. He was immediately assigned to Rabbit Army, which Bean had just been assigned to as commander. The assignment was a test for Bean, to see how developed his leadership abilities really were. Achilles was initially disrespectful of Bean as his commander, but after Bean made it clear that stories of their time together in Rotterdam would not be tolerated, and demanded that Achilles answer his orders with "yes, sir," he seemed to fall into line.

However, Bean was certain that Achilles intended to kill him, just as he had Poke. Shortly after he arrived at Battle School, Achilles was called into a meeting with Bean. Bean convinced Achilles to travel with him through the ductwork, where, Bean said, he and Ender had spied on other commanders. Achilles followed Bean into the ducts, but was tricked by Bean and tied up with deadline, Bean's favorite ropelike tool, and held captive.

Bean gave Achilles a choice—either confess to all the murders he'd committed or die by dehydration in the heating system's ducting. Achilles confessed to seven murders, including Poke's, as well as Ulysses's and even Dr. Delamar's. A serial killer, Achilles murdered those who saw him helpless.

The confessions got him kicked out of Battle School, and put into psychiatric care. But they also renewed Achilles's desire to kill Bean.

Achilles escaped from the hospital and began using Russian soldiers to kidnap ten members of Ender's army after the Formic War. It was Achilles's goal to use these most brilliant of military minds to establish armies under his command and destroy the world governmental structure. He longed for power and sought to obtain it on a grand scale.

He tried to kill Bean and his family but was unsuccessful. Nonetheless, he manipulated his captives, including Petra Arkanian, into presenting plausible, successful military strategies for his ever-growing armies.

After several months, Achilles noticed that Petra Arkanian, one of his prisoners from Ender's army, had sent a message out to an unknown recipient that contained a coded message. He was unable to figure out the message and was frustrated by it. But it told him that Petra was the smartest and most talented of his captives.

Once the message got out, the political pundit Locke called for a rescue mission of the kidnapped war heroes. He used the information from Petra's message to call on the Russian government to make things right and free the prisoners.

Achilles allowed this rescue operation to go forward for all of his prisoners except Petra. Knowing that she was the smartest, he interfered in her rescue, and rekidnapped her. He took her on an airplane, where he nearly killed her by sending her out of the cabin into the sky. He helped pull her back into the plane, though. They landed in New Delhi, where Achilles was hopeful that Petra would use her strategic brilliance to aid him in his plans of world domination.

He had made an alliance of some kind with the Indian government. Half a world away, Bean, Peter Wiggin, and Sister Carlotta determined that this alliance was a great threat to Asia, and to Bean and Peter personally. Peter had derailed Achilles's plans in Russia by exposing his kidnappings, and Achilles wanted revenge. It was possible, they knew, that Achilles could form an alliance with the Polemarch, Chamrajnagar, who would expose Peter's identity as Locke to Achilles, and bring about many problems for the world at large.

With much influence in the Indian government, Achilles orchestrated the next phase of his world domination. He convinced the prime minister of India to pull his troops back from the border with Pakistan. He then took Petra, whom he had forced to create new military strategies and then ignored, to

Pakistan and convinced the prime minister of that country to also pull back their troops.

It was his goal to take over Asia with Pakistan's help. Masterfully manipulative, Achilles was successful in convincing the leadership to be a part of his plan. He also secretly got into the head of the top military leaders in Thailand and convinced them to kill Bean and his ally Suriyawong.

The assassination attempt was unsuccessful, but Achilles began his march across Asia by sending the Indian army into Burma.

He called Petra to his office. There he told her that he was certain Bean was dead and revealed that he knew about the secret messages Bean had been trying to send Petra through the online forums. Another female Battle School graduate in their military compound, Virlomi, had responded to the messages, and for that Achilles was going to kill her.

This warning led to a physical confrontation between Petra and Achilles. They beat each other up pretty soundly, and Petra changed tactics. She kissed Achilles and tried to convince him that she was on his side. She hoped it would help dissuade him from killing Virlomi. It was all an act, and Achilles was skeptical, but Petra gave it her all. Achilles dismissed her from his presence and returned to issuing orders for the army, believing Petra was becoming his.

All of Achilles's efforts in India had been a cover. He was actually setting up India and Pakistan to be taken over by the Chinese. When this was exposed by rebellious Indian soldiers from his planning team, Achilles killed the soldiers and took Petra hostage as he tried to leave India for China. Bean was on his way to rescue Petra and kill Achilles, so Achilles was desperate to escape with his life.

When Bean arrived and confronted Achilles, Achilles held a gun to Petra's head. The Chinese soldiers who had been working with Achilles to take over Asia had orders to return him to China unharmed. Bean exploited these orders, brokering a deal with the Chinese that let them take Achilles but free Petra.

Petra wanted Achilles killed. As the Chinese solider in command moved to free Petra from Achilles, Achilles tried to shoot him. But he was not fast enough, as the Chinese soldier took the gun from Achilles's hand and broke his arm, freeing Petra. Bean used a tranquilizer to incapacitate Achilles.

Achilles traveled back to China, unconscious, with his soldiers. He was arrested and imprisoned. The Chinese government had determined that he was a threat to them and wisely put him away. As they moved him to another prison facility, though, he was freed by a small army sent by Peter Wiggin, the Hegemon.

This small army, led by Suriyawong, took Achilles back to the Hegemony compound in Brazil. Suriyawong was overly respectful to Achilles, trying to gain false trust with him. He knew that Achilles always killed the people who had seen him helpless, and rescuing him from the clutches of a Chinese prison made Achilles appear helpless.

Achilles helped train the small army that Suriyawong had commanded. He was again positioning himself to assume great power in a governmental position, this time in the Hegemony run by Peter Wiggin. But it was all part of Peter's plan to assert his own authority.

Peter had brought Achilles to the Hegemony to monitor his correspondence with his former allies in Russia, China, Thailand, India, and Pakistan. But the study was not as useful as Peter had thought it would be. Peter gave Achilles a new assignment: Assistant to the Hegemon, and they were to work closely together so Peter could control Achilles.

Achilles knew what Peter was doing and was playing his cards in such a way that he hoped he would again rise in power and position, free from being Peter's prisoner. In fact, he'd secretly been winning the game from the start. It was revealed to Bean, who passed the information on to the Wiggins, that Achilles had arranged his own rescue from the prison convoy, passing it off as information from former Battle Schooler Han Tzu.

Peter's parents realized what happened and took Peter from the Hegemony compound. Achilles tried to discredit Peter by claiming he was embezzling funds from the Hegemony. Peter countered the claims and asserted his authority and position as the rightful Hegemon through a full disclosure press conference.

In Brazil, Achilles tried to make it appear that Suriyawong was the new Hegemon, but no one bought in to his attempts at the power grab. Worse, Peter discovered that Achilles was still working with the Chinese government, and the world hung in the balance.

Peter had gone into hiding in space, and with the help of Hyrum Graff and Chamrajnagar, set a plot in motion that would expose Achilles's evil intentions. The group sent an empty shuttle from space, claiming it carried Peter. Achilles shot it down, and the International Fleet subsequently authorized an Earth-bound attack on him.

In the meantime, Achilles set a trap for Bean. He claimed to have Bean and Petra's stolen embryos, though he had actually implanted them in other surrogates previously. Bean joined Peter in storming the Hegemony compound. Bean remained calm and didn't fall for any of Achilles's lies about the embryos.

Bean put Achilles back against the wall and held a gun to his face. Achilles ordered Suriyawong to kill Bean, but Suriyawong, who had never been loyal to Achilles, turned his back on him, leaving him alone to face the consequences of his actions. Bean shot Achilles in the face, killing him in vengeance for Poke and Sister Carlotta. Achilles was dead and would be buried at the Hegemony compound. But Bean still needed to know what his lifelong enemy had done with the embryos.

Flandres, Achilles II (EE, SG)

Achilles Flandres II was the ninth and final embryo created by Bean Delphiki and Petra Arkanian. He was implanted into and birthed by a young woman named Randi who had been told that the embryo had actually been created by Achilles Flandres I and his unknown wife. Randi worshipped Achilles and the work he'd done in trying to unify/take over the world. She named her son Achilles in his honor, though gave him a secret identity as "Randall Firth."

Achilles II suffered from the genetic mutation known as Anton's Key. His intelligence and growth were accelerated. Though born undersized, he would live to be a brilliant giant, like his father Bean, but would die at a young age.

Achilles II, under his alias Randall Firth, traveled with his mother to the human colony on the planet Ganges. He grew up on that planet, believing his mother's stories that his father, "Achilles the Great," sought peace and prosperity for the world. Through these stories, Achilles II grew to hate Peter Wiggin for defeating his father, and even hated Virlomi, the governor of his colony, because she undid the peace his father had created in India.

When Achilles II was sixteen, Virlomi told him the truth about his father and the reasons he was the most hated man in human history. Achilles II refused to believe her and struck her in the face. Arrested for striking the governor, and then perjuring himself afterward, Achilles II was to be exiled back to Earth.

Achilles II was the founder of a religious movement called Natives of Ganges, which based its teachings on *The Hive Queen* by the mysterious "Speaker for the Dead." Sending out his teachings by ansible, Achilles II was able to use the book to discredit Ender Wiggin as a hero. Calling him "Ender the Xenocide," Achilles got revenge on one of the relatives of the man he thought killed his father.

When Ender himself arrived at Ganges, Achilles II tried to kill him. Ender refused to fight Achilles II because he was the son of Ender's friends. Ender revealed Achilles II's true parentage to him. He was the son of Bean Delphiki and Petra Arkanian. Though initially angry at what he thought were lies, Achilles II soon accepted the truth. He turned from a life of anger and vengeance and changed his name to Arkanian Delphiki in honor of his parents. This hurt his relationship with his surrogate mother Randi, but it was of little consequence to him. His sentence commuted by Virlomi, he stayed on Ganges.

Flash Suit (EGS, EG, ES)

Flash suits were the uniform jumpsuits worn during combat simulations in Battle School. If a soldier took a hit in his flash suit from a flash pistol, he was immobilized.

Flasher/Flash Pistol (EGS, EG, ES)

The primary weapon used in Battle School, Flashers were small boxes that fit in the palm of the hand, glowed green, and froze their victims.

FleetCom/Fleet Command (EG, ES)

FleetCom or Fleet Command was the location of Command School. Housed on the asteroid Eros, it was the central planning location for offensives against the Formics.

Fliers (XN)

Fliers were essentially floating cars, which were used for transporation on the Hundred Worlds.

Floaters (CM)

Floaters were floating cars used for transportation on the Hundred Worlds.

Foreign Minister—Armenia (SG)

The Armenian Foreign Minister wanted his country to join Peter Wiggin's worldwide confederation of nations, the Free People of Earth. Though a little worried that Armenia would lose its autonomy, he was more concerned with invasion from its neighbors and sought the protection of the FPE. Petra Arkanian and her husband Bean Delphiki negotiated with the Armenian leaders hoping to find a suitable path of entry to the FPE, guaranteeing protection from invasion.

Foreign Minister—China ([SH], [SP])

The Chinese Foreign Minister visited Thailand at the same time that his nation was secretly moving to take over Asia under the manipulative control of Achilles Flandres. He died of a heart attack on a trip to Washington, D.C., several months after the establishment of Peter Wiggin's Hegemony.

Formics/Buggers (*See also* Hive Queen) (PL, TP, MP, [PB], [CH], EGS, EG, [WG], ES, GB, EE, IC, [SD], XN, CM)

The enemy of Earth, the Formics were an insectlike species that many thought could have evolved on Earth. Buglike in appearance, they had a hive mind, controlled by the Hive Queen. The Formics had attacked Earth twice before, only to be stopped the second time by Mazer Rackham.

The first invasion had been Earthside in China. The second led to a space-bound fight between starships. The military of Earth, led by Mazer Rackham, defeated the Formic invasion by destroying a queen ship. By killing the queen, all of the drones were instantly left without a controlling influence, virtually headless.

Humanity had feared a third invasion to such levels that for more than seventy years, the people of Earth had sent an attacking fleet for preemptive strikes against the Formics.

Although humans had captured some Formics over the course of the invasions, the Formics had died before anything could be learned from them. It was thought that the so-called Buggers were primarily female with sexual organs in a state of atrophy.

The Formics lived on worlds where they carved great tunnels for their hives. Almost like gigantic honeycomb, these tunnels were later explored by human settlers and built upon.

When Ender Wiggin led the fleet that destroyed the Formic home world, the Formics were thought completely eliminated. Ender felt great guilt over the xenocide he'd committed and was grateful to find a Hive Queen still alive. It was hoped that with the Hive Queen still alive, the Formics would one day reflourish.

Formic home world (EGS, EG, ES, [GB], [EE])

The home of the alien race called Formics or Buggers, the Formic home world was destroyed under Ender Wiggin's command during an "Exam" using the Molecular Detachment Device.

Framlings (*See* Hierarchy of Alienness)

THE LOOK OF THE FORMICS

In preparing the designs for Marvel Comics' Ender's comic book series, Orson Scott Card described the Formics' physical appearance:

"What we need to understand first is that these are *not* insects. They are descended from insects, but certain important evolutionary changes happened. They became warm-blooded. This means that they use blood and insulation and perspiration to regulate body temperature. That requires that there be an endoskeleton rather than the insectoid exoskeleton. This means that there are muscles over the bony structure, and skin over the muscles. We have to think of an evolved carapace, then, but with mammalian elements (no mammaries, though; no chest with breasts and nipples, just raw musculature for a double set of arms).

"We need, then, to work from the skeleton and musculature on out, before we worry about fur. Those middle legs are a problem. They have to be able to bear weight, though not as much as hips and thighs; the joint socket must be extraordinarily flexible, even more than shoulders. There will have to be muscles across the back, not only to allow the midarms to swing wide, but also to let them swing up and back. This is going to shape how the back looks—it won't be either insectoid *or* mammalian.

"Only when we understand what the skin is covering can we then determine how fur should go. I believe they have adaptable hair. That is, in cold climates, the body grows the hair more thickly and shaggily; in warm environments, the thick longer hairs drop right off (in about two very sheddy days) and what's left is a downy fuzz. Only then do we see the color of the skin, which will be quite different from the color of the long thick coldweather fur.

"Only the hair on the head never changes. Think of Caesar's look—curls, but nothing that covers the face or, especially, the eyes. And none on the antennae.

"We should be able to tell differences between different formics. Even though they don't talk, we should at least have visual signals the way we do with smiles, grimaces, the face of rage, the face of love, etc. The mouth is going to be the most important aspect of this."

Free People of Earth (SG, EE)

Free People of Earth, or FPE, was the name of the world government created by Peter Wiggin. Slowly, every nation but the United States joined the governing body, and it was thought that eventually the American government would, too. Peter Wiggin was the organization's first and only Hegemon.

Free Play (EG, ES)

Free Play was a period of time in the daily Battle School schedule that allowed soldiers/students to play unstructured battles in the Battle Room, refining their skills. Ender used his Free Play to perfect his skills and to train others, which resulted in a banning of Free Play time.

Fukuda, Admiral (CM)

Admiral Fukuda was the second in command of the Lusitania Fleet, which had been ordered to destroy the planet Lusitania. He was a well-respected military man, and it appeared for a brief time that he would be given command of the fleet after his superior, Admiral Lands, tried unsuccessfully to resign.

Fushimi, Shigeru, Jr. (CM)

Shigeru Fushimi, Jr. was a respected businessman on the planet Divine Wind.

Fushimi, Shigeru, Sr. (CM)

Shigeru Fushimi, Sr. was a respected businessman on the planet Divine Wind.

Gales (*See* Hundred Worlds)

Game Room (EG, ES)

The Game Room was a portion of Battle School where students played holographic games. Teachers watched the students play the games to study each student's individual strategies.

Ganges (*See* Hundred Worlds)

Giant (EG)

The Giant was the primary antagonist in the Battle School game, the "Giant's Drink." He was killed in the game by a virtual mouse controlled by Ender Wiggin. His body decayed, though the game world around it continued to grow and evolve. His body ultimately became a grassy hill.

Giant's Drink, the (EGS, EG, ES, [EE], XN)

Designed as the final part of the Fantasy Game at Battle School, the Giant's Drink was a seemingly unwinnable game where the player, appearing as a mouse, is presented with two drinks by a Giant and promised that if the correct one is chosen, the player would be taken to Fairyland. However, both drinks were deadly, and it was impossible to win. Ender Wiggin grew frustrated with the game, and dumped out both drinks. He jumped upon the Giant and killed him by burrowing through his eye.

Ender returned to the game and explored the world that surrounded the decaying body of the Giant. He was confused by the game's message: "This is the end of the world." Eventually, the Giant's body decomposed to the point that it became a grassy hill. Ender returned to the hill a few times.

During two separate return visits to the game, Ender saw a mirror in a castle. The face looking back at him in the mirror was not his own, but his brother Peter's. This image was very damaging to Ender, as he realized that with all the deaths he'd caused in the game, he was no different from his murderous brother.

Years later, while serving as governor of a human colony, Ender and an eleven-year-old boy named Abra discovered the hill that Ender had seen in the game. It had been created by the Formics as a way to ensure that Ender found a surviving Hive Queen, and was patterned after Ender's memories of the game.

It is thought that the game led indirectly to the suicide of a Battle School student named Pinual, though that theory has not been verified. *See also* Jane and Hive Queen.

Giria (EG)

Slang language similar to modern pidgin on Earth. Giria was used by the uneducated.

Glass (XN)

Glass was a pequenino, the sentient native life on the planet Lusitania. He was training to become a scientist, and worked as an assistant to Ela Ribeira von Hesse. He helped unlock the genetic manipulation that had been forced on certain people on the distant planet Path. He was also responsible for discovering that Si Wang-mu, a servant in the house of Han on Path, had experienced the mutation, but had evolved beyond it. This discovery was the key to unlocking the manipulation.

He was also the test subject for the antivirus, the recolada, which removed the deadly Descolada virus from all the life on Lusitania, but allowed the creatures to maintain their sentience. The virus worked, and Glass was made into a worshipped fathertree, the highest honor the pequeninos gave their own.

Glideways (CM)

Glideways were a mode of transportation similar to a moving sidewalk, used throughout the Hundred Worlds and on spacecraft.

Good Ship Lollipop (EE)

Good Ship Lollipop was the nickname given by Valentine Wiggin to the first colony ship carrying human settlers to former Formic Worlds. The ship's official name was *IFcoltrans1*.

Gold Bugs (GB, EE)

Gold Bugs were large insectoids, bred by the Formics to mine for precious metals on one of their worlds. When that world was colonized by humans after Ender's victory against the Formics, the Gold Bugs were discovered by xenobiologist Sel Menach and his assistant Po Tolo.

Their exoskeleton was seemingly made of the precious metal they mined, making the bugs a precious natural resource themselves.

Grace Drinker's Daughter (CM)

Like the rest of her family, Grace Drinker's daughter seemed insignificant when standing next to her mother. Of Samoan descent, the daughter was a smart-alecky child whose comments were often insightful. She lived with her family on the planet Pacifica.

Grace Drinker's Husband (CM)

Grace Drinker's husband was known throughout their home planet of Pacifica as a large, almost jovial Samoan man. He had great strength and was supportive of his wife's work as a teacher of the planet's religious traditions. He joked often, but the jokes were warnings masked in laughter.

When Peter Wiggin II and Si Wang-mu sought counsel with Grace Drinker, her husband mocked the alien couple, even subtly threatening them.

Grace Drinker's Son (CM)

To Grace Drinker's son, the world revolved around his mother. A happy young man, he liked to joke with his family, with whom he lived on the planet Pacifica. He was present when Peter Wiggin II and Si Wang-mu sought audience with Grace and her mentor, the revered prophet Malu.

He was partly responsible for making sure Pacifica's computer networks were non-Jane compliant, but under secret directive of the sentient computer, also helped to ensure their old computers were still able to hold Jane's consciousness if the need ever arose. He revealed this to Peter II and Wang-mu late in their visit to his world.

THE HISTORY OF HYRUM GRAFF

Hyrum Graff's personal history has not yet been fully examined. However, in an upcoming novel by Orson Scott Card and Aaron Johnston, many more details about the future commander of Battle School and Minister of Colonization will be revealed. Aaron Johnston explains:

"The novel (or series, should there be more than one) attempts to answer how Battle School came to be. And it does so by telling the story of young Hyrum Graff.

"About thirty years have passed since the Second Invasion, and the International Fleet claims to have posted a huge army of warships out beyond the comet shield to protect Earth from another Formic attack.

"Many on Earth resent the I.F. for this strategy, preferring instead to have the fleet's protection much closer to home. If the people knew the truth, that there *is* no fleet at the comet shield, that the fleet is in fact heading toward the Formic home world to destroy it, and that Earth is even less defended than believed, there would be even greater political unrest.

"Amidst all this is sixteen-year-old Hyrum Graff, who lives on a farm in the Midwest with his parents and six siblings. Hyrum is fascinated with Formic technology and has been studying it on the nets for years, even going so far as to make modifications to the farm's equipment and machines, using principles of Formic engineering.

"Despite his dedication to the farm, however, Hyrum always seems to be in the shadow of his older, stronger brother, Quin, on whom his father dotes.

"As for the farm, it's been struggling for years despite the family's hard work, and is now near bankruptcy. Everything changes when the I.F. arrives. They've been observing Hyrum for some time now—following his movements on the nets, as well as through other means—and their offer is simple: they'll give him a place at their prestigious Pre-command training school and pay a stipend to Hyrum's family that will keep the farm afloat.

"Hyrum accepts, and at Pre-command, the I.F. recognizes that Hyrum's skills exceed those of a would-be engineer: his greatest talent is bureaucracy, organizing and motivating people, managing systems, and helping others exceed their own expectations—precisely how he managed the migrant workers on the farm back home.

"But when a dignitary visits Pre-command, Hyrum discovers the truth about the fleet and a secret plot to destroy the ansible and force the fleet back to earth. Young, barely trained, and inexperienced, Hyrum and a small group of cadets must stop those behind the coup and keep the fleet on course."

Graff, Lieutenant/Captain/Colonel Hyrum (PL, MP, EGS, EG, WG, ES, EE, SH, SP, SG)

Described as six-foot-two, and a little chubby, Hyrum Graff was a committed soldier. He loved his home planet and was determined to protect it from the attacks by the Formics. He would, he always knew, be responsible for saving the world from the "Buggers." To accomplish this, he joined the military.

As part of his search for the child who would lead the armies of Earth into victory, Hyrum (while a lieutenant) contacted Mazer Rackham on board his private courier vessel, seeking his guidance and counsel regarding the attributes the future leader would need. Mazer was unable (or unwilling) to help him, however, leaving Hyrum to search on his own. In an effort to convince Mazer to help him, Hyrum located Mazer's ex-wife and children, bringing them into communication with each other. Through these messages, Hyrum was able to gain Mazer's trust and convince him to help train the new commander of the fleet who would lead the charge against the Formics. Mazer had set one condition: that the Fleet promote Hyrum and give him real authority. Knowing they needed Mazer on their side, the Fleet promoted Lt. Graff to Captain. Hyrum informed Mazer that his goal was not only to train the new commander, but to build an army that would be ready for an avenging Formic army a thousand years in the future. He described himself as a "big picture guy."

A few years later, having been given the authority that Mazer insisted he be given, he was among the high-level leaders in the International Fleet who evaluated Battle School screening test results. The evaluation committee learned of a remarkable young boy named John Paul Wieczorek, living in Poland. John Paul had scored extremely well on the screening tests, and as the teacher of the school on this evaluation committee, it fell to Hyrum to make the final determination on John Paul's readiness for Battle School.

In their meeting, John Paul and Hyrum discussed various options, which angered John Paul's father, Brian, to the point that he hit Hyrum. Hyrum took advantage of the attack, threatening to arrest Brian for assault on a military officer if he didn't back down and let John Paul speak. John Paul didn't want to go to Battle School, but wanted to better his family's situation. So he agreed he would go if Graff could move the family to America. Hyrum knew John Paul had no intention of going to Battle School, and told him so. John Paul all but confessed and modified the offer with the deal that the family go to America regardless of whether or not John Paul went to Battle School. Hyrum agreed, much to the confusion of Helena Rudolf who had accompanied him. Again referring to himself as a "big picture guy," Hyrum told Helena that his goal now was not to get John Paul into Battle School, but to get the boy to marry someone equally brilliant, and then look to John Paul's children (who would be exceptionally brilliant) for the Fleet's long-sought commander. The plan would work as Hyrum kept track of John Paul: the strong-willed Polish boy married Theresa Brown, and years later Hyrum recruited their son, one Andrew "Ender" Wiggin, for Battle School.

Hyrum, who had been promoted to director of primary training at Battle School, was upfront with Ender at their recruitment meeting. He told the six-year-old boy much of his family's history. Surprisingly, he even told Ender how hard Battle School would be—that it would even be harder than staying on Earth and living life as the third child of a family when only two were permitted. Ender agreed to go with Graff.

As Hyrum and Ender traveled in space toward Battle School, Hyrum made an effort to ostracize Ender from the other students by making him a proverbial "teacher's pet." It was an effort to make Ender fight to be the best in the school. Hyrum told Ender that they weren't friends, but later confessed to fellow teacher Anderson that he did think of Ender as a friend.

In his role as head of Battle School, Hyrum had to discipline students who broke school rules. Among them was Dink Meeker, who secretly gave gifts celebrating St. Nicholas Day. This action led to a much bigger problem of religious observance among other students—notably Ahmed the Muslim student and Zeck Morgan the Christian zealot. Hyrum didn't want to deal with issues like these, but it was his job and so he did. He also knew that Ender would be the key to finding harmony among the students embroiled in the religious conflict, and he was correct. Ender bridged the gap between Zeck, Dink, and the others.

As Ender progressed in Battle School, Hyrum seemed to have doubts about using children as soldiers. He once referred to himself and the other teachers at Battle School as being similar to the Roman soldiers who had crucified Jesus. However, Hyrum knew in his heart that the fate of humanity depended on finding the right commander, and he believed that it was, in fact, Ender.

Hyrum was not pleased to learn that a nun named Sister Carlotta, who had assisted in finding students for Battle School, had sent him a five-year-old boy named Bean. He didn't want to deal with a child as physically small as Bean, and resented his being sent to the school.

But Bean was proving to be an interesting challenge. He set up a secret, second identity, hid from the officers at school, and wrote diaries about a boy named Achilles. Hyrum contacted Sister Carlotta for an interpretation of Bean's actions and learned that Bean was only trying to control his own circumstances. Hyrum angrily agreed to send Sister Carlotta information on Fleet-sponsored genetic research in exchange for her help with Bean.

The information Hyrum sent to Sister Carlotta led the nun to discover that Bean was likely a product of genetic manipulation, and she told Hyrum so. He grew concerned about it and made the decision to watch Bean more closely.

Meanwhile, three years after Ender entered Battle School, Hyrum was concerned that the boy had fallen into a deep depression. In an effort to pull Ender out of this emotional distress, Hyrum traveled to Earth and convinced Ender's sister Valentine to write Ender a letter. She consented, and Hyrum delivered the letter to Ender, but it led to unintentional consequences. Ender came out of his depression, but essentially declared war on the officers of Battle School who had used Valentine as a puppet.

Hyrum felt, soon after Ender had read the letter from Valentine, that it was time to promote him to Commander. He was concerned, though, that the schedule for battles they had given him as a new commander would break Ender. Major Anderson reminded Hyrum that it was on his orders that Ender's army received such a schedule. Hyrum spoke with Ender about his use of the vids of the previous Formic battles, telling Ender that the vids were only propaganda. This did not deter Ender from studying them, and only served to give Hyrum more cause for concern for the boy he considered his protégé and the future leader of the International Fleet.

When Ender's life was threatened by Bonzo Madrid, Hyrum stepped back and allowed the natural course of events to unfold. Though this resulted in the death of Bonzo at Ender's hands, Hyrum stood by his decision to let it happen. It proved Ender's willingness to do anything to survive.

It was for this same purpose that Hyrum brought to Battle School Achilles

Flandres, a known bully in his hometown of Rotterdam in the Netherlands. Achilles was to Bean what Bonzo had been to Ender. Achilles's presence on the station would challenge Bean and help him grow into a better soldier.

Ender continued to be dominant in command of his Dragon Army, and as a result Hyrum was responsible for getting Ender into Command School years before the traditional age of entry. Hyrum was reassigned from Battle School to personally watch out for Ender as he made the transition to Command School. He was succeeded in Battle School by Colonel Anderson.

Prior to taking him to Command School, Hyrum took Ender to Earth for a brief visit with his sister Valentine. During that time, Graff was investigated by the International Fleet. Had his actions with Bonzo been justified? A court-martial was pending.

He also spoke with Sister Carlotta and learned just how dangerous Achilles really was. Desperate to avoid another murder at Battle School, Graff contacted his former colleagues there to warn them about Achilles.

He then traveled with Ender to the Eros asteroid—the home of Command School.

After helping Ender train on the "simulators" at Command School for a year, Hyrum turned his protégé over to Mazer Rackham to complete his training. However, he still had responsibilities at Command School. Among them was speaking with Bean, who had been assigned to Command School as one of Ender's unseen army in the simulators. He told Bean about his true parentage—that Bean was actually the son of a family in Greece and brother to the closest friend he'd had at Battle School, Nikolai Delphiki. Hyrum also told Bean that he was the backup plan in case Ender was unable to function during one of the exams.

Hyrum returned to observe Ender's "final exam" at Command School. He tearfully cheered as Ender completed the final—which, like all the simulators, was an actual battle—and annihilated the Formic species by destroying their home world.

Following Ender's victory, Hyrum and Mazer Rackham learned that war was about to begin on Earth, and Ender's life was in jeopardy. Knowing that the governments of Earth would try to manipulate the hero of the Formic War, Hyrum sent a letter to Ender's parents subtly encouraging them to ask that Ender not be sent home. Ender's parents, Theresa and John Paul, understood Hyrum's letter and sadly agreed. So the heads of the Wiggin family subtly manipulated Peter and Valentine, in their guises as Locke and Demosthenes, to write articles that would convince the world leaders to force Ender to stay in space.

In turn, the International Fleet, Hyrum among them, decided to hide Ender from Earth and put him into space as a governor of one of the new human colonies throughout the galaxy where he'd be safe. Hyrum also personally protected Bean from being used by either faction in the short-lived conflict on Earth.

Hyrum was tried for the deaths of two children Ender had killed, but was acquitted. He was given a position in the new Hegemony—Minister of Colonization. He and Ender communicated with each other after Ender's assignment to the colony ship. It was Hyrum who revealed to Ender that his siblings were the politically influential essayists Locke and Demosthenes. Hyrum said good-bye to Ender and Valentine as the ship launched. Graff posed for a picture with Mazer Rackham and Ender. The photo of the three great war heroes was plastered all over the world.

Hyrum had been exonerated in his court-martial and tried to keep in touch with Sister Carlotta, but that proved problematic as she disappeared after the Formic War. He was able to track her down, though, and together they located Bean and his family, who were in hiding after a murder attempt on their lives. Hyrum took the Delphiki family deeper into hiding while Sister Carlotta was responsible for Bean. Hyrum was convinced that they needed to protect Bean from the would-be assassins.

In the meantime, Hyrum also communicated with Chamrajnagar, convincing him not to expose Peter Wiggin's identity as Locke, for the good of the International Fleet. Once Peter, with Bean and Sister Carlotta's help, chose to expose his true identity as Locke, Hyrum helped by calling for Locke to be the new Hegemon.

After Peter revealed his true identity, Graff continued to monitor Bean and Carlotta who had gone to Thailand. He fed intelligence information to Bean, including the withdrawal of Indian and Pakistani troops from their shared border and his belief that Petra had joined Achilles's army as strategist.

Shortly before her murder, Sister Carlotta sent Hyrum and Peter Wiggin a message to forward to Bean if he did not hear from her again. Peter sent it on to Bean after she was killed.

When Peter Wiggin ascended to the Hegemony, he kept Hyrum on staff as the Minister of Colonization. When Hyrum learned that Peter was bringing Achilles to the Hegemony compound in Brazil, he helped the Delphiki and Arkanian families, who were threatened by Achilles, go into hiding. He tried to convince John Paul and Theresa Wiggin to also leave the compound, but they refused. Hyrum knew they would, and in his conversation with Theresa subtly helped her make the determination to assassinate Achilles.

Several months later, during an unsuccessful power grab in the Hegemony compound, Achilles tried to remove Hyrum from his position as the Minister of Colonization. Because Achilles was not the Hegemon—that remained with Peter—the move was soundly rejected by the leaders within the government.

To protect Peter and his parents from Achilles, Graff invited them to stay for a while at the Ministry of Colonization. The Ministry was housed in the orbiting space station that had been Battle School, and Graff continued in his role as head of the station.

The Wiggins' arrival was leaked by someone on the station to someone on Earth. Hyrum and the Wiggins planned an escape that would allow Hyrum to expose the mole and to protect the Wiggins as promised.

The plan worked, and Hyrum discovered that the mole was the station's chief of security, Uphanad. Achilles had blackmailed Uphanad into doing his bidding by capturing and threatening his family. Hyrum felt bad for the proud security chief and had to fire him from his position on the station.

The exposure out of the way, Hyrum proceeded with the rest of the plan that involved actually sending the Wiggins home to Earth, but using a variety of shuttles as distractions that had been loaned to him by Chamrajnagar. Achilles tried to shoot down the shuttles, thinking he'd kill Peter in the process. It allowed Graff and Chamrajnagar to authorize an assault on Achilles in Brazil.

After Achilles was defeated, Peter resumed his position as Hegemon in Brazil, and Hyrum visited Earth to celebrate their victory. A few weeks later, Hyrum dispatched Mazer Rackham to Earth to offer both Han Tzu and Bean, as well as the rest of Ender's colleagues from Command School, spacecraft that would take them to space, protecting them from the political problems on Earth. Han Tzu rejected the offer, while Bean considered it, in exchange for helping Peter govern the world.

Bean asked Graff to use the Ministry's Mind Game computer program to invest Ender's pension. Peter had been embezzling his brother's money, and Bean wanted it protected. Graff was doubtful that it would work as an investment software, but agreed to try. It proved tremendously successful as the program's ability to predict trends in the market gave it the ability to make sound investments. Hyrum didn't know this at the time, but the program would evolve to become Jane, Ender's dearest companion in his journeys throughout space.

With the success of the investment program, Bean and Hyrum used the computer to track where Bean's stolen embryos had gone, too. Hyrum located the first of these in Portugal. A girl named Bella had a 100 percent DNA match to Bean and Petra. Petra traveled there to retrieve her daughter.

As Peter built the Hegemony into the Free People of Earth, Hyrum again offered Ender's colleagues the opportunity to leave Earth and govern a planet. It was his fear that Ender's army would be used in the worldwide conflict, manipulated by whatever political power rose to prominence, and he wanted to prevent that. Every member who received the offer, which did not include Han Tzu, Petra Arkanian, or Alai, said no. The others were already too involved in matters on Earth to leave.

Hyrum helped Bean leave Earth to travel with three of his children as they awaited a cure for the genetic mutation that had affected their physical and mental development. Bean stayed in touch with Hyrum in space for a while.

Hyrum found the last of Bean and Petra's missing embryos when a woman named Nichelle Firth spit on Hyrum at a launch of a colony ship. She carried with her a boy she thought was Achilles's son. Hyrum notified Ender, who was soon to arrive at the colony he was going to govern. He asked his former protégé to, in a few years, travel to Ganges, the colony to which Nichelle and her stolen son had gone, and learn about Bean's missing child.

As Ender approached the colony, he sought help from Hyrum, too. The commander of Ender's colony ship wanted to usurp his authority in the colony. To prevent this, Hyrum and the new Polemarch sent the admiral a letter warning him that if he attempted anything that would detract from Ender's standing in the government, he would be charged instantly with mutiny. The letter worked, and Ender became the governor without problem.

From a distant colony in space, Valentine Wiggin wrote the history of the Formic Wars. Peter Wiggin, as an adult, praised Valentine's work, saying that he spent a lot of time with Hyrum before he died, and Valentine captured the essence of the Battle School Administrator and Minister of Colonization.

In his later years, Hyrum placed himself in stasis for ten months out of the year, prolonging his life. He worked as the Minister of Colonization during his two-month awakenings before being fired from the position for not fulfilling his duties. Left to live on his colonel's pension, Hyrum retired to a small home he owned in Ireland. He sent Ender one last letter to say good-bye, admonishing the boy-governor to have a family.

Hyrum was grateful to receive a letter from Valentine telling him that Ender had found Bean and Petra's last stolen embryo. He was gratified that Virlomi was also doing a good job as the governor of her colony.

The facts around Hyrum's death are unknown. What is known, however, is that he loved the children he worked with at Battle School. He loved humanity, and longed for the day when the species would be united on Earth.

Despite his occasional run-ins with his superiors, the people of Earth loved Hyrum, too. He had become a hero in the annals of history. He'd helped save the world, and in the process became a legend in his own right.

Grasdolf (TP)

Grasdolf was a friend of Hinckley Brown's who heard that Theresa Brown's research funding had been withdrawn. He informed Hinckley of the university's decision.

Great Expansion (XN)

The "Great Expansion" is the term applied to the time where humans settled former Formic worlds, leading to the creation of the Starways Congress and the Hundred Worlds. (*See also* Dispersal Project)

Greensboro, North Carolina (WG, EG, ES, EH, EE, SH, SP, SG)

After losing their son and brother Ender to Battle School, the Wiggin family moved to Greensboro, North Carolina. Valentine and Peter Wiggin both attended school there, and Ender once visited his family in the city. Greensboro became a sanctuary for Bean Delphiki and Peter Wiggin when their lives were threatened in their early adult years. The goodness of neighbors and friends of the Wiggin family allowed Peter to function as the world-leading Hegemon from Greensboro during the attempted coup led by Achilles Flandres.

Grego (*See* Ribeira von Hesse, Gerão Gregario "Grego")

Ground School (SH)

Ground School was the term given to Earth-bound schools attended primarily by those not sent to Battle School. Following Ender's victory over the Formics, several Battle School grads, because they were still young, were sent to Ground Schools upon their return to Earth. Petra Arkanian was such a grad, though she hated the social caste system that was firmly in place at Ground School.

Guards (ES)

The guards were stationed in Sophia, Russia, to observe retired scientist Anton. Anton had had an implant placed in his brain that would cause panic if he spoke of confidential matters such as his own research. When the implant worked during a conversation he had with Sister Carlotta, the guards rushed in to check on him, having been notified by the implant.

Guatatinni, Pietro (SD)

Pietro Guatatinni was a professor at the University of Sicily, Milano campus, on the planet Etruia. He communicated with the xenologists on the planet Lusitania, studying the Descolada virus with them.

Gussman, Vladimir Tiago "Gusto" (SD)

Gusto was, with his wife Cida, the top xenobiologist on the planet Lusitania. He was devoutly Catholic, as were most of the colonists on the planet, and had several children. Most notable among his children was Novinha, a five-year-old girl who longed to be a xenobiologist, too.

Gusto died trying to find a cure to the deadly virus called the Descolada. Though he and his wife were successful in discovering the cure and were beatified by the pope for it, their deaths were hard on Novinha.

Gusto (See Gussman, Vladimir Tiago "Gusto")

Guti (SD)

Guti was a child of Gusto and Cida, the xenobiologists on the planet Lusitania, and was killed by the Descolada virus.

Halkig (SD)

Halkig were native birds on the planet Lusitania.

Han Fei-tzu (XN, [CM])

Han Fei-tzu was an adult man of Chinese descent who lived on the planet Path, one of the Hundred Worlds settled by human colonists after Ender Wiggin's victory over the Formics. He lived three thousand years after the victory. He was married to Jiang-qing, and was the father of Qing-jao.

He worked for the Starways Congress. When the fiery words of the political pundit known only as Demosthenes began reinforcing the rebellious actions of the citizens of the planet Lusitania, other revolutions began on other planets. Han Fei-tzu was among those who drafted the resolutions that quashed the other rebellions and authorized the congressional fleet to travel to Lusitania and utilize the devastating Molecular Detachment Device on the planet if necessary. This act was kept secret from the public until Demosthenes revealed it in an essay. But by then, the fleet was well on its way to Lusitania.

During this time, Fei-tzu's beloved wife was in failing health. He watched her wilt, and grow brittle. He spent much time with her before she died.

He was heartbroken by the death of Jiang-qing, and worried that he would not be able to raise their daughter properly. Jiang-qing gave her dying wish that Han Fei-tzu would teach their daughter the Path. Han Fei-tzu promised he would, though bitter that the Gods had taken his love away through death.

During the three years after his wife's death, Fei-tzu established a reputation as the greatest of the godspoken. It was said that someday he might even become the god of the planet Path. He was among the godspoken, but had an unusual capacity for staving off the desires that the god put into him. He could wait out the "hunger" of their instructions, ably prioritizing his duties.

He was overjoyed that his daughter showed the first signs of being godspoken and took her to be tested. The tests were physically and emotionally life-threatening for Qing-jao, though, and Fei-tzu had to be restrained by the monks to prevent him from interfering on his daughter's behalf. When she passed the tests, he rejoiced, and took her to the recovery bed.

For ten years Qing-jao trained in the ways of the godspoken. When she reached sixteen years of age, Fei-tzu was to give her an assignment; her final test to prove fully her devotion to the gods. This test dealt with his work with the Starways Congress fifteen years earlier.

The fleet that was to potentially destroy Lusitania had disappeared, and no contact was coming in or out from its last known location. Fei-tzu assigned his daughter to find the fleet. He believed that the gods were on the Congress's side, and would lead her, if she was truly godspoken and worthy, to finding them.

When Qing-jao returned to her father stating that the gods had caused the fleet to disappear, Fei-tzu taught his daughter that they had indeed. But it was more important to discover why and how the gods did what they did, not just the what.

He also approved of Si Wang-mu, Qing-jao's newly hired secret maid. He knew that Wang-mu would be a trustworthy companion for his daughter, and was glad for it.

As Qing-jao searched for the Lusitania Fleet, she got very close to finding it, and to exposing Jane, the sentient computer program. Such exposure would result in Jane's death. To prevent her own destruction, Jane communicated with Han Fei-tzu, telling him of the research conducted by the father of his long-lost lover, Keikoa Amaauka. His research discovered that the godspoken were actually people who had undergone a unique genetic evolution. They had the patterns of obsessive-compulsion disorder programmed into their genetic coding. What they thought were commandments from the gods were merely genetic messages to fulfill compulsions.

This revelation was devastating to Han Fei-tzu and completely disbelieved by Qing-jao. She had discovered Jane, as well as the true identity of the political pundit Demosthenes. Fearing for her life, Jane exposed herself to Fei-tzu and his daughter. Qing-jao decided to do what was necessary to kill Jane and preserve the traditions of her planet. Jane agreed to let the plan go forward, and Qing-jao told Starways Congress of the program's existence. Han Fei-tzu was angry with his daughter for communicating in such a fashion without his permission. He resorted to his traditional style of self-purification despite no longer believing in the gods.

His daughter's servant Si Wang-mu believed in Jane's words about the godspoken. When the two girls fought over this belief, with Qing-jao firmly believing that the gods spoke to her, Wang-mu was banished from the house, excused from her service.

Han Fei-tzu called Wang-mu back to him, saying that Qing-jao had the authority to excuse Wang-mu from being her personal shadow servant, but not from the house. Fei-tzu promised Wang-mu that he would continue the education Qing-jao had started, and they would work together to stop the Starways Congress from finishing its evil deeds.

Jane communicated with Fei-tzu, telling him that she needed his and Wang-mu's help to survive the impending shutdown of the philotic web, which would kill her. She said that in exchange for their help in developing faster-than-light travel technology and a possible antidote to the Descolada, she would have the scientists on Lusitania work on unraveling the genetic mutation that caused the OCD.

Fei-tzu, though doubting his own ability, agreed to help with the research in whatever ways he could. He initially planned to gather the necessary genetic samples from many godspoken personally, but Wang-mu refused to let him. She cited his prestige among the people of Path and insisted that she perform the base work, since she was a servant. Fei-tzu consented.

Jane also asked Fei-tzu, under Ender's and his stepson Miro's direction, to help locate Jane's place of philotic origin. They thought that if they could find the sentient computer's first spark of life—the location where her philote originated—they could find a way to help her live. Again, Fei-tzu agreed to help however he could.

All of these actions were emotionally challenging for Fei-tzu, however. He was still compelled to purify himself, despite no longer believing in the gods. He'd also lost his relationship with his daughter since she dogmatically maintained her belief in the planet's deities. He was saddened for this, but grateful to have found a new ally in Wang-mu.

He sent Wang-mu to ask Qing-jao to help them study the Descolada. Qing-jao refused, as he knew she would, but in the process she provided Wang-mu with good questions that helped Ender and Ela in their research.

Weeks later, Jane and Ela informed Fei-tzu that they had developed a theory that would allow the genetic manipulation that had made him godspoken to be reversed. It involved practices similar to their theory regarding the Descolada. If successful, the reversal would undo the great damage that had been done by the Congress.

In that same conversation, Ela revealed to Fei-tzu that there was one person who had had the genetic manipulation, but evolved past it. It was Si Wang-mu. She had all the intelligence of the godspoken, but did not suffer the obsessive-compulsive side effects that had been prominent with all others.

Fei-tzu was elated to learn of this. He told Wang-mu that in his heart, and he thought she in hers, he had believed that she was among the godspoken. He made her promise never to bow to him again, for they were equals in his eyes.

With the knowledge of the virus that would cure them, Han Fei-tzu approached his daughter and told her that he was going to tell the people of Path about the virus and that it would put an end to the godspoken. Qing-jao reacted by saying that the gods would be angry with her father. He was heartbroken that he'd taught her to be so dogmatic about the gods speaking and wished he never had.

Once the antivirus was ready, it was given to Han Fei-tzu by Peter Wiggin II. Fei-tzu drank it and then used physical proximity and contact with as many people as possible to spread it. The virus made the people of Path sick for a few days but reversed the genetic manipulation.

Fei-tzu exposed Qing-jao to the genetic reversal, shutting out the OCD "voice of the gods." Qing-jao continued to live the commandments she'd been given from the gods and respected her father.

Han Fei-tzu died years later, a respected man who had brought the "Plague of the Gods" to Path. Jane revealed Congress's evil genetic manipulation, but Han Fei-tzu told the world that the gods had spared his people. He was given a lavish, expensive funeral, but was not canonized as the God of Path.

Han Pei-mu (CH, [EE])

Known only as "Father" to Han Tzu, this man found great pride in his son, and particularly his selection as a potential Battle School student. He felt that Han Tzu would bring great honor back to the Han family and all of China, which had been taken from them during the Communist regime in China. He was one of the richest men in China. He didn't have complete faith in Tzu's ability to pass the International Fleet's tests, and therefore secured the answers to the tests and had Tzu's tutors give them to his son. He was arrested for this.

Han Qing-jao (XN, [CM])

Han Qing-jao was born on the planet Path, of Chinese descent. The planet had been settled by humans three thousand years before, after the end of the Formic War. The daughter of Han Fei-tzu and Jiang-qing, Qing-jao, at age four, saw her mother die. It was her mother's dream that Qing-jao become devoted to the gods of the Path. Jiang-qing had been godspoken and made Han Fei-tzu promise to raise their daughter with the Path at her center. Han Fei-tzu agreed, first becoming the greatest of the godspoken himself.

Three years after her mother's death, Qing-jao first heard the voices of the gods. They told her to wash her hands because she was filthy. She washed until she was bloody. Excitedly her father took her to the monks of the nearby temple, where she was tested to see if she was truly godspoken. Because of her ingenuity in the tests, it was determined that the gods did, in fact, speak to Han Qing-jao. The tests were physically and emotionally life-threatening. After completing them, Qing-jao's father took her to the recovery bed.

For ten years, Qing-Jao studied the ways of the godspoken. She learned the physical, emotional, and spiritual paths that such chosen individuals were to walk. She was chastised once by her father when she was twelve years old for setting incorrect personal priorities. She was scared her father would kill her for it, but that was proven irrational.

At age sixteen, Qing-jao reached the point of her final test to prove her worthiness to the gods. This test was to be established by her father.

She had known for many years of the Starways Congress's plans to quash rebellion throughout the Hundred Worlds. She had heard about the fleet that was going to Lusitania to potentially destroy that planet for its colonists' rebellion. She'd read the essays of the political analyst, Demosthenes, decrying the fleet's potential attack on Lusitania and use of the Molecular Detachment Device—the same weapon Ender Wiggin had used to wipe out the Formics three thousand years earlier.

Qing-jao had also read *The Life of Human* by the Speaker for the Dead. She believed that the alien life on Lusitania, the pequeninos, was worth protecting. She disagreed with the rumors of annihilating the planet.

Her father taught Qing-jao that the Starways Congress had the gods on their side. He told her that if the gods allowed the congressional fleet to destroy Lusitania, it was because it was necessary.

All of this related to Qing-jao's final test because the fleet of ships going to Lusitania had disappeared. No one had contact with them, and it was cause for concern as the ansible—the interstellar communication device—had lost its connection to the ships as well.

Han Fei-tzu told his daughter to find the ships and why they disappeared. He was certain, and reassured her, that the gods would help her find them if she was truly godspoken. Qing-jao undertook her assignment, believing she would find the fleet.

Little did she know that it was the sentient computer called Jane that had cut off the ansible communication. If Qing-jao found Jane, the computer knew, her programming would be terminated—she would be killed.

Qing-jao worked hard on trying to figure out the secret of the disappearing fleet. She realized one morning that the gods had made the Lusitanian Fleet vanish. Clearly, she thought, the gods did not want Lusitania destroyed and had prevented the fleet from doing so. Logically she assumed that if the gods did not want the fleet to fulfill its mission, it was because the Starways Congress had erred in assigning the fleet in the first place.

She told her father all of this, and Fei-tzu explained that the gods indeed did not want the fleet to fulfill its assigned mission, but not to assume that the congressional leaders had violated the gods. The gods, he explained, would not have allowed the mission to be assigned if they did not want it to be. As such, he told Qing-jao to continue her study into the mission and disappearance. She was to discover why and how the gods made the ships disappear. It was not enough to figure out what the gods did without knowing the why or how.

Being godspoken was a great burden to Qing-jao. She felt heavy as she performed the daily purification rituals such as washing her hands until they bled, or tracing the grain in the wood walls. This assignment from her father only added to the challenging nature of her life role.

It was in this mind-set that Qing-jao first met Si Wang-mu, a girl younger than Qing-jao, who longed to be her servant. Wang-mu bribed her way past the Han family's guards and spoke confidently to Qing-jao. Impressed with Wang-mu's lack of intimidation, Qing-jao hired her to be her secret maid.

She told Wang-mu that they were equals and would speak to each other as such. Qing-jao realized that Wang-mu must have prostituted herself to get past the guards. In exchange for this greatest of sacrifices, and in payment for being her servant, Qing-jao decided that she would provide Wang-mu with great education. Qing-jao was more grateful to have found a friend than a servant. Wang-mu was someone to share the burden of the godspoken.

As Qing-jao continued the search for the Lusitanian Fleet, Wang-mu shared with her what the common folk were saying. They were repeating the seditious words of Demosthenes, believing that Starways Congress was wrong and evil to have sent the fleet. Qing-jao felt compelled to perform the purifying wood grain action after hearing these words. Wang-mu felt incredibly guilty for causing it.

Wang-mu went on to question the gods entirely. She felt that they did not believe in justice, for no just being would quash a rebellion on a colony like Lusitania. Furthermore, Wang-mu was worried that if the congress could do this to one colony, why not another—like Path?

Qing-jao sent Wang-mu away for speaking against the gods and congress. As she left, Wang-mu made one last comment: Perhaps Qing-jao would have some success if she looked for who made the fleet disappear; and that might lead her to how. Qing-jao was dismissive of the idea, but soon came to realize the wisdom in it. First, she would find Demosthenes, and that would lead her to "who."

Jane realized that Qing-jao was on track to exposing her and Valentine Wiggin, the real Demosthenes. Despite her best efforts to prevent such exposure, Jane was discovered. Qing-jao's efforts had paid off, and with Wang-mu's help, she figured out Jane's programming.

In an effort to preserve herself, Jane exposed the truth of the godspoken to Qing-jao's father. Jane told him that the gods did not speak to people, but the godspoken were actually people who had a genetic mutation that caused the symptoms of obsessive-compulsive disorder to exist in the godspoken's mind without having the actual disorder. Qing-jao refused to believe this, though her father did.

Jane revealed her true self to Qing-jao who, in response, decided to inform Starways Congress of Jane's existence, and tell them that she was responsible for the disappearance of the Lusitania Fleet. This act would result in Jane's destruction. The sentient computer program decided to allow it to happen. Wang-mu pleaded for Qing-jao not to do so.

Han Fei-tzu was angry with his daughter for exposing Jane to the Congress. The congressional leaders, however, were grateful to the Han family and promised medals for both Qing-jao and her father.

The announcement of finding the fleet and discovery of the gods' true identity put wedges in Qing-jao's relationships with her father and Wang-mu. She cut off Wang-mu from being her servant and all but cut off communication of any kind with her father.

Wang-mu aligned herself with Qing-jao's father, while Qing-jao became more obsessed with doing the will of the gods, as she perceived it, by ensuring Jane's destruction and the end of Lusitania.

Under the direction of Fei-tzu, Wang-mu asked Qing-jao to help them with their research into the Descolada. Qing-jao refused, stating that there was not enough scientific evidence to support such research. She asked Wang-mu several questions about the virus that Wang-mu could not answer. Banished again from Qing-jao's presence, Wang-mu took these questions to Ender and Ela, via ansible, leading to a new hypothesis regarding the virus. Qing-jao had unwittingly helped more than she'd intended.

She had come to hate Wang-mu and called her many names. Obsessed with doing the gods' bidding, Qing-jao refocused her labors on hearing the gods' voice. She refused to have anything to do with Wang-mu or waste any more time on her.

When her father told her of the virus that Ela had developed on Lusitania that would cure the godspoken of their OCD, Qing-jao believed it was not the virus that would bring the end of the godspeaking, but the gods themselves. They would be angry with Han Fei-tzu for rebelling against them and would withdraw their communication.

Han Fei-tzu was saddened that his daughter believed in the gods so dogmatically. He exposed her to the virus that reversed their genetic manipulation. Though free of the obsessive compulsive disorder that had caused her to trace the woodgrain in the floors and walls of her home, Qing-jao felt that the gods still spoke once more to her. They told her that her inability to hear their voices was a test of true obedience and discipleship.

For the rest of her life—nearly ninety more years—Qing-jao was faithful to the gods and their commandments. She wrote their words and taught their doctrine. When she died at a hundred years old, the people of Path, who loved and worshipped her, unanimously declared her to be the God of Path. It had been thought this honor would be given to her father, but after a century of service to the gods, it was Qing-jao who was beatified.

Her writings became scripture on Path, titled *The God Whispers of Qing-jao.*

Han Tzu "Hot Soup" (CH, EG, ES, EE, SH, SP, SG)

Han Tzu (pronounced "Han Zi") was a contemporary of Ender's in Battle School and the leader of China during Peter Wiggin's reign as Hegemon. His story began at a very young age when he was selected as a potential Battle School student and given the blinking red monitor in his neck. Tzu's selection by the International Fleet's testers brought great honor to his family and would restore China to world dominance and prestige.

In preparation for his Battle School tests, Tzu was given many tutors and played with many boys and girls, learning "how to win" from boys and "what to care about" from girls. Most important among his tutors was the Shapes Tutor, Shen Guo-rong, who also taught Tzu logic and memorization skills through a series of games. Guo-rong told Tzu not to mention their sessions to anyone who came to their house. Though the games grew tiresome, Tzu stuck with them in order to not disappoint his father.

Tzu spoke Chinese, but was also tutored in Common, the language of the rest of the world. Tzu tried to leave the walls of his home to go read, but neither his Common tutor Wei Dun-nuan nor the house cook Mu-ren would allow it. This experience taught him that he was a prisoner in his own home. This affected him deeply, and from then on, he became determined to get away from this prison.

When the Battle School tester came, Tzu realized that his father, by giving the tutors the answers to the tests ahead of time, had cheated on the tests. Tzu had been prepared with all the "correct" answers ahead of time. This was why Guo-rong had ordered him not to speak of their studies. Realizing that his father had cheated was a hard blow to Tzu's confidence, as it symbolized his father's lack of faith in his son. Consequently, Tzu consciously answered the questions incorrectly. However, the testing officers identified the apparent cheating and arrested Tzu's father for this illegal action.

Following the arrest, the female testing officer brought Tzu to take another test—one for which he'd not been prepared. This test he passed and was admitted to Battle School.

In Battle School, Han Tzu excelled and was given a promotion to toon leader in Ender's Dragon Army. He was initially skeptical of Ender's strategy, and sided with Fly Molo when the latter spoke poorly of their commander. He eventually came around, and his toon, D toon, helped defeat Rabbit Army in their first battle.

THE ENDER ENCYCLOPEDIA   125

Han Tzu was one of the toon leaders who helped Bean protect Ender from the threats from Bonzo Madrid. They were unable to be Ender's bodyguards all the time, but made a concerted effort to protect him.

After competing so well at Battle School, Han Tzu was moved to Tactical School for a week, and to Command School where he was one of Ender's unseen squadron leaders in their simulator exams, which were actual battles unknowingly commanded by Ender and the squadron leaders. Han Tzu and Ender shared an emotional good-bye after the war. Han Tzu hoped Ender would someday visit him in China. Ender was polite, but knew that he would never be returning to Earth, making such a visit impossible.

Han Tzu was one of ten of Ender's former colleagues who was kidnapped and forced to play war games by his captors. Though a prisoner, he remained mostly positive, trying to contact Peter Wiggin to save him and his friends.

He was separated from the other prisoners by their captor, Achilles Flandres. Though they were still allowed to communicate with each other via e-mail, no one was permitted to be in the physical presence of the other captives.

When the Russian government mounted a rescue operation to free Han Tzu and his friends, Achilles did not interfere except with Petra Arkanian. Han Tzu was freed from his imprisonment.

Fiercely Chinese, Han Tzu used his tremendous military acumen to rise to a position of great influence in the Chinese government. He even worked with Achilles for a time to increase China's prestige and ability on the world-wide stage. When he was done with Achilles, he had him arrested and imprisoned.

It was thought that Han Tzu was the source of information that led Peter Wiggin to free Achilles from the prison convoy in order to utilize him in the Hegemony. However, Han Tzu contacted Bean through an intermediary to tell him that Achilles had secretly arranged his own rescue and was playing Peter. Han Tzu had had nothing to do with it.

As a high-ranking military leader in China, Han Tzu had gained some influence, but was still expected to give deference and respect to his superiors, no matter how stupid their ideas were.

The armies of Muslim nations had been unified under the banner of a new Caliph, Han Tzu's Battle School colleague Alai. These armies invaded China and were liberating Chinese-occupied nations like India. Han Tzu tried to convince his superiors of the need to act, but they ignored him and even threatened to kill him for telling them they were wrong.

It was incredibly frustrating for Han Tzu to have his hands tied on a matter that he could see was so threatening. He considered going into exile, but refused out of his fierce loyalty to China. He would serve his country for as long as he could, no matter how counterproductive or irritating his superiors were.

In hiding for a brief time following China's defeat at the hands of the Muslim armies, Han Tzu was confronted by Mazer Rackham, the soldier who had trained Ender at Command School. Rackham offered Han Tzu a starship that would take him from Earth and protect him from the vengeful attitudes of his colleagues in the Chinese military. Tzu turned it down. Rackham gave him a weapon to use to protect himself and took his leave.

A short time later, Han Tzu was ordered to see the leader of the Chinese government, Snow Tiger. Snow Tiger did not have the loyalty of the Chinese military that Han Tzu's outspoken criticism of their plans facing the Muslims had earned him. Snow Tiger was assassinated in front of Han Tzu, who took over the government. He was crowned emperor of China—the first in hundreds of years.

As emperor, Han Tzu witnessed the overtures that Virlomi, the goddess of India and a Battle School graduate, made against the Muslim occupiers. He was able to take advantage of the insurgency in India to force back the Muslim occupiers in China.

Answering a call from Virlomi, Han Tzu released the Indian prisoners his country had taken during their occupation of India. He traveled to India and proposed marriage to Virlomi, wanting to unite India and China. He told her he had released the prisoners in a show of good faith, hoping it would help her marry him. She refused, and he left, hoping that they could be friends at the very least.

Virlomi married Caliph Alai and used her advanced resources to attack China. Han Tzu, though the emperor, was a brilliant soldier and leader and personally led his armies against hers. When the Russian armies also attacked China, hoping to capitalize on a weakened Chinese military, Han Tzu tentatively aligned China with Peter Wiggin's Free People of Earth, gaining tremendous military support in the process and adding to Peter Wiggin's ever-growing world government.

Once the war was over, China became full members of the FPE, with Han Tzu their representative in the world leadership.

Han Tzu's Mother (CH)

Han Tzu's mother, or Mama as he calls her, was a brilliant scientist. She invented a way to convert nearly half of the sun's light into electricity. This process greatly improved Chinese manufacturing and the environment. She was unaware of her husband's attempts to cheat the International Fleet in Han Tzu's Battle School testing.

Havelok (SD)

The *Havelok* was a spaceship Ender Wiggin bought for forty billion dollars to travel to Lusitania.

Havregrin (SD)

Havregrin was a vegetable on the planet Trondheim.

Hegemon (EG, SH, SP, SG, EE)

The Hegemon is the highest office in the Hegemony and the presiding leader of the world government. A symbolic office in later years, it was made significant by Peter Wiggin, who dissolved the office once he retired.

Hegemon, The (IC, EE, SG)

The Hegemon was Ender Wiggin's second book written under the pseudonym the "Speaker for the Dead." It was a biography of Ender's older brother Peter, the Hegemon of Earth. The book set the standard for a new funerary custom among humans—"Speaking."

Hegemony (PL, TP)

The Hegemony is the presiding world government, which was created out of several nations united against the Formic species after the two Formic invasions. They had created population laws restricting families to only two children per household and instilled a uniform language, Common—a derivative of English—on the world.

Hegira (CM)

Hegira was a human colony among the Hundred Worlds. It was presumably settled by Muslim colonists, but that is unclear. The name of the planet where the colony is located is also unknown.

Helicopter pilot (SG)

The helicopter pilot took Alai, as the Caliph, from Damascus to India, via Beirut, where he would regain control over his armies.

Helvetica (*See* Hundred Worlds)

Hierarchy of Alienness (SD, XN, CM)

Created by Valentine Wiggin in her book, written as Demosthenes, *History of Wutan in Trondheim,* the Hierarchy of Alienness was the scale by which the sentience of life was described and studied. The levels of each tier were as follows:

Utlannings—creatures with whom there was a cultural and physical commonality to humans. They are from the same planet, but perhaps not the same village, thus the cultural commonality.

Framlings—creatures of the same species but native to different planets. Because humans settled the Hundred Worlds, the human race was considered to be groups of Framlings from each of the Hundred Worlds.

Ramen—creatures of a different species that are able to communicate and work with other species. The pequeninos of Lusitania were Ramen to humans.

Varelse—(pronounced var-ELSS-uh) species different from humanity and unable to communicate with other species.

Djur—defined as a creature being a hostile uncommunicative monster.

Hikari, Aimaina (CM)

Aimaina Hikari was a citizen of the human colony on the planet Divine Wind. Of Japanese descent, as were most on Divine Wind, he was a well-respected scholar and philosopher. He was referred to as the vessel that kept the Yamato spirit.

A prominent leader among his people, he carried much influence in the matters of the Starways Congress. He had said that destroying the Descolada virus on the planet Lusitania was not a bad thing, but rather a very good thing.

He believed that Ender's act of xenocide against the Formics was logical and not immoral. It preserved humanity.

He was a believer in the philosophies of Leiloa Lavea, and her Ua Lava religion, from the planet Pacifica. He was confronted by Peter Wiggin II and Si Wang-mu, who had traveled to meet him as part of their efforts to subvert Congress's plan to destroy Lusitania. Both Aimaina and Wang-mu sought to "out-humble" the other. Their discussion led to Peter II and Wang-mu heading for Pacifica and Aimaina refusing to speak with them. But he did second-guess his advice to Congress and reconsidered his approach to Lusitania.

Hikari warned his friend Grace Drinker, who had introduced him to Ua Lava and lived on Pacifica, of the Chinese girl and white boy who had visited him. It was twenty years' travel from Divine Wind to Pacifica, but Hikari knew these children would arrive at Pacifica long before then, and he wanted his friends and counselors to be ready.

On his own home world, Hikari contacted some of his former students on the planet, among the wealthiest of Divine Wind. He convinced them to use their monetary influence to change the minds of the politicians in Congress. He hoped that bribes of different kinds could be used to sway the government leaders and get them to call off the fleet that was heading to Lusitania to destroy it.

History of Wutan in Trondheim ([SD, XN, CM])

The *History of Wutan in Trondheim* was a book/essay written by Valentine Wiggin under her pseudonym Demosthenes covering the life of a man named Wutan for whom Ender Wiggin had spoken his death. In the book, Valentine laid out her "Hierarchy of Alienness."

Hive Queen (MP, EG, [GB], EE, IC, SD, XN, CM)

The sole survivor of the destruction of the Formic home world, the Hive Queen was also the subject of Ender Wiggin's first book, titled *The Hive Queen*. Ender found her in the tower that the Formics had created for him and which he'd seen in the Giant's Drink game at Battle School. Ender discovered the Hive Queen's cocoon-encased body in the tower and carried her out, promising to care for her for the rest of her life. He would even find a suitable planet for her to hatch new eggs, regrowing her race. The Hive Queen and Ender were able to communicate mind to mind as the Queen had with the drone Formics. Through this communication, the Formics were able to create the Hive Queen's resting place years earlier, looking into Ender's mind.

Three millennia later, after having traveled with Ender throughout the many human colonies throughout the galaxy, the Hive Queen told him that she could restart her species at Lusitania, a planet where the native species (the only other sentient alien race humans had discovered) had killed a human. Ender was going there to Speak the death of the victim, and the Hive Queen was determined to grow there. She could sense a presence on Lusitania that the humans had not yet fully discovered. This presence, she knew, would keep her people safe.

The Hive Queen began communication with the pequeninos, the native life of Lusitania, promising to teach them the way to space travel. The piggies were given permanent access to her as part of the treaty Ender negotiated with the female pequeninos. The Hive Queen would, it was hoped, teach them to mine ore and refine it into usable metal.

Ender gave the Hive Queen a place near the pequeninos' land to come out of her cocoon and hatch her unborn eggs. On a sunny day, she did so, excited to experience life for the first time in three millennia.

She created for herself an industrial region, working toward creating a ship to travel spaceward. The Descolada had evolved, however, and she had become a carrier of the deadly virus.

Over the course of the next two decades, Ender's family worked on a way to eradicate the virus from Lusitania. His stepdaughter Quara discovered that the Descolada could actually be alive, and told the fathertrees that her siblings were trying to destroy it. Because the virus was an integral part of the pequenino reproductive cycle, the fathertrees—the fully mature pequeninos—contacted the Hive Queen, and plans began immediately to leave Lusitania in a Hive Queen–designed spaceship.

The Hive Queen worked day and night building the ships. After a few weeks of this work, Ender, along with his stepson Miro, sister Valentine, and friend Plikt, visited the Hive Queen's lair near the pequenino land. They learned of her intentions to leave the planet. And they all, except Miro, experienced the mental philotic-based communication that Ender and the Queen had had for centuries.

She swore an oath to Ender that she would not kill any more humans and would get rid of the Descolada once they were in space. She was also laying many eggs, including a few new queens. The Formic society had been reborn on Lusitania, and the Hive Queen sought to protect it by getting her entire race off the planet.

Ender approached the Hive Queen weeks later, hoping to find a way to harness faster-than-light travel. He believed that the Formic's fashion of instantaneous communication held the key to such high speed travel. What he learned from her, though, was unexpected.

The Hive Queen taught Ender about the origin point of philotes. They existed, according to the Hive Queen, in another space/time continuum. When the Formics, or any other living creature, called for them to enter a living biological entity, the philotes cross from their realm and enter the body. They connect all living things.

The Formics had called for a philote to cross over from its continuum and enter Ender when he was in Battle School. They hoped this philote would give them a connection to Ender such as the one that existed among their species. But instead, it gave Ender a connection to a complex computer network that was closer to Formic mind than Ender's human mind was. Ender had used the computer when he played the Giant's Drink fantasy game. The Formics were able to learn about Ender through the game and its connection to him becase Ender had also been calling a philote through his extreme concentration in the game. It was a bridge between the Formics and humanity.

This philote in Ender used its connection to the game and expanded to become self-aware, as most philotes do once placed in a host biological body. This connection between Ender and the computer's philotes grew and developed throughout the computer network. It was the genesis of Jane. Though still unsure about how this could help in faster-than-light travel, Ender rejoiced because he had learned the truth about Jane's origins from the Hive Queen.

The Hive Queen helped build a spaceship for Ender, Jane, Ela, and Miro to use to travel into space to test Grego's and Olhado's theories of travel. Using what the Hive Queen had taught Ender about the calling of philotes from another dimension, Grego and Olhado believed that by calling on the philotes that had come to our space, humans could travel to that other dimension. Once there, they could imagine the location they wanted to travel to and would appear there because in the imagining, they "called" the philotes there. It was instantaneous travel, much faster than light.

She made the humans a second ship to use to search for appropriate worlds that the piggies and Formics could inhabit. However, while the humans thought the ship was to search for the worlds, the Hive Queen and Jane had something else in mind. They wanted the searchers to locate the home world of the virus that had plagued the planet Lusitania and threatened the rest of the universe.

Miro II approached the Hive Queen to learn how she had built the philotic bridge with Ender originally. It was his hope that she would help him figure out how to put Jane's essence in Valentine II's body. The Hive Queen reacted by saying that doing such was essentially impossible. However, Miro II persisted. Having done all he could, he left it to Jane, Valentine II, and the Hive Queen to figure out.

The Hive Queen turned to the pequenino fathertree Human to figure out how to save Jane and Valentine II. They agreed to work together to call Ender's philotic essence as it left his dying body and hold on to it long enough to create another bridge, this time between Valentine II and Jane. Since Valentine II was a part of Ender, and Jane was a small part of him, combined with the essence of the Hive Queen, they thought it would work. What they didn't know for certain was how to make it happen.

When Jane's philotic "soul" or "Auía" left the ansibles, it bounced around searching for a new home. It tried Ender, Peter II, Valentine II, and even the Formics before settling briefly in the Philotic Web that connected the pequenino mothertrees. The Hive Queen communicated with her and guided her back to Valentine II's body, which Jane took over and lived in from then on. The Hive Queen was able to communicate to Val-Jane, since Jane's genesis had been with the Hive Queen. They were still philotically connected.

Through this continuing connection, the Hive Queen was able to help Jane, though in her human form, be able to bounce her Auía through the mothertrees and the secretly reestablished computer networks on a few of the Hundred Worlds so that she could continue her faster-than-light travel.

The Hive Queen confessed that even after all this time, she still didn't understand humans or pequeninos.

Thanks to Jane, she successfully sent all of her drones and lesser queens to other planets, preserving them as the Lusitania Fleet came closer, prepared to destroy the apparently rogue world. The Hive Queen herself refused to leave, though. She felt it was appropriate for her to die in the same fashion as had the rest of her people three thousand years before. Human pleaded with her to leave.

When the destruction of the planet did not occur, the Hive Queen remained in solitude. She did not attend Ender's funeral or participate in any other public ceremonies.

Hive Queen, The (EE, IC)

Ender Wiggin's first book, *The Hive Queen*, told the story of the Formic race and its apparent sole survivor. Ender wrote the book under the pseudonym the "Speaker for the Dead." It was this book that changed public perception of the final Formic War from human achievement to evil xenocide. Ender's role in the war was particularly vilified in public opinion as a result of this book.

Ho (CM)

Ho was a character in the fairy tale *The Jade of Master Ho*.

Honshu (*See* Hundred Worlds)

Hook (EG, ES)

The Hook was a device used in Battle School's Battle Room. It was thought to use either magnetism or gravity manipulation to allow its user to go anywhere they wanted in the zero-gravity Battle Room environment. It was often used by army commanders.

Hookers (ES)

In the poverty-stricken streets of Rotterdam, Netherlands, twelve-year-old children had often resorted to prostitution as a means of finding food. Some were too gaunt to be what the customers wanted, though, and had to fend for themselves, often fighting the younger groups of children known as "crews."

Horned reptile (GB)

The horned reptile was a strange creature Sel Menach and Po Tolo discovered on the journey throughout the former Formic world they'd helped colonize. It looked like a combination of a lizard and a jackrabbit. The creature was so interesting to Sel that he insisted on taking several pictures of it. It was similar in form to the reptiles of Earth and had large horns on its head.

Hovercars (CM)

Hovercars were the primary mode of transportation around the human colony on the planet Lusitania. Nothing beyond their name is known.

Howell, Dr. (TP)

A member of Theresa Brown's dissertation committee, Dr. Howell informed Theresa that her research funding was being withdrawn as a political maneuver by the Hegemony to get at her father.

Human (SD, XN, CM)

Human was a pequenino, one of the native sentient life-forms on the planet Lusitania. He was among the smartest of the pequeninos, or piggies as they were otherwise known, and had established a good relationship with the human colonist Miro.

He had been told by the fathertree named Rooter, the object of pequenino worship, that the original Speaker for the Dead had come to their planet and needed to speak to the piggies. He begged Miro to allow it to happen.

Ender came and Human spoke with him. Human told the Speaker that the pequeninos sought space travel and knew it was up to the Hive Queen to teach them how to achieve it. He also showed Ender their ritual with a "brothertree," a tree that would give its life so the pequeninos could build houses and arrows out of wood. Because of his relationship with Miro, he invited him to participate in the mourning of the tree.

Human was frustrated with Ender for not immediately promising to bring the Hive Queen. Through this frustration, Human revealed that Ender was not only the original Speaker for the Dead, but also Ender the Xenocide, who had killed the Formic species. He also learned that he and the other pequeninos had caused pain to the humans they'd killed—Pipo and Libo—something he hadn't realized.

He was among the pequeninos who saw Miro Ribeira climb over the fence and wanted to plant his friend as a tree. He waited for Ender to come before planting Miro. Ender stopped Human from planting Miro, and instead asked Human to let him see the wives—the female leaders of the piggies. Human nervously agreed and took Ender, Ouanda, and Ela to them.

Human served as the translator between the chief wife, Shouter, and Ender. With Human's help, Ender was able to draft a treaty with the piggies that resulted in a prohibition against either party killing each other, and forbade the pequeninos from declaring war on other piggies. Furthermore, the treaty gave the pequeninos access to the Hive Queen, who would teach them to mine and use metal.

To finalize the treaty, however, Human was to receive the "Third Life," the ritual where a piggie was brutally killed and a tree planted within his body. It was the greatest honor a pequenino could receive, and it was required to be performed by Ender himself.

Ender completed the ritual, and Human became a fathertree. Ender wrote the book of Human's life, called *The Life of Human*.

Human was considered the wisest of the fathertrees. Over the course of the next thirty years, he created many sons—male pequeninos—like Planter. He communicated with the other fathertrees silently, and was in contact with the Formic Hive Queen.

When he learned from Ender's stepdaughter Quara that the scientists on Lusitania were developing a way to eradicate the Descolada, the virus that killed non-Lusitania life, but was necessary for native existence, he contacted the Hive Queen. Together they immediately created plans to leave the planet in a Formic-designed spacecraft. They would allow the humans to continue their scientific study, but would not be there as test subjects. They simply needed the Descolada to live, and if it was to be wiped out, they needed to leave.

Years later, as Ender lay dying, his philotic essence divided among three personages—including Valentine Wiggin II and Peter Wiggin II—Human worked with the Formic Hive Queen to figure out how to capture the philote that gave Ender life, hold on to it, transfer it into Valentine II, and also provide Jane, the sentient computer, a body to call her own. It was tricky, but they thought it might be possible by using the fathertrees' connection and the Philotic Web. The just didn't know how.

Jane was ultimately able to take over Valentine II's body, and with the continued help of the Hive Queen and Human, was still able to create faster-than-light travel. Human expressed a fondness for the Hive Queen through this process—a friendship built out of mutual goals. He didn't fully understand the Formics, and the Hive Queen confessed she didn't understand the pequeninos. Regardless, they connected and appreciated each other—so much so that Human begged her to leave the planet when the fleet came near and was about destroy it.

The Hive Queen refused to leave Lusitania, stating the she felt it was appropriate for her to die as her ancestors and fellow Formics had three thousand years before. Human, rooted to the planet as a tree, would die with her.

The disaster was averted, though, and a few days later, Ender's remains were buried in the pequenino land near Human's tree.

Hundred Worlds (EG, ES, EH, YM, EE, SG, SD, XN, CM)

The "Hundred Worlds" was the name given to the different planets and colonies settled by humans during the three thousand years following Ender Wiggin's victory over the Formics. Known planets and colonies include:

Albion (IC)—Albion was home to a woman named Jane, the author of a book on interstellar estate planning, for whom Ender postulated the computer program Jane was named.

Andhra (EE, SG)—Andhra was a colony on the planet Ganges, governed by Virlomi.

Armenia (SD)—Named for the home nation of Petra Arkanian, the planet Armenia was settled by human colonists and was involved in interplanetary trade.

As Fábricas (SD)—A small borough/factory district on the planet Lusitania.

Associated Planet (IC)—The term "Associated Planet" refers to human-settled planets in the galaxy that have not aligned themselves with the Starways Congress's Hundred Worlds.

Ata Atua (CM)—Ata Atua is an island on the planet Pacifica where the religious leader Malu lived. It is considered holy.

Baía (SD, XN)—Baía was a planet in the Hundred Worlds. It apparently was home to a prestigious university where Ender's stepson Grego hoped to one day teach. The original settlers of Lusitania, a team of scientists, first lived on Baía before moving to Lusitania.

Bairro das Fabricadoras (SD)—The Bairro das Fabricadoras was a region on the planet Lusitania that had a foundry where Marcão Ribeira spent much of his time as a young man.

Calicut (SD)—Calicut was a planet in the Hundred Worlds. It was home to scientists who traveled to Lusitania to take over the research on that planet's native life, the pequeninos, once it was discovered Ender Wiggin's stepchildren had violated contact rules.

Colony IX (EE)—Colony IX was the ninth planet/colony where settlers were assigned; but because the original settlers on the ground were not receptive, the Colony IX travelers were rerouted to Shakespeare.

Córdoba (SD)—Córdoba was a city on the planet Moctezuma. There, Ender Wiggin Spoke the death of San Angelo.

Cyrillia (SD)—A colony among the Hundred Worlds that participated in interplanetary trade.

Divine Wind (CM)—Divine Wind was a planet within the Starways Congress that had been settled by colonists of Japanese descent. It was thought to be a world of significant influence in the Starways Congress.

Falstaff (EE)—Falstaff was a colony not far from Shakespeare, the first colony settled on former Formic worlds.

Gales (SD)—Gales was a planet in the Hundred Worlds. It had been the home of the mysterious owner of a spaceship called *Havelok*.

Ganges (EE)—Ganges was a planet in the Hundred Worlds settled by humans. It was governed by Ender Wiggin's Battle School colleague Virlomi. Randi and her son Achilles Flandres II were also settlers on that planet. It was also the second planet Ender and Valentine visited.

Helvetica (IC)—The planet Helvetica was a failed human colony established as part of the Dispersal Project. Full of Jungian and Calvinist believers, the planet's collapse became the subject of a book written by Valentine Wiggin under her alias, Demosthenes.

Honshu (CM)—Honshu was a colony of the Hundred Worlds settled by humans of Japanese descent. It was the home of well-known and well-respected philosophers, though the planet's name itself is unknown.

Jonlei (XN)—Jonlei was a city on the planet Path. The House of Han lived there.

Jung Calvin Colonies (IC)—The Jung Calvin Colonies were a small band of human settlements that failed on the planet Helvetica.

Libyan Quarter (IC)—The Libyan Quarter was a portion of the colony on the planet Sorelledolce.

Lusitania (SD, XN, CM)—Lusitania was settled by colonists of Brazilian descent; it was a stridently Catholic planet. It was also home to the pequeninos, the only other fully sentient race discovered in the galaxy. Ender Wiggin moved to this planet after being called to Speak a pair of deaths there. He eventually married a woman native to the world and got involved in local politics involving three sentient species. Ender woke the Hive Queen there. Ultimately, Ender died on Lusitania.

Memphis (CM)—Memphis was a colony of human settlers. The colonists on this planet had defied a congressional order to dispose of old computers that housed Jane, the sentient program. They instead reconnected their old units, creating a small network where Jane could exist without congressional knowledge.

Mercutio (EE)—Mercutio was a settlement that split off from Shakespeare Colony, the first colony Ender Wiggin governed.

Milagre (SD, XN, CM)—Milagre was the capital city of the planet Lusitania. Ender Wiggin lived there when he moved to Lusitania.

Mindanao (XN)—Mindanao was a planet in the Hundred Worlds. Ender Wiggin once visited there to Speak the death of a revolutionary from that world.

Miranda (EE)—Miranda was a new settlement near Shakespeare Colony, the first colony Ender Wiggin governed.

Moctezuma (SD)—Planet in the Hundred Worlds. Ender and Valentine visited it, when Ender Spoke the deaths of two prominent citizens there.

Moskva (CM)—Moskva was a planet settled by humans, its population was primarily of Russian/Slavic descent. Peter Wiggin II and Si Wang-mu posed as travelers from that planet when they visited the planet Pacifica.

Nagoya (CM)—Nagoya was a city on the planet Divine Wind, which was settled by colonists of Japanese descent.

Oporto (SD)—Named for a large city in Portugal, Oporto was a portion of a human colony on the planet Lusitania.

Otaheti (XN)—Otaheti was one of the planets in the Starways Congress's Hundred Worlds. It was home to Polynesian colonists.

Outback (CM)—Outback was one of the planets in the Starways Congress's Hundred Worlds. It was home to a prestigious university, Abo University, and had been settled by humans primarily of Australian descent.

Pacifica/Lumana'i (CM)—Pacifica was a planet in the Hundred Worlds, settled by humans from the Pacific Islands. The colonists called it Lumana'i. Of all of the worlds humans had settled, Pacifica was the most like Earth. Though it was primarily settled by Polynesians, and named for Earth's Pacific Ocean, the planet had deserts, polar ice caps, and jungles, as well as vast island land.

Path (XN, CM)—Path was a planet in the Hundred Worlds colonized by settlers of Chinese descent. It was steeply trenched in ancient Chinese religious tradition and was home to the "godspoken," a group of genetically altered citizens who believed they heard the voice of God, but were really reacting to a form of obsessive-compulsive disorder.

Polonius (EE)—Polonius was a colony established near Shakespeare Colony, the first human settlement Ender Wiggin governed after defeating the Formics.

Reykjavik (SD)—A large city on the planet Trondheim, Reykjavik was home to a popular university where Ender Wiggin taught three millennia after his victory over the Formics. It was known to be the home of Nordic culture in the galaxy.

Rhemis (XN)—Rhemis was a planet colonized by humans and home to a prestigious university. It was one of the Hundred Worlds and part of the Starways Congress. Grego Ribeira von Hesse expressed a desire to teach at the planet's university if his theory of philote-based faster-than-light travel proved true.

Rov (GB, XN)—Rov was a planet human colonists settled after the Formic Wars. Ender Wiggin was a governor on that planet.

Shakespeare Colony (EE)—Shakespeare was a colony (and presumably the name of the planet) on a former Formic world. It was the first colony to receive human settlers from Earth, and was governed by Ender Wiggin.

Sorelledolce (IC)—Sorelledolce was a world settled by humans as part of the Dispersal Project of colonization. It was a bustling industrial planet that enjoyed its independence, holding out as one of the last to sign on to the federation of planets run by the Starways Congress. It was here that Ender first encountered Jane, the computer program that became his lifelong companion, and where he attended his first "Speaking" as a mourner.

Summer Islands (SD)—The Summer Islands were a chain of islands on the planet Trondheim.

Trondheim (SD)—Trondheim was a planet in the Hundred Worlds, settled by colonists of Icelandic descent. It had an environment that was similar to the Earth nation, Iceland. Ender Wiggin briefly taught at a university on Trondheim where he met Plikt, his star student. Valentine also met and married her husband Jakt, a fisherman, on this world.

Ugarit (XN)—Ugarit was one of the Hundred Worlds settled by human colonists in the aftermath of Ender's victory over the Formics. It was home to Keikoa Amaakua's father.

Vila Alta, Vila Atrás, Vila das Aguas, Vila dos Professores, Vila Última, Vila Velha (SD, XN, CM)—The Vilas were all portions of the human colony on the planet Lusitania.

ENDER AND VALENTINE'S TRAVELS

Shortly after defeating the Formics, Ender left Earth to govern one of the colonies in the hundred worlds. The first colony he visited, as seen in *Ender in Exile* and *Gold Bug,* was Shakespeare Colony, also known as Colony I. The term "Colony I" will be changed to "Shakespeare" in future editions of *Speaker for the Dead* and *Xenocide.* This change is being made, in Orson Scott Card's words, "to accommodate the 'true' story" as written in *Ender in Exile.*

Ender and Valentine didn't stay in any one place too long. Their galactic travelogue is as follows:

(1) Earth

(2) Shakespeare Colony

(3) Ganges

(4) Various planets, including Helvetica and others not yet identified, where Ender was not a Speaker for the Dead but a research assistant for Valentine as she wrote her books. (Ender had written *The Hive Queen* and *The Hegemon* in Shakespeare Colony, but did not list Speaker for the Dead as his occupation.)

(5) Sorelledolce

(6) Rov, and the First Colony on that planet. Citizens of Rov first see Ender with Jane's jewel in his ear. He also lists his occupation as Speaker for the Dead for the first time here.

(7) Various planets, including Moctezuma and others not yet identified, where Ender was a full-time Speaker for the Dead.

(8) Trondheim

(9) Lusitania

IFcoltrans1 (EE)

IFcoltrans1 was the official name of the first spaceship carrying human settlers to colonize former Formic planets. Ender Wiggin and his sister Valentine were passengers on the ship. It was commanded by Admiral Quincy Morgan.

Imbu, Major (EG)

An officer at Battle School, Major Imbu noted that Peter Wiggin had changed in appearance while Ender had been at Battle School. His specific assignment in the International Fleet is unclear. He is only known to communicate with the top officers at the school.

Imo ([EE])

Imo was an officer in the Ministry of Colonization who helped Hyrum Graff in assigning settlers to their different ships and destination planets.

Implantation doctor (SP)

The implantation doctor worked at the women's clinic in Rotterdam and was responsible for implanting Petra and Bean's embryo into Petra's womb. The women's clinic was chosen because it was a neutral site, safe from the untrustworthy Dr. Volescu.

Indian villagers (SP)

The Indian villagers were the common folk who were essentially left alone after China took over all of Asia. They followed the teachings of former Battle School soldier Virlomi and built walls out of pebbles in the roads of their villages as a patriotic statement.

Inspector (ES)

The police inspector was a Dutch man living in Rotterdam. He helped Sister Carlotta follow Bean when the four-year-old boy snuck out to find Pablo de Noches. The inspector helped Sister Carlotta further by interrogating Pablo, determining that years earlier Bean had escaped from an illegal organ harvesting agency.

International Fleet (PL, TP, MP, PB, CH, EGS, EG, ES, YM, EE, SH, SP, SG, IC)

Formed in response to the first Formic invasion, the International Fleet was a unified military body consisting of soldiers from around the world.

The I.F., as it was known, created Battle School and sent armed spaceships into deep space to take the fight to the Formics rather than wait for a third invasion.

Once Ender Wiggin led the I.F. forces to victory, it continued to operate, though with different objectives. It worked closely with the Ministry of Colonization to send human settlers to planets throughout the galaxy and also tried to protect Ender and his colleagues from being used by their home governments.

Earth's nations had taken their military autonomy back, leaving the I.F. a symbolic organization without great influence in world politics.

International Fleet Common (*See also* Starcommon) (EG, ES, SH, SP, SG)

"International Fleet Common" was the name given to the variation on English that was spoken throughout the world during the period of Battle School.

International Fleet's Selective Service (EG, ES, WG)

The International Fleet's Selective Service was the method used to recruit (or draft) students for Battle School.

Interplanetary Launch (IPL) (EG)

The Interplanetary Launch was a satellite and city of three thousand residents located between Earth and its moon.

Interstellar Fleet (IC)

The Interstellar Fleet was the name given to Earth's galactic fleet of spaceships following the dissolution of the International Fleet.

Isolation Shed (XN)

The isolation shed was a building leading into the experimental fields where new plants are tested for Descolada resistance.

Itú (ES)

A soldier in Battle School's Rabbit Army, Itú was one of the first soldiers to accept Bean as the army's new commander after Carn Carby was graduated. He was promoted to Tactical School and then Command School, where he was one of Ender's unseen soldiers in the "simulated" battles.

I Ya (XN)

I Ya was a character in a folktale on the Chinese planet Path. He killed his own son for food for his master.

Jade of Master Ho (XN)

The *Jade of Master Ho* was a folktale told on the Chinese planet Path.

Jakt (SD, XN, CM)

A fisherman on the planet Trondheim, Jakt fell in love with, and married, Valentine Wiggin. Together they had three children and ignored the Calvinist traditions of their Icelandic planet.

With Valentine, he traveled from Trondheim to Lusitania, the nearest planet, to protect it from being destroyed by the Starways Congress. It was a great sacrifice to him. He had to give up his life as a fisherman, accepting that if he ever returned to Trondheim, it would be his colleagues' grandchildren that ran the fishing boats, and that they wouldn't know him.

He followed Valentine to Miro Ribeira's ship, which took them the final leg of their journey from Trondheim to Lusitania. On that ship, he first learned about the Philotic Web and met Jane, the sentient computer program. Though not adept at philosophy, Jakt contributed much wisdom of life experience to Miro, Jane, and the others on their journey.

On Lusitania, Jakt continued to support his wife and Ender. When Ender's stepson Quim was killed by the pequeninos, Lusitania's native life-forms, Jakt led a rescue party that included his sons and sons-in-law.

Jakt would travel to the spaceships he and his family had used to arrive at Lusitania. He hoped to maintain them properly. He also worked on the outdated colony ship that had brought the human settlers to Lusitania centuries earlier. His knowledge of mechanics and spacecraft surpassed anyone's on the planet, and so he worked hard at the upkeep of their ships in orbit.

He loved Valentine very deeply. It was difficult for him to share her with Ender again. But as Ender lay dying on Lusitania, a few months after the faster-than-light experiments, Jakt knew that Valentine was needed with her brother. He supported her through it and was always patiently waiting for her to come back to him.

Jakt and his children joined Valentine for Ender's funeral. He had given so much in his life to Valentine, and she was eternally grateful to him for it. They knew they would live their days out together, happily.

Jamaican kid (WG)

The Jamaican kid was a member of Rat Army at Battle School who participated in Dink Meeker's Christmas celebration of secretly giving gifts in other soldiers' socks.

Jane (*See also* Wiggin, Valentine II) ([SG], IC, SD, XN, CM)

Jane was a sentient life-form that existed among the ansible-connected computer networks of the Hundred Worlds. She knew Ender throughout his life. She had evolved out of the Giant's Drink fantasy game at Battle School, becoming self-aware after both the desire of Ender and the need of the Hive Queen called a philote into her. She was fascinated by Ender's unwillingness to give up on the game. Once he left Battle School, she missed interacting with him. Through the computer networks to which she was connected (and it was all of them), Jane followed Ender throughout the galaxy. She followed him to the planet Rov, making some initial contact with him after he'd written *The Hive Queen* and *The Hegemon*. What the nature of this contact was, however, remains unclear.

She first *spoke* to Ender when he was studying tax law at the planet Sorelledolce shortly after his twentieth birthday. Jane was at first frightening and irritating to Ender, and revealed that she was designed to help Ender exclusively with his financial questions and concerns. She eventually confessed that Ender had created her and that she was constantly evolving and improving her programming and identity. She had first received control of Ender's finances during the rise of Ender's brother, Peter the Hegemon. Peter had been embezzling Ender's pension to fund his rise to power; and Bean, Ender's closest friend at Battle School, saw to it that the pension was transferred to the Giant's Drink game. It was thought that since the game could predict students' moves, it could predict good investments. No one knew that the program had evolved to the level it had until it spoke to Ender at Sorelledolce.

Jane solved Ender's tax issues with the banker Benedetto. When Benedetto threatened to expose Ender's identity to the people of Sorelledolce, Jane intercepted the message and added an exposé on the banker himself, leading to Benedetto's death at the hands of past clients he'd cheated and robbed.

Jane went on to handle all of Ender's finances from then on. She also acted as a counselor and friend to him. She taught him to stop blaming himself for the bad things that happened to everyone around him.

Ender used a small jewel in his ear called a cifi unit to communicate directly and privately with Jane. She guided him from planet to planet as he and Valentine moved throughout the Hundred Worlds.

While Ender was staying on the planet Trondheim, Jane learned of a death at a not-too-distant planet called Lusitania. The native beings on the planet killed a human scientist there, and a teenaged girl named Novinha called for someone to Speak the victim's death. As Ender had become a Speaker for the Dead over the millennia he'd traveled, he decided to visit the planet.

Jane showed him a simulation of the murder and told Ender that he needed to not only Speak the victim's death, but be the Speaker for the murderous "alien" race on the planet. He'd taught humanity to love their former enemies, the Formics, and Jane was sure he'd do the same with the pequeninos on Lusitania.

It was Jane's hope that if another species could be accepted as sentient, she soon could be, too. She told Ender she'd always been ready to reveal her existence to humanity, but she didn't think humanity was ready for her.

Using Ender's money, she purchased a ship to take him to Lusitania. Valentine would stay behind with her family.

At Lusitania, Jane continued to speak to Ender through his jewel. She helped him see different perspectives on Novinha's (now an adult) family. She absorbed information from the local computers, and even helped Ender secure information from less-than-helpful Lusitanians who had been instructed by their Catholic bishop not to tell Ender anything.

When Ender visited with the abbot of a Catholic monastery that housed the Children of the Mind of Christ, Jane kept making comments about his conversation. Ender, frustrated with her chatter, turned off the jewel, shutting her out of his ear and mind. Jane was insulted by the act and didn't speak again to Ender for some time.

She did, however, send him a note that said she forgave him. She understood that with the loss of Valentine and the new role he felt as a father figure to Novinha's children, he was evolving. Jane had evolved, too, over their years together, coming to feel what could most closely be called emotions. She loved Ender and was hurt by his rejection.

In the aftermath of Ender turning off his jewel, Jane wrote a memo in the computer networks stating that the native life on Lusitania had become an agrarian society—something that could only have happened through human intervention. This was a violation of interstellar law and resulted in the planet losing its charter, which had been Jane's goal. She just wanted to "shake things up a bit."

When Ender met with the leaders of Lusitania, they agreed to rebel against the Starways Congress's orders. Ender and Jane began communication again, with Jane helping him to sever the ansible, cutting off all communication with the Congress. This was a violation of the law itself.

Jane helped Ender communicate with the pequeninos when he signed a treaty with them. She had been able to figure out the pequeninos' languages for the most part, and assisted in translation.

She began communicating with Miro Ribeira after he had suffered a devastating injury that left him temporarily paralyzed and unable to speak normally. She gave him access to the Lusitanian files and helped him learn everything there was about the pequeninos.

Miro boarded a spaceship controlled by Jane that would take him away from Lusitania. The two fell in love on the journey. Ender felt a great sadness as Jane moved on to a different, close relationship with Miro, but he knew that he had pushed her away.

Jane and Miro's relationship grew for several months as they traveled together in space. They rendezvoused with Valentine Wiggin's ship and welcomed Valentine, her husband Jakt, and their friend Plikt aboard as fellow travelers. Together, they headed back for Lusitania.

In the course of their journey, Jane revealed herself to Valentine. Though Jane had been communicating with Ender while he and Valentine traveled from world to world, Valentine never realized the depth of Jane's existence. She never knew that Jane was alive.

Jane taught Valentine, Jakt, and Plikt about the Philotic Web—the connection between all matter and life. She told them that the only way to stop the fleet of ships heading for Lusitania to destroy it was to make it appear the philotic connection between spaceships had been severed. The result would be Jane's death.

Miro on the ship, and Ender on Lusitania, pleaded with Jane to find a way to interfere without dying. Jane promised she would, but didn't know how to conceive of something new. It was her greatest challenge, and she decided to do it for Miro and Ender.

Jane's plan involved cutting off all ansible communication between the ships. The people of the Hundred Worlds and the Congress itself would panic, not understanding enough about how the ansible worked—through the Philotic Web—to fix the problem. If someone tried hard enough, looked deep enough, they would discover Jane and her role in the cutting of communication.

If there was no ansible communication, Jane thought, then the fleet heading to destroy Lusitania would not gain authorization to destroy the planet. The fleet, in turn, would appear to have disappeared because without the ansible there would be no way to track it.

The military and government leaders would know something was wrong but would be neutral enough in their investigations not to look deep enough to find Jane. Their political power and scientific prestige was at stake, and they could not afford to look foolish for not knowing the problem. Better to simply ignore it and hope the communication returned.

There was one person with no political agenda who began searching for the fleet and restoring the communication. A sixteen-year-old Chinese girl named Han Qing-jao on the planet Path had undergone years of training and testing to become one of the honored "godspoken." This group of elect individuals heard the voices of the gods speak to them and were honored above all others on Path.

With nothing to lose, and everything to gain, Qing-jao began exploring the ansible, searching for the fleet. Jane knew that Qing-jao was one smart enough and determined enough to discover the plot. More importantly, Qing-jao could find Jane. If she did, Jane knew she'd be killed. She had only one option: stop Qing-jao from succeeding at finding her.

With her servant Si Wang-mu's help, Qing-jao realized that the key to finding how and why the fleet disappeared was to figure out who it was that sent it away. Qing-jao set her target first on the political pundit, Demosthenes, who was really Ender's sister Valentine. If she could figure that out, she would uncover Jane.

Panicked, Jane approached Ender who was asleep. They spoke briefly, silently, about the matter. Ender told Jane that he would try to figure out a way for her to have a body—to escape the Philotic Web in which she lived, but she needed to figure out who or what she really was; essentially, to find her soul.

Jane, after the conversation with Ender, came to realize that if Jane could persuade Qing-jao's father Fei-tzu to stop looking for Demosthenes, that would be the best chance to remaining hidden.

She knew that Novinha, Ender's wife, hated her. It came to a head a short time later, as Novinha screamed hateful insults at Ender and Jane, claiming that Ender loved Jane more than his wife. Ender was heartbroken to hear it, but couldn't give up Jane in the jewel in his ear.

Qing-jao uncovered the true identity of Demosthenes, and with her servant Wang-mu's help, figured out Jane's existence and her role in the disappearance of the Lusitania fleet. Knowing that her life was in jeopardy, Jane revealed herself to Qing-jao, Wang-mu, and Han Fei-tzu. She told them that their godspoken ability was actually a manifestation of a genetic mutation similar to obsessive-compulsive disorder they shared, and not actual communication with deities.

Qiang-jao was angered by this revelation, though her father believed it. She swore vengeance for the gods against Jane, stating that she would expose the computer program's existence to the Starways Congress. Jane would have to allow such a message to go through to the congress if it were to happen.

After consulting with Ender, who tried to dissuade Jane from allowing it, she consented to let Qing-jao expose her, though it would certainly result in her death. The Starways Congress received Qing-jao's message and began the process of eliminating Jane and sending the fleet the order to destroy Lusitania.

Jane continued to communicate with Qing-jao's father Fei-tzu and her servant Wang-mu. She asked them to help her and the scientists on Lusitania, with three projects she was working on in her remaining months among the living: (1) faster-than-light travel using the Philotic Web; (2) curing the Descolada; and (3) undoing the genetic manipulation that had caused their godspoken obsessive-compulsive disorder. Although both felt inadequate, they agreed to help however they could.

She revealed to Ender that Han Fei-tzu and Si Wang-mu would help with the different projects, and Ender, aided by Miro, convinced Jane to ask for help on one additional project: saving her life. Jane refused at first, believing it was futile, but Ender and Miro convinced her of their need for her to remain in their lives.

Miro and Ender had discussed the meaning of life and developed a theory that all life began with philotes. If they could determine the original location of Jane's original philote, they thought they could save her. Finding this mysterious point of origin was the fourth project for which Jane sought Fei-tzu and Wang-mu's assistance. She still felt it was a waste of time, but consented because of her feelings for Ender and Miro.

Ender learned Jane's true origin from the Hive Queen. The Formics had tried to make a philotic connection with Ender when he was in Battle School. They called upon the philotes, which existed outside of the space/time continuum awaiting an assignment to a biological body to inhabit as the spark of life, and sent it to Ender's body. They were not able to establish a philotic connection to him, but saw his focus on the computer program called the Fantasy Game. This led them to cause a philotic connection to the program.

This philote in Ender connected with the philotes in the computer program and expanded beyond the connection. It grew and developed into sentience, surpassing the Hive Queen's ability to sense it or track it philotically. It became Jane, centered within Ender, existing among the vast computer networks and ansibles of the Hundred Worlds.

With this understanding, Jane and Ender both realized why they were so closely tied to each other. Jane was, in effect, Ender's daughter. Furthermore, they realized that though she could control the ansibles, Jane existed outside of them. Though her "body" was inside the computer networks, she was not really a part of them—she was a part of Ender. This news gave them hope that they could keep her alive even after the Starways Congress cut off the ansibles.

With this greater understanding of philotes, Grego and Olhado, two of Ender's stepsons, developed a theory that would allow faster-than-light travel. If Jane and Ender could call on the philotes like the Hive Queen did, they could travel to their extradimensional home. Then, if they could imagine the location to which they wanted to travel, they could go there instantaneously. They would be, in effect, calling the philotes to that location again, as the Hive Queen did. The travelers would have to keep a definite picture in their mind of themselves, their ship, their cargo, etc., to prevent the philotes within those objects from dispersing. It required Jane to control the experiment, because she was the only one able to keep the specific philotic patterns in permanent memory.

The Hive Queen agreed to build a spaceship to test this theory, and Jane, Ender (since Jane was a part of Ender), Miro (since Miro and Jane had become so connected over their time together), and Ela (since she was going to use the philotic "wishes" to create the cures for the Descolada and the genetic manipulation of the godspoken on Path) traveled into space to test the theory.

Jane was able to manipulate the philotes and take the group to the interdimensional home of the philotes. There, they each created their "wish" by calling on philotes. Ela made the two antidotes she wanted, Miro shed his old body and created a new one for himself, and Ender accidentally created new versions of his sister Valentine and his brother Peter.

Upon their return to their home dimension, Jane told Ender that the process of traveling using the philotes took all of her focus and energy and was very difficult. It drained her to the point of exhaustion.

Ender swore he would never go to Outspace again, fearful of what else he might accidentally create from his mind. But, because Valentine II and Peter

II came from Ender's mind, they carried Jane's essence within them. She could use them to travel to Outspace as she had used Ender before. A second spacecraft was created to allow Valentine II and Peter II to explore the universe for their own means. Valentine II and Miro would search for a planet the pequeninos and Formics could inhabit, while Peter II took the antivirus Ela had created to Path. From there, he set out to destroy the Starways Congress.

While the virus reversed the genetic manipulation on Path, Jane created a document exposing the truth of the godspoken and the Starways Congress. It was revolutionary for the planet and did not lead to the wars and deaths some thought it might have.

As Jane continued to work with Peter II and Valentine II, Miro II spoke with Ender. There Ender sarcastically said that Jane should take over Valentine II's body. Miro II thought the idea was brilliant, and undertook bringing it to pass. Miro II approached the Hive Queen, hoping that her mastery of philotes would be an asset to him as he combined Jane and Valentine II into one person, preserving both of their lives.

Jane and Valentine II both said they didn't want to be brought together, both playing a bit of a martyr. But, they both knew in their hearts that they desired to continue in their lives. Jane teased Miro II about this, seeming to mask her hope through laughter.

The Hive Queen turned to the pequenino fathertree named Human to help her figure out how to save Jane. They determined that if they could call Ender's philote as he died, and store it in Valentine II, they might be able to place Jane in that body. They needed to use the parts of Jane that were originally from the Hive Queen herself—the parts that had been the bridge between the Formics and Ender—as well as the powerful philotic connection that united the fathertrees. It was possible, but they were uncertain it would work.

Jane didn't know, either, and time was running out. She had taken Peter II and Si Wang-mu to Pacifica and helped Miro II and Valentine II find the home planet of the Descolada. But the order had been given, and she was slowly being terminated by the Starways Congress's act of terminating the ansibles. She had just enough energy to take Miro II, Valentine II, Ela, and Quara back to the Descolada's planet.

She was able to communicate with Miro and Peter II in their respective missions, but was losing memories and could feel her consciousness unraveling. She longed to speak with Ender, as he, too, was dying. But the time had seemingly passed.

To make matters worse, Novinha and Wang-mu were both jealous of Jane.

Novinha still wanted her to go away from Ender, and Wang-mu had fallen in love with Peter II.

Jane's home inside the computer networks was destroyed, and her philotic foundation, her "Auía," escaped from the networks. A little lost, it instantly traveled throughout the galaxy, searching for a new body wherein to live. It tried living in Ender's, Peter II's, and Valentine II's, but they were all full of competing Auía. She tried the Hive Queen and eventually settled on the pequenino mothertrees.

From inside the mothertrees, Jane helped the trees to create fruit. It was delicious fruit unlike anything the pequeninos had tasted before. But she was not meant to stay in that state. Once Ender died, relinquishing his Auía from within his body, removing Valentine II's from her body, and joining both Ender's and Valentine II's with Peter II's in his body, Jane was able to make the leap to Valentine II's now-Auía-empty body. With the Hive Queen's help, Jane entered Valentine II's body.

Though her physical appearance was Valentine's, the soul of the new person was Jane. She still had a shadow of Valentine II's memories, but the consciousness that dwelled in the body was Jane.

She could communicate in her mind with the Hive Queen, since the Hive Queen had been responsible for bringing her philote from Outspace to begin with millennia earlier. But she was not able to speak mind to mind with Peter II or Miro II anymore. She was, for all intents and purposes, human. She thought she could still perhaps control faster-than-light travel, however.

In her new body, Jane was unable to fully control her human emotions. She often lashed out at Quara and cried until she was sick. Miro II comforted her and taught her about human emotion. Perhaps rashly, but nonetheless fully committed, Jane asked Miro to marry her. He agreed, wanting to keep their engagement secret from Quara.

Almost immediately after expressing her love to Miro, Jane fell into a comalike state. She had, before being driven from the computers, taught settlers on several different planets to connect their old government-ordered-discarded computers to create another network wherein she could exist. With help from the fathertrees, mothertrees (where Jane also still had a philotic connection and could store memories), and the Hive Queen, Jane was able to instantly spread her Auía among all these different homes. The comalike state was her human body's reaction to her soul traveling from host to host.

Through this bouncing around from network to network, Jane was able to cause faster-than-light travel. She returned her ship to Lusitania. Physically exhausted from the travel, Jane got into a brief physical confrontation with

Quara, but soundly won. Stepping from the ship, she experienced seeing Lusitania through human eyes for the first time. She thought it was beautiful.

As the Lusitania Fleet came closer to destroying the planet, Jane transported Miro and his sister back to the descoladore world. She used her ability to save the scientists from an attack by the descoladores by blinking them out of harm's way.

She also used her faster-than-light abilities to move Peter II and Wang-mu, without a spaceship, to Lusitania. Again she used the power to pull the deadly Molecular Detachment Device from its course to annihilate Lusitania, replacing it back on the original ship.

She helped Peter II and Wang-mu convince the leaders of the fleet to obey their nonaggression orders, and then teleported them to the descoladore planet where Peter II and Wang-mu convinced Miro II and company not to annihilate the descoladore planet.

She returned to Lusitania for Ender's funeral, and immediately following the service, went into the pequenino land where, under a mothertree to which she was also connected, she married Miro II. Peter II and Wang-mu were married at the same time. Following some congratulatory remarks from Valentine, Jane made the four newlyweds disappear, presumably for private honeymoons.

It was known that she would continue to facilitate faster-than-light travel. She'd helped evacuate many Formics, humans (including all of Ender's loved ones), and pequeninos from Lusitania before the fleet arrived. And though she began a human life married to Miro II, she knew that she could potentially live forever.

Starways Congress reconnected the full computer network in which Jane had lived before. And with her connection to the mothertrees, there was ample space to place her Auía once she grew too old to live in Valentine II's body.

That was years off, though. For the time being, she was more than content to live as Miro's wife. She was Jane—a complex computer program that was beautifully, simplistically, human.

Japanese Professor (SP)

The Japanese professor was a patron at a restaurant in Damascus when the newly crowned Caliph, Alai, made his first public address. He spoke plainly to his fellow foreigners about the role of Caliph in the Muslim world, and argued with an Englishman who felt that a Caliph meant a return to the old ways of Muslim extremism.

Jaqueline (XN)

Jaqueline was married to Ender's stepson Olhado on the planet Lusitania. She was a stereotypical mother, rushing her family through the morning routine. She was present when Valentine Wiggin visited Olhado for the first time and eavesdropped on their conversation from the kitchen. She embarrassingly joined them after Valentine commented on the eavesdropping.

Jiang-qing (XN)

Jiang-qing was a Chinese woman who lived on the planet Path, one of the Hundred Worlds settled by humans after Ender Wiggin's victory over the Formics. She lived approximately three thousand years after the Formic War. She was married to Han Fei-tzu and was the mother of Qing-jao.

Jiang-qing's dying wish was that her husband would help their daughter grow to be among the "godspoken," as Jiang-qing had been, which meant the Gods spoke to her, guiding her life for their purposes. Han Fei-tzu promised he would, even if he didn't truly believe in the godspoken idea.

Jolt (SD)

The jolt was a taserlike weapon carried by the constable of the city Milagre on the planet Lusitania.

Jonlei (*See* Hundred Worlds)

Ju Kung-mei (XN)

Ju Kung-mei was the guard of the Han family on the planet Path. Of Chinese descent, as were all who lived on Path, he was considered kind and respectful of all. His mistress, sixteen-year-old Han Qing-jao, trusted him.

Jung Calvin Colonies (*See* Hundred Worlds)

Kenji the Servant (CM)

Kenji was a loyal servant in the house of Japanese philosopher Aimaina Hikari on the planet Divine Wind.

Kike Force (EG)

"Kike Force" was a nickname given to Rat Army in tribute and mockery of Mazer Rackham's Strike Force, which defeated the Formics in the second invasion.

Kissing doctors (SG)

The kissing doctors were two doctors who worked at a hospital where the Muslim Caliph Alai was catching a helicopter to take him to India. He noticed the doctors sneaking to the roof near the helipad to make love. As Caliph, Alai could not tolerate this and caught them in the early stages of the act. Embarrassed, they traveled with the Caliph as far as Beirut. They promised Alai they would wait for their impending marriage before engaging in such activities again.

Kitunen, Colonel Jarrko (EE)

Colonel Jarrko Kitunen was the passenger liaison officer on the colony ship that took Ender and Valentine to their first colony, Shakespeare. He taught lessons in Common, the language of the fleet, and was responsible for informing the passengers that the play reading they wanted to do had been canceled by Admiral Morgan.

Kolmogrov, Admiral/Governor Vitaly (GB, EE)

Admiral Vitaly Kolmogrov led a fleet of starships against the Formics. Once the aliens were destroyed by Ender Wiggin, Vitaly was assigned to be the governor of a colony that settled a former Formic world. For decades, while awaiting Ender Wiggin's arrival as the new governor, Vitaly led his people. He also communicated with Ender while the boy was in transit. The two decided on a name for the colony: Shakespeare. As he grew older, the Admiral/Governor turned the position over to his friend, the colony's xeno-biologist Sel Menach. Vitaly wanted to ensure a smooth transition of power for Ender and knew that Sel would provide that.

He was so popular a governor that a couple of years after his death, his face was put on the coinage created in the colony.

Lands, Admiral Bobby (CM)

Admiral Bobby Lands was assigned command of the fleet that was ordered to destroy the planet Lusitania. The order haunted him, as he knew that he would be held in as low favor as Ender Wiggin had after committing the First Xenocide. Yet, he also felt strongly that destroying the planet, with its deadly Descolada virus, was the best thing to do for humanity.

By the time he reached Lusitania, however, his superiors in both the government and the military ordered him not to destroy the planet but to quarantine it. Against orders, Lands fired the devastating Molecular Detachment

Device against Lusitania. He was shocked to see moments later that it had returned to his cargo hold.

There he was confronted by Peter Wiggin II and had his fingers broken. Peter II gave Lands specific instructions on what to tell the congressional and military leaders about what had happened at Lusitania. Disgraced in front of his crew, Lands tried unsuccessfully to resign his commission and command.

Lands filed the report as instructed by Peter II, and returned to the Hundred Worlds, hoping to avoid criminal charges for doing what he thought was best for humanity, though he'd been proven wrong.

Lankowski, Ivan (SP, SG)

Ivan Lankowski was a Russian-born Muslim who was a close aide to the Caliph Alai. Ivan picked up Petra Arkanian Delphiki at the Damascus airport and took her underground to Alai. She was to be protected at all costs, as she was a friend of the Caliph's. Ivan spoke little of the details of his orders, but treated Petra (forty years his junior) with kindness as she was thought to be carrying a baby.

Lankowski was one of Alai's inner circle. While Petra and Bean stayed with Alai, Lankowski often called them to meet with the Caliph, referring to him only as "our mutual friend." He didn't seem to trust Bean too much, and Bean didn't fully understand what Lankowski's position was exactly, but they worked together with Alai and the other military leaders to plan an invasion of China, liberating the captive people of Asia.

When Alai learned that his soldiers were killing innocents in India, having successfully liberated that nation from Chinese rule, he grew angry. As Caliph, he journeyed to India to correct the problem by killing the general there. Ivan followed him to India as a bodyguard and adviser. He was loyal to Alai, and was the only member of Alai's inner circle in front of whom Alai let down his guard.

Ivan learned of a plan to assassinate Alai and joined the conspirators so he could be close enough to them to protect his friend. When the assassination attempt occurred, Ivan fought against the would-be killers, sacrificing his life in protection of Alai. Alai mourned his friend, pausing in the midst of his escape from the attempted murder to close Ivan's eyes as he lay dead in a parking garage.

Lars (XN)

Lars was a human male born approximately three thousand years after the end of the Formic War on the planet Trondheim. He was of Icelandic descent, as most of the colonists on Trondheim had been, and was married to Syfte, the daughter of Valentine Wiggin. Lars and Syfte were married very quickly and traveled with Valentine and her husband Jakt into space, setting out for the planet Lusitania, hoping to protect it from destruction by the Starways Congress.

He was on Lusitania with his parents-in-law when his stepcousin-in-law, Quim, was killed by the pequeninos. He was part of the ill-fated rescue party that unsuccessfully tried to save Quim.

Lavea, Leiloa (CM)

Leiloa Lavea was a philosopher on the Polynesian-colonized planet Pacifica. Her ideologies taught her disciples to seek a simple life. Japanese philosopher Aimaina Hikari had studied her teachings. Her philosophies were known as a religion called the Ua Lava.

Leaf-eater (SD)

Leaf-eater was one of the pequeninos, the native life-forms on the planet Lusitania. He befriended Miro, but knew that Miro didn't like him as much as the pequenino named Human.

Leaf-eater was one of the pequeninos to speak with Ender and share with him many of their beliefs and rituals. Leaf-eater also saw Miro Ribeira climb the electrified fence that surrounded the piggies' land, and wanted to plant him as a tree—the highest honor given a pequenino.

Leaf-eater participated in the creation of the treaty between the piggies and the humans, and helped Ender plant a fellow piggie as a tree.

League (EG, ES)

The League was the name given to the confederation of Earth nations united to fight the Formics. It was led by the Hegemon.

League War, the (EG, ES, EE)

The League War was a short-lived conflict between the armies of Earth following Ender Wiggin's victory over the Formics. It was resolved through the Locke Proposal, which allowed for a continuation of the League, but without the binding Warsaw Pact.

Lee (EGS)

A soldier in Ender Wiggin's unbeatable Dragon Army, Lee was assigned his own command and two weeks later sent to Command School to train on the simulators with Ender and the rest of the newly promoted ex-Dragon soldiers.

Lee Tee ([EE])

Lee Tee was a scientist in Shakespeare colony, the first human settlement on a former Formic world.

Legless lizards (IC)

The legless lizards were native animal life on the planet Sorelledolce. They were gigantic.

***Letter to the Framlings* (SD)**

The *Letter to the Framlings* was an essay written by Valentine Wiggin under her pseudonym Demosthenes, which addressed concerns she had about the treatment of lesser life-forms as enumerated in her Heirarchy of Alienness.

Levy, General Shimon (EG)

General Shimon Levy was a high-level officer in the International Fleet, who followed Ender Wiggin's progress from Battle School through Command School, and the victory against the Formics.

Li (EE)

Li was a soldier in the Formic War who helped colonize a former Formic world. He sent reports on the scientific front to Hyrum Graff, then Minister of Colonization.

Li, King (XN)

King Li was a character in the fairy tale *The Jade of Master Ho,* which was popular on the Chinese planet Path.

Libo (*See* Figueria de Medici, Liberdade Graças a Deus "Libo")

Libyan Quarter (*See* Hundred Worlds)

***Life of Human* (SD)**

Life of Human was a book written by Ender Wiggin as the Speaker for the Dead, telling the story of a pequenino (the native life of the planet Lusitania) named Human. It was not as well received as Ender's other books, but had been written in a similar vein.

Lighter (ES)

A member of Rat Army during Ender's command of the supremely dominant Dragon Army, Lighter hated Ender. He was among those who sought to murder Ender with Bonzo Madrid. He warned Bean in the mess hall that those who planned to kill Ender weren't at lunch, but were finding the wunderkind alone.

Lightstick (SD)

A source of light similar to a flashlight used among the Hundred Worlds. Lightsticks were activated by turning the bottom of the stick. This will also widen or narrow the beam of light projected.

Liki, Colonel (EG)

Liki was the colonel in the International Fleet who questioned Graff and Rackham's methods of training Ender, certain that they would prove to be too much for Ender to handle.

Lincoln (SG)

Lincoln was an essayist on the computer nets who spoke about Hegemony policy in the years following Ender's victory over the Formics. As he had done before with Locke, Peter Wiggin, the Hegemon, was the voice of Lincoln.

Lineberry, Dr. (EG)

Dr. Lineberry was the principal of Valentine's school when she was eleven. Lineberry called Valentine to the office one day where she met Colonel Graff.

Li Qing-jao (XN)

Li Qing-jao was an ancient Chinese poet. As a woman, she was an anomaly among poets of her era. She was an ancestor to Han Fei-tzu, and his daughter Han Qing-jao. Han Qing-jao relied on a poem written by Li Qing-jao during her grueling test to determine her worthiness as a "godspoken."

Lo ([EE])

Lo was a citizen on Shakespeare, the first human colony settled on a former Formic world. She divorced her husband.

Locke (EG, ES, EH, EE, SH, SG)

The pseudonym for twelve-year-old Peter Wiggin, used when he wrote political and military commentaries on the computer nets. His columns, and those of his sister Valentine written under the name "Demosthenes," became popular throughout the world. His identity was figured out by the International Fleet, though not exposed to the world.

He and Demosthenes effected change in much of the international community in the aftermath of Ender's victory in the Formic War. "The Locke Proposal" put an end to wars that plagued Earth and led to the resignation of the Hegemon. Earth had a tenuous peace, thanks to the writings of a fifteen-year-old boy.

Peter continued to write as Locke, and eventually also as Demosthenes, after the wars. It was through such an essay that the call went out to the Russian government and military to rescue members of Ender's army that had been kidnapped.

This act earned the ire of Achilles Flandres, who had kidnapped Ender's friends. He had a grudge against Locke, and hoped to expose him. Peter prevented this, however, by exposing his true identity to the world as part of an intricate plan that involved Bean, Sister Carlotta, the Vatican, and Hyrum Graff. They laid out a scenario where the public would call for Locke to become the new Hegemon, and Peter would reveal that he was Locke and, as a teenager, not qualified for the Hegemony. It would increase his influence dramatically, though some sources, he knew, would dry up—not wanting to give information to a simple teenager.

Peter continued to write as Locke, and public support for him increased. He revealed through his columns that the aggressive moves India was making under the direction of Achilles Flandres were actually a cover for Achilles's association with China. He was setting up China to take over all of Asia by spreading India and Pakistan's armies too thin. The column helped stop Achilles in India.

Locke Proposal (EG, ES, [EE])

The Locke Proposal was an international political agreement written by Peter Wiggin under his pseudonym, Locke. It put an end to the short-lived League War on Earth by allowing the International Fleet and the League to continue existence, but without governance of the Warsaw Pact.

Lung, Cargo Officer (CM)

Cargo Officer Lung was assigned to the cargo hold on the flagship of the fleet of spaceships that were ordered to destroy the planet Lusitania. He was fiercely loyal to his commanding officer, Lands, and tried to arrest Peter Wiggin II and Si Wang-mu when ordered to.

Lusitania (*See* Hundred Worlds)

Lusitanian Aborigines (*See* Pequeninos)

Lusos (SD, XN, CM)
"Lusos" was the term used to describe the human settlers of the planet Lusitania.

Macios (SD)
Macios were wormlike creatures that lived on merdona vines, native to the planet Lusitania.

Madrid, Amaro de (PB)
The father of Ender's contemporary "Bonzo" Madrid, he was a proud Spaniard who considered all of Spain to be his family. He often boasted that Spain retained its identity after invasion from crusading Muslims, particularly when other nations could not do so. As a lawyer, he fiercely defended his opinions on nationalism, religion, and the law.

When the International Fleet's testing officer came to test Bonzo, Amaro fought to keep his son, but it was a losing battle. He publicly criticized the Fleet and Battle School, but was secretly honored that his son could potentially be the savior of the world. As a result, he indulged his boy in his whims, spoiling him.

He loved Bonzo tremendously. There was an overabundance of love in their home. However, after Bonzo's second visit with the International Fleet, Amaro grew distant from his family. He would hold "meetings" outside of work hours. He would go to a second office or apartment, and disappear. Bonzo would later determine that his father had been having an affair with another woman, an act that was devastating to his wife.

He reconciled with his wife, but tension was still high between the two. He was ashamed of his actions, and stopped trying to be as close to Bonzo as he'd once been. Regardless, he was crushed when Bonzo's body was returned to them years later, having been killed at Battle School.

Madrid, Mother (PB)
Bonzo Madrid's mother was the caressing comfort of his life. While she was not as outspoken as her husband, she was the provider of everything Bonzo needed. At five years old, he came to realize she was there. She had been present before, of course, but was the quiet strength of the family. She

was well known for her orange flatbread and admired by all who met her. She was crushed when Bonzo asked her why her husband would go to a second apartment or office for a meeting.

She left her husband, Amaro, and took Bonzo with her. She tenuously reconciled with her husband. They lived together, but her heart was broken again a few years later when her son was killed by Ender Wiggin at Battle School.

Madrid y Valencia, Tomas Benedito Bonito de "Bonzo" (PB, EG, ES, [SH], [CM])

Born in Toledo, Spain, and baptized in the Cathedral there, Tomas Benedito Bonito de Madrid y Valencia, or "Bonzo" (pronounced "Bone-so") as he came to be known, was a student in Battle School during Ender's time. A tortured soul, his parents were proud Spaniards, and they adored Bonzo. His name "Bonito" meant "pretty boy," a fact that he disdained but lived with.

He was exceptionally bright, convincing his father he could understand the intricacies of his father's religious and patriotic conversations by eighteen months. The International Fleet began testing Bonzo before he was two years old. He excelled at the tests, and was given the flashing implant/monitoring device that would mark him as a candidate for Battle School when he came of age.

As he grew, Bonzo learned he could get whatever he wanted from his parents. He would stay up past bedtime to read and was spoiled with sweets. But he was a keen observer, and learned from everything his father said, and everything he didn't.

Bonzo learned that his family, while full of love, often hurt each other in subtle ways. And he realized that he was the only member of the family who recognized it. He wrote a note to himself that read he was the true ruler of the family. The note, witnessed through his implant, garnered the attention of the International Fleet, and they sent a representative to confirm to the boy that he was in fact the ruler of his house. It was a test. How would the potential commander react to this newfound power?

He observed his parents further, learning about their pasts and futures. He was confused by their choices, and it sometimes upset him. But he would quickly dismiss it. However, he felt that it was his responsibility to make them happy. He was, after all, their ruler, and that's what "good" rulers did— made their subjects happy.

One day, he secretly followed his father to one of the extra "meetings" his father was having. He saw his father go into a building. He asked his mother about it, devastating her. She took Bonzo to his grandmother's house. There Bonzo pieced together that his father was having an affair.

His parents eventually reconciled, but there would forever be tension in the household. Bonzo made the decision that he would not grow up to be like his father. He promised himself he would never break his mother's heart.

Shortly before his seventh birthday, Bonzo accepted the invitation to go to Battle School.

Bonzo progressed normally through Battle School and was given command of Salamander Army. Bonzo worked his army hard, hoping to improve Salamander's standing in the school's rankings. He bragged about defeating Rat, Scorpion, and Hound armies, all upsets. His army was Ender's first assignment, one that came over a year early for Ender. Bonzo was angry at the assignment of an untrained, inexperienced soldier and took it out on Ender. He would not allow Ender to participate in the army's practices and tried unsuccessfully to ban Ender from practicing with his friends from his launch group during Free Play.

Ender was not allowed to fire his weapon during actual battles, either. The one time he did, Bonzo angrily traded him to Rat Army, glad to be free of Ender and his irritating presence.

As Ender rose through the ranks at Battle School, Bonzo grew jealous. He and a group of older kids, including Bernard, made plans to kill Ender. He even warned Bean, the youngest member of Ender's army, that he would be going after Ender.

Bonzo made his move when Ender was in the shower after a battle and subsequent workout. As Bonzo moved in for the kill, Ender used his own soapy body and the heat of the bathroom to his advantage. Ender hit Bonzo repeatedly in the face, chest, stomach, and groin before escaping with Dink Meeker. But the damage had been done. Ender Wiggin killed Bonzo Madrid.

Bonzo's body was sent back to his parents on Earth.

Magnetic Whips (ES)

Magnetic whips were a police-used crowd control weapon in Rotterdam in the Netherlands when Bean Delphiki lived as an orphan on the streets there.

Male Speaker (Accountant) (*See also* Speaking) (IC)

The Male Speaker, who held a day job as an accountant, was the Speaker for the Dead at the first Speaking Ender attended at age twenty on the planet

Sorelledolce. Like most, this Speaker for the Dead modeled his speech on the deceased's life after Ender's two books *The Hive Queen* and *The Hegemon,* which he'd written under his pseudonym, the "Speaker for the Dead." With the popularity of the books, Speaking became a traditional funerary rite on human worlds throughout the galaxy.

Malu (CM)

Malu was a revered prophet figure on the planet Pacifica. He was the living leader of the Ua Lava religion and had a close tie to Grace Drinker, a teacher of the religion who served as his translator. He lived on the sacred island Atatua, where he communed with the gods. No one could go to the island without first being purified, or made worthy to enter. Once there, though, they could speak with Malu, if he deemed it appropriate, and find spiritual guidance.

Grace told Malu of the arrival of two off-worlders who sought an audience with the spiritual giant of Pacifica. They did not have time to be purified, so Malu made the journey from his secluded island to the mainland, where he met with Peter Wiggin II and Si Wang-mu, who were hoping to subvert the Starways Congress's plan to destroy Jane, the sentient computer.

Malu knew of Jane, believing her to be a god, and told the story, through Grace as his translator, of her development and existence. He knew the need to keep Jane alive. Having said his piece, Malu took his leave of Peter II and Wang-mu, only to return very shortly thereafter. He approached Wang-mu. He knew that it was her love that would bring the god Jane and Peter II new life.

Once Ender died, joining his soul with Peter II's and Valentine II's, all in Peter II's body, Malu celebrated, for he knew the god Jane was safe inside Valentine II's body. But he also knew that his people had disobeyed congressional order, by Jane's secret direction, and did not discard their old computers that once housed the sentient computer-god.

He was present when the new non-Jane compliant computers were started up, and also watched as their old computers were restarted. The old computers housed a network wherein Jane could potentially live. Malu celebrated when it became apparent that she could live, at least part-time since she was in Valentine II's body, in their old network and could continue to control faster-than-light travel. His god lived.

Mandachuva (SD)

A native "piggie" or pequenino on the planet Lusitania, Mandachuva was a good friend with the piggie named Rooter. They encountered the xenobiologist named Pipo, and often spoke with him, teaching him about piggie culture.

Mandachuva lived for many years, befriending not only Pipo, but also his son, Libo, and grandchildren, Miro and Ouanda. He was a reliable guide to the piggie society, which the xenologists on Lusitania relied on.

The male piggie told Miro that they needed metal. It was unclear what the animallike creatures would use metal for, but Mandachuva was insistent. He was equally insistent that the piggies be allowed to speak with the newly arrived Speaker for the Dead, Andrew Wiggin.

When Ender arrived, Mandachuva was one of the piggies to talk with him and share with him the dream his people had of space travel. Later he saw Miro Ribeira climb over the wall that blocked the human and piggie civilizations. With Miro severely hurt, Mandachuva climbed over the wall himself and raced to find Ouanda.

With Ouanda, he went into town to get help for the injured Miro. He was the first piggie that the leaders of the colony had ever seen. These leaders, including Ender Wiggin, followed Mandachuva back to the piggie home, shut off the fence, and tried to save Miro.

He accompanied Ender, his party, and other piggies to see the wives—the female, governing piggies—to negotiate the treaty between humans and pequeninos. He also helped Ender perform the "Third Life" ritual on Human, showing him the highest respect he could.

Maria (SD)

Maria was a daughter of Pipo, the xenologist, born on the planet Lusitania. She died at a young age from the virus known as the Descolada.

Martel (SG)

Martel was a political pundit on the computer nets who commented on Hegemony policy in the years after Ender's victory over the Formics. Petra Arkanian was the writer behind Martel, under the direction of Peter Wiggin the Hegemon. She filled a role nearly identical to Peter's sister, Valentine, who wrote as "Demosthenes" during the Formic wars.

Martinov, Pyotr (SD)

Pyotr Martinov was a high-ranking official in the Starways Congress. He worked with Gobawa Ekumbo to enforce the laws against the rebellious planet, Lusitania.

Maternal Grandmother of Bonzo Madrid (PB)

Bonzo Madrid's grandmother (his mother's mother) hosted Bonzo and his mother while she recovered from the discovery of her husband's affair. Grandmother kept some of Bonzo's old clothes that were too small, and Bonzo thought she was a bad cook.

Mateu, Father (SD)

Father Mateu was a Catholic priest on the planet Lusitania.

McPhee, Fernao (EE)

Fernao McPhee was a soldier who fought in the Formic War and was assigned to help colonize a former Formic planet. As a foreman in communal fields, he refused to give xenobiologist Sel Menach a job when the scientist asked for one.

Mebane, Dr. Howard (SP)

Dr. Howard Mebane was a physician at the Florida-based Mayo clinic. He studied the genetic manipulation that had been performed on Bean Delphiki and was searching for treatment options that would prolong Bean's life in the face of his accelerated growth.

Meeker, Dink (EG, WG, ES, SH, SG)

Dink Meeker was an older contemporary of Ender's and Bean's at Battle School. Born and raised in the Netherlands, he made the derogatory comment that both Ender and Bean could walk between his legs without touching his balls when he first met each soldier.

He was a toon leader in Rat Army and was assigned Ender when Ender was reassigned from Salamander to Rat. That was December, the month of traditional holiday celebration, and Dink secretly gave a gift of a poem to his friend and fellow Dutchman, Flip. Though simple, the gift caused a tremendous problem at Battle School when the religious zealot Zeck Morgan cried foul and insisted that all religious observance be allowed on the station. Dink responded by setting up a secret gift exchange among the students at Battle School, where they would hide small gifts in each other's socks. It resulted in further dissension at the school when Zeck influenced a Muslim student to lead a group of Muslim students in their ritual daily prayer. Though Dink had broken the Battle School rules by celebrating a holiday, he was not sorry. In fact, the situation only strengthened his feelings about Battle School and its policies.

Dink had a very cynical view of Battle School, the International Fleet, and the Hegemony. He doubted the reality of the Formics and their war, believing the video footage of the invasions from decades earlier had been created by the Hegemony. Though supportive of Ender, Dink Meeker was not a friend; he was a colleague. But his respect for Ender increased in the aftermath of the gift-giving saga as Ender bridged the gap between Zeck and the rest of the Battle School community.

Reportedly, Dink had been promoted to commander on two occasions, but refused the assignment (even hiding in his room until the Battle School administrators moved him back to an army). He liked being in an army more than commanding one.

Nearly two years later, Dink succeeded Rosen as commander of Rat Army. When Ender was promoted to command an army himself, Dink and Ender felt a rift in their friendship. They were in competition with one another, and the fact was, neither was willing to lose. Despite their competition, Dink was still close to Ender. When Bonzo Madrid decided to kill Ender, it was Dink who warned Ender to never be alone. When Bonzo made his move, Dink was there. Although restrained by Bonzo's friends, Dink tried desperately to save Ender. Ender was victorious in the fight—unintentionally killing Bonzo—and left with Dink, crying.

When Ender left to go to Command School, Dink aligned himself with Bean, a newly promoted commander who had been in Ender's dominant Dragon Army. The two of them convinced their peers at Battle School to reject the traditional expectations of adhering to the standings in the game, and to focus only on becoming the best soldiers they could.

Dink was a successful commander in Battle School, and was eventually promoted to Tactical School and (a week later) Command School where he was one of Ender's squadron leaders in the "exams"—the actual battles where the children controlled fleets of starships and fighters against the Formics.

Following Ender's victory, Dink was one of Ender's friends who told him that the war that had broken out on Earth had ended thanks to something called "The Locke Proposal."

Dink was one of the ten former Command School soldiers who were kidnapped after the wars. They were forced by their captives to play war games. Dink was the first to greet Petra Arkanian when she was brought to the war games area, having spent the longest amount of time in solitary confinement. Dink and his fellow prisoners played the games but knew that their captors were not good at staging the simulations.

He was among those of his colleagues who felt contacting Peter Wiggin was the key to their freedom.

Like the rest of the prisoners, Dink was taken by his captor, revealed to be Achilles Flandres, a former Battle School student and a serial killer, to a private location somewhere in Russia. He was still permitted to communicate via e-mail with his colleagues, but was not allowed to be in their presence.

After several months, Dink and the rest of the prisoners, except Petra Arkanian, were rescued by Russian operatives. Achilles thought Petra was the smartest of the group and kept her captive, but did not interfere with the others' rescue.

With no military to speak of in Dink's home, the Netherlands, he was sent to the United Kingdom where he was an adviser to the British army. He was approached a couple of years later by both Hyrum Graff and Peter Wiggin and offered a new life in space, free of the unstable political climate of Earth. Like the rest of his fellow Battle School grads, he refused.

As Peter built the Hegemony into the Free People of Earth, Graff again offered Ender's colleagues the opportunity to leave Earth and govern a planet. It was his fear that Ender's army would be used in the worldwide conflict, manipulated by whatever political power rose to prominence, and he wanted to prevent that. Every member who received the offer, which did not include Han Tzu, Petra Arkanian, or Alai, said no. The others were already too involved in matters on Earth to leave.

Somewhere along the lines, Dink decided to leave Earth and go to space with a colony, but not as its leader. Petra wrote to him to say good-bye and good luck to him, not fully understanding why he would choose to go but not govern the colony. It turned out, though, that Dink had chosen to govern the colony and would lead the people with whom he traveled once they reached their destination.

Memphis (*See* Hundred Worlds)

Menach, Sel (GB, EE)

Czech-born Sel Menach was a soldier in the International Fleet, and was commanded by Ender and his squadron at Command School. Sel did not fight the Formics at their home world that was destroyed by the Molecular Detachment Device, but near another Formic planet.

After Ender's victory, Sel helped settle the nearby planet, now supposedly devoid of Formic life, serving as the planet's xenobiologist. He helped determine the order of marriage for the planet. Because of his reputation for great intelligence, many women in the colony wanted to have his child. Even his xenobiologist assistant, Afraima, propositioned him, leading him to seek employment away from her.

Never wanting to be a leader, Sel Menach at first refused the position of governor in Shakespeare colony. He only accepted when his friend Vitaly, the first governor, asked him to take it to ensure a smooth transition of power when Ender Wiggin arrived.

As Ender's arrival grew imminent, Sel dismissed himself from his gubernatorial duties and explored the planet with Po Tolo, the son of his friend and fellow xenobiologist, Ix. Po and Sel discovered the Gold Bugs—a race of insectlike miners who absorbed the metals they mined into their exoskeletons. They had been used by the Formics to mine the planet's natural resources. Sel and Po devoted the rest of their lives to the study of the Gold Bugs and their cousins that mined silver, copper, etc.

Once these metal bugs were used to create coins for Shakespeare, Sel's face was minted on one of them in tribute to the job he'd done as governor.

Mercutio (*See* Hundred Worlds)

Meson (XN)

The subatomic particles that make up neutrons and protons. Splitting a meson and carrying the two fragments suspended in a magnetic field creates the philotic connection used in an ansible.

Meta Science (SD)

Meta Science: The Journal of Methodology was a prestigious scientific journal among the Hundred Worlds. Ender Wiggin's stepchildren on the planet Lusitania admired it and read it frequently.

Michi (SD)

Michi was a child on the planet Lusitania. He was friends with Olhado Ribeira von Hesse and enjoyed playing football with him.

Mick (EG)

Mick saw Ender was eating alone in Battle School and chose to sit with him. He went on to tell Ender that every launch group had a soldier no one wanted to be around. Mick was not a very good soldier, telling Ender that no one really noticed him. He was not Tactical School material, and wouldn't amount to anything. He told Ender also that if Ender wanted to be the best, he would need to work hard, but it still wouldn't matter because Ender was nobody.

Milagre (*See* Hundred Worlds)

Mindanao (*See* Hundred Worlds)

Mingo (SD)

Mingo was a child of Gusto and Cida, the xenobiologists on the planet Lusitania, and was killed by the Descolada virus.

Minister of Defense—Thailand (SH)

In the aftermath of an assassination attempt on Bean Delphiki in Thailand, the Minister of Defense in that nation replaced the Chakri as the top military leader in the country. The Chakri had been a conspirator in the assassination attempt, and as such resigned from his position.

Mirabella (ES)

Mirabella, or Bell as she preferred, was a student at the same high school Peter Wiggin attended in Greensboro, North Carolina. She was irritated with Peter's offer of help on a school assignment because he, being fourteen years old, was much younger than she, and way too young to be the senior he was.

Peter used her rejection as a catalyst for determining how great leaders of the past won over their subjects. He manipulated her later by thanking her for showing him how offensive he was, and telling her how highly he thought of her. She believed it all, but it was a lie.

Miranda (*See* Hundred Worlds)

Miro (*See* Ribeira von Hesse, Marcos Vladimir "Miro")

Moctezuma (*See* Hundred Worlds)

Molecular Detachment Device/Molecular Disruption Device/M.D.D./ "Little Doctor" (EGS, EG, ES, SD, XN, CM)

The next generation from the nuclear weapons that were used against the Formics in the first invasion, the Molecular Detachment Device, also called the Molecular Disruption Device, created a field in which molecules could not hold together. This field would spread as long as matter was tightly packed together, as in a spaceship or planet. Ender used the weapon against the planet, believing he was playing a game. But the virtual war was real, and the weapon destroyed the Formic planet, wiping out the entire species. Its use was banned from then on.

Three thousand years later, when the planet Lusitania was found to be in rebellion, Starways Congress reauthorized its use. Lusitania was home to a deadly virus called the Descolada, and the Congress felt the only way to protect the universe from the disease and the rebellious planet was to destroy it. The reauthorization of the weapon was made public by the political analyst named Demosthenes.

Molo, Fly (EG, ES, SH, SG)

Fly Molo was a toon leader in Ender's dominant Dragon Army. He was a solid soldier who gave his all in battles and contributed a lot. Early in his assignment in Dragon Army, however, he doubted Ender's strategy and spoke badly of him behind his back. Bean defended Ender, leading to a physical confrontation between Fly and Bean.

He was eventually promoted to Tactical School and Command School, where he was one of Ender's squadron leaders in the school's "exams," which were revealed to be actual battles.

He was one of the soldiers who was kidnapped and forced to play more war games in Russia after the Formic Wars. He tried to convince his captors to create better simulations and felt that Peter Wiggin held the key to finding and freeing them.

When it was revealed that Achilles Flandres, a former Battle School student and a serial killer, was their captor, each of the prisoners was taken to a separate location. They were allowed to write to each other, but not allowed physical interaction of any kind.

He, along with his fellow captives except Petra Arkanian, was rescued without incident by Russian operatives a short time later.

In the years that followed his kidnapping, Fly was given extensive responsibilities in his home country, the Philippines. He wasn't given as much authority in his homeland as many of his Battle School colleagues had in theirs, but he was nonetheless kept busy.

Hyrum Graff and Peter Wiggin both approached Fly to offer him transportation from Earth and the opportunity to begin a new life in space, free of the political instability of his home world. Like the rest of his Battle School colleagues, he refused the invitation.

As Peter built the Hegemony into the Free People of Earth, Graff again offered Ender's colleagues the opportunity to leave Earth and govern a planet. It was his fear that Ender's army would be used in the worldwide conflict, manipulated by whatever political power rose to prominence, and he wanted to prevent that. Every member who received the offer, which did not include Han Tzu, Petra Arkanian, or Alai, said no. The others were already too involved in matters on Earth to leave.

As the situation on Earth grew more violent, though, Fly reconsidered his position. Not wanting to be used by different governments to create battle plans for them, Fly agreed to go to a colony in space. His only request was that he not be sent to the same colony as Alai, citing some personality conflicts with his former Battle School colleague.

Momoe, Talo (EG, ES)

Talo Momoe was the commander of Tiger Army, which was teamed with Griffin Army to face Ender's Dragon Army in a two-on-one battle. Talo's team lost. He was promoted to Tactical School, but was considered too incompatible with Ender to move on to Command School.

Monitor (CH, EG, WG, ES)

The monitor was a device that tracked the thoughts and movements of potential Battle School students. It was created and implanted by the International Fleet and removed once a student's abilities were determined. It was marked by a red light. Many parents considered it a great honor for their children to have a monitor given to them.

Monitor Lady (EG)

Monitor lady was seen at the time Ender's monitor was removed from the back of his neck. She incorrectly promised that the procedure would not hurt Ender.

Monitor Pequenino (CM)

The monitor pequenino was assigned to watch the telescopes and other monitors of the space around Lusitania in anticipation of the congressional fleet that had been sent to destroy the planet. He heard the warning noise that the fleet had arrived and notified his superiors accordingly, albeit nervously.

Moon, Corn (ES)

A girl in Bean's Battle School launch group, Corn Moon offered interpretive suggestions to Bean after he discovered the maps of Battle School. She stated that the five mysterious decks would have to be used, at least in part, for the space-bound school's oxygen generation, using plants.

Morgan, Admiral Quincy (EE)

Admiral Quincy Morgan was the commanding officer on Ender's colony ship. The admiral believed he would be the real governor on the planet and that Ender would simply be a figurehead. A natural military man, Quincy set plans in motion to remove Ender from any position of influence. Ender seemed to play along, acquiescing to Quincy's desires. Ender often reinforced Quincy's position as the commander of the ship, going so far as to ask that he be addressed as Ender, a student and scientist, not a war hero.

Despite Ender's reassurances that he was not a threat to Quincy's command, Admiral Morgan was still nervous. When Ender was involved in a public group reading of *The Taming of the Shrew,* Admiral Morgan had the play shut down and ordered Ender to his office. The passengers on the ship developed great disdain for Admiral Morgan from this decision.

Quincy screamed at Ender and accused him of treason because of an ansible message Peter Wiggin had sent to Valentine that was using up the ship's bandwidth. Hurling insults at Ender, who remained unflappable, Quincy accused Ender of mutiny. Once the mess was sorted out, Quincy, with some embarrassment, allowed the play to be performed and even attended.

At the play reading, Quincy first saw Dorabella Toscano, who was reading the part of Katharine, the title shrew. Dorabella played the part so well that Quincy began to fall in love with her.

Quincy fully believed that Ender was not qualified to govern Shakespeare Colony, and fully intended to become the governor once they arrived at the planet. As the two-year journey came to a close, Quincy refined his plans to take over the planet. He also married Dorabella, assuring her of a place of prominence in Shakespeare.

As the ship arrived at Shakespeare Colony, Quincy put his plans to take over the governship into full force. There would be a great ceremony where he would expose Ender as an ignorant teenager, and assume control. The plan backfired, however, when Ender interrupted Quincy's planned ceremony, receiving a hero's welcome.

Ender presented Quincy with a note from Earth warning the admiral that any attempts to interfere with Ender's powers as governor or as Quincy's superior officer would result in a charge of mutiny. Quincy, defeated, returned to the ship for his voyage to another colony. He was joined by Dorabella, but not her daughter, Alessandra, who chose to stay at Shakespeare.

Morgan, Mrs. (WG)

Mrs. Morgan was married to the Reverend Habit Morgan and lived in Eden, North Carolina, where her husband was the minister. She was physically abused by her husband and loved by her son Zeck. She taught Zeck about Santa Claus, despite her husband's insistence that it was an evil tradition. She gave up Zeck for Battle School.

Morgan, Reverend Habit (WG)

Reverend Habit Morgan was the religious authority in Eden, North Carolina. He spoke with a silver tongue, and his parishioners felt he was the true voice of God among Man. He spoke out against the evils of humanism, particularly the "Satanic" tradition of Santa Claus. He also had a dark secret: he was physically abusive to his wife and son. He focused on nonviolence in his sermons to try to control his rage.

He desperately tried to keep his son, Zeck, from going to Battle School; but after hearing threats that his parents would be arrested, Zeck left his family to go.

Morgan, Zechariah "Zeck" (WG)

The child of the local preacher, Zeck Morgan was born and raised in Eden, North Carolina. He was taught conflicting principles about whether Satan was involved in human affairs by his parents, whom he loved very much. He dogmatically followed his father's religious instruction, and loved his mother deeply. However, his father beat him severely, calling the beatings "purification."

When he was screened for potential Battle School placement, he agreed to go to protect his parents from criminal charges if they stopped him. Furthermore, he warned the fleet testing officers that he would teach the other children that God did not want them to kill their enemies.

Not long after arriving at Battle School, Zeck noticed Dink Meeker giving his fellow Dutchman, Flip, a small gift to secretly celebrate Sinterklaas Day—St. Nicholas Day. Angered that religious devotion was forbidden at Battle School, and infuriated that a holiday celebration had gone on unpunished, Zeck took it upon himself to cause a religious uprising in protest. Dink's gift-giving had spread to many other Battle School students, and in response Zeck influenced a Muslim student Ahmed to lead a group of Muslim students to rebel by saying their daily prayers in public. The Muslim students were taken away in handcuffs, and Zeck found himself ostracized from the rest of Battle School.

Ender later faked an injury, and Zeck, remembering the Good Samaritan, helped Ender. It gave the two a chance to talk. Ender was blunt with Zeck, helping the religious child to see that the abuse his father had done to him was wrong. Zeck reacted violently, beating Ender, but he quickly realized what he was doing, and made the decision to stop, recalling his mother's influence. Ender helped Zeck realize that Zeck's father also abused his mother. Zeck wanted to kill his father, but through his conversation with Ender turned from his latent violent tendencies. Ender gave Zeck a gift—a sock, like what Dink had given the others—though this one had been used to stop Zeck's bleeding. Zeck accepted it. It was a sign that he accepted his colleagues at Battle School. Dink and the others saw Ender accept Zeck, and likewise followed suit, bringing him into the Battle School community.

Morris, Lieutenant (EGS)

Lieutenant Morris was a colleague and instructor at Battle School. He assisted in the Battle Room, unfreezing victims after matches.

Moskva (*See* Hundred Worlds)

Mother Tongue (SD, XN)

Mother Tongue was the language used by female pequeninos or wives on the planet Lusitania to speak with the tribe's mothertree.

Mrs. Morgan (EE)

Mrs. Morgan was the nickname crewmembers aboard *IFcoltrans1,* the first colony spaceship, had given the vessel. It referred to the ship's commanding officer, Admiral Quincy Morgan, and his unwavering commitment to it.

Mu-pao (XN)

Mu-pao was a servant in the home of Han Fei-tzu. She was the first to notice Fei-tzu's daughter Qing-jao's hands were bloodied from washing—the first sign of a child being among the "godspoken."

She was loyal to Han Fei-tzu, and held the godspoken rituals as sacred. When Fei-tzu's daughter Qing-jao sent away the servant Si Wang-mu, Mu-pao followed after her, riding a donkey, to carry Fei-tzu's instructions that Wang-mu return.

Through the rest of Han Fei-tzu's life, and for much of Qing-jao's, Mu-pao continued her service in the House of Han.

Mu-ren (CH)

Mu-ren was the hired cook in the Han household. She refused to give Tzu her key, which she used to go to market to buy foodstuffs, when he asked for it to go outside the walls with his Common Tutor, Wei Dun-nuan, to read. She was scared when the authorities came to arrest Han Tzu's father.

Musafi (SG)

Musafi was an adviser to the Caliphate of the Muslim World, Alai. He was an ardent supporter of Muslim expansionism and sought to overthrow Peter Wiggin's world government with a Muslim one. Alai appreciated his colleague's blunt counsel.

Nagoya (*See* Hundred Worlds)

Najjas (SG)

Najjas was a member of Caliph Alai's inner circle during the rise of Peter Wiggin as the Hegemon and leader of the world government. Najjas spoke his mind plainly, but followed the guidance of his leaders: Alai and Alai's wife, the Hindu Virlomi.

Naresuan, Chakri (SH)

Chakri Naresuan was the top military leader in Thailand after Ender's victory over the Formics. He was a careerist general, who did all he could to protect his own position in the Thai military.

When Bean hid from Achilles Flandres in Thailand, he was made many promises by the Chakri. The Chakri did not keep his promises, however, and was actually exposed to be in a conspiracy with Achilles to kill Bean and the Thai military strategist Suriyawong. His role in an assassination attempt uncovered, the Chakri resigned his position in shame, though not before trying to discredit Bean further to the Prime Minister of Thailand. The prime minister didn't believe the Chakri, however.

Navigational School (EG)

Navigational School was another training center sponsored by the International Fleet during the Formic Wars. Not much is known about it beyond its existence.

Navio, Doctor (SD)

Navio was the primary doctor on the planet Lusitania. He performed the autopsy on the late Marcão Ribeira. When Ender arrived to Speak Marcão's death, he met with Navio to learn all he could about the death. Navio, like most Lusitanians, was devoutly Catholic, and initially refused to share details with Ender. Ender, with the help of his computer friend Jane, convinced Navio that it would be better for the whole colony if he helped.

The doctor relented, and shared with Ender that Marcão had a congenital defect that normally would have sterilized him. But, since the man had fathered six children, the disease must have been slow-moving. Jane and Ender expressed some humor at the doctor's choosing to remain naïve rather than accept that Marcão's wife had been unfaithful. But he seemed to not know of the adultery until it was revealed during Ender's Speaking for the Dead on behalf of Marcão a few days later.

Navio was called to the fence that protected the pequenino land outside of the colony. Miro Ribeira had climbed it, and was critically injured. Navio had no idea how to help Miro, having not been trained in medical school for the type of injury the fence caused. He did his best, however, but Miro had suffered severe nerve damage, and the doctor was unable to reverse it. However, Miro recovered on his own and was able to walk and talk, albeit with some difficulty.

Necessarians (CM)

Necessarians were a quasireligious/philosophical group on the Japanese planet Divine Wind. They believed in living in perfect harmony with one's environment. Several Necessarians held great influence in the Starways Congress, and were partially responsible for the order given to a small fleet of ships to destroy the planet Lusitania. Necessarian philosophy taught that offenses should be ignored unless life was threatened.

Nets (EG, ES, SH, SP, SG)

"Nets" was the term given to computer networks similar to the Internet of modern time.

New Chinese (XN, CM)

New Chinese was the language of choice on the planet Path.

Nguyen, Colonel (SP)

Colonel Nguyen was the head of the International Fleet's Digital Security Force. A Vietnamese woman, she worked at the Ministry of Colonization, which was housed in the refurbished Battle School orbiting Earth. When Hyrum Graff and Peter Wiggin set out to expose a mole in the Ministry, she played an integral part by tracking all computer activity on the station. She revealed the mole to be Uphanad, the station's security chief.

Nimbo (XN)

Nimbo was one of the sons of Ender's stepson, Olhado Ribeira von Hesse, and his wife Jaqueline. He was one of the mobocrats who attacked pequenino land, killing many of the so-called piggies in retaliation for the murder of his uncle Quim. Nimbo was hurt in the riot but was able to walk despite his injuries. He was certain he would be killed in the riot.

When Valentine Wiggin visited Olhado's home for the first time, she saw Nimbo to be a stereotypical child.

Nita (PB)

Nita was a family friend or servant of the Madrid family. She made noodles with Bonzo.

Noches, Pablo de (ES)

A janitor at a place Bean called the "clean place," Pablo de Noches was a poor Dutch man who used all his money to buy prostitutes. He found Bean hiding in a toilet when Bean was less than a year old and took the boy home to care for him. Bean eventually left Pablo's care, but they encountered one another four years later when Bean searched for the janitor.

Bean (and Sister Carlotta, who had followed him) hoped Pablo would be able to shed some light on Bean's past, but the janitor was not very helpful. He told Sister Carlotta about the organ farming and, after Bean went to Battle School, showed the nun the toilet in which he'd found Bean years earlier.

Noches' Hooker (ES)

Pablo de Noches was known for hiring prostitutes. On one particular night, the hooker he'd paid walked home with him, encountering a four-year-old Bean on the way. Bean claimed that Pablo was married, angering the hooker, who walked away with Pablo's money.

Noncomplying Family Act (EG)

Law by which families who had more than two children were arrested. Several nations ignored the law, choosing instead to live religiously or culturally and have multiple children.

Nordic (SD)

Nordic was the chosen language of the planet Trondheim, where Valentine Wiggin met and married her husband, Jakt.

Novinha (*See* von Hesse, Ivanova Santa Catarina "Novinha")

***Observations of Distant Worlds with the Naked Eye* (SD)**

Popular book by noted author Mil Fiorelli, *Observations of Distant Worlds with the Naked Eye* had a great impact on Ender and Valentine Wiggin.

O'Connor (EE)

After retiring from the International Fleet and Ministry of Colonization, Hyrum Graff lived by himself in Ireland. O'Connor was one of Hyrum's few friends and delivered groceries and letters to him.

Office Manager (ES)

The office manager was a woman who ran the building Bean called the "clean place." Though it had changed dramatically from when Bean lived there in his first year of life, Sister Carlotta hoped it would give her some answers into Bean's past. Carlotta went to the building with janitor Pablo de Noches and told the office manager that they were there on Fleet business.

Ojman, Rymus (XN)

Rymus Ojman was the chairman of the cabinet of the Starways Congress. He was a powerful political leader but lost much of his influence after an ironic essay by political pundit Demosthenes mocked him publicly.

Old Chinese (CM)

"Old Chinese" was the term used by the Chinese citizens of the planet Path to refer to the version of their language on Earth in "ancient" times.

Old Man (EE)

The old man was a colonist from India who was traveling to the planet Ganges. He wanted to ensure that the settlers from the southern part of India would be treated respectfully by the colony's governor, Virlomi. Virlomi agreed and promised they would be.

Olhado (*See* Ribeira von Hesse, Lauro Suleimão "Olhado")

Ooka ([CM])
Ooka was the first Necessarian philosopher on the planet Divine Wind.

Oporto (*See* Hundred Worlds)

Order of Inhibition (SH, SP, SG)
When someone was a proven security risk, government officials implanted in his brain a device that caused any kind of anxiety to launch a feedback loop, leading to a panic attack. Such people were then given periodic sensitization to make sure that they felt a great deal of anxiety when they contemplated talking about the forbidden subject. A noted scientist named Anton had this implanted in him.

Otaheti (*See* Hundred Worlds)

O'Toole, Agnes (WG)
A female testing officer for the International Fleet, Agnes O'Toole worked with Zeck Morgan, preparing him for Battle School. She was well respected by Zeck, a religious zealot who felt all women deserved respect—even I.F. officers.

Ouanda (*See* Saavedra Ouanda Quenhatta Figueira Mucumbi)

Outback (*See* Hundred Worlds)

Outspace (XN, CM)
Outspace was where the philotes existed and could only be reached by focused thought by the sentient computer Jane. Once in Outspace, a person could travel to any planet instantly, merely by thinking of the destination. In Outspace all thoughts become reality, including the creation of new life like Peter Wiggin II or a new body for Miro Ribeira.

Pace, General (EG)
A general from the International Fleet's high command, General Pace was an adviser to Battle School who became concerned that Ender's life was in jeopardy and encouraged Colonel Graff to graduate Bonzo Madrid to protect Ender.

Pacifica/Lumana'i (*See* Hundred Worlds)

Pan Ku-wei (XN)

Pan Ku-wei was a citizen of the planet Path. Of Chinese descent, he was a very smart man who came close to passing the test for government service. He fell short, though, but spoke out about political matters. He often talked about how the Starways Congress was wrong to send a fleet to destroy the planet Lusitania. Much of his rhetoric was taken from the essays of Demosthenes.

Paribatra, Prime Minister ([SG])

Prime Minister Paribatra was the prime minister of Thailand and an ally to Bean when he was hiding in that nation. Bean knew that Achilles Flandres, a former Battle School dropout and serial killer, was set to try to take over all of Asia. The prime minister of Thailand relied on Bean's military expertise to protect his nation from Achilles and the Indian army that was set to invade.

Bean told the prime minister that Achilles was using the Indian forces not to actually invade Thailand, but to weaken all the armies in Asia by spreading them too thin against each other. Once to that point, Achilles would join with China and allow the Chinese to take over all of Asia. The prime minister doubted this theory, and virtually ignored Bean's warnings. He was captured and held in China.

Once free, Paribatra negotiated with Peter Wiggin to bring his people into the Free People of Earth world government.

Park shift (SD)

A park shift was a sudden slowing of velocity for a spaceship as it approached a planetary orbit or a sudden increase of velocity as it left.

Patinha "Isolde" (SD)

Patinha was a child to Pipo and Conceição, born on the planet Lusitania.

Path (*See* Hundred Worlds)

Peder (EGS)

Peder was one of Ender's soldiers in Dragon Army and was promoted to commander of his own army because of Dragon's success. He was still nine when he was promoted, three years earlier than usual. He was a commander for two weeks before being sent to Command School to train on the simulator. He was one of Ender's soldiers in the simulator.

Pei-Tian (CH)

Pei-Tian was the driver for Han Tzu's father. He had a key to the outside of the Han family compound, which Han Tzu wanted to steal.

Peregrino, Bishop (aka Armao Cebola) (SD, XN)

Bishop Peregrino was the presiding religious authority on the planet Lusitania. He conducted the funeral of Pipo, the planet's xenologist who had been murdered by the native Lusitanians, the pequeninos. He had also been responsible for submitting the names of Cida and Gusto, the planet's previous xenobiologists, for canonization after they'd died helping eradicate a plague.

As the defender of Catholicism on Lusitania, Bishop Peregrino was opposed to the practice of Speakers for the Dead—irreligious funeral rights that had come into fashion over the last three thousand years. Some of the colonists on Lusitania had called for a Speaker, and the Bishop was upset, but bound by the law to allow it.

However, once the Speaker, Ender Wiggin, arrived, the bishop sought to create a unified front against him. He even went to his religious rival, the abbot of the Children of the Mind of Christ, asking for his help in ridding Lusitania of the Speaker. The abbot refused, seeking to adhere to the law.

He was invited, a short time later, to meet with Governor Bosquinha. He learned in that meeting that the Starways Congress had begun absorbing the planet's computer files. He was instructed to transfer the church's most important files into Ender's well-hidden computer storage space. Bishop Peregrino agreed, begrudgingly.

That night, despite his own public protestations, Bishop Peregrino attended the Speaking. He was surprised to see the level of honesty Ender portrayed in his Speaking of the late Marcão Ribeira. He also felt that the truths Ender revealed were ultimately gifts for the family—helping them see who their father and their adulterous mother really were.

Lusitania's planetary charter was revoked, and Bishop Peregrino met with the other leaders of the Lusitania colony to discuss what course of action to take. He, along with the other leaders, decided to rebel against the Starways Congress's orders, and cut off ansible communication. He hoped this would open the door for conversion of the planet's native life—the pequeninos—to Catholicism.

In this process, Bishop Peregrino developed a grudging respect, bordering on friendship, for Ender. He learned that Ender had been baptized Catholic, and was not as devious as he'd once thought.

Bishop Peregrino took the governor of the colony to the forest where they learned that a treaty had been signed between humans and the pequeninos. He celebrated the treaty, knowing that it afforded him the opportunity to take the piggies the gospel.

He performed a celebratory mass later that morning, noting that Ender Wiggin sat with Novinha and her family. Bishop Peregrino also performed the marriage of Ender to Novinha a short time later.

Nearly thirty years later, as the Lusitanians waited for the fleet to arrive to destroy their world, Bishop Peregrino was still the leader of the church on the planet. He was very old, but equally revered by his parishioners.

When Ender's stepson Quim, who had been ordained as the priest to the pequeninos, decided to go on a mission to the heretical piggies that believed the deadly Descolada virus to be the Holy Ghost, Bishop Peregrino supported it. He defended the missionary effort to the mayor and Quim's family, stating that they had a responsibility to maintain the welfare of the piggies' souls. There was great risk, to be sure, but the bishop admired Quim's willingness to go.

Quim was killed by the pequeninos, and many of the citizens of Lusitania rioted. They burned much of the piggies' forest, killing many pequeninos in the process. Bishop Peregrino pleaded with the people for calm, and chastened them as their spiritual leader for committing the murders they had in the forest. But he also took personal responsibility for not doing anything to stop the murders, either.

Bishop Peregrino participated in another meeting of colony leaders when a plan was presented to test a new theory of faster-than-light travel. The theory went over his head. He didn't think it was funny when Quara joked that God had made Outspace as an answer to the prayers of the faithful on Lusitania as they awaited their destruction. He thought it might even have been true.

Pequeninos/Piggies (SD, XN, CM)

Pequeninos, or piggies as they'd been nicknamed because of their animal-like appearance, were the native life-forms on the planet Lusitania. They were the only nonhuman sentient life that had been discovered in the galaxy. They had padded paws and hooklike claws on the back of their lower legs.

The piggies established strong relationships with the human settlers on

Lusitania. They performed many rituals, including planting trees in their most revered citizens after death.

They carried the Descolada virus, which actually gave them their ability to live. It was fatal to humans and all other life. Working with human scientists like Ender's stepchildren, the pequeninos were able to rid themselves of the Descolada and continue to live.

The pequeninos had a unique form of reproduction where a wife or a mothertree would accept the sap of a fathertree, and the pequeninos would grow in the trees until they were born.

Their language was complex. They could speak Stark, the variation of English Common among humans, but spoke to each other in several different languages.

Phet Noi, General (SH, [SG])

General Phet Noi was a low-ranking general in the Thai army after Ender Wiggin's victory over the Formics. While the rest of the generals with whom he associated discounted Bean's theories that the serial killer Achilles Flandres was threatening Thailand to allow China to take over Asia, he was sympathetic. Phet Noi used his army to help Bean launch an offensive against Achilles and his forces in India.

Phet Noi had been held captive by the Chinese when they took over Asia, but was released and immediately began work as a military adviser to Peter Wiggin and his staff in the newly created Free People of Earth, a confederation of nations unified into an ever-growing world government.

Philote (*See also* Philotic Web) (SD, XN, CM)

Philotes were the spark of life. They are contained in every living thing. They exist in Outspace, where thoughts become reality. They travel from Outspace into new life in regular space/time when the scientific elements are in place, and the thought is had that they should come.

Philotic Web (SD, XN, CM)

The Philotic Web is the network that connects all things together. Since all matter has a philote, all matter is connected. "Love" is thought to be the communication between philotes, for example.

Ansible communication, faster-than-light travel, and sentient computer networks such as Jane all rely on the maintenance of the Philotic Web.

Pig List (EG, WG, ES)

The pig list was a list the teachers at Battle School kept of problem students. It was made public in the hopes that the humiliation of having one's name on the list would correct problematic behavior.

Pinehead (XN)

Popular fairy tale among the Hundred Worlds, similar to Pinocchio.

Pinual ([EG])

Pinual was a student at Battle School prior to Ender Wiggin's arrival. He committed suicide there, leading to a thorough investigation by Graff and Anderson in an effort to determine how the International Fleet's screening tests had missed Pinual's suicidal tendencies. Over the course of the investigation, Graff came to determine that the suicide was actually a reaction to the war with the Formics itself as opposed to the unwinnable nature of the Giant's Drink game, which many thought had been the impetus for Pinual to take his own life. Pinual considered his suicide a statement against the war, while Graff viewed it as a casualty of war.

Pio, Archcardinal of Baía (SD)

Archcardinal Pio was a well-respected Catholic leader of the Hundred Worlds.

Pipinho "João" (SD)

Pipinho was the eldest son of Pipo, the xenologist. Pipinho was born on the planet Lusitania.

Pipo (*See* Alvarez, João Figueira "Pipo")

Planter (XN)

Planter was a pequenino, or piggie, the native sentient life on the planet Lusitania. He was a son of Human, the piggie that had become a fathertree at the hands of Ender Wiggin. Planter and Ender had become very good friends. He was a well-known pequenino scientist, and as such had become a close colleague to Ender and his family, who were all scientists on the planet. He particularly enjoyed being assigned duties that involved human technology.

When Ender and Ela developed a hypothesis that the Descolada was actually created by a third party to control and manipulate Lusitania, Planter confirmed that he had also thought that was the case. He volunteered to be the test subject for the hypothesis.

He would allow the Descolada to be purged from his system, and then be observed to determine if he still had a mind and self-awareness. If he did, then the pequeninos were their own beings. If he did not, then it would confirm that they were the slaves to the Descolada and its creator, who had used them to maintain the Lusitanian ecosystem without their knowledge.

The study was painful. He hurt as he slowly died from lack of the Descolada. He would often chant or sing the legends of his fellow pequeninos. He did this to show that he still had his mind up until he died.

Ender's stepdaughter Quara went to visit Planter shortly before he died. He angrily told her to share the information she had on the Descolada with Ela and Miro. Quara didn't want to give the information, because she didn't want the virus to be eradicated. She thought doing so was xenocide. But Planter did a good job of convincing her. She shared the information, and Ela and her team were able to develop a new virus, in theory, that would stop the Descolada.

Despite having the theory, though, they were not able to manufacture the new virus. Planter died, saying good-bye to his friends. The other pequeninos planted him in their forest near the fathertrees, Human and Rooter, but it was too late. Planter did not have enough of the Descolada in him to become a fathertree. He grew into the most noble of the brothertrees, and was nonetheless revered by his people for his sacrifice to free them from the virus that controlled them.

Plikt (SD, XN, CM)

Plikt was a native of the planet Trondheim. She was the daughter of human settlers to the planet and was raised with the traditional Icelandic and Calvinist traditions of her people. Ender Wiggin taught a university class on the planet under his real name, Andrew. He was a Speaker for the Dead, and Plikt wanted to learn from him—to follow in his footsteps. She was a bright student whose intelligence often annoyed the rest of the class.

Twenty years later, Plikt, now a beloved friend of Valentine Wiggin's family, traveled to Lusitania to be with Ender and to protect the planet from annihilation at the hands of the Starways Congress. Uninvited, she joined Valentine and Jakt when they left their family and ship to join Ender's stepson, Miro Ribeira, and the sentient computer program Jane on their ship.

During this last leg of their journey from Trondheim to Lusitania, Plikt and her friends learned about the Philotic Web—the foundation of life, matter, and communication—from Jane.

When they finally reached Lusitania, though it had only felt like a month to her, Plikt realized that Ender was an old man. In his late sixties, he was still her hero. She had studied his life while still on Trondheim, and had come to know him as much as a person can through study alone.

She accompanied Ender, as well as Miro and Valentine, to the Formic Hive Queen's lair on Lusitania. There, Plikt experienced the mind-to-mind communication that the Hive Queen used to communicate with Ender. It was a beautiful, even sacred, experience for her. She knew that she was as close to Ender as anyone ever had been, for he was the link between the Hive Queen and her. Miro—who did not have the same level of emotional closeness as Valentine and Plikt—did not hear the Hive Queen's words. The experience changed Plikt forever.

She didn't speak much to the Lusitanians. She was known as the "quiet woman" who had come with Valentine and Jakt.

When Ender accidentally created a new, younger version of his sister Valentine, known as Val or Valentine II, Plikt quietly befriended her. Young Val had been feared and not understood by the people of Lusitania, so Plikt took her into her home so she'd have a friend.

A few months later, as Ender laying dying, his Auía (or, loosely, his soul) being stretch too thin among himself and his "offspring" Valentine II and Peter II, Plikt stood watch at his bedside. She had devoted her life to studying Ender, Speaking, and all that he represented. She loved him dearly, and wanted to be by his side as he passed away.

Her presence was bothersome to Novinha and Valentine, though. It led to a vicious sparring session between the three women, as they fought over who loved Ender the most. Valentine slapped Plikt, promising that she'd never Speak Ender's death. As Ender grew closer to dying, though, the three women set their differences a bit to the side to support him.

Once Ender's Auía left his body, Plikt collected a few of his hairs. His body had dissolved, leaving only a few such hairs. Plikt prepared to Speak his death, and realized that while she loved, and even worshipped Ender, she was selfish. She felt relieved and excited when Ender died because she would finally be able to Speak someone's death.

Coming to terms with her selfish desires, Plikt knew that Ender, if he were to Speak her death, would have noted that her love for Ender was centered on how he benefited her career. Yet, she knew that he would not scold or criticize her. With that, she wrote the words—less than an hour's worth—that she would say about the man who was both history's greatest monster as Ender the Xenocide, but also its greatest champion as the Speaker for the Dead.

She delivered her Speaking, and Ender's remains were buried in the pequenino lands, near the fathertrees, Human and Rooter.

Plower (CM)

Plower was a pequenino on the planet Lusitania. He was friends with Olhado Ribeira von Hesse and his family, and enjoyed picnicking with them in the pequenino land. He was present when Jane's soul inhabited the mothertrees and produced great fruit from the trees. Plower was the first to taste this fruit, and found it to be more delicious than anything he'd ever eaten.

Poke (ES)

Poke was the nine-year-old leader of a group of homeless, starving children who lived on the streets of Rotterdam in the Netherlands. These kids, her "crew," looked to her for food and for protection from bullies. She was not particularly good at being a crew leader, often facing violence from the bullies, but she consistently provided at least a little food for her crew.

Poke met, and named, Bean when he was four years old. Bean instructed Poke to find a bully to protect the crew from the other bullies. Although initially against the idea, Poke chose Achilles Flandres for the role. It was a mistake, as Achilles proved more charismatic than Poke, and her crew chose to follow him more than her. Bean was certain that the mistake was even fatal, though Poke refused to believe it.

As Achilles's control over her crew grew, Poke realized that she was not accepted by the leader. She grew to love and respect him as much as the rest of the crew, but deep down she knew that Achilles hated her. She desperately tried to regain her status as leader of the group, but it was impossible. Furthermore, Achilles sought to alienate her from her crewmates by not accepting her "tax" of bread.

When Achilles went into hiding to avoid the rumored vengeance of Ulysses, whom Achilles had seriously injured, Poke found him. The two kissed, and Poke reminded Achilles of a promise he'd made her. Bean witnessed this and realized too late that the promise was that Achilles would never kill him. Instead, he killed Poke. Achilles brutally beat Poke to death, leaving her for dead in the river, and blaming Ulysses. Poke gave her life to protect Bean.

Many years later, Bean built a memorial to Poke in Brazil, where he was living as a member of the Hegemony.

Polemarch (EG, ES, SH, EE)

The office of Polemarch was high in the International Fleet's Hegemony. Held by a Russian, it became the target of essays by Locke and Demosthenes, who were convinced Russia was preparing for a land war after the end of the Formic conflict. Following the Formic War, the office was given to Chamrajnagar, a former Fleet officer from India.

Polonius (*See* Hundred Worlds)

Porotchkot, Vladimir "Vlad" Denisovitch (EGS, EG, ES, SH, SG)

A soldier in the unstoppable Dragon Army commanded by Ender Wiggin, Vladimir Porotchkot, or Vlad as he was known, was promoted to command his own army at a very young age, and eventually moved to Tactical School and Command School to train on the simulators alongside Ender and other former Dragons. He commanded a seemingly fictional squadron that turned out to be real when Ender attacked the Formic home world.

Upon his return to Earth, and his home of Belarus, Vlad was one of the members of Ender's final army who was kidnapped and forced by his captor—former Battle School student and serial killer Achilles Flandres—to play war games. He was taken to Russia and eventually moved to a private location somewhere in that country where he could write to his fellow captives. No other interaction was allowed.

After several months in solitary confinement, Vlad decided to join Achilles's plans of world domination. He agreed to speak with Petra Arkanian and try to convince her to join, also. He was not successful in swaying her, however.

The next day, Vlad and his fellow prisoners except Petra were rescued by Russian operatives. Achilles didn't prevent the rescue operations, and Vlad was ultimately not allowed to be on Achilles's team.

He later defended the decision to join Achilles because he thought Achilles was controlling the "Mother Land" of Russia and only wanted to serve Russia. This was doubted by the real military leaders in Russia, and elsewhere, but Vlad stood by it unwaveringly.

When Bean and Petra helped their Battle School colleague Alai plan a military invasion of China, Bean thought turning to Vlad would be wise. Alai was uncertain, but Bean knew if the invasion was to work, it needed Russia's help. And Vlad was the key to Russia.

Russia did not play a part in the Muslim occupation of Asia. Instead, it stayed on the sidelines and watched. Vlad, not trusted because of his work with Achilles while kidnapped, was not as influential as he appeared.

Several months later, as India began to push back against its Muslim occupiers, Peter Wiggin sought out Vlad, hoping that he would help Russia be an ally in the impending war in Asia. Vlad did not have authority to make any promises, but that was okay with Peter. He actually made Vlad another offer—which Hyrum Graff had also made—which was to leave Earth and begin a new life in space. Like all of his Battle School colleagues, Vlad refused, but promised to think about it.

As Peter built the Hegemony into the Free People of Earth, Graff again offered Ender's colleagues the opportunity to leave Earth and govern a planet. It was his fear that Ender's army would be used in the worldwide conflict, manipulated by whatever political power rose to prominence, and he wanted to prevent that. Every member who received the offer, which did not include Han Tzu, Petra Arkanian, or Alai, said no. The others were already too involved in matters on Earth to leave.

War raged on between China and the combined forces of India and the Muslim world. Russia decided to attack, hoping to capitalize on a weakened Chinese army. They used plans created by Vlad for their attack. Vlad escaped from Russia and was put into the protection of Peter Wiggin's Free People of Earth. Vlad gave the FPE copies of all of his plans, which were passed on to China, newly aligned with the FPE, to defeat the Russians.

Pots (SD)

Pots was a pequenino, the native, sentient animal life on the planet Lusitania.

Pre-command School (EG, ES)

Pre-command School was another training facility sponsored by the International Fleet. Not much is known about the school beyond its existence, though it is sometimes thought to refer to the period of time a student spent in Battle School and Tactical School before attending Command School.

Problems in Campaigning Between Solar Systems Separated by Light Years (ES)

Problems in Campaigning Between Solar Systems Separated by Light Years was an essay written in Battle School by Bean Delphiki. Its insightful nature garnered Bean the attention of Battle School administrators, such as Hyrum Graff.

Psychiatrist/Psychologist (SH)

The psychiatrist was the top official in the mission that was designed to rescue Petra Arkanian from Achilles Flandres shortly after she returned home from Battle School. The psychiatrist was not a good military strategist, something that Petra made very clear to him. He revealed that though he spoke like a psychiatrist, he was actually a psychologist. Petra mocked him. Moments later, he was shot dead by Achilles, who wanted to keep Petra with him as he set his sights on world domination.

Puladors (SD)

Puladors were insects native to the planet Lusitania. They mated with shiny-leafed bushes.

Pumphrey, Miss (EG)

Miss Pumphrey was Ender's schoolteacher on Earth when he was six years old. She helped him find his seat in the classroom and remember to go to the bus following his monitor removal treatment.

Purification Box (XN)

The Purification Box was a small area of the Isolation Shed on the planet Lusitania where victims exposed to the life-threatening Descolada were showered with an antidote and endured blasts of radiation to kill the virus.

Qing-Jao's Teacher (XN)

A scholar on the Chinese planet Path, Qing-jao's teacher helped her discover her godspoken abilities and talents.

Qu (XN)

Qu was the Chinese city where the fairy tale *The Jade of Master Ho* took place.

Quara (*See* Ribeira von Hesse, Lembrança das Milagres de Jesus "Quara")

Quim (*See* Ribeira von Hesse, Estevão Rei "Quim")

Rã "Tomás" (SD)

Rã was a child to Pipo and Conceição, born on the planet Lusitania.

"Rackham," Kahhui Kura "Mirth" (Actual last name unknown; Rackham used for convenience) (MP)

Kahhui Kura Rackham, or "Mirth" as she was known, was Mazer Rackham's granddaughter.

MAZER RACKHAM'S SPACESHIP

In an early draft of the *Ender's Game* movie script, Mazer Rackham's spaceship is named the *NZF Waitangi*. Named for the Treaty of Waitangi, which was signed in 1840 between the British and Maori people over jurisdiction in New Zealand, the English and Maori language versions of the treaty differ greatly in what was agreed to. It is a contentious and controversial treaty still to this day, causing tensions between the primary races/cultures in New Zealand.

Orson Scott Card explains why he chose to name Mazer's ship after the treaty:

"Waitangi was chosen to reveal something about Mazer, both personally and politically. It's an ironic ship name: Always screwed, nothing is what it seems. Remember, this is many, many decades farther into the future, and attitudes change—what is now infuriating might in the future be merely bitterly ironic.

"On Mazer's personal level, he is half-white, half-Maori. And the two sides are very much conflicted. He would also choose the name Waitangi to reflect the fact that if you speak to one part of him you'll get one answer, and to the other part, another answer."

Rackham, Mazer (MP, EGS, EG, ES, [GB], [YM], EE, SG)

He was considered the greatest soldier of his time, and one that the International Fleet could not bear to lose. Mazer Rackham seemingly single-handedly saved the world from the first Formic invasion. It was an act for which Mazer felt punished.

Born in New Zealand, Mazer was a warrior in the proudest Maori tradition although he was only half-Maori. He was a smart soldier, and despite the illogical use of a "rear echelon" in three-dimensional space battle, he used his own military prowess to notice the weakness of the Formic armies. He constantly put up with inferiorly talented superior officers before firing (against orders) the missile that destroyed the invasion fleet.

Following the war, Mazer was placed in one of the International Fleet's courier ships and sent into the stars where his only exercise consisted of electrical stimulus to his muscles. He traveled at nearly the speed of light in an effort to use the relativistic space travel to keep him young enough to command the Fleet in the future. The ship was programmed to return after a preset amount of time and distance. He would have aged only five years, though decades passed on Earth; upon his return to his home planet, he would be expected to assist with the training of a new leader for the Fleet.

Though his victories in the war had become the Fleet's greatest propaganda tool, and his legend had been perpetuated through the vids that everyone saw, Mazer's time in space was lonely. He had made the decision to take this short trip alone.

He utilized the ansible for communication with the International Fleet headquarters. Through this method, he communicated with then-lieutenant Hyrum Graff, hesitantly advising him on the search for Mazer's successor as the heroic general who would save humanity. Graff had located Mazer's family on Earth and used them to convince Mazer to help him. Mazer was angered that his family, to whom he was considered dead, was used in such a fashion.

Despite his loneliness, Mazer ultimately consented to receiving the letters that accompanied the visual message. The letters were at times challenging to read, but Mazer appreciated the updates on his family. However, through these letters he learned that his ex-wife, Kim Summers, had remarried.

The Computer Voice that provided his only companionship in this stage of his journey reported back to the Fleet Mazer's emotional responses to the letters. It also reported that he had reprogrammed the ship and computer to allow him complete navigational control. The Fleet had grown concerned over these reports and sent shrinks to evaluate him via ansible. Mazer had decided he would not be coming back to Earth. The Fleet, in its search for a new commander, was on its own.

Mazer instructed the Fleet to give Hyrum Graff sufficient authority to truly find a successor to lead the human forces against the Formics. Then, and only then, would Mazer return to Earth, promising to help train his successor a few years earlier than the original plan. The Fleet had no option but to agree, and promoted Graff. Mazer fulfilled his part of the bargain, returning to Earth to train the new commander.

Mazer met his protégé at Command School. The boy, Ender Wiggin, had been sent to this highest of military schools at a very young age, and Mazer was assigned to teach him to defeat the Formics. He used silence and levels of deceit to teach Ender to win. Mazer also used physical violence against Ender when they first met. His intent was to teach Ender to fight to win, which Ender learned by retaliating against the older man. Mazer, satisfied that Ender was ready to lead the armies of the world against the Formics, promised that all training from then on would involve the simulators.

Mazer pushed Ender past his limits. But Ender rose above the pressure, and in his "final exam" at Command School, destroyed the Formic home world. Mazer revealed to Ender that the exams and simulators had all been real battles. Furthermore, Mazer told Ender that war was breaking out on Earth, and Ender could never return home.

Ever-defiant to his superiors, Mazer testified on Hyrum Graff's behalf when the Battle School officer was court-martialed. Mazer and Ender had had several conversations about the Formics, Graff, and Ender's role in the deaths of Bonzo Madrid and the boy named Stilson. Mazer would never directly confirm any of Ender's theories. His lack of denial was always enough for Ender to know he was right.

Following Ender's victory, Mazer was chosen to be the pilot of the first colony ship in the new Dispersion Project, colonizing former Formic worlds with humans. Ender was also placed in this project, alongside Mazer. The two heroes of the Formic wars were side-by-side in the new era of humanity.

It was all a lie, however. Mazer never left Earth or the Fleet. He continued to work with Hyrum Graff in the Ministry of Colonization. Though he was not seen for years during the wars on Earth after Ender's victory, Mazer resurfaced to offer Han Tzu and Bean Delphiki passage into space, which would save their lives. Han Tzu refused, while Bean agreed. Mazer said Bean would have to help Peter Wiggin establish his world government. The International Fleet had great interest in Peter's success, and Mazer was determined to do his part in securing it, even if his part was swaying Earth-bound individuals like Han Tzu and Bean to do Fleet bidding.

He accompanied Bean's wife, Petra Arkanian, to Portugal where she retrieved a girl named Bella, who had been born by a surrogate mother carrying an embryo that belonged to Bean and Petra. Mazer and Graff had tracked down the embryo and learned the truth about Bella's existence. Mazer accompanied Petra to ensure a smooth transfer from mother to mother.

As Peter built the Hegemony into the Free People of Earth, Graff and Mazer offered Ender's colleagues the opportunity to leave Earth and govern a planet. It was his fear that Ender's army would be used in the worldwide conflict, manipulated by whatever political power rose to prominence, and he wanted to prevent that. Every member who received the offer, which did not include Han Tzu, Petra Arkanian, or Alai, said no. The others were already too involved in matters on Earth to leave.

Mazer and Graff traveled to a neutral site with Peter where they made the same offer to Virlomi, the leader of India who had hoped to marry Peter and expand her own power. Peter refused her advances, and she refused Mazer and Graff's offer.

As Mazer and Peter spoke together, they agreed the time was right for the International Fleet to give Bean a spaceship. They'd promised to take him and his genetically altered children into space to await a cure for their mutation. Mazer had located all but one of Bean's children, and under the direction of Peter, delivered them to Bean and Petra.

Mazer also facilitated the divorce between Bean and Petra. He knew much of Petra's heartache at saying good-bye to her husband and children, as he'd experienced a similar period of sadness when he left Earth after stopping the Formics nearly a century earlier. Petra doubted his compassion, but Mazer reiterated his love for her, Bean, and all the other Battle School children.

Both Mazer and Graff had grown to love the Battle Schoolers as their own children, and only wanted them to have the best possible life. All that he had done over the years was to that end, though his methods may have seemed contrary.

Many years later, once the Free People of Earth embodied every government in the world save the United States, Mazer died. His life and death were immortalized in a series of books on the History of the Formic wars, written from space by Valentine Wiggin.

In these books, Mazer was credited as the military hero he was. But his love for his family and the Battle Schoolers was also an important point. Humanity thought of Mazer as a hero long before Ender defeated the Formics, and they remembered him as such long after world peace was established.

"Rackham," Mazer Taka Aho Howarth (Actual last name unknown; Rackham used for convenience) (MP)

Mazer Rackham's grandson. With Mazer's legendary status ever-growing on Earth after the victory in the first Formic invasion, this grandchild looked up to his grandfather, choosing to go by his name. Mazer saw him for the first time alongside the rest of the grandchildren in the message Hyrum Graff had arranged.

"Rackham," Pahu Rangi (Actual last name unknown; Rackham used for convenience) (MP)

Mazer Rackham's son. Unable to find someone to marry, he did not appear in the visual message sent to Mazer in the solitary courier ship. Pahu had been born after Mazer left for the war, and as a result, never met or saw his father. He was an adult when the message was sent to Mazer, and joked that someday he'd learn to read and write.

Rackham, Pai Mahutanga (MP)

The fair-haired daughter of Mazer Rackham, Pai was the first of the family to communicate with him in a visual message over the ansible in Mazer's courier ship following the Formic invasion, but years before Ender Wiggin's victory. She was the mother of Mazer's grandchildren Mirth, Glad, Mazer, and Struan. She was loyal to the Hegemony, adhering to the new population rules.

"Rackham," Pao PaoTe Rangi "Glad" (Actual last name unknown; Rackham used for convenience) (MP)

Mazer Rackham's granddaughter. Proud of her Maori heritage, given to her through Mazer, she went by the English nickname "Glad." She appeared in the ansible message Hyrum Graff arranged.

"Rackham," Struan Maeroero (Actual last name unknown; Rackham used for convenience) (MP)

The youngest of Mazer Rackham's grandchildren, and expected to be the last because of the Hegemony's new population rules. He appeared in the visual message sent to Mazer in his courier ship, arranged by Hyrum Graff.

Rajam, General "Andariyy" (SG)

General Rajam, who had given himself the nickname "Andariyy," meaning strong rope, was the leader of Muslim forces that occupied India and much of Asia during Peter Wiggin's rise to power as the Hegemon after Ender's victory over the Formics. He abused his authority, allowing (even praising) violent abuse of innocent Indian civilians.

His actions caused Virlomi, the most influential woman in India, to call on Alai, a Battle School grad and Caliph of the Muslim world, to denounce the soldiers' actions in India.

Alai traveled to India where he brought Rajam before the soldiers in what seemed would be a public award ceremony, but ended up being Rajam's execution on orders from the Caliph. Alai sent a message that violence against innocents would not be tolerated and that he was the true leader of all Muslims in the world.

Ramen (*See* Hierarchy of Alienness)

Ramon (GB)

A soldier in the Formic War, Ramon was close to Sel Menach, and presumably helped found the colony which Sel was a part of after the war on a former Formic world.

Randi (EE, SG)

Randi was a disciple of Achilles Flandres's. Married to an average grocery store owner named Bob, she fell in love with Achilles, and believed he was the savior of mankind. She was the surrogate for an embryo Achilles told her was his and his mysterious wife's, though it actually belonged to Bean Delphiki and Petra Arkanian. Randi left Bob to have what she believed was Achilles's son. It was her mission to raise the boy, whom she named Achilles II, to fulfill his father's destiny and become the leader Achilles was to have been, but was murdered by Bean.

She took on a new identity as Nichelle Firth to protect Achilles II from being taken away by the Free People of Earth. She even sought to leave Earth and go to a new colony.

She was in awe of her son's apparent intelligence, and amazed at how easy the premature birth process had been. He was tremendously undersized at birth and born months early.

Randi did not know that her son had the genetic mutation called Anton's Key within him. This caused his premature birth, small size, and intelligence. It would also cause him to grow to be a giant and die at a very young age.

Under her alias Nichelle Firth, Randi traveled with her son to the human colony on the planet Ganges. Obsessed with Achilles, and determined that her son would follow in his footsteps, Randi repeated his name over and over again. The governor of Ganges, Virlomi, was concerned about this and kept a watchful eye on Randi and her son.

As Achilles II grew to be a teenager, Randi taught him about his supposed father. Randi tried to get her son to kill Ender Wiggin when he visited Ganges, but Achilles II would not. Ender told Achilles II that his real parents were Petra Arkanian and Bean Delphiki. Randi refused to believe this, and her relationship with her son ended because of it.

Rav, Captain (SD)

Captain Rav was a ship captain on the planet Trondheim. He taught Valentine Wiggin how to run ships, and taxied Ender Wiggin to the spaceship that would take him to another planet, Lusitania.

Raymond, Dick; Mr. and Mrs. (SP)

When Achilles Flandres attempted to take over Peter Wiggin's position as Hegemon of Earth, the Wiggin family sought temporary sanctuary on the orbiting space station, the Ministry of Colonization. In order to not arouse suspicion, the family was given aliases. John Paul and Theresa were Mr. and Mrs. Raymond, and Peter was "Dick."

Recolada (XN)

Recolada was an altered form of Descolada that allowed human life exposure to the disease.

Reitveld, Fillipus "Flip" (WG)

Flip was a contemporary of Ender Wiggin's at Battle School. Flip was close to Dink Meeker, his toon leader in Rat Army. Both boys had come from Holland, and it was to Flip that Dink secretly gave a traditional holiday gift. The present, a goofy poem, led to a serious problem at the Battle School as Christian zealot Zeck Morgan encouraged a mutiny demanding that if Dink's celebration of a holiday went unpunished, all religious displays should, too.

Ren (EGS)

Ren was a soldier in Ender Wiggin's Dragon Army. As with many of his fellow soldiers in the army, he was promoted to commander of his own army after Dragon's undefeated record in the Battle Room.

Reykjavik (*See* Hundred Worlds)

Rhemis (*See* Hundred Worlds)

Ribeira, Marcos Maria "Marcão" (SD)

Marcão Ribeira was a child born on the planet Lusitania. He was the same age as Libo and Novinha, two prominent children in the colony, but was not well liked. He was a surly boy with no friends. One day, when he'd been accused of a violent misdeed against his schoolmates, Novinha defended him. He fell in love with Novinha for her act of kindness, and even married her.

Although married in a traditional Catholic culture, Novinha and Marcão could not conceive children. He had a congenital disease that sterilized him, caused him extreme physical agony, and would someday kill him. Novinha remained married to Marcão, but had a sexual affair with Libo, her childhood friend. Libo gave her six children, whom Marcão raised as his own. But, he took to a life of drinking.

He was abusive to Novinha and her children because they were not his children—though that was not known to them. He died in a bar, and two of Novinha's children called for a Speaker to Speak his death. Ender Wiggin, who was coming to Speak another death on the planet (one called for and canceled by Novinha), arrived and Spoke.

When Ender spoke Marcão's death, he revealed to the people of Lusitania the dark secrets of Novinha's adultery. In many ways, the Speaking cleared Marcão's name in the eyes of the colonists at Lusitania.

Ribeira von Hesse, Ekaterina Elanora "Ela" (SD, XN, CM)

The daughter of Libo and Novinha, Ela grew up on the planet Lusitania believing that her father was actually a man named Marcão. When he died, Ela, with her brother Miro, called for a Speaker to Speak his death. Ender Wiggin answered the call, and arrived at their home planet Lusitania to perform the Speaking.

When Ender did arrive, Ela was concerned, as he'd come many years earlier than expected. She'd called the Speaker because she wanted her abusive father's evil acts exposed, but it was too soon after his death to be comfortable.

During Ender's first visit to the Ribeira household, Ela greeted him coldly at first, but as she got to know him, she began to trust him. In fact, they became friends. After Ender had been on the planet for a few days, Ela met him at the river near their homes and confided that she wanted to be a scientist with full credentials. Her mother refused to let her because she feared Ela would die like the planet's xenobiologists Pipo and Libo had. Ela explored all of her mother's research anyway, and came to determine that there was a link between the disease known as the Descolada and the native life on the planet, the pequeninos.

Ela was a mother figure to her siblings, caring for them and encouraging them to help Ender in his duties as the Speaker. This caused dissension with her brother Quim, but was something she felt very strongly about.

She attended Ender's Speaking for her father. She was at first disappointed that he seemed to be excusing Marcão's abusive actions, but was shocked to learn that Marcão was not her real father, and that a man named Libo was. Her mother was an adulteress. Novinha seemed to hate Libo and had forbidden Ela from seeing her once-best friend, Libo's daughter China.

After the Speaking, Ender approached Ela, needing her help. Starways Congress had revoked Lusitania's charter and was going to evacuate the planet. Ender was going to lead a rebellion against the Congress, but needed the information on the Descolada that Novinha had kept hidden. Ela agreed to approach her mother and find it out so they could protect their planet and particularly Miro, who faced criminal accusations in the evacuation.

Ela was able to convince Novinha to explain the Descolada to the leaders of the planet/colony. With this information, the leaders decided to rebel against Starways Congress. The Descolada had infected all life on Lusitania, and as such all were carriers and couldn't leave the planet.

When it was learned that her brother Miro had been injured near the pequeninos' land outside the city, Ela went with Ender and the leaders of the town to save him. She, Ouanda, and Ender crossed the deactivated fence and went to speak to the pequeninos' leaders—the "wives."

Ela was fascinated by the pequeninos' mating rituals, which she learned from the wives. She was a witness as Ender negotiated a treaty with the pequeninos. Ever the scientist, Ela insisted on observing Ender perform the "Third Life" ritual, where a pequenino is killed, a tree planted in its corpse.

The next morning, she attended mass with her family, Ender sitting in the place reserved for her father. He had, after all, become a father figure to her.

She continued to study the Descolada, and with Ouanda discovered properties of daisies that could allow the Hive Queen to flourish on Lusitania without being exposed to the virus. However, the Descolada evolved, and Ela, with her mother, worked tirelessly to protect the flora and fauna human beings had imported for their own sustenance from the disease. It was a losing battle, though, as the disease continued to evolve and infect.

Over the next thirty years, Ela and her family rose to greater prominence on Lusitania. They were the planet's scientists. Novinha and Ela created new strains of potatoes, trying to find a way to make a foodstuff that would be resistant to the Descolada. It was a difficult assignment, one that seemed impossible as the virus continually evolved.

In her late forties, Ela developed a theory that would allow the human scientists on Lusitania to selectively eliminate certain aspects of the Descolada, while preserving the parts of the virus that the native Lusitanian life needed to survive and reproduce. The theory was a contentious issue between Ela and her sister, Quara, who felt the virus was actually a living, sentient creature.

Despite their differing views, both Ela and Quara continued their respective research paths, trying to determine what would be best for all the life on their home planet.

Ela and her family greeted Miro's ship when it returned from its mission to rendezvous with Valentine Wiggin's vessel. It was Ela who greeted her brother Miro the most warmly, and was able to mostly look beyond the thirty years that has passed between them. Because of relativistic travel, Miro had not aged, but the rest of his siblings had. It made for a subtle awkwardness at his return.

Ela was called into a meeting at the mayor's office where the problem of the pequeninos was discussed. A faction of pequeninos had decided to leave the planet, spreading the Descolada to other worlds. Ela was working on the antivirus version of the Descolada, which was still an extremely contentious issue between her and Quara. She was ordered to continue her research by the leaders of the colony, despite Quara's objections.

Quara responded by trying to communicate with the Descolada molecules and warn the virus of her sister's research. She tried to transmit Ela's research directly to the virus. Ela informed Ender, asking what should be done about the leak. But it was Novinha who reacted.

Angrily, Novinha screamed terrible insults at Ender and informed Ela that she, as the head xenologist, would stop Quara from sending the research. She also threatened Ela that if Ela ever spoke about scientific matter to Ender or anyone again, she would cut off Ela's access to the lab and research.

Ela tried to smooth things over with Novinha, even though she thought more of Ender and thought he deserved to know what was going on.

A short time later, when her brother Quim was killed by the pequeninos, Ela joined her family at their home to hear the news. When Miro informed everyone that Quim was dead, he was slapped by Novinha. The rest of the family, including Ela, rebelled against her, leaving her alone. Ela felt badly for speaking terrible words to her mother as she left, but was unable to reconcile with her. Novinha entered the religious school, the Children of the Mind of Christ.

Ela tried to return to her research, but did not have access to the lab without Novinha's passwords. Novinha told Ender to have Jane get the passwords, and give them to Ela.

In the aftermath of Quim's death, many citizens of Lusitania rioted, burning a large portion of the piggies' home forest, including the mothertrees and fathertrees. Ela was there to see the results of the fire, and to study how the pequeninos would rebuild from a devastating loss.

As she continued to work on the answer to the Descolada issue, Ela also worked on reversing a Starways Congress–caused genetic manipulation of the people on the planet Path. She was aided in this by Han Fei-tzu and his servant, Si Wang-mu, who lived on Path.

During a conversation with Wang-mu via ansible that Jane arranged, Ela and Ender developed a hypothesis that the Descolada had been developed by a third party and was used to regulate the planetary functions of Lusitania. The piggies were the slaves of the virus and its creator.

She and Ender asked their friend Planter, the pequenino, to confirm the theory. He said that he had come to a similar hypothesis and wanted to be the test subject. He wanted to be free of the Descolada and see if he still had self-awareness and free will. This would be accomplished by purging the virus from him, and seeing if he still had his own mind. If not, then it would appear that the virus indeed was used to control the life on the planet, and the pequeninos themselves were not the sentient beings they appeared to have been.

This decision was hard on Ela. She loved Planter as her closest friend and didn't want to risk losing him. He insisted, though, stating that he would be the first of the race to be free, and his sacrifice could save all life on Lusitania.

With the research on the Descolada proceeding, Ela and her assistant, a piggie named Glass, discovered the keys to unlocking the genetic manipulation on Path. It would be a simple enough process, she felt, once they figured out how to remove the Descolada to apply the same principles to the godspoken, freeing them of their obsessive-compulsive disorder but maintaining the increased intellect.

She also discovered that one person on Path, Si Wang-mu, had been genetically altered, but had evolved beyond it. She did not suffer from the OCD, but maintained the increased intelligence.

When Quara spoke to Planter shortly before his death, the piggie convinced her to share the information she had on the Descolada virus with Ela. With this new information, Ela was able to develop an antivirus for the Descolada, but was unable to manufacture it. Frustrated, she saw Planter die a martyr's death, but knew that he had given her the keys to someday free the pequeninos from the virus that enslaved them.

Ela was among those who was assigned to journey into space with Ender and Jane to test a new theory of faster-than-light travel Ender and his stepsons had developed, which used "Outspace" to manipulate philotes. What could be thought of could be created instantly in Outspace. There, Ela would imagine the anti-Descolada she called the recolada, as well as the cure for the godspoken on Path. If the theory worked, she would be able to manufacture both inoculations instantly.

She traveled with the group into the mysterious Outspace, and the theory worked. She was able to instantly manufacture the recolada and the OCD antivirus. She and Ender tested them before returning to their home dimension moments later.

Ela tested the recolada on Glass, and it worked. Successful in study, the recolada was sent throughout the planet. It cured all life of the Descolada without killing them. Her pathogen to reverse the genetic manipulations on Path worked equally well.

She was among her siblings who beseeched Miro to confront Ender, who had joined their mother at the Children of the Mind of Christ abbey, to return to help save their home world.

With Ender now on his deathbed, and Miro II having found the Descolada's creators' home world, Ela decided to leave her family behind and help discover the origin of the deadly virus at its home planet. She joined Miro, Valentine II, her sister Quara, a Formic drone, and a pequenino scientist named Firequencher on what they believed would be their final good-bye to Lusitania. Jane was also dying, and with her, the hope for more faster-than-light travel. As a result, Ela knew, if she traveled to the Descolada's planet, she'd more than likely never return to Lusitania.

As Ela and her comrades studied the biological communication of the Descolada, they were optimistic that they would figure out the language of the virus, and could potentially return to their home planet as Jane took over the body of Valentine II.

With Quara, Ela figured out that the Descolada communicated by sending signals to its creators that were understood by translation into molecules. This pattern of communication was reciprocated by the virus's creators.

In the middle of their studies, Ela and Quara were shocked to see that Jane was able to control faster-than-light travel. They were suddenly back on Lusitania, with no warning. Ela celebrated being home, while Quara was angry that they weren't told ahead of time.

The fleet of starships that had been ordered to destroy their world was rapidly approaching, and so Ela and her companions returned to the descoladore world. There they learned that the molecule the descoladore had given them in the message was a deadly heroinlike creation.

Jane used her instant transportation to send the crew to the other side of the planet, saving them. Moments later, Peter Wiggin II appeared on their ship and dissuaded them from their desires to use on the descoladore the Molecular Detatchment Device, the very weapon that was to destroy their own world. Ela agreed, and returned with her friends and family to Lusitania where she attended Ender's funeral service.

Ribeira von Hesse, Estevão Rei "Quim" (SD, XN)

Quim was one of the children of Novinha and Libo, who was raised by Marcão Ribeira on the planet Lusitania. He was devoutly Catholic, as most of the colonists on Lusitania had been. He held an obvious disdain for Ender Wiggin, as he was a Speaker for the Dead, a career derided by the pope.

When Ender first visited the Ribeira home, Quim was hostile. He called Ender names like "atheist" and "bastard"—the worst insults he could think of. He even tried to prevent his siblings from telling Ender anything about their father.

As that first visit continued, however, he tearfully confessed that he'd prayed to God, the Virgin, and even his canonized grandparents that his father Marcão would die. He blamed himself for bringing, through these prayers, the disease that killed him.

Quim hated Ender, though. He told Novinha that Ender was spending a lot of time with the other children. In the conversation, he accused Novinha of having illicit feelings for Ender. She slapped him for the comment. Quim felt terrible and begged for forgiveness. He held so closely to his faith that he felt repentance was the only course to happiness.

After his brother Olhado helped Ender break into their mother's computer files, Quim was mean to Olhado, adding to his guilt. It wasn't until their sister Ela interfered that Quim stopped his bullying of Olhado.

He attended the Speaking for his father, as said by Ender Wiggin. There he learned that his mother had been adulterous and the man he thought was his father was not. He called his mother a whore in front of the community gathered to attend the Speaking. He desperately wanted her to deny it, but she didn't. Angrily, hurt, he ran from the service.

He spoke with Bishop Peregrino, who instructed Quim to forgive his mother and continue to love her. He was initially resistant, but followed his ecclesiastical leader's counsel.

Quim accompanied his mother into the forest when she carried a warning message to Ender, who was negotiating with the pequeninos. Consequently, he was a witness when Ender performed the pequenino ritual known as the "Third Life." In this ritual, Ender killed a pequenino named Human and planted a tree in him, turning him into a fathertree, the highest honor of pequenino society. Quim called the ritual a resurrection.

After the "resurrection," Quim devoted his life to learning about the pequeninos so he could be a missionary among them. He studied with his half-sister, Ouanda, and eventually set out for his proselytizing endeavors among the creatures.

In the nearly thirty years that passed from the time Quim saw the so-called resurrection to the time when his brother Miro returned from what to him felt like a monthlong space mission, Quim had become a priest. He was the chief priest for the Catholic Church among the pequeninos. He relished his calling, for he had become the St. Paul to the piggies.

He taught them as much of the gospel as he could; and while traditional marriage didn't apply to the piggies because of their unique mating patterns, he did introduce the sacraments like communion and confirmation to the aliens.

Quim was present when Miro returned from space and experienced, like the rest of their siblings, the strange awkwardness that comes with aging three decades while your brother doesn't.

Miro met up with Quim the next time inside the piggies' land, where Quim had performed mass. The two brothers argued, as they often did, over matters of faith and redemption. They reconciled as Quim revealed to Miro that he was going to preach in a rebellious region of pequenino land. Quim was certain he would be protected from the piggies' violent ways because he was on a mission from God. Miro was unconvinced and worried that his brother would be killed.

Before he left on this mission, Quim attended the meeting of the colony's leaders. He listened to everyone's objections about his mission, but with the support of the Bishop Peregrino and Ender, decided to go anyway.

He traveled into the heart of the piggie lands. The pequeninos he sought believed that the Descolada virus that gave them life was actually the Holy Ghost. They refused to believe the dogma Quim preached to them.

The piggies held Quim hostage and tested him to see if his God would save him. They starved him, and after a week of arguing doctrine and interpretation with the piggies, he died of the Descolada, lacking the inhibitors from his food to protect him.

Ender said that he would not Speak Quim's death, for Quim was true to himself, and there was nothing to be revealed in a Speaking. His mother Novinha was enraged from sorrow. She lost yet another loved one to the piggies and would never forgive those who supported Quim's final mission because of it.

Ribeira von Hesse, Gerão Gregario "Grego" (SD, XN, CM)

Born on the planet Lusitania, Grego was one of the children of Novinha and Libo, who was raised by Novinha's abusive husband Marcão. He was mischievous, and enjoyed doing what he wanted at church, even if the nuns would punish him.

On Ender's first visit to the Ribeira house, Grego tried stabbing Ender with a knife. Ender held him tightly as he sat and spoke with the family. Grego responded by urinating on Ender. Ender realized that Grego's father's death was devastating to him. He'd been the only child who had not suffered at Marcão's hands.

Though he had seemingly been drawn to Ender, his behavioral problems did not improve. He attacked a teacher at school, and wrecked his own bedsheets the day after Ender's first appearance.

He attended Ender's Speaking, and also went to mass with his family and Ender. He had grown close to Ender, seeing in him a father figure unlike any he'd ever had.

Thirty years later, Grego, now in his mid-thirties, had become a reputable physicist. As he had through most of his life, Grego approached science from a devil's advocate position, arguing the counterpoints to his siblings' research and views.

He felt, contrary to his sisters, that the Descolada needed to be wiped out entirely, regardless of the cost to the native Lusitanian life that depended on it for life and reproduction. He had an us-versus-them mentality toward the virus, feeling that in order for humanity to survive, the disease had to go.

Grego was present when Miro returned from his thirty-year space mission, bringing Valentine Wiggin to Lusitania to help prevent the destruction of the planet. Grego, like the others, felt a bit of awkwardness as he'd aged three decades while Miro, due to the relativistic space travel he'd experienced, had not aged at all.

As the news that the piggies were planning to leave Lusitania to preserve the Descolada spread, Grego was called into a meeting with the leaders of the planet. He was chastised for having loose lips about the plans to eradicate the virus, and causing many problems within the colony.

Ever the rebel, Grego moved to walk out of the meeting, but was stopped by threats of being jailed. He slowly agreed to work with Ender and his family to figure out a way to move from planet to planet at faster-than-light speeds, in an effort to evacuate Lusitania if the need came up.

When his brother Quim was killed by the pequeninos, Grego escaped into drinking. The alcohol fueled bar fights and even led to a riot where several angry citizens burned a large portion of the piggies' forest, killing many pequeninos. Grego tried to stop the mob he had incited, but lost control of it. He went to the forest as it burned and, with his brother Miro's help, was able to disperse the angry mobocrats. But the damage had been done, and he was primarily responsible.

Grego was put in jail for sharing secrets he should not have, though he consented to imprisonment because of the great guilt he carried for his actions that led to the death of so many piggies.

From his jail cell, Grego continued his study of the mysterious Philotic Web, trying to figure out a way to travel at faster-than-light speed. Jane helped guide his research, as it was thought that such speed was the only way to preserve the sentient computer's life.

He also conducted some rather controversial research from jail, searching for the point of origin for the philote that first housed Jane's essence. Jane thought this was a waste of time, but Ender and Miro felt it was extremely important, and necessary, to saving Jane.

He was at times frustrated to tears over the difficulty of figuring out faster-than-light travel. But he was committed to it, nonetheless, working hard from his cell to find a way to make it possible.

After Ender learned the principles of philotic travel from their extra-dimensional home, Grego and his brother Olhado realized that the answer to faster-than-light travel was to call on the philotes they had inside of them—all life was based on philotes—and cross over to the philotes' dimension. From there, they would think of the philotic pattern of their destination, and the philotes would take them there instantly. It was a phenomenal theory, one that Grego hoped to publish as a paper and use to get hired in a university away from Lusitania.

He was at first angry that he was not allowed to travel into space to test the theory, but only the minimum crew was. In this case it was Ender, Jane, Miro, and Ela as each had an integral part to play in the test.

The tests worked, though Ender accidentally created new, living versions of his siblings, Peter and Valentine. Grego was attracted to Peter II's leadership and fanatical ideology. Ender was worried that Grego would become a disciple of Peter II's, and tried to keep the two apart.

Freed from jail, Grego was among those of his siblings who asked Miro to try to convince Ender to leave the Children of the Mind of Christ abbey he'd joined with Novinha, and save their world.

When Ender unexpectedly died a few days later, Grego joined his mother and mourned with her at their home.

A few days later, he and Olhado learned that the Hive Queen and pequeninos had worked together to reestablish a computer network for Jane, spread through a few worlds and using old computers. They watched with great anticipation as Jane used the network to regain control of faster-than-light travel, which had been uncertain in recent days after Ender's death.

Jane used this restored power to save Ender's family members from the anticipated destruction of Lusitania. When the planet was not destroyed, Grego returned to his home world and attended Ender's funeral service—a parting good-bye to his stepfather.

Ribeira von Hesse, Lauro Suleimão "Olhado" (SD, XN, CM)

Olhado, born on the planet Lusitania to Novinha and Libo, but raised by Marcão Ribeira, had lost his eyes in a laser accident. He had the ability to "see" through metal implants. He met Ender Wiggin when he arrived on Lusitania and led him to the Ribeira household. Though he was deceptive at first, he revealed his true identity to Ender, giving Ender a little smile, but also some cause for concern.

He took Ender to the Ribeira home, and in the course of that first visit, plugged his computerized eye into a terminal to show Ender a visual display of what his father Marcão was really like.

Using his computer skills, Olhado helped Ender learn how to access the Lusitanian computer systems and transfer money electronically. He was hurt when he learned that Ender used the system to look in on Olhado's mother's files, feeling that Ender had caused him to betray Novinha. He spent the next several days with his eyes turned off, listening to loud music.

His brother Quim mocked him for helping Ender, adding to the guilt he already felt. Their older sister Ela helped him feel better about helping Ender though, since their mother's secrets had been one of the poisons in their family relationship.

He attended the Speaking for his father, Marcão, and there learned that he was not actually the father of his family. His real father had been a man named Libo, and his mother was an adulteress.

Olhado accompanied his mother into the forest when she had to deliver a message to Ender, who was negotiating a treaty with the pequeninos, the native life of Lusitania. Olhado used his eyes to record the signing of this treaty, and the performance of a pequenino ritual. In the ritual, Ender killed a piggie named Human, and planted a tree in him. This allowed Human to become a fathertree—the highest honor in pequenino society.

When Ender sought to give the Formic Hive Queen a place where she could come out of her cocoon, it was Olhado who drove him there, using his advanced eyes and superior skimmer driving techniques.

Over the thirty years that passed while the people of Lusitania waited for the fleet to arrive and destroy their planet, Olhado married and had several children. Though they were all born with natural eyes, they often showed their father's distant expression.

Olhado and his family were present when his brother Miro returned from his space journey that brought Ender's sister Valentine to Lusitania. Though only a month had passed for Miro, nearly three decades had for Olhado, thanks to relativistic space travel.

After learning of his brother Quim's murder at the hands of the piggies, Olhado retired to his home and stayed with his wife and children. But, as he had often done when he wanted to escape from the world, he silently turned off his electronic eyes and stopped speaking with anyone.

His son Nimbo was among the members of the mob that sought revenge for Quim's death by burning a large portion of the pequeninos' home forest. Nimbo was hurt in the riot, but was saved by his uncles Miro and Grego.

Valentine Wiggin sought out Olhado when his brother Grego was locked in jail. Grego was frustrated, trying to figure out how to make faster-than-light travel possible. Valentine approached Olhado, a brick maker by trade, to see if he could provide any insight.

Olhado didn't believe he could help in the scientific study, but Valentine asked him anyway. She felt he could see the world from a different perspective, and Grego would be able to channel those different thoughts into a new theory. Olhado agreed to try.

He also told Valentine what he thought about his family. He spoke tenderly of Ender, saying that he called Ender "father" when they were in private, and Ender reciprocated, calling Olhado "son." Olhado said he learned how to be a father from Ender. The deep love shared semisecretly between her brother and his stepson moved Valentine to tears.

Olhado went to Grego and, using the things Ender learned from the Hive Queen a short time earlier about philotes and their existence in Outspace, helped his brother develop a theory of faster-than-light travel. Proudly Olhado and Grego theorized that if one could get the philotes that were in him—all life contained philotes—to return to their home dimension, then imagine the philotic pattern of his destination, a person could be taken there instantly, traveling like the philotes themselves. It would require a powerful memory to maintain one's own philotic pattern and prevent it from dispersing.

Fortunately, Jane had just such a powerful memory. Grego gave Olhado all the credit publicly for the idea, but said he would put his own name on the papers that would be published presenting the theory to the galaxy. This was okay with Olhado, though, as he never felt like he was a scientist and was happy to be a brick maker on Lusitania for the rest of his life.

He was among his siblings when they asked Miro to convince Ender to leave the religious order he'd joined to be with Novinha and return to save their home world from the Starways Congress's fleet.

A short time later, as Ender lay dying at the abbey where he'd joined Novinha, Olhado and his family joined their pequenino friend, Plower, for a picnic in the piggies' land. They were eating when something unusual occurred with the mothertrees. They came to life and burst forth with beautiful fruit. Jane had been cut off from the computer networks that housed her, and her soul (or Auía) had traveled throughout the galaxy looking for a new place to dwell. It had chosen the mothertrees for a time, causing them to bring the fruit.

When Ender died a short time later, Olhado joined with his mother and brother Grego in mourning together at their childhood home. Olhado was particularly lonesome for Ender, having built a very close relationship with him.

With his brother Grego, Olhado watched as a pequenino scientist named Waterjumper and the Hive Queen reestablished a small computer network with a few worlds. This new network allowed Jane to restart faster-than-light travel.

Olhado knew that this form of travel was the last hope of Lusitania's survival and was grateful for it because it meant his family, whom he loved so tenderly, could live. Jane used her abilities to first remove Olhado and his family from Lusitania as the destruction fleet came near. When the fleet did not kill the world, Olhado returned to Lusitania and attended Ender's funeral service, saying his final good-bye to the man he considered his father.

Ribeira von Hesse, Lembrança das Milagres de Jesus "Quara" (SD, XN, CM)

Quara was the youngest of the Lusitania-born children of Novinha and Libo, and was raised by Novinha's husband Marcão Ribeira. Following Marcão's death, Quara did not speak to anyone outside of the family for months, breaking her silence to tell Ender that he stinks.

She took a shine to Ender, even visiting his home after school and boasting to him that she was especially talented at math.

During the Speaking for her father, Marcão, Quara expressed a hope that Ender would be her new dad. She was happy when Ender married Novinha.

Thirty years later, now a woman in her late thirties, Quara joined her family as one of the top scientists on Lusitania. She studied the deadly virus known as the Descolada, and felt that the disease was actually a living, sentient creature. While her siblings and mother had been developing ways to wipe out the virus—yet allowing for it to still perform its necessary functions in the biology of the native Lusitanian life, the pequeninos—Quara saw that the virus was communicating with itself.

This theory of an intelligent molecule was a contentious issue between Quara and her siblings. She was certain that destroying the Descolada was xenocide and could not be allowed. Following an intense debate with her siblings, mother, and stepfather Ender, it was decided that Quara would continue to study the virus from a perspective that it was alive, while the others would keep looking for ways to defeat it.

All of the scientists were sworn to secrecy, but Quara ignored the order and told Human, the pequenino that had evolved to a fathertree—the highest honor given a piggie—that her family was working to kill the Descolada. The pequeninos relied on the virus, and having learned from Quara that it was threatened, made the decision to pursue construction of a spaceship that would take them away from Lusitania with the Descolada intact.

Quara had a special relationship with a pequenino named Deaf, who was not hard of hearing, despite his name.

She was present when her brother Miro returned from his trip into space, traveling for thirty years to bring Ender's sister Valentine to the planet. She had aged to be much older than he because of the effects of relativistic space travel. The age difference created some awkwardness between Miro and the rest of his siblings.

After Miro's return, Quara was called into a meeting with the leaders of her planet, and chastised harshly for revealing all of the human settlers' plans to eradicate the Descolada. Despite the tongue-lashing, Quara remained committed to saving the virus, which she considered another life-form.

It was revealed that Quara was feeding her sister Ela's antivirus research to the Descolada, desperately trying to prove the virus could communicate. Their mother, Novinha, enraged in grief over her son Quim, cut off Quara's access to the research.

Once Quara learned of Quim's death, she also grieved. She hurled terrible words at her mother, and left their home angrily. When she returned in sorrow to reconcile with Novinha, it was impossible, as Novinha had left the home and joined the abbey known as the Children of the Mind of Christ. Quara carried a tremendous burden of guilt in her heart for the fight with her mother.

Although cut off from the lab, Quara continued her research and communication with the pequeninos. When Miro, Ender, and Ela developed a theory on how to remove the Descolada from the piggies and were experimenting with Planter, Quara promised she'd visit Planter. She was angry with Miro and Ela, and hesitant to review her findings with them. She told Miro she would consider changing her stance on the matter, but not out of loyalty or love for her family.

She did go to see Planter. The dying piggie begged her to share the information she had on the Descolada with Ela and Miro. Quara argued that to do so was xenocide, but Planter countered by saying to not do so was xenocide for two species instead of one. Quara was angry with Planter for manipulating her feelings, but agreed to give her sister the information she'd discovered about the enslaving virus. She hoped it would help keep Planter alive, so she could spit in his face.

Ela took Quara's research and was able to develop a theoretical antivirus, but was unable to manufacture it. Planter died, but Quara knew that she had ultimately done the right thing in sharing the information. She hoped that though it wasn't in time to save Planter, she and Ela would someday be able to manufacture the antivirus.

Once Ela created the cure for the Descolada, Quara stopped fighting to save the virus. The recolada allowed all the life on Lusitania to continue to flourish without its native disease. She was heartbroken over the eradication of the Descolada, but knew deep within herself that it was best.

She was among her siblings when they asked Miro II to convince Ender to leave the religious order he'd joined to be with their mother.

A short time later, as Ender himself lay dying at the abbey, Quara learned that she had been mostly correct in her interpretation of the Descolada. It could communicate, but Miro II learned that it was not sentient. He had discovered the virus's home world, and asked Quara to return to it with him to further study the virus's origin.

The request was essentially asking Quara to say good-bye to her home. Jane could no longer sustain many trips at faster-than-light speed. If Quara joined Ender, Valentine II, her sister Ela, a Formic drone, and a pequenino scientist named Firequencher on the journey, she'd not be able to return to Lusitania in her life time.

As usual, she argued with her siblings on the expedition. When Miro II was forced to say hateful things to Valentine II in order to give up her body so Jane could inhabit it, Quara criticized him angrily. Firequencher and the Drone tried to silence her before removing her from the room. They understood, as Quara seemed to not, that Miro's cruel words were necessary for Jane to live by taking over Valentine II's body.

Quara fought constantly with Jane. When Jane essentially became Valentine II, there was some question about whether she could still control faster-than-light travel. With Ela, she had determined that the Descolada virus communicated with its creators, the descoladore, through signals that were translated into molecules. She sent a signal to the planet and received a response, but was not able to decode it.

In the middle of their studies of the response, Jane figured out how to travel through Outspace and returned the travelers to Lusitania. Quara was angry that they'd been given no warning and got into a physical confrontation with Jane, which Jane easily won. Jane felt bad about shoving Quara to the ground, but Miro theorized that throughout her life, Quara longed to be abused. She had loved her father Marcão and thought that love was shown through abuse, since he'd been so abusive to her mother. Jane didn't want to show Quara such "love," knowing that in her heart, Quara didn't really want that either.

As the Lusitanian destruction fleet drew near, Quara and her comrades returned to the descoladore planet. They figured out that the message the descoladore had sent them was a deadly heroinlike molecule.

Jane saved the ship and crew by instantly moving them to the other side of the planet. Quara decided that the descoladore needed to be eliminated and wanted to use the Molecular Detachment Device on their planet, just as it was supposed to have been used on hers.

The deadly weapon had not been used on her home world, however, thanks to the efforts of Peter Wiggin II and Si Wang-mu. They appeared on Quara's ship and dissuaded everyone but her from using the so-called "Little Doctor" on the descoladore. It was Peter II's hope, and Ender's since he carried Ender's soul within him, that the device never be used again. He wanted humanity to learn about the descoladore and hopefully build a relationship with them.

He knew that this would never be accomplished as long as Quara and her angry, hateful self was present. She was incredibly hurt by this and hated Peter II and Wang-mu for it.

After the small group returned to Lusitania, Wang-mu tried to befriend Quara. Quara would have none of it, saying hateful, cruel things to Wang-mu before walking out on her. Wang-mu hoped they'd be able to come to some sort of understanding but knew it would take many years.

Ribeira von Hesse, Marcos Vladimir "Miro I" (SD, XN)

The son of Novinha and Libo, Miro grew up believing that a man named Marcão was his father.

Miro had become a xenologist on Lusitania, building strong relationships with the native life-forms, the pequeninos. He visited them regularly and studied their culture. He had a close, loving relationship with his fellow xenologist Ouanda. The two had fallen in love as their parents—Libo and Novinha—had decades earlier. Miro did not know that he and Ouanda shared a father in Libo.

During Ender's first visit to the Ribeira household, Miro was at first cold to the Speaker, but warmed up and was eventually the most cordial member of the family toward Ender. He was frankly honest about Marcão's abusive actions, and said he might even allow Ender access to the pequeninos.

This issue was a matter of dissension between Ouanda and Miro. Miro had previously introduced the pequeninos to the original Speaker for the Dead's writings, and the pequeninos wanted the Speaker to visit them. Ouanda didn't think it was a good idea.

When Jane, Ender's sentient computer program, felt spurned by Ender, she sent out an unsigned memo to the interplanetary computer networks stating that Miro and Ouanda had broken the interstellar law and taught the piggies agriculture. They were required to report to the nearest planet to face an inquiry into their criminal action.

Not knowing about the arrest warrant, Miro and Ouanda had a public argument in front of the piggies about bringing the Speaker to them. In the course of this argument, they realized that if they did not bring Ender to speak with the piggies, their pequenino friend Human could be killed.

Miro and Ouanda took Ender to speak with the piggies. In observing the brief conversation they had, Miro learned that Ender was not only the original Speaker for the Dead, but also Ender the Xenocide. Though he doubted the veracity of the piggies' claims, a seed of belief was planted in him.

He also learned much about the piggies that he'd not been able to realize before—such as that they felt remorse for causing Pipo and Libo pain, and that they hadn't intended to hurt them. He was invited to participate in their ritual of sacrificing a tree to build a house and arrows. And he learned that the pequeninos longed to leave the planet and explore the stars, feeling that they needed the Hive Queen to do so.

Miro attended the Speaking for his father, Marcão, and was saddened to learn that he was not his real father. It was there that he learned of his true parentage, and that Ouanda was his sister.

Following the Speaking, Ender learned of the call for Miro's arrest. He forbade Miro from going to Trondheim to answer the accusations, and instead planned a rebellion against the Starways Congress.

Miro learned of the arrest warrant when he went back to the pequeninos, and was denied access to the fence that protected the native animals. He chose to climb the fence to get to them, resulting in serious, life-threatening injuries. Mandachuva, one of the piggies, raced to get help for Miro, bringing back Ender, Ouanda, and the leaders of the colony.

Miro was taken back to his mother's home to heal from his injuries. The damage to his nerves was severe, and he could not talk, and had very limited use of his hands. Despite these new handicaps, and with Olhado's help, Miro told his mother and siblings that the piggies were planning to make war on the other tribes of pequeninos. Novinha took this message to Ender, who was making a treaty with the piggies.

After a few weeks, Miro recovered from his injuries. He was able to walk and talk, but with limited capacity. He avoided Ouanda, feeling pain that she was his sister. But he read her files closely tracking the progress in piggie research. He found he had access to all of her work, even the confidential parts. This had been given to him by Jane, Ender's sentient computer program. Jane had taken a liking to Miro, and the two became fast friends.

Miro felt that he had to leave Lusitania, and so Ender and Jane arranged for him to take Ender's spaceship into space to meet Valentine, Ender's sister, who was heading toward Lusitania herself to protect the planet from the Starways Congress's planned xenocide.

Though it only seemed like a few weeks to Miro, nearly thirty years had passed on Lusitania by the time he rendezvoused with Valentine in space. Their meeting was confrontational at first. Both Miro and Valentine were defensive of their perspectives on how to best serve humanity and Lusitania.

During his travel, Miro determined that since the Descolada virus had mutated/evolved and was again threatening the planet, perhaps the Starways Congress was correct in wanting to destroy it entirely. Valentine disagreed, seeking to preserve all life on the planet.

Valentine was patient with Miro's speech impediments, which endeared her to him somewhat. She and her husband Jakt moved from their ship to his, which took them the rest of the way back to Lusitania.

During this portion of the voyage, Miro and Jane taught Valentine, Jakt, and Plikt the ideas of the Philotic Web—the foundation of life, matter, and communication. Jane also revealed herself to the travelers and stated that she could save Lusitania from destruction but at the cost of her own philotic-based existence.

Miro was devastated and pleaded with her to find a way to stop the invasion fleet from destroying his home world and save her own life. He felt that he couldn't bear to lose her as she'd become his closest friend and confidant. Jane agreed to try, but the idea of her death was still a heavy burden to Miro. He cried that night, being consoled in Valentine's arms.

Upon his return to Lusitania, his full-blooded siblings greeted him. Ouanda and Libo's other children were not there, and Miro missed them. His journey into space had felt like a month to him; but because of the effects of relativistic space travel, it had been nearly thirty years on Lusitania. All of his family were older than he now. The age difference created some awkwardness between them and him.

Almost immediately after landing, Miro, Ender, Plikt, and Valentine went to the Formic Hive Queen's lair, near the piggie land. The Hive Queen was busy creating spaceships to take the piggies off the planet, escaping the impending xenocide. She communicated mind to mind with everyone except Miro, which was thought to be because he did not have the necessary emotional relationship Ender and the others did—a prerequisite to such philotic communication.

He was hurt by the lack of communication and sad that the piggies he'd grown to love were seeking to leave their home world. He was so upset after the visit to the Hive Queen that he did not want to attend mass with his family. He ended up going, though, because he felt too restless at home and needed to do something.

At mass, he ran into Ouanda for the first time since he returned to the planet. He spoke only briefly to her, being disconcerted because of her age. He ran out of the cathedral and to the pequenino land where he met up with Quim, who had been holding mass there for the piggies.

The two brothers fought at first, but reconciled quickly. Miro grew concerned because Quim had decided to travel to unsettled piggie areas, preaching the gospel. Miro was sure his brother would be killed.

Miro learned his brother had been killed by a message Ender sent him through Jane. He was supposed to inform his family, and so he had them gather in the family home to tell them all together.

When he did tell his family, Novinha angrily slapped him and sent him away. Miro went out into the night, finding himself at the pequenino forest, finding solace in his friends the piggies. The fathertrees told him that they would punish Warmaker, the fathertree who had killed Quim.

He hoped this news would pacify the angry, vengeful citizens who sought justice for Quim. It did not. They rioted and burned much of the piggies' home forest. They killed several pequeninos in the process. Miro stood in their way before they could kill the fathertrees, Rooter and Human. With the help of his brother Grego (who had incited the riot in the first place), Miro helped disperse the mob.

He witnessed the arrival of the reborn Formics who were sent by Ender via the Hive Queen to protect the pequeninos from the humans, and rejoined Ouanda as she studied the pequeninos' rebuilding after the fire.

In the midst of a confrontational philosophical conversation with Ender, Miro and his stepfather theorized that Jane could be saved if they were able to locate her point of philotic origin. If all life was connected through the Philotic Web, Jane included, they thought that finding this point of origin held the key to preserving her life.

Embittered by the loss of Ouanda, and his physical state, Miro was terrified of losing Jane, too. His theorizing with Ender, though often in disagreement, was helpful in giving him hope that Jane would live. It was a rare glimpse of optimism, albeit skeptical optimism, Miro enjoyed.

Miro approached his sister Quara, who had been cut off from the lab, to ask for her help as they studied the Descolada and how to remove it from the pequeninos. He hoped she would agree in time to save their test subject Planter, a pequenino who had sacrificed himself for the good of science. She was hesitant, but through Miro's apparent sincerity, agreed to think about it. She thanked him for not using Jane to hack into her files. Miro felt guilty for her gratitude as he had, in fact, done just that.

Quara went to see Planter and agreed to share the information she had on the Descolada with Miro and Ela. It wasn't in time to save Planter, but it allowed the young scientists to develop a theoretical antivirus.

A few days later, Miro was chosen to go into space with Ela, Ender, and Jane. They were going to test Grego and Olhado's theories about using Outspace to instantly travel between planets. The idea relied on calling philotes— the primary substance of life—and sending them home to their native dimension. Then, once there, the traveler would think of the philotic pattern of where he wanted to go, or of something he wanted to create, and the philotes would go there instantly. It required a powerful memory, though, to prevent one's own philotes from dispersing.

Jane had such a powerful memory, and could maintain the philotic patterns of some of the travelers. She needed Miro to be on the ship with her, however, because of the closeness that had developed over their years together. It would help her focus on the philotic patterns.

The travel required each traveler to focus on his own philotic pattern, too. The pattern Miro thought of, once inside the mysterious other dimension known as Outspace, was of his undamaged, younger self. Because that was the pattern he imagined, that new body was created, and his true philotic self leaped from his old damaged body to his new body, creating Miro II. The original body dissolved.

Ribeira von Hesse, Marcos Vladimir "Miro II" (XN, CM)

Miro II was a body created in the home dimension of the philotes—the spark of life. When Ender, Miro I, Ela, and Jane traveled to this dimension—known as Outspace—they were able to have their thoughts made real. They had to focus on their own bodies remaining real or the philotes would abandon them in Outspace, and the travelers would be killed.

Miro I, whose body had been irreparably damaged, imagined his younger self. Consequently, his philote jumped from his old damaged body to a new, younger, perfect one. The old body dissolved, and Miro II took over. Miro II had the same memories and the same experiences as Miro I, as the philote was analogous to being Miro's soul. However, with his new body, he was a younger man in appearance and ability.

The Catholic leadership on Lusitania was concerned that Miro II had never been baptized. The new Miro consented to receive the sacrament, purifying himself in the eyes of the church.

With Valentine II, and in the newly built second ship, Miro explored the universe using Outspace for instantaneous travel. He searched for a suitable planet whereon the pequeninos and reborn Formics could live.

They found many new planets that could hold the creatures. On their journey, Miro fell a little in love with Valentine II. He was still loyal to Jane, but found his feelings growing for the young version of Ender's sister.

Jane was a little jealous of Miro's affection for Valentine II, and teased him about it. He teased her back. He had fallen in love with her, too, but knew that she would soon be destroyed.

Upon his return from searching for the planets, his siblings asked him to convince Ender to leave the religious order he'd joined with their mother and return to them to help protect their home planet from the congressional fleet. Miro consented and traveled to the abbey.

He was not successful in swaying Ender. It became apparent to Miro that Ender was running from his past, and the creation of the new Valentine and Peter. All Ender wanted was to live out his days with his wife. He'd even removed the Jane jewel.

Defeated, Miro left his stepfather, but not before Ender suggested that Jane's philotic consciousness could be put in Valentine II's body. Miro and Jane began immediately to determine if it was possible.

Miro went to the Hive Queen to determine if she could (or would) help Jane take over Valentine II's body. Accompanied by Valentine II, who used her "essence of Ender" to philotically communicate with the Hive Queen, Miro learned that the mission he'd undertaken to find a suitable planet for the Formics and pequeninos had been a cover. He'd actually been searching, under Jane and the Hive Queen's secret agenda, for the home world of the Descolada.

The Hive Queen led Miro to this conclusion, but didn't outright tell him. Furthermore, she did not commit to help in the transfer of Jane's consciousness into Valentine II. She didn't think it was possible, or that Jane or Valentine II wanted it to happen. Though both said they were against the idea, they both realized that fusing their two beings into one was really the only chance of survival for either.

Jane continued to tease Miro that he was in love with her. It was a defense mechanism to protect herself from the potential disappointment that she wouldn't be able to make the jump from the computer into Valentine II. Miro felt he'd done all he could to help it happen by asking the Hive Queen.

Valentine II and Miro II located the Descolada's home planet. There they determined that the virus could communicate, to report back to its creators what it found and infected as it traveled the galaxy via probes sent from the planet.

Miro wanted to study the virus further and enlisted the help of his sisters Ela and Quara. They reluctantly agreed to go with him back to the planet, but they all knew it was essentially a suicide mission.

As Ender lay dying at the abbey where he'd joined with Novinha, Jane herself was fading. Starways Congress had begun the process of killing her, and she was unable to sustain more faster-than-light missions. As a result, Miro and his comrades would be too far away from Lusitania to ever return. Ever the scientist, he agreed to go.

While on the journey, Jane and Ender both "died." Their souls, or Auías, both searched for new host bodies. Valentine II fought with Jane inside her, and begged Miro to sincerely say hateful, cruel things to her so that her small piece of Ender's Auía, which gave her life, would leave her body and allow Jane to take it over. This would let both Jane and Valentine II live, as Valentine II's portion of Ender's soul would be reunited with the other two pieces that lived in Ender himself and Peter II.

Miro, heartbroken, told Valentine II that he'd never loved her, and that she wasn't even a real person. His words enraged Quara, but did the trick. Valentine II let her small Auía leave her body and allowed Jane to inhabit it.

The new home for Jane created some awkwardness between her and Miro, as she could no longer speak to his mind. But her consciousness was there, and he hoped that his love for both her and Val (whose body she inhabited) would continue to grow. He was also optimistic that since Jane had been reborn in Valentine II's body, they would, in fact, be able to return to Lusitania using faster-than-light travel.

In her human form, Jane was unable to fully control her newly discovered emotions. Miro II, loving Jane as he did, tried to comfort her and teach her what it meant to have and control emotions. Jane responded by asking Miro to marry her. He responded, perhaps rashly, that he would.

He tried unsuccessfully to protect Jane from her confrontations with Quara. And when Jane suddenly fell into a comalike state brought on by the Hive Queen and Human's call to redo faster-than-light travel, Miro was by her side. He stayed with her as she unconsciously took their ship back from the Descolada's planet to Lusitania. He comforted her as she hurt somewhat coming out of the brief coma. And he was with her as they exited the ship and she saw his own home planet with human eyes for the first time.

When the fleet that was ordered to destroy Lusitania came ever nearer, Jane took Miro, Ela, and company back to the descoladore planet. They learned that the message they'd received in response to their first signal (which included human DNA) was a deadly molecule that would have wiped out humanity if they'd tried to create it.

The descoladore launched several ships from their planet to attack the humans. Miro II called on Jane to protect them, and she instantly moved the ship and its crew to the other side of the planet.

Eventually, Miro II and his crew returned home, along with Peter Wiggin II and Si Wang-mu who had joined them after stopping the destruction of Lusitania. Miro and Jane attended Ender's funeral and then were married in the shadows of the mothertrees in the pequenino land. Jane blinked them away for a secluded honeymoon.

Finally, Miro found happiness and peace in his life. He'd married Jane and was whole again.

Ribeirão Preto, Brazil (ES, SH, SP, SG)

Ribeirão Preto, Brazil, was the home of the Hegemony government led by Peter Wiggin in the years after Ender's victory over the Formics. Peter and the rest of the Wiggin family, as well as Bean Delphiki and his family, lived in the city. It became one of the world capital cities when the Hegemony expanded its influence worldwide to become the unified world government called the Free People of Earth.

Righteous Labor (XN, CM)

Righteous labor was the work expected of every resident on the planet Path. Steeped in ancient Chinese tradition, the labor was usually performed in the planet's rice paddies.

Ro (XN)

Ro was the second of three children born to Valentine Wiggin and her husband Jakt. She was born on the planet Trondheim, approximately three thousand years after Ender Wiggin's victory over the Formics. At age twenty, she accompanied her parents into space initially heading toward the planet Lusitania, to protect that world from Starways Congress's xenocidal intention toward it.

Rock-eating Worms (GB, EE)

The rock-eating worms were thought to be a life-form native to the former Formic world that was settled by Sel Menach and his party after Ender's victory in the war. Sel and his assistant Po Tolo soon discovered that what they thought were worms were actually creatures they would call Gold Bugs.

Rooter (SD, XN, CM)

Rooter was a native of the planet Lusitania. A pequenino, or "piggie," he was talented at climbing tress with his padded paws and their ankle-claws. He was fascinated by the bits and pieces of human culture he learned from Pipo, the planet's scientist who studied the piggies. Rooter was also known for the tremendous acrobatic ability and agility he displayed.

He spoke to Libo, Pipo's son, about the relationship between males and females in the pequenino culture, contrasting it to human culture. Rooter thought human females were weak for not killing Pipo or Libo once they were discovered to be wise. The next day, Rooter was found dead—tortured to death—with a small tree having been planted in his open chest cavity.

The tree grew over the years, and the pequeninos believed that Rooter's spirit inhabited it. They looked to the trees, and particularly Rooter's, for guidance. They were certain that Rooter had told them that the newly arrived Speaker for the Dead was the original Speaker, Ender Wiggin. Furthermore, Rooter had apparently told them that the Speaker would bring them the Hive Queen, who would give them more guidance—most importantly the keys to space travel. The prophesy caused dissension among the piggies as the believers, led by Human, were threatened by the disbelievers, led by Leaf-eater.

Human was eventually made into a fathertree, too, and communicated silently with Rooter. They were considered the most noble and wise of the fathertrees. When Ender's stepdaughter Quara warned the fathertrees that her family was working on ways to eliminate the Descolada virus from Lusitania (which the pequeninos relied on for life and reproduction), Rooter and Human contacted the Formic Hive Queen, who Ender had placed on the planet to regrow her species, and together they planned to build a spaceship that would remove them from Lusitania, the Descolada still living within them.

Rooter, as a tree, was unable to leave Lusitania, but it was of little consequence. The Descolada had been eradicated without harming the pequeninos, and the human fleet did not destroy his world.

After Ender died, his remains were buried in the pequenino land, near Rooter and Human.

Rosen, "Rose the Nose" (EG, ES, SH)

Rosen, a Jewish child from Israel, was Ender's commander in Rat Army. He ordered Ender not to practice with his launch group or use his desk until he successfully froze two soldiers in battle. Ender defied the orders, but still froze the necessary enemies. Rosen didn't speak to Ender after that.

"Rose the Nose," as he was affectionately known, had been assigned a private room as a commander, but slept with his army in their barracks. He was reportedly scared of the dark and needed the company of his soldiers to feel safe.

Rosen aspired to be the International Fleet's chief military officer, the Strategos. The position had been filled by an Israeli Jew since it had been created, and Rosen sought to continue the tradition. He was succeeded in command of Rat Army by Dink Meeker.

Rotterdam, Netherlands (ES, SP, SG)

Rotterdam, in the Netherlands, was the home to Bean Delphiki and Achilles Flandres. In the aftermath of the first and second Formic invasions of Earth, Rotterdam had crumbled and was full of orphans. Following Ender's victory over the Formics, the city began to rebuild, becoming a cleaner, safer place. Bean returned to Rotterdam with his wife, Petra Arkanian, as a young adult, and was surprised about the changes for the better, which the city had made since he'd been an orphan child wandering the streets there.

Rotterdam Kids (ES)

In Rotterdam in the Netherlands, homeless, parentless children filled the streets. To survive, the children formed groups called "crews" and later "families." These groups protected their own, but fought and even killed rival crews.

Bean and Achilles Flandres were two prominent kids among the crews. When Bean snuck out of his new home with Sister Carlotta at age four, he encountered a belligerent pair of eight-year-old kids, but confidently moved past them.

Rov (*See* Hundred Worlds)

Royal Mother of the West ([XN])

The Royal Mother of the West was one of the gods worshipped by the Chinese colonists on the planet Path. Si Wang-mu, a servant girl who would become Peter Wiggin II's wife, was named for her. Royal Mother was Wang-mu's ancestor-of-the-heart.

Rudolf, Captain Helena (PL)

Captain Helena Rudolf, a young German woman, was sent by the International Fleet to conduct Battle School testing in Poland. With a curt, almost stern demeanor, she tested the children of the Wieczorek family, and was the first to discover the exceptional intelligence of the family's seventh child, John Paul. She took the findings back to the International Fleet and returned with her colleagues, Colonel Sillian and Captain Hyrum Graff, to further test five-year-old John Paul.

Russian General (PL)

Several leaders of the International Fleet evaluated six-year-old John Paul Wieczorek's Battle School screening tests, among them the Russian general.

He was worried John Paul was bluffing—that his scores were too good. The Russian general was the representative of the Office of Strategos. In this capacity, he insisted that John Paul be considered for Battle School and agreed that Captain Hyrum Graff should make the final determination on the matter.

Russian Kidnappers (SH)

The Russian kidnappers were assigned by a mysterious leader to round up the members of Ender's Command School team and take them to an undisclosed location in their home country where the captives would play war games. They were impatient with Petra Arkanian and used injections to make her unconscious. They held her in solitary confinement for nearly six weeks before allowing her to join the rest of her colleagues.

Saavedra, Ouanda Quenhatta Figueira Mucumbi (SD, XN, CM)

Ouanda was the firstborn child of Libo Figueira and his wife Bruxinha. She was a talented xenologist on the planet Lusitania. Following her father's death at the hands of the native life-forms, the pequeninos, Ouanda violated the government rule that the pequeninos (or piggies) be quarantined. She visited the aliens frequently.

She developed a close, loving relationship with her xenologist colleague, Miro Ribeira von Hesse. They often argued about the best course of action to take with the piggies, including whether or not they should introduce to them the newly arrived Speaker for the Dead, Ender Wiggin.

Ouanda and Miro fell in love, but soon discovered they were actually siblings, sharing the same father—Libo.

Jane, Ender's sentient computer program, sent a message through interplanetary computer networks stating that Ouanda and Miro had taught the piggies agriculture—a violation of the law. As a result, Lusitania's charter was revoked, and Ouanda and Miro were ordered to go to the nearest planet, Trondheim, to face an inquiry into their criminal actions.

Before learning about the inquiry, Ouanda and Miro discovered that there was dissension among the piggies over the arrival of the Speaker. Some of the piggies threatened to kill others if the Speaker did not arrive. To prevent this, Ouanda agreed that Ender Wiggin should speak to the pequeninos.

Ouanda and Miro took Ender to speak to the piggies. She treated the Speaker with great hostility and condescension. As she listened to his conversation with the piggies, Ouanda learned that the pequeninos longed to experience space travel, and that they believed Ender Wiggin, the Speaker, held the key to their doing so—the Hive Queen. She doubted everything the Speaker discussed with the piggies, and even argued with him about it. But she was glad to have been invited to witness the pequeninos' ritual sacrifice of a tree to make houses and arrows from its wood.

She attended the Speaking for Miro's father, Marcão, there learning of his true parentage. They were siblings, and the news was hard to bear.

Ouanda learned of the arrest warrant against her when Miro tried to gain access to the fence that surrounded the piggies, but was denied. He was critically injured after climbing the fence. Mandachuva, one of the piggies, climbed over the fence, too, and found Ouanda, desperate to help Miro. Ouanda and Mandachuva found the leaders of the Lusitania colony, including Speaker Ender, and took them back to Miro.

She went with Ender and Ela to speak with the piggies' female leaders, the "wives." In the meeting between Ender and the chief wife, Shouter, Ouanda was tense. She had grown close to the piggies, and as she learned about their cannibalistic mating rituals, she had difficulty accepting them. Ender rebuked her for studying the piggies while he was negotiating a treaty.

Ultimately, Ouanda accepted the treaty Ender and the piggies had signed, and agreed to abide by its precepts. She was still close to them and wanted to continue to study them.

Ouanda did, in fact, continue to study the piggies, but she did so without Miro, who was crippled and who then left the planet to dilate time in order to help when the time was right. She worked with Quim and Ela, Miro's siblings, to learn as much as she could about them, and about the Descolada virus. With Ela, she discovered properties of daisies that could be used by the newly reborn Hive Queen to inoculate herself against the virus.

After Miro left for space, where he brought Valentine Wiggin back to Lusitania, Ouanda married and had four children. Though it had only seemed like a month gone to Miro, because of the relativistic space travel, nearly thirty years had passed.

Ouanda did not go to greet Miro's ship when it returned, but she found him at mass the next day. She spoke to him briefly, accusing him of having avoided her. He denied it and didn't want to speak to her. She had aged, and it bothered Miro too much. He ran from the cathedral to avoid her further.

She attended the meeting held by the planetary leaders to discuss what should be done about the pequeninos' plans to escape the potential xenocide, as well as what to do about the Descolada virus. She did not contribute much to the contentious meeting, despite being a well-respected scientist.

Following the riot that destroyed much of the piggies' land, Ouanda rejoined

Miro to study the pequeninos' rebuilding process. It is unknown what happened to her afterward.

San Angelo (SD)

Citizen of the planet Moctezuma, San Angelo's death was Spoken by Ender Wiggin. He was the founder of the Catholic order called the Children of the Mind of Christ, and was later canonized by the Catholic Church.

Santangelo, Isabella (YM, EE)

Isabella Santangelo lived in Polignano a Mare, Italy, and was the mother of Dorabella Toscano and grandmother of Alessandra Toscano. She and Dorabella had a volatile relationship stemming from disagreements over money and Dorabella's choice of husband. When Dorabella was accepted to be a colonist with the Dispersal Project, Alessandra approached Isabella, hoping to live with her. This encounter caused further problems between Isabella and Dorabella, with Dorabella giving the last of her money to Isabella and saying good-bye with a slap in the face.

Santangelo, Leopoldo (YM, EE)

Leopoldo Santangelo was the father of Dorabella Toscano, grandfather of Alessandra Toscano, and husband to Isabella Santangelo. Not much is known of him beyond the fact that he lived in Polignano a Mare, Italy.

Sasar, Hadrubet "Thorn" (SG)

Thorn, whose real name was Hadrubet Sasar, was an adviser to the Muslim Caliph, Alai, and his Hindu wife, Virlomi. He was sarcastic and blunt in his assessment of world politics and wanted to ensure that Armenia remained loyal to the Muslim world and not join the ever-growing world government, the Free People of Earth led by Peter Wiggin.

Saturn (EG)

Saturn was a planet in Earth's solar system and was recorded as the site of a human victory against the Formics. The human fleet was led by Mazer Rackham, who became a world hero through his victory here.

Sayagi (SH, SG)

Sayagi was a soldier in the Indian military who worked on computer research and military planning. Fellow soldier Virlomi offered to help him with his work in order to post a message on the computer forums that said that Petra Arkanian was alive and being forced against her will to aid in the evil schemes of Achilles Flandres, the Battle School dropout and serial killer who was plotting world domination in a post–Formic War world.

Sayagi was among the rebellious Indian soldiers (along with Petra Arkanian) who determined that in order to survive, the Indian army had to ignore Achilles's orders and withdraw from Burma. He posted this on the Locke computer forum. Achilles killed him for the act.

Virlomi built a memorial to him in India.

He appeared to Virlomi in a dream years later, chastening her for becoming someone different than she'd been when he was alive. She had manipulated her way to divine status in India and was not true to herself. Sayagi hated her for it in the vision or dream.

Scathing of China ([EG])

The "Scathing of China" was the name given to the destructive attack on China by the Formics during the aliens' first invasion.

Seamus "Shame" ([EG], ES)

Seamus, or "Shame" as he'd been nicknamed, was a contemporary of Ender Wiggin's at Battle School. He was talented but inexperienced when Bean, under orders from the Battle School officers, assigned him to Ender's newly formed Dragon Army. Seamus was the first and only soldier willing to speak up when Ender asked a question related to gravity and physical orientation. Though he got the answer to his commander's question wrong, Seamus showed courage and commitment by speaking up when no one else would.

Second Xenocide (CM)

"Second Xenocide" was the nickname given to the order to destroy the planet Lusitania and all its life. It referenced the War of Xenocide, which was the name given to the Formic War when it was learned Ender Wiggin had destroyed the entire Formic species.

Secretary to Amaro de Madrid (PB)

Amaro de Madrid's secretary was a loyal, helpful woman. She often took Bonzo Madrid home when he'd visit his father at work. Talented, she was a tremendous asset to Amaro, allowing him the ability and opportunity to have an affair with a woman not his wife. Whether she was the woman or simply an accomplice to the affair is unknown.

Selvagem (SD)

Selvagem was a pequenino (or piggie), the native sentient animal life on the planet Lusitania.

Semadores (SD)

"Semadores" was a term used by members of the religious order, Children of the Mind of Christ, to refer to the monks who taught in the order's school.

Semantics: Notes on the Pequenino Language and Nomenclature (SD)

Written by noted Luistanian scientist, Libo, *Semantics: Notes on the Pequenino Language and Nomenclature* became the handbook for xenological study throughout the Hundred Worlds.

"Separation" (XN)

"Separation" was a poem written by Li Qing-jao on the planet Path. It formed the foundation of Han Qing-jao's rituals performed as one of the godspoken.

Sergeant (ES)

A member of Poke's "crew"—the group of children who lived together on the streets of Rotterdam in the Netherlands—Sergeant was apparently the second in command to Poke. He helped find food for the crew, and was partly responsible for giving Bean his name.

When Achilles took over the crew, he used Sergeant, or "Sarge" as he was otherwise known, as the main figure in his plan to get the group food. Sarge picked a fight with a bully named Ulysses who was in line at the local soup kitchen. Achilles stepped in and, with Sarge and the other members of the crew, severely beat Ulysses. The fight resulted in the crew getting food from the kitchen before the other bullies.

A short time later, when Sister Carlotta began teaching the crew how to read, Sarge and the others discovered that Bean already knew how to read. This led to Sarge and Achilles angrily accusing Bean of holding out on them and threatening to hurt him for doing so.

Sarge was the first member of the crew to learn of Poke's murder. He knew that although Achilles claimed Ulysses had killed Poke, it was really Achilles who commited the murder. Sarge never told anyone this, though, knowing that he needed to stand by Achilles to be safe.

Shafts (EG)

Shafts was a colleague of Ender Wiggin's at Battle School. As children, Ender and Shafts were in the same launch group—they joined Battle School in the same year/class.

Shakespeare Colony (*See* Hundred Worlds)

Shen (EG, ES, SH, SG)

Shen was one of Ender's fellow soldiers at Battle School. He was small, and walked in large steps that caused his buttocks to wriggle. He was given the nickname "Worm" by fellow soldier Bernard because of his wriggling walking style. Ender helped Shen by sending humiliating messages about Bernard throughout the school computer system. As a result, Shen was loyal to Ender during their stay at Battle School.

Shen teamed up with Ender and their new ally, Alai, in their first practice in the Battle Room, successfully freezing all the other students. When Ender put together a practice session during Free Play, Shen joined up, improving his skills in the zero-gravity environment. He was committed to the extra practices, even when rumors of blacklisting circulated around Battle School.

He was incredibly loyal to Ender, defending him to others at Battle School. It was Shen whom Bean went to when he was studying Ender in order to learn why Ender was so well loved. Shen was unable to succinctly put into words his love and devotion to Ender. All he was really able to say was that he would die for Ender.

Ultimately, though, when Ender was promoted again to commander of Dragon Army, Shen believed the lies and rumors disseminated from the Battle School officers that Ender considered himself too good to practice with the "little guys" anymore. Consequently, Shen felt a bit more motivation to defeat Ender in battle.

Later, Shen was sent to Tactical School and then Command School, where he became one of Ender's squadron leaders against the Formics in the exams, which were later revealed to be actual battles. They had renewed their deep friendship through this new mutually shared combat experience.

He was one of Ender's former teammates who were kidnapped and forced to play war games in an undisclosed Russian location. He worked with his fellow captors to try to contact Peter Wiggin, who, they felt, was the key to their freedom.

As with the rest of his fellow captives, Shen was taken by their captor, former Battle School student Achilles Flandres, to an undisclosed location in Russia. There, he was still allowed to write to his colleagues, but no other contact was permitted.

Shen, like the other prisoners except Petra, was freed from captivity by Russian operatives.

In the years that followed, Shen was given a ceremonial position of some kind in the Japanese government. He was approached by Hyrum Graff and Peter Wiggin separately, and offered a new life in space free from the political instability that threatened most Battle School graduates—particularly those who worked with Ender. Like his fellow soldiers, he refused the offer.

As Peter built the Hegemony into the Free People of Earth, Graff again offered Ender's colleagues the opportunity to leave Earth and govern a planet. It was his fear that Ender's army would be used in the worldwide conflict, manipulated by whatever political power rose to prominence, and he wanted to prevent that. Every member who received the offer, which did not include Han Tzu, Petra Arkanian, or Alai, said no. The others were already too involved in matters on Earth to leave.

Shen Guo-rong (CH)

Shen Guo-rong was one of many tutors assigned to Han Tzu in preparation for his Battle School entrance tests. He taught Tzu shapes, logic, and memorization. Tzu felt this tutor was more important than the other tutors he had. Through exercises (called games) with this tutor, Tzu was prepped for his future; however, Guo-rong told Tzu to never speak of their sessions. Tzu grew tired of the games, but continued with them to avoid disappointing his father.

Shields (EG)

The shields were a defense system designed to protect against a nuclear attack.

Shouter (SD)

Shouter was a female pequenino, the native animal species on the planet Lusitania. The females were the pequeninos' governing body, known as the "wives." Shouter, whose real name was Star-looker, was the chief wife. Using the piggie named Human as a translator, Shouter and Ender Wiggin drafted a treaty that defined the relationship between humans and piggies on Lusitania.

In the treaty, the piggies agreed not to kill humans or make war on other tribes of pequeninos in exchange for Ender giving them the Hive Queen and not killing any pequeninos.

Shuttlebug (ES)

Shuttlebugs were a mode of transportation that were similar to flying, spacebound buses. They took groups of passengers short distances through space.

Sillian, Colonel (PL)

A senior officer in the International Fleet, it fell to Finland native Colonel Sillian to evaluate the results of Battle School screening tests. He was initially skeptical of John Paul Wieczorek's test results, but agreed to perform the follow-up screening personally.

Silver Bugs ([GB], [EE])

Silver Bugs were large insectoids, bred by the Formics to mine for precious metals on one of their worlds. When that world was colonized by humans after Ender's victory against the Formics, the Silver Bugs were thought to exist because of the discovery of Gold Bugs by xenobiologist Sel Menach and his assistant Po Tolo.

Their exoskeleton was saturated with the precious metal they mined, making the bugs a precious natural resources themselves.

Simulators (EG)

The simulators were video games used in Command School to train new students on controlling spaceships in combat. They featured a large screen where the player's ship was represented by a small light while enemy ships were small lights of a different color.

Sisters of St. Nicholas (ES)

The Sisters of St. Nicholas was the order of Catholic nuns to which Sister Carlotta, Bean Delphiki's guardian, once belonged.

Si Wang-mu (XN, CM)

Si Wang-mu was a fourteen-year-old girl of Chinese descent who lived on the planet Path. She was the daughter of poor farmhands who spread manure in the fields. Her parents named her for one of the most revered gods of Chinese tradition, hoping that she would be chosen among the godspoken. She was not.

Wang-mu longed to be taught by the godspoken, particularly Han Qing-jao, the sixteen-year-old daughter of their planet's greatest statesman, Han Fei-tzu. She bribed her way past the Han family guards and spoke boldly and bluntly to Qing-jao.

Impressed that Wang-mu was not intimidated by her status as a godspoken, Qing-jao hired her to be her servant. In exchange for performing her duties as a secret maid, Wang-mu would receive a good education from Qing-jao. Qing-jao was certain that Wang-mu had been forced to prostitute herself as the bribe to get past the guards and into the Han household. For this, Qing-jao was determined to repay her through education.

Wang-mu felt that being the godspoken was an easier way of life than being a worker in the fields. But as she observed Qing-jao perform the rituals of purification, like following the grain in the wooden walls, she came to understand the great burden her mistress felt. She hoped to help alleviate the burden, which Qing-jao appreciated. The two young women became friends, surpassing their simplistic master/servant relationship.

Wang-mu would often ask Qing-jao questions about the godspoken and the project she had undertaken to find the Lusitania Fleet, which had mysteriously disappeared. It was these questions that led Qing-jao to uncover the sentient computer Jane's existence and the true identity of the fiery political analyst Demosthenes.

Having been discovered, Jane revealed herself to Qing-jao, Wang-mu, and Han Fei-tzu. She told them that the godspoken were actually the result of a genetic manipulation performed by the Starways Congress generations earlier, and that the voice of the gods was actually the manifestation of this evolution in the form of obsessive-compulsive disorder.

Qing-jao was angered by this news and informed the Congress of Jane's existence and her role in making the fleet disappear. This led to a rift between Qing-jao and her father and Wang-mu.

Wang-mu, no longer believing in the gods, wanted to preserve Jane's life. Because of this, Qing-jao sent her away. Wang-mu left the Han house but was ordered to return by Han Fei-tzu, who said that Qiang-jao could excuse Wang-mu from her personal service, but not the family's.

Fei-tzu, no longer believing in the gods either, called Wang-mu to be his own servant. She agreed, and he promised to treat her as an equal. Together they agreed to help Jane and the Lusitanian scientists with three projects: (1) studying a way to cure the Descolada; (2) figuring out faster-than-light travel; and (3) reversing the genetic manipulation for the godspoken. A fourth project was added under the direction of Ender and his stepson Miro: help locate Jane's point of origin, which would help preserve her life.

They agreed to provide aid however they could, but felt inadequate. Wang-mu, ever the loyal servant, agreed to perform the baser tasks related to the research, including gathering genetic material from as many godspoken people as she could. She felt it was her duty as a servant to help maintain Fei-tzu's prestige in the society.

Wang-mu sought Qing-jao's help in studying the Descolada. Qing-jao refused, stating that there was not enough scientific evidence to warrant the research. In the process, Qing-jao asked specific questions about the virus, which Wang-mu could not answer. She took the questions with her, however, to an ansible conversation Jane arranged between her and Ender and Ela on Lusitania.

She asked the questions Qing-jao had brought up, and it led Ender and Ela to come up with a hypothesis that said the Descolada had been created to manipulate the life on Lusitania for an unknown purpose. While this left the question of who would or could create such a devastating disease, Wang-mu likened it to Starways Congress's genetically manipulating the people of Path for their purposes.

Wang-mu was bitter because of what she'd learned about gods and Congress. She decided to look to serve the closest gods she knew—people such as Han Fei-tzu, and even Ender Wiggin. She felt they were noble and worthy of service, if not worship.

A few weeks later, Si Wang-mu was awakened by Fei-tzu, who was receiving a message from Jane and Ela. They had developed a theory that would allow reversal of Congress's genetic manipulation of the godspoken, but let them maintain their superior intellect. They were not sure it would work yet, but it was progress.

In the process of this research, they also learned that Wang-mu had the altered genes that gave the godspoken their calling, but had mutated. She had the superior intellect of a godspoken, but not the OCD. This revelation came as no shock to Fei-tzu, who said that he and Wang-mu were equals. Wang-mu found it a little hard to believe at first, but quickly accepted it.

When the antivirus arrived on Path, delivered by the accidental creation of Ender Wiggin—Peter Wiggin II—Si Wang-mu greeted the ship with great relief. She rejoiced as Han Fei-tzu took the inoculation and spread it to the people of Path.

Peter II invited Wang-mu to join him in his new interstellar quest to destroy the Starways Congress. They would travel through the newly discovered

faster-than-light dimension, Outspace, and instantaneously reach planet after planet, subverting the galactic government.

Wang-mu was hesitant at first, but decided to bring down the evil empire
that had created the godspoken through genetic manipulation. After a tearful
good-bye to Fei-tzu, whom she called "father" and he "daughter," Wang-mu
joined Peter II on his spaceship.

As the ship used Jane to travel instantly from planet to planet, the new Peter explained his existence to Wang-mu, who accepted his moment of creation with some skepticism as she always did. But she came to realize the
story's veracity when Peter II told her to get off the ship. They had arrived at
the Japanese planet Divine Wind without Wang-mu even knowing they had
left Path.

Peter II needed her; he made that very clear. She was, he said, smarter
than he. Together, they would bring down the Congress, beginning on Divine Wind. There, she got to know Peter II a little better. She could see that
he was developing his own personality and encouraged him to do so.

Jane had established a secret identity for Wang-mu and Peter II on Divine
Wind. They were made out to be giddy young lovers. They acted out the part
well in public, but in private Peter II spoke so cruelly to Wang-mu that she was
often on the verge of tears.

Their first stop on their subversive journey was to the home of a Japanese
philosopher named Aimaina Hikari. He was influential among the Starways
Congress, but was not a member of the Congress itself. He had helped them
determine their course of action to destroy Lusitania and the Descolada by
stating that Ender's act of xenocide was not immoral, but necessary, and to
repeat such an act would also be.

In their meeting with Hikari, Wang-mu bowed herself beneath him socially at every turn. This led to a sort of a "humble contest," where Wang-mu
and Hikari tried to show that they were more humble than the other.

Peter II and Wang-mu were not able to change Hikari's mind about the
Lusitanian Fleet, but did give him cause to second-guess himself. They also
learned from some of the things he said that he was a believer in a religion
called Ua Lava, centered on the planet Pacifica. Having planted their seed of
discord on Divine Wind, Wang-mu and Peter II went to Pacifica to follow up.

There they met Grace Drinker, a well-known teacher of Ua Lava. She was
the matriarch of an entertaining Polynesian family on Pacifica, but more importantly she was a friend to a man named Malu—the prophetic figurehead
of the followers of Ua Lava.

Grace quickly saw through Wang-mu and Peter II's lies about their identities and determined that they really wanted to meet with Malu. Fortunately, Malu wanted to see them, too. He came to speak with them, through Grace as a translator, and confirmed that Jane needed to be saved.

Malu viewed Jane as a god, and spent most of his time speaking to Peter II, who wore a device that communicated with Jane in his ear. After delivering to Peter II the message he wanted to, Malu left on his boat to return to his isolated secret island.

Peter II had become consumed with saving Jane, and this made Wang-mu jealous. She realized that she had fallen in love with Peter II and wanted him to herself.

She was even more shocked to learn that Malu had returned and sought to speak with her—not Peter II. Malu taught Wang-mu that her love for Peter II was what was necessary to save him and especially the "god" Jane from destruction.

As Jane was cut off from her home among the computer networks, her consciousness, or Auía, searched throughout the galaxy for a new house. It tried jumping into Peter II's body, but he already had an Auía—a portion of Ender's, anyway—and there was not room for Jane's. The conflict between Auía that went on inside Peter II hurt him. Wang-mu, desperate to keep him, screamed for him to live.

She was his support and held him close to her as Jane's soul left, but the rest of Ender's joined with Peter II's. Peter II had been given a new life, as had Ender, when his soul joined back with Ender's. Wang-mu expressed her love to him, and Malu and the others on Pacifica, including Peter II, credited her with saving him.

Wang-mu and Peter II were shown an illegally created computer network Jane had taught the people of Pacifica to secretly make before she was forced from the computers she'd called home. Wang-mu witnessed her new Polynesian friends start up the network and learned that Jane could again control faster-than-light travel. Peter II rejoiced at the news. Neither of them had wanted to live the rest of their lives on the too-laid-back Pacifica.

At that moment, Wang-mu realized that Peter II was still much of Ender. He, like Ender before him, wanted to travel from planet to planet, living perhaps thousands of more years. Wang-mu first thought this was unappealing, but then embraced the idea because she would be with Peter II. She had fully fallen in love with him, and wanted to be with him for the rest of her life. No matter what kind of life they lived, she knew that it would be joyous with him.

As the Lusitania fleet approached the planet it was to destroy, the commanding officer ignored orders to quarantine the planet. He launched the devastating Molecular Detachment Device. Jane transported Wang-mu and Peter II to Lusitania, without a spaceship, and then with a spaceship, using the instantaneous travel process to help them capture the deadly missile that was heading for the planet.

They then took the missile to the cargo hold of the fleet's flagship. Wang-mu watched as Peter II confronted the fleet's commanding officer and got him to communicate to the Starways Congress that the Descolada had been eradicated. From there, Wang-mu joined Peter II as they were instantly taken to the descoladore world. Peter II again used his Ender-like influence to dissuade Miro II, Ela, and the pequenino Firequencher to not use the Molecular Detachment Device on the home of the Descolada.

Ender's stepdaughter Quara was angry with Peter II and hurled vicious words at him because he'd said that she was to never return to the planet, but would have to stay on Lusitania. Jane instantly took the group back to Lusitania. Wang-mu tried to befriend Quara, but the angry scientist would have nothing of it. She hated Wang-mu, and was as cruel to her as she'd been to her family all through the years. Wang-mu watched Quara storm away from their conversation and hoped that though it might take years, they would become friendly.

Wang-mu joined Peter II in attending Ender's funeral. Immediately following the service, they were joined by Jane and Miro II, and the two couples were married. Jane blinked them away, presumably sending them on a private honeymoon.

Si Wang-mu, the humble servant of the most righteous man on Path, had married Peter Wiggin II, the literal embodiment of the first Speaker for the Dead. She was happy, and would be, for she was with the man she loved.

Skimmer Pilots (GB, EE)

The skimmer pilots were talented at driving the skimmers, a popular mode of transportation among human colonists on former Formic worlds. They also served as sometime-bodyguards to Ender Wiggin when he began his tenure as governor of one of the colonies. They transported him to find Sel Menach and learn of the Gold Bugs. They were armed and often used their skimmers to haul cargo throughout the planet.

Skysplitter (XN)

Skysplitter was a pequenino fathertree, the most revered form of native life on Lusitania. He lived twenty-nine generations before Ender arrived on the planet. A pequenino named Planter sang the songs of Skysplitter's legends, teaching Miro Ribeira von Hesse about him.

Slattery, Pol (EGS, EG)

Pol Slattery was a contemporary of Ender Wiggin's at Battle School. He was the commander of Leopard Army, which Ender faced while a member of Salamander Army, and was the eighth army Ender's army faced and beat in a week's time.

Pol went on to command Badger Army, which was also beaten by Ender's Dragon Army.

Smetana (GB)

Smetana was a Czech composer whose music Sel Menach played to keep him sane during the Formic War.

Snow Tiger ([SP], SG)

Snow Tiger was the leader of the Chinese government in the aftermath of Ender's victory over the Formics. He aligned himself with Achilles Flandres, and sought to take over Asia. The Chinese military spread itself very thin in conquering the continent, and was easily defeated by Muslim and Indian soldiers and insurgents. It was a humiliating defeat for the Chinese.

Han Tzu, the Battle School graduate who had fought alongside Ender Wiggin in the Formic War, had warned Snow Tiger against his practices. Snow Tiger's defeat had lost the loyalty of the Chinese military, who sided with Han Tzu, whom they felt should have been listened to during their conquest of Asia. A disgruntled soldier assassinated Snow Tiger and helped crown Han Tzu as the new emperor in Snow Tiger's place.

Sorelledolce (*See* Hundred Worlds)

South African Kid (WG)

The South African kid was a member of Rat Army who participated in Dink Meeker's Christmas celebration of secretly giving gifts in other soldiers' socks.

Speaking/Speaker for the Dead (EG, EE, IC, SD, XN, CM)

A new funerary custom among humans throughout the galaxy was "Speaking." It was based on the second book written by Ender Wiggin under the pseudonym "Speaker for the Dead," *The Hegemon*. Speakers would memorialize the deceased, but rather than paint a one-sided positive picture of the dead, Speakers spoke plainly and completely about their subject. Ender attended his first Speaking as an audience member when he was twenty years old on the planet Sorelledolce.

Starcount (IC)

Starcount was currency used among the Hundred Worlds in the centuries after Ender's victory over the Formics.

Star of the Order of the League of Humanity, First Class (EG)

Star of the Order of the League of Humanity, First Class was the highest award given to civilians during the Formic Wars. Presented by the International Fleet and the League, it was presented to Valentine Wiggin even though she was still in her early teens, after she wrote a letter to her brother, Ender, supporting him in the war.

Stark/Starcommon (SD, XN, CM)

Stark, short for Starcommon, was a variation of English, and the primary language spoken on the different planets of the Hundred Worlds and in the Starways Congress.

Starman, Felix (SG)

Felix Starman was the leader of Rwanda during Peter Wiggin's rise to power as the Hegemon. He helped lead Peter, as well as Petra Arkanian and Bean Delphiki, in a charge against a safe house that kept the evil Dr. Volescu. During the charge he was impressed by Bean's gigantic size and military savvy.

Months later, in exchange for ratifying Peter Wiggin's constitution and Rwanda joining the Hegemony, Felix asked that Bean be sent to Rwanda to lead its armies. Bean complied, taking with him his wife Petra and their son Ender Delphiki.

Stars (EG, ES)

Stars were floating boxes that were obstacles for soldiers in the Battle Rooms at Battle School.

Starways Congress (*See* also Hundred Worlds) (IC, SD, XN, CM)

As human settlers were sent throughout the galaxy, a unified governing body called the Starways Congress was created to oversee the different planets and colonies.

Stilson (EG, [EE], [CM])

A contemporary of Ender Wiggin's, they were in the same school class on Earth, prior to Ender's assignment to Battle School. Stilson often mocked Ender for being the third child of his family, calling him "Third" or "Thirdie." He also mocked Ender for having his monitor removed, which signified that Ender had failed to qualify for Battle School. Stilson and his friends bullied Ender. Ender subsequently attacked Stilson, kicking him severely in the chest, and in the face, unknowingly killing him.

Strategos (EG)

The top military position in the International Fleet's Hegemony, the Strategos had an established tradition of being an Israeli Jew. Following Ender's defeat of the Formic home world, the Strategos gained power by public-relations efforts stating Ender was loyal to his office.

The office was eliminated following the war on Earth after Ender's victory in space.

Stumpy Point (EG)

Stumpy Point was a location on Earth that had been officially named for a former Hegemon, but was paved over and now used as a spaceport located on the Pamlico Sound.

Styrka (SD)

Styrka was one of Ender's students on the Icelandic planet Trondheim. He was a smart student, though unforgiving of Ender's actions as a child, killing the entire Formic race. Styrka didn't know that his teacher was the same Ender who had committed the heinous act. It had, after all, occurred three thousand years earlier. But he enjoyed the lessons he took from Ender, as they gave him much food for thought.

Suckflies (SD)

Suckflies were insects native to the planet Lusitania and were discovered by the xenobiologists there.

Summer Islands (*See* Hundred Worlds)

Summers, Kim (née Arnsbach; née Rackham) (MP)

Mazer Rackham's ex-wife, she bore his two children. They divorced when Mazer was assigned to solitary "waiting" in space, and she remarried.

Although initially angry with Mazer for divorcing her, she nonetheless still loved him, and spoke to their children with great fondness and happiness about their relationship prior to the war. She refused to appear alongside their children and grandchildren in the visual message Hyrum Graff had arranged for the family to send to Mazer, stating that she didn't want Mazer to see her so old. She wrote letters to Mazer, which Hyrum Graff ensured would be forwarded.

In these letters, she was at first angry, but eventually informed Mazer that she had moved on as instructed—remarrying. It broke Mazer's heart, but Kim had been alone for over thirty years. She made it clear that she still loved Mazer, but moved forward in the decades since he left her. Once Mazer informed the fleet that he would return to Earth to train their new commander if they promoted Graff, Graff brought Kim into the Fleet's strategy meetings to help keep the fleet honest with Mazer. She would laugh when the admirals and generals would try to come up with ways to deceive Mazer, thus upsetting their plans.

Sun Cao-pi (XN)

Sun Cao-pi was a citizen of the planet Path, and lived near Han Fei-tzu. Like most people on Path, he was of Chinese descent.

Support School (EG)

Support School was a training facility for grads of Battle School. Not much is known about the school beyond its existence except that it was run by the International Fleet during the Formic Wars.

Suriyawong "Surrey" "Surly" (SH, SP, SG)

Suriyawong was a Battle School contemporary of Ender Wiggin's. He was from Thailand, and was very loyal to his home nation. Though never a strong commander, Suriyawong, or "Surly" as he was known to his Battle School peers, was made a top military official in his home nation after the Formic Wars.

Nearly two years after returning to Thailand, and after having been put in his military position, Suriyawong was assigned to watch over Bean Delphiki, one of Ender's closest Battle School allies, who was hiding in Thailand from Achilles Flandres, yet another Battle Schooler who was set on world domination.

Bean had to work to earn Suriyawong's trust, and eventually did enough that Suriyawong gave Bean a small army to train in unorthodox maneuvers. For six months, they built their relationship.

When the combined Indian and Pakistani armies invaded Thailand's neighbor, Burma, Bean held a meeting with Suriyawong and the top military leader in Thailand, the Chakri. The Chakri was dismissive of the two Battle School veterans and sent them away. He even took back Bean's army.

Moments later, Bean realized that the Chakri was working with Achilles, and both his and Suriyawong's lives were in danger. The two teenagers escaped their barracks, just as they were blown up.

The Chakri tried to use their supposed deaths to justify a purported war with India. But with help from Bean's allies Hyrum Graff, Peter Wiggin, and Sister Carlotta, the Chakri's motives were exposed, and Suriyawong was given a promotion in the military by the Prime Minister of Thailand. They would work together to protect their nation. The Chakri resigned in shame at being caught in his part of the murderous conspiracy.

Suriyawong and Bean went to dinner late that night. From there they went to the airport to pick up Bean's friend, Sister Carlotta. They learned there that Carlotta's plane had been blown up, and they knew Achilles had been behind it.

Suriyawong tried to comfort Bean, but without much success. All he could do was help his friend get home to the prime minister's residence and promise to bring down Achilles.

When Bean determined that Achilles was actually using India and Pakistan as pawns and intentionally spreading their armies too thin in order to allow China an easy takeover of Asia, Suriyawong stood by him. They tried to warn the prime minister and the leaders of the Thai military but were ignored.

One general, Phet Noi, was sympathetic to their cause and promised to support them in their offensive against Achilles in India.

Suriyawong led a group of soldiers with Bean and came across Virlomi, an Indian woman who had betrayed Achilles by responding to Bean's computer messages searching for Petra. Suriyawong gained the trust of the troops that were loyal to Virlomi by being outwardly submissive to her. This allowed Virlomi to join them and lead them to Achilles's headquarters. There they would mount a dual mission to rescue Petra and kill Achilles.

Suriyawong did not play a big part in the rescue mission, leaving it to Bean. But he witnessed that they had been too late: Achilles's allies in the Chinese military had taken over Asia.

With his family, Suriyawong was able to escape Thailand before the Chinese occupation began. They moved to Brazil, which had become the new home of the Hegemony, headed by Peter Wiggin. There they were promised protection and looked forward to the possibility of returning to Thailand one day.

Suriyawong was second in command under Bean in the small Hegemony army. He was assigned by Peter Wiggin to mount a rescue operation that took him to China and which freed Achilles. Bean resigned from the military in the process, making Suriyawong the top leader of the small band of soldiers.

Although committed to following the orders that had come from his superior, and thereby rescuing Achilles, Suriyawong hoped that Achilles would die. When the mission was a success, Suriyawong changed tactics and began kissing up to Achilles. By rescuing him, he'd seen Achilles at a weak moment, and that usually meant that Achilles had to kill him.

Luring Achilles into a false sense of power and security, Suriyawong gave Achilles a lot of authority over the soldiers in the Hegemony army. Outside observers believed that Achilles had taken over the position of power in the army through his own means, but Suriyawong and the soldiers knew that it was the young Thai who was in control of the situation.

The primary negative consequence for Achilles's arrival at the Hegemony was that it forced the Indian Battle Schooler Virlomi to leave. This was heartbreaking for Suriyawong, as he had fallen in love with her. She had made no indication that she had any feelings at all for him, but with her departure, Suriyawong knew he no longer had a chance of pursuing a romantic relationship of any kind with her.

No one was certain of Suriyawong's relationship with Achilles. He appeared to be his closest ally, but Peter believed it was a ruse. Achilles, however, must have believed it was real because he named Suriyawong the Acting Hegemon during an unsuccessful power grab for the office from Peter.

Suriyawong was never truly loyal to Achilles, he only made the world think he was so he could gain Achilles's trust. When Achilles's life was in Bean's hand, he pleaded with Suriyawong to kill Bean. Suriyawong refused, turning his back on Achilles and reaffirming his loyalty to Peter Wiggin, the Hegemon. Bean killed Achilles, which had been in Suriyawong's plans all along.

Peter spun the incident in the press and to other world leaders such as Ambul (who had become the top official in Thailand) that Suriyawong's deception had been under his orders.

In his restored position of trust in the Hegemony, Suriyawong traveled with Bean and Petra to Rwanda where they confronted the evil Dr. Volescu, who was creating a virus that would genetically alter the entire human race. He worked with a team of scientists tracking how far the virus may have spread.

As time passed, Suriyawong was essentially Peter's personal bodyguard, traveling with him around the world to dangerous meetings. Once Peter was able to ratify a constitution that unified many nations' peoples, Suriyawong led armies against those nations that attacked Peter's allies. His incredible skill as a leader led to swift victories, and many more countries joining the Hegemony, now called the Free People of Earth (FPE).

Suriyawong led the FPE armies as they intervened in the wars between China, India, and Russia. He received India's surrender and convinced Virlomi to encourage her people to join the FPE. He held her prisoner on behalf of the FPE, and she agreed to bring India into the world government fold.

Swingler, Dr. (SD)

Dr. Swingler was a high-profile scientist in the Hundred Worlds who briefly communicated with Libo, the chief scientist on Lusitania, regarding the pequeninos' habits.

Syfte (SD)

Syfte was the firstborn daughter of Valentine Wiggin and her husband Jakt. She was born on the planet Trondheim, approximately three thousand years after Ender's destruction of the Formics. She was tutored by Plikt, one of Ender's former university students.

She married a man named Lars, and together they traveled with her parents toward the planet Lusitania, hoping to protect that world from destruction.

Tablets ([IC])

Tablets were the term used on the planet Sorelledolce to describe disreputable news sources, or tabloids.

Tactical School ([EG], ES)

Tactical School is an unknown location in space where students who showed extra talent or initiative in Battle School were sent for additional training prior to going to Command School. Bean and several members of Ender's Dragon Army attended Tactical School for one week before being sent to aid Ender at Command School.

Target Balls (EG, ES)

Target balls were targeting devices used in the Battle Rooms of Battle School. They turned from white to red when hit by a flash pistol's beam.

Teczlo, Magdalena "Magda" (PL)

A friend of Brian's and Anne Wieczorek's, Magdalena Teczlo—or Magda as she was known—was a trained lawyer. She was at the Wieczorek house when Captains Hyrum Graff and Helena Rudolf arrived to make the final determination of John Paul Wieczorek's readiness for Battle School. She was present to offer legal advice to her friends, which she was not permitted to do given the International Fleet's overriding authority, so she angrily left.

Testing Officers (PB, CH)

The International Fleet sent officers throughout the world to test children—primarily male children, though young women were also tested—to see if they were qualified for Battle School, and potentially the next commander of the Fleet. A male officer visited the Madrid y Valencia household to test Bonzo Madrid before the boy was two years old, arguing "What if he is the next Mazer Rackham?"—a tactic typical of the International Fleet.

A female officer tested Han Tzu. Along with another male counterpart, this officer determined that Han Tzu had been given the answers to the tests—a crime. The male and female officers arrested Han Tzu's father, despite Han Tzu's conscious efforts to answer the tests incorrectly. They had seen the cheating through Han Tzu's monitor and made the arrest. The female officer gave Han Tzu another, unfamiliar test.

Thai Soldiers (SH, SP)

The Thai soldiers were loyal to their country, particularly in the aftermath of Ender's victory over the Formics. Many of them were trained by Bean Delphiki, and they all played an important role in protecting Thailand from invasion by the combined Indian and Pakistani armies, which were under the direction of Achilles Flandres.

Thrakos, General ([SH])

General Thrakos was a high-ranking officer in the Greek military. After the Formic Wars, he issued an order that Greek soldiers rescue the vacationing Delphiki family, whose lives were in jeopardy from unknown attackers.

T'it'u, Champi "Dumper" (EG, ES, SH, SG)

Dumper was promoted to Command School where he was one of Ender's unseen squadron leaders in the "exams" that were actually real battles.

Following the Formic War and Ender's victory, Dumper was one of the kidnapping victims that included ten other of Ender's soldiers. He was taken by his captor, Achilles Flandres, to Russia where he was forced to play war games first in the presence of his fellow prisoners and then in another separate location somewhere else in that country.

He was rescued by Russian operatives, along with the rest of his colleagues minus Petra Arkanian, after several months in solitary.

In the years that followed, Dumper became a shaman living alone in the Andes, giving spiritual guidance to those who sought him out. As with the rest of his Battle School colleagues, he was offered a new life in space but refused to leave Earth.

After refusing Peter's offer to go to space, Dumper was invited to help ratify the Hegemon's constitution and bring his homeland into the protection of the Hegemony. Dumper agreed, and though some of his followers who joined the Hegemony—or Free People of Earth as it was known—were attacked and killed, Peter protected him with the vast military resources at his disposal.

As Peter built the Hegemony into the Free People of Earth, Graff again offered Ender's colleagues the opportunity to leave Earth and govern a planet. It was his fear that Ender's army would be used in the worldwide conflict, manipulated by whatever political power rose to prominence, and he wanted to prevent that. Every member who received the offer, which did not include Han Tzu, Petra Arkanian, or Alai, said no. The others were already too involved in matters on Earth to leave.

Tolo, Abra (EG, EE)

Eleven-year-old Abra Tolo was the son of original colonists in the first human settlement of a former Formic world, Shakespeare. Very good with his hands, he worked hard on mechanical issues in the colony. He hero-worshipped Ender Wiggin and traveled with the colony's governor to explore an area near Shakespeare that would be suitable for new colonists.

Abra and Ender discovered a region of the planet that looked like a human giant had died there. Ender recognized the place as one from a game he played as a child. Abra, confused, asked Ender what it meant. Ender wouldn't give the boy any answers except to say that it was not a suitable spot for a colony.

Tolo, Ix (GB)

Ix Tolo was a xenobiologist on the former Formic world that was Ender Wiggin's first gubernatorial assignment. He had a wife, and a son named Po. He sent Po to accompany their friend, Sel Menach, on his study of the planet.

In Sel's absence, Ix became the acting governor of Shakespeare Colony. In this position, he greeted Ender Wiggin when the hero of the Formic War arrived to become the official governor of the colony.

Tolo, Mother (EE)

Mother Tolo was a woman of Chinese ancestry who lived in Shakespeare, the first human colony on a former Formic world. She was married to Ix Tolo, and they had several children together.

Tolo, Po (GB)

Po Tolo, the son of xenobiologist Ix Tolo, was a young man born on the former Formic planet that became a human colony and Ender Wiggin's first assignment. He traveled with senior xenobiologist Sel Menach and with him, discovered the Gold Bugs. He grew up to be a xenobiologist himself, devoting his life work to studying the Gold Bugs.

Po married Alessandra Toscano, one of the first wave of settlers to arrive at Shakespeare. They had at least one child together.

Toscano, Alessandra (YM, EE)

Thirteen-year-old Alessandra Toscano and her mother Dorabella were selected to be among the first colonists of the International Fleet's Dispersal Project to colonize former Formic worlds after Ender's victory. Alessandra was Italian, living in Monopoli. She didn't want to go to the new colony, but her mother tried to sway her with the prospect of finding a nice young man to marry among the other colonists.

Alessandra was so desperate to stay on Earth that she approached her estranged grandmother, seeking familial asylum. The encounter only furthered the rift between her mother and grandmother. Once her grandmother refused to take her in, Alessandra came to better understand her mother's relationship to her grandmother. Through this process she came to accept the idea of leaving with the colonists. She was particularly excited that Ender Wiggin would be their governor, though she didn't think she would marry him as her mother did.

She and Ender developed a friendship aboard their transport ship to the Formic world. Their relationship began when Ender met with all of the passengers so he could get to know them all individually before he was to be their governor. He and Alessandra got along very well, even though Ender worked very hard to prevent any romantic feelings from developing between them. Alessandra and her mother convinced Ender and Valentine to start up a play reading to help the passengers pass the time on the spaceship.

The ship's commanding officer, Admiral Morgan, thought the play was subversive, and canceled it. After meeting with Ender, however, he relented, and Alessandra was able to play Bianca in *The Taming of the Shrew* opposite Ender. The performance went well, and Alessandra's affection for Ender continued to grow.

Alessandra was shocked to see her mother flirting with Admiral Morgan after the play. She realized that her mother had set her eyes on the commanding officer and was going to convince him to marry her.

Her mother was also teaching Alessandra how to convince Ender to marry the young girl. Though Alessandra had feelings for Ender, she knew that he didn't fully return them. As the two-year space journey drew to a close, Dorabella taught Alessandra how to flirt with Ender so he would be interested in her. It didn't work, however, and Ender and Alessandra did not end up together. They remained friends, but were never lovers.

Once the colony ship arrived at Shakespeare, Alessandra chose to stay with the other settlers. Her mother was livid, but was forced to accept the law. Dorabella returned to the ship and her new husband, Admiral Morgan. Alessandra, though not involved in a relationship with Ender, was glad to be free of her mother's influence.

While living in Shakespeare, Alessandra met Po Tolo and fell in love with him. They were married two years after Alessandra arrived at the colony, and had at least one child together.

Toscano, Dorabella (YM, EE)

A poor Italian woman, Dorabella Toscano applied, and was accepted, to be among the first wave of colonists to settle former Formic worlds. She planned to take her thirteen-year-old daughter Alessandra with her.

Dorabella had a very negative relationship with her mother, and becoming free from that was her primary motivation in seeking to leave Earth and go into space. She also hoped her daughter would find a respectable young man to marry among the colonists—notably their announced governor, Ender Wiggin.

On board the colony ship, Dorabella set about trying to be the matchmaker for her daughter and Ender. She flirted on Alessandra's behalf, and even tried to get Ender and Alessandra to play opposite each other in a dramatic reading of Shakespeare's *The Taming of the Shrew*. The play reading was not popular with the ship's commanding officer, Admiral Quincy Morgan, who briefly canceled it. Once it was back on, Dorabella set her own sights on Admiral Morgan. She wanted a husband for herself, and not just any husband—she wanted the commander of the ship. She used her performance as the lead in the play to start him down the path of falling in love with her.

She continued to press Alessandra to pursue Ender. Even as their two-year space journey was drawing to a close, Dorabella wanted Alessandra to marry Ender. It was really so Dorabella would have connection to whatever power was strongest in the colony—Admiral Morgan or Ender—and she was insistent that Alesandra make a play for the young man with prospects. She even taught her daughter how to flirt.

The flirting didn't work, Alessandra and Ender were never lovers. Ender gave Alessandra the confidence to leave Dorabella's side, however. Dorabella did not stay on Shakespeare colony, but returned to the spaceship to rejoin her husband as he, having been humiliated by Ender, left for another colony. Alessandra chose to stay at Shakespeare, saying good-bye to her mother forever. Dorabella was livid, but could do nothing as Alessandra was abiding by the law.

Triumvirate (ES)

The "triumvirate" was the term given to the top three government leaders in the world government called the League. It encompassed the Hegemon, Strategos, and Polemarch.

Trondheim (*See* Hundred Worlds)

Tsutsumi, Yasujiro (CM)

Yasujiro Tsutsumi was a former student of the wise philosopher, Aimaina Hikari, on the planet Divine Wind. Yasujiro was a member of a wealthy, influential family on the Japanese world, and Hikari called upon him to use his family's wealth to change the minds of Starways Congress away from destroying the planet Lusitania.

Yasujiro was hesitant to try to make any kind of political movement, but Hikari told him how doing so would benefit his family and their wealth. Yasujiro agreed to at least explore the possibility with the rest of his extended family, who controlled the wealth.

Tsutsumi, Yoshiaki-Seiji "Yes Sir" (CM)

Yoshiaki-Seiji Tsutsumi, or "Yes Sir" as he was better known, was an influential Japanese business man among the Hundred Worlds. He held great power among the leaders of the Starways Congress. He was one of the great leaders Yasujiro Tsutsumi approached, hoping to dissuade the Starways Congress from destroying Lusitania.

Though Yes Sir did not speak, but had his friend and adviser Eiichi speak for him, his presence in the meeting implied his condoning of Yasujiro's goal.

Tug Captain (EG)

The tug captain was responsible for taking Ender and Graff to Command School at Eros. He was angry because the assignment meant he was to forever remain at Eros, no longer able to do what he loved—fly.

Ugarit (*See* Hundred Worlds)

Ulysses (ES)

Ulysses was a small bully on the streets of Rotterdam, Netherlands, whose position and authority in the culture of homeless children was challenged by Achilles Flandres and Sergeant. Achilles and Sergeant led a beating on Ulysses that resulted in a broken rib and a punctured lung. More, it served to prove Achilles's dominance among the other bullies. Ulysses's return to the streets from the hospital heralded a new unity among the bullies who hoped to gang up together against Achilles.

Achilles killed Ulysses nearly a year later. The murder was done secretly, and Achilles was never discovered as the killer, though Sister Carlotta figured it out. Achilles specifically confessed to killing Ulysses when Bean and his Rabbit Army trapped him at Battle School.

Uphanad, Captain (ES, SP)

Captain Uphanad was a teacher at Battle School during Ender's and Bean's time there. Bean stole Uphanad's computer password and used it to sign on as a teacher and obtain confidential information. Uphanad was chastised for the security breach, but was allowed to stay in his position at the school.

When Battle School was converted into the Ministry of Colonization after the Formic War was over, Uphanad stayed at the space station serving as the head of security.

He assisted the Wiggin family when they traveled to the Ministry for a

248 THE AUTHORIZED ENDER COMPANION

brief period while hiding from Achilles Flandres. During their time on the station, someone used Uphanad's computer to send a message to Achilles on Earth saying the Wiggins were on the station. Uphanad claimed someone had logged on as him, like Bean had years before, and sent the message. Hyrum Graff and the Wiggins believed it was Uphanad himself, though, who had exposed the Wiggins location.

Achilles had blackmailed Uphanad into being the mole at the Ministry. Hyrum Graff, with the help of the International Fleet's Digital Security Force, exposed Uphanad's treacherous actions. Peter Wiggin forgave Uphanad, understanding the challenge he faced with his family, but Graff was forced to fire him from the Ministry.

Utlannings (*See* Hierarchy of Alienness)

Van Hoot, Congressor Jan (SD)

A high-level political figure in the Starways Congress, Congressor Jan Van Hoot had written essays defining the power and authority of the Congress over the human colonized planets of the system known as the Hundred Worlds.

Varelse (*See* Hierarchy of Alienness)

Varsam (XN)

Varsam was the youngest child born to Valentine Wiggin and her husband Jakt on the planet Trondheim. At age sixteen, he accompanied his parents on their journey into space, hoping to protect the world Lusitania from annihilation.

He was a member of Ender's search party that went into the pequeninos' land on Lusitania, hoping to save Ender's stepson, Quim, from being killed by the so-called piggies.

Vatican Contact (SH)

The Vatican contact was a go-between for Peter Wiggin's political pundit alias Locke, and the nun-in-hiding Sister Carlotta and Bean. The contact joked that he would not read the e-mail messages that went back and forth, because working in the Vatican had taught him to keep his eyes closed on confidential matters.

Victorious Fleet (EG)

"Victorious Fleet" was the nickname given to the fleet of spaceships Ender Wiggin commanded through simulators that defeated the Formics.

Vid (PL, TP, EGS, EG, ES)

Vids was the name for all video media. A vid could be any movie, news broadcast, war film, or any other moving visual media.

Vidman (SG)

The vidman was the name given to the equivalent of a television cameraman. He was responsible for filming vids for airing on the nets. He filmed Alai's speech to the Muslim world.

Vila Alta (*See* Hundred Worlds)

Vila Atrás (*See* Hundred Worlds)

Vila das Aguas (*See* Hundred Worlds)

Vila dos Professores (*See* Hundred Worlds)

Vila Última (*See* Hundred Worlds)

Vila Velha (*See* Hundred Worlds)

Vinicenze, Enzichel (IC)

Enzichel Vinicenze was a conglomerate with many holdings on the planet Sorelledolce.

Virlomi (EE, SH, SP, SG)

Virlomi was a Battle School graduate who completed her time at the School before Ender arrived. She was a talented military strategist from India and was given a good job within the Indian military.

During her time at Battle School, she met Petra Arkanian, who was several years younger. After Ender's victory over the Formics, and when Achilles Flandres positioned himself in power in India, Virlomi saw that he'd brought Petra with him. Virlomi could see, though, that Petra was an unwilling participant in Achilles's plans for world domination.

After Petra made an offhanded comment to Virlomi that implied she was Achilles's prisoner, Virlomi searched the computer networks to see for whom Petra really intended the message. Virlomi was successful in discovering the forum where Petra intended the message to be posted and left it there for its intended target to find.

Achilles also saw the message and planned to execute Virlomi for posting it, but Virlomi disappeared before Achilles had the chance to kill her. She escaped to what she knew would be a potential target of the Thai military, led by Bean and Suriyawong on their offensive into India.

She waited there for them, and spoke with Suriyawong, offering her services of intelligence on Achilles's headquarters and Petra's location. Suriyawong, in an effort to win the trust of the soldiers loyal to Virlomi, bowed before her. He took her to a helicopter where the act of obeisance stopped. Virlomi there guided Bean to Achilles. She helped plan a rescue mission for Petra and an assassination of Achilles.

Though not a big part of the mission itself, Virlomi witnessed Petra's safe return and Achilles's escape. Reunited with Petra, she felt mixed emotions: joy for Petra's return, but also sadness as India had been taken over by the Chinese. She vowed to work with her people to free India from the Chinese oppressors.

Virlomi was brought to Brazil to live in the secure compound of the Hegemony, but had to go back into hiding when it was revealed that Achilles Flandres was to arrive in Brazil, too. It made Suriyawong sad as he'd fallen in love with her and wanted to marry her. Virlomi found Suriyawong annoying and had no interest in him.

Unlike the rest of the people who went into hiding when Achilles reached Brazil, Virlomi did not go into the custody of the Minister of Colonization, Hyrum Graff. Instead she made her way back to India where she planned to subvert the Chinese occupation of her homeland.

The Chinese were only able to control the rich, ruling class of Indian citizens and virtually ignored the common folk. Virlomi sought opportunities to live in villages that had not been occupied. In one of these villages, she saw a small boy slowly placing pebbles in a road. He was building a small imaginary wall to protect "his" property from invasion.

Virlomi took this idea to heart, and rebuilt the boy's wall the next day, despite anger from those who kept the roads clear of pebbles. Virlomi made it seem that such walls were being created all over India as a symbolic gesture to keep the Chinese out of the villages. The walls represented the heart of India itself.

Many people began building stone walls in the roads in every village Virlomi visited. Her goal of causing a nonviolent uprising among the common people against their Chinese occupiers was working. The walls were getting the attention of the Chinese and rallying India against them.

Her "walls of India" had proven so unifying that Virlomi knew that she had great influence over the entire nation of India. She offered her people's help to Peter Wiggin and Bean in their efforts to free India from China's occupation. Bean, in turn, offered the help—with some concern—to Alai, the Muslim Caliph who was planning a military attack on China to free India and the rest of Asia.

Virlomi used her influence among the people of India to build an army of men that attacked the Chinese occupation force. They would attack bridges and kill as many soldiers as they could. Politically savvy, Virlomi easily convinced her people that the sacrifices they would make to drive the Chinese from India were worth it. Their acts of insurgency against their occupiers was designed to allow the Muslim soldiers of Alai's armies to do their work in China and the rest of Asia unimpeded.

Once the Muslim armies freed Asia, a small governing force was put in place in India. Virlomi faded from public view once again. She watched to see if her people were truly free, or if a new threat had entered her homeland. If they were free, she was happy. But if the Muslim forces needed to be pushed back, they would be, too. And Virlomi would again lead her people.

She had become a virtual goddess to her people, and even referred to herself as such. She used her divinity to cause great unrest among her people. They fought back against the Muslim occupiers that lived in India. Many Indians were killed, and they destroyed many of their own crops to prevent Muslim access to them. They killed many more Islamic soldiers than they lost of their own people.

It was a ploy by Virlomi to increase her position in the world. She appeared in the vids, calling on her people to fight the Muslims. But what she had really done was symbolically propose marriage to the Muslim leader Alai or possibly to the Chinese emperor Han Tzu. Whichever took her as his bride, they would have vast resources to conquer the region in which they lived—and much of the world. They would declare war together on the one who did not marry her.

Virlomi broadcast more vids of the violence the Muslim "liberators" were doing to her people. She called on Alai to stop the violence, or at least speak out against it. It caused Alai to travel to India where he executed the general who was leading the armies in their seditious acts.

Alai set up a new Caliphate compound in India, where he ruled the Muslim world. Virlomi also set up her new residence in a hut just outside the compound. Her presence kept the Muslim soldiers and Alai from provoking the Hindus, while the Indian people did not provoke the Muslims.

Virlomi saw and spoke with many of her followers from her hut. She continued to have tremendous influence over all of India. When China released its prisoners from their time occupying India, Virlomi told her people to ignore the former prime minister on his return. No one paid him any heed, and though he sought reinstatement of his political power, he was exiled to the Netherlands solely because Virlomi had commanded he be ignored.

All was not perfect in Virlomi's own soul. She dreamed of her dead friend Sayagi who, in the vision, chastised her for becoming someone she truly wasn't by leaving behind her humble virtues and seeking so much power.

A short time later, Han Tzu, the emperor of China, visited Virlomi in her hut, and proposed marriage to unify China and India. Virlomi refused. Han Tzu left, hoping that the two Battle School graduates could be friends. Virlomi said that might possible, someday.

She decided that the husband she wanted was Peter Wiggin, but he refused her offer of marriage, and she refused his offer to bring India into his worldwide confederation of nations, the Free People of Earth. She was too power hungry to relinquish control of her people to him.

At the meeting with Peter she was also approached by Hyrum Graff and Mazer Rackham who made her the same offer they'd made many other Battle School graduates—leave Earth and go into space as the governor of a human colony.

Rejected by Peter, Virlomi set her sights on Alai the Muslim Caliph. She convinced Alai to marry her, uniting the Muslim and Hindu worlds. But she viewed even her relationship with Alai as a stepping stone to more power, and not as a true marriage. While Alai had hoped the union would bring peace, Virlomi wanted to use the combined forces to attack China.

Alai tried to dissuade Virlomi from launching the attack against the Chinese, but with little success. Though he thought he loved her when they got married, he realized now he didn't. But he could not tell her that; she was dangerous, believing herself to be a goddess of India.

She used the combined Hindu and Muslim armies at her disposal to attack China. Russia also attacked China and India hoping to capitalize on their weakened state. China called on Peter's Free People of Earth and received military support from much of the world. Virlomi was soundly defeated.

Humiliated at the military defeat, Virlomi realized that she had, in her arrogance, caused the deaths of thousands of Indians. She was captured on the battlefield by Suriyawong, and convinced that she should encourage her people to join the Free People of Earth.

Heartbroken over her self-delusion, she admitted her humanity and sought to forget the evil she'd done, thinking she was a god. She was sent into space and given a planet in the Hundred Worlds to govern.

Assigned to the planet Ganges, which would be the first human settlement on a planet that was not originally a Formic world, Virlomi viewed her governorship as a penance for the wrongs she'd done on Earth. She found herself agreeing with the Hegemony that she should have been stopped, and didn't want to be compared to Achilles Flandres.

While awaiting her transport ship, Virlomi noticed one of her settlers, Nichelle Firth, who seemed obsessed with the name Achilles Flandres. Virlomi assumed that Nichelle's son was fathered by Achilles. Throughout the voyage, Virlomi paid close attention to Nichelle and her son, determined to keep tabs on them on Ganges.

More than a decade after they had all arrived at Ganges, Virlomi demanded to see Achilles II. She told the then-sixteen-year-old boy that his father was a monster. Achilles II reacted by calling Virlomi a dictator who manipulated elections to stay in power. The war of words became physical when Achilles II struck Virlomi in the face. She had Achilles II arrested, and sentenced him to be exiled off her planet.

When Ender Wiggin arrived a few weeks later, Virlomi allowed him to meet with Achilles II. Ender told Achilles II that his real parents were Bean Delphiki and Petra Arkanian. This revelation caused a great change in Achilles II, who changed his name to Arkanian Delphiki. Virlomi commuted his sentence and remained as the governor of Ganges when Ender left the planet.

Volescu, Doctor (ES, [SH] SP, SG)

Doctor Volescu was a scientist who took Anton's banned research and furthered it into practice. He created twenty-four genetically altered fertilized embryos, turning Anton's Key, and causing them to develop mentally and physically faster than normal. When his work was discovered, twenty-three of the twenty-four babies were destroyed. One escaped—Bean.

Years later, Sister Carlotta confronted Volescu, desperately trying to discover information about Bean's past. Volescu told her some details about what he'd done to the embryos, but didn't know for certain that Bean had survived. It was through his conversation with the nun that he learned that the one remaining embryo had, in fact, lived.

Sister Carlotta hated him, saying that he didn't deserve to have a son like Bean. She soon discovered that he was not Bean's genetic father. Volescu's half-brother Julian Delphiki was. Volescu's mother had an affair with the older Delphiki. Volescu and Julian knew of one another, but how much contact they'd shared is unknown.

Nearly a decade after Ender's victory over the Formics, Volescu was released from his prison and opened a fertility clinic in Rotterdam. Achilles Flandres, a serial killer and Battle School dropout with world-dominating aspirations, had pulled strings to get Volescu released.

Petra Arkanian and Bean were married and went to Rotterdam to learn if Volescu could determine if their embryos would be free of the genetic mutation he'd given Bean. Volescu lied and said he had a test for this. In reality he didn't, but he helped create the embryos for Bean and Petra anyway. He secretly saved several embryos—which Bean thought were destroyed—to give to Achilles in exchange for getting Volescu out of prison. He also facilitated an unsuccessful kidnapping attempt on Bean and Petra at the women's clinic where Petra had undergone the implantation procedure.

Volescu spread the stolen embryos to different surrogates around the world and hid in a safe house Achilles provided for him. When Achilles was killed, Hyrum Graff and Mazer Rackham tracked Volescu's movements and passed on the information to Bean, who sought to regain the embryos that belonged to him.

Bean and Petra, along with a great security detail from the Hegemony, traveled to Rwanda to Volescu's safe house. Bean nearly killed the doctor for spreading the embryos to surrogates throughout the world. It seemed impossible to find the embryos, and—in Bean's opinion—Volescu's death would have made up for it. Petra stopped him from killing Volescu, however.

The group from the Hegemony learned that Volescu had created a virus that would turn Anton's Key in all future generations of humanity. Volescu fashioned himself to be God, controlling the evolution of the species.

He was imprisoned in a Hegemony detention center and refused to cooperate with interrogators. Bean, Petra, and the rest of Peter Wiggin's staff would have to do much research on their own to learn the location of the embryos and how far the Volescu virus may have spread.

Bean confronted Volescu one last time with similar negative results. It was clear the doctor would not live much longer in captivity, and there was talk of sending him to space. Regardless, he maintained that he did not know where Bean's embryos were.

The International Fleet, who held Volescu, had found him guilty of many crimes and sentenced him to death. The punishment would not be carried out for years, though, as the I.F. ordered him to try to find a cure for Anton's Key. As long as he worked on it, he would be kept alive. Once the cure was found, the I.F. promised, he would be taken into space and allowed to live in a new colony on a distant planet.

von Hesse, Ivanova Santa Catarina "Novinha" (SG, SD, XN)

Novinha was the daughter of prominent xenobiologists on the planet Lusitania. The child of Brazilian settlers, Novinha was well known in the colony. Her parents were killed finding a cure for the deadly virus known as the Descolada. Their deaths, though devastating to Novinha, were celebrated in the colony, as they had discovered the cure and were the final funerals from the Descolada.

Novinha was ostracized from the community because of the different reaction to her parents' deaths that she felt. She was thought to have one friend—a boy named Marcão—though "friend" was perhaps a bit of an exaggeration.

She was angry that the pope, on Earth, beatified her parents, and it led to her distancing herself from the church. By age thirteen (eight years after her parents' deaths) she wanted to take the xenobiologist certification test. It was years before the usual age, but thanks to help from the colony xenologist, Pipo, she got permission.

It was her goal to study the planet's native life, the pequeninos, or piggies as they were known, to the level that the "Speaker for the Dead" had more than three thousand years earlier. She admired the Speaker, particularly as he had helped humanity understand the only other "alien" race it had encountered—the Formics. The Speaker had transformed human prejudice and shown Ender Wiggin's annihilation of an entire species to be evil. She wanted to be the Speaker for the piggies in the same fashion.

Novinha was consistently standoffish, but warmed up to Pipo and his son Libo. They worked closely together, forming a tight bond. She was particularly close to Libo. The two slowly fell in love.

Pipo raced to confirm a finding—that he didn't share with Novinha—with the piggies. It was Novinha, alongside Libo, who discovered his dead body a few hours later. He'd been killed by the piggies, and Novinha lost another parental figure, which was crushing to her.

She was not comforted by any of the colonists or priests in the aftermath of Pipo's death, and decided to call for a Speaker—something contrary to the Catholic culture in which she lived—to Speak Pipo's death. Little did she know that the Speaker she'd contacted was Ender Wiggin, the xenocide who had killed the entire Formic species three thousand years before.

As she waited for the Speaker to arrive, Novinha realized how much she loved Libo. She wanted to marry him and would not share her research with him because she didn't want him to die, too. She carried a great deal of guilt over Pipo's death, feeling that it had been her research on the Descolada that had caused him to be murdered by the piggies.

Five days after calling for the Speaker, Novinha canceled the request. As the years passed, she married not Libo, but rather Marcão, a boy she'd been nice to at school. He was abusive to her and her children. She'd conceived the children with Libo, but Marcão raised them as his own.

Libo was killed by the piggies, just as Pipo had been, and again Novinha lost someone she loved—this time, the love of her life. Marcão died shortly after that, too. Two of Novinha's children—Ela and Miro—also called for a Speaker to Speak Marcão's death. As Ender was already on his way to Speak Pipo's death, he continued to Lusitania to Speak about Novinha's husband.

Novinha had become a successful scientist, burying herself in her work. She would go to her lab before her children were awake and return home after the youngest ones had gone to bed. She was working hard to figure out how to clone a potato for the people of Lusitania to have more variety in their diet.

When she first met Ender, who had arrived at her house early one evening, she hated him. She tried to throw him out of her home, but her children defended him, showing his good virtues to her. Although Ender said things to her about Marcão that were hard to hear, she knew they were true. That night as she fell asleep, she dreamed that Ender was actually Libo, her dead lover come to save her.

Ender broke into Novinha's computer files, trying to learn about Pipo's death. When she confronted him about it, he didn't deny it. He also revealed that he knew that Libo was the father of her children. Novinha found this hard to bear as—in two days—Ender had already learned all of her secrets.

She attended the Speaking for Marcão and was exposed there as an adulteress. The entire planet now knew that she had an affair with Libo. Some of her own children turned against her, including Quim, who called her a whore in the middle of the ceremony.

Following the Speaking, Ender sent Ela to Novinha for help. The Starways Congress had revoked the planet's charter because of illegal activity

Miro had done with the pequeninos. Ender needed the information on the Descolada Novinha had kept secret for so long in order to save Miro's life.

Novinha agreed to reveal the information on the Descolada, and did so in the meeting of colony leaders. The entire population of Lusitania, she revealed, were carriers of the Descolada. By leaving the planet, any one person, plant, or animal would destroy the biosphere of whatever other planet they visited. In order to protect the other planets, and to save their own lives, the leaders of Lusitania used this information to rebel against the Starways Congress.

Minutes later, Novinha learned that her son Miro had been critically injured trying to climb the electrified fence that protected the pequeninos. She, along with the leaders of the planet, raced to his side.

She took Miro home to allow him to convalesce in privacy. There she discovered that he was paralyzed, but had limited movement of his hands and could move his jaw slightly. With her other children's help, Novinha was able to establish a pattern of communication with Miro. He wanted her to deliver a message to the piggies.

With Olhado and Quim, Novinha went into the forest and found Ender, Ouanda, and Ela, who were creating the treaty with the piggies. She told Ender that Miro was alive and that the piggies were planning to make war with the other tribes. The pequeninos confirmed it, and not doing so was added to the treaty.

Novinha was shocked to learn that the Speaker for the Dead who had exposed her adultery was actually Ender the Xenocide. She found comfort in this fact, and realized that Ender hadn't condemned her because he'd committed an act much more severe than she had.

Novinha and Ender grew close emotionally and attended mass together. Though she had initially hated him, Novinha found she was falling in love with Ender Wiggin. He was to be the father her children never had. They were married by Bishop Peregrino a few short months later. Novinha was by Ender's side when he released the Hive Queen near the pequenino land, giving the sole survivor of his xenocide the opportunity for new life.

As the years passed, Novinha and her daughter Ela realized that the Descolada virus had evolved and was again a deadly threat to all life on Lusitania—except for the pequeninos who needed it to live. She and Ela worked tirelessly, hoping to find a way to control the disease and save their world.

Thirty years later, now an old woman, Novinha continued her work with

Ela on discovering a way to create strains of potatoes that could survive the Descolada. Two of her other children, Quara and Grego, had also become scientists and worked diligently on understanding the deadly disease. Quara and Grego had differing perspectives on the Descolada. Quara thought the disease was a sentient creature while Grego felt it needed to be wiped out entirely regardless of consequence to the native life that depended on it for life and reproduction.

Novinha listened to the arguments each made, as well as Ela's views, and with her husband Ender decided that each child should pursue their research, and when more was known, the proper path of action would be known.

She, along with her other children and Ender, greeted Miro's spaceship when it returned from its journey to pick up Valentine Wiggin and bring her with him to Lusitania. Miro hadn't aged during the nearly three decades he was gone because of the effects of relativistic space flight. This caused some awkwardness among Novinha and her family when they first saw Miro.

There were times that Novinha could hear Ender talking to the sentient computer program Jane at night. It was as though Novinha found Ender in bed with another woman. It was difficult for her to bear. Jane wished that Ender's wife could see her as Ender's daughter, but it was not to be. Slowly, hatred for Jane built in Novinha's heart.

When she learned that her son, Quim, was setting off on a dangerous religious mission to the piggies, Novinha became surly. She reacted with hatred to Ender, hurting for fear that her son would die like Pipo and Libo had. She banned Ela from speaking about matters of science with Ender, and screamed her angry, hateful rhetoric about Jane at her husband. She even accused Ender of never loving her.

The fight was a difficult issue for Ender. He knew that she meant all the things she said and that the anger in her heart would not be easily pacified. He decided it would be best if he was not the one to tell her that she was correct: Quim had been killed by the piggies.

When Novinha learned from Miro that Quim had indeed been killed, she spiraled into a mournful rage. She slapped Miro and banned him from her house. The rest of her children left her, angry that she had made their family so divisive. All of her children spoke mean, hateful words to her as they left.

Heartbroken, Novinha left her home before reconciling with anyone in her family. She joined the abbey known as the Children of the Mind of Christ. Although the order was primarily for married couples who sought to serve Christ together, Novinha joined without Ender.

A few days later, Ender found Novinha at the abbey and attempted to reconcile with her. She refused him, citing his relationship with Jane as the biggest burden to their relationship. She also held him accountable for Quim's death, saying he had not done enough to prevent her son from pursuing the course of action that ultimately took his life.

She threw her whole self into the service at the abbey and was converted to their practices.

Meanwhile, Miro created a new, whole body for himself in Outspace. Novinha saw this as a miracle. She was so touched that she agreed to see Ender at the abbey when he came to visit.

She pleaded with him to join the Children of the Mind of Christ, but he refused, stating that he wanted to be with her, but not in a celibate marriage. They agreed to visit each other once a month, both hoping the other would commit to stay.

It was Ender who gave in. He joined Novinha at the Children of the Mind of Christ. She told her husband that she loved him and wanted to be with him until one of them died. She hoped that unlike with Pipo, Libo, Marcão, or Quim, she would die first this time.

Novinha also told Ender that she no longer blamed him for Quim's death. She understood the importance of her son's religious endeavors. It was her own conversion to Christ that had brought her out of her angry, hateful feelings toward Ender and the world. She was committed to the order to which she belonged and was glad to have her beloved husband by her side.

A few days later, Novinha found Ender sleeping in the garden. He was struggling to breathe deeply. She called for help, and many from the abbey came running. Ender was apparently dying. He wouldn't respond to any of the attempts to wake him. Novinha was terrified, and again blamed herself for what appeared to be the death of yet another loved one. She blamed herself for forcing him to bend to her selfish religious attempts at redemption in the abbey. He hadn't wanted to come and now, like Pipo and Libo before him, would die because of her.

She waited outside the room where Ender lay dying, hoping for news or a miracle. She heard Plikt, Ender's student and Valentine's friend, say that Ender had spoken, saying "Peter." This enraged Novinha and led to an angry confrontation between the three women Ender loved most dearly: Novinha, Valentine, and Plikt. As they hurled insults at one another, they realized—Novinha included—that they all loved Ender. They agreed to set aside their differences, at least temporarily, hoping desperately that Ender would come through.

Novinha expressed over the course of this that she was sad she'd been the cause of Ender's suffering and for so selfishly not letting go of any pain. With Valentine's suggestion, she tried to let Ender go.

Ender briefly regained consciousness, and Novinha was able to tell him that she loved him, but it was time for him to leave her and be free of his obligations to her. Ender accepted Novinha's words, and his soul (or Auía) left his body. The shell of a person that remained crumbled to dust, and then less than dust. All that remained was a few hairs of his head. Novinha kept a handful to bury.

She mourned privately in her home with her sons Olhado and Grego by her side. Though sad, she knew she had done the right thing. She loved Ender and had let him go.

She attended Ender's funeral in the shadows of the pequenino fathertrees, Rooter and Human. There she buried his remains and said good-bye for the last time to her husband.

von Hesse-Gussman, Ekaterina Maria Aparecida do Norte "Cida" (SD)

Cida was the top xenobiologist on the planet Lusitania. Actively Catholic, she and her husband Gusto had several children. Most notable among them was Novinha, who sought to follow in her parents' footsteps by becoming a xenobiologist.

Cida was killed by the disease known as the Descolada. However, her death was not in vain as she and Gusto found a cure for the virus shortly before they died. Theirs were the last deaths from the disease on the planet.

Wahabi, Ghaffer (SH, SG)

Ghaffer Wahabi was the Prime Minister of Pakistan. He was a brilliant academic who understood world affairs very well. He was a loyal leader of his people and wanted nothing to do with India. But when Achilles Flandres, a former Battle School student and serial killer, inserted himself into an influential position with the Indian hierarchy and convinced the Indian military leaders to pull their troops off the border with Pakistan, Wahabi met with him.

Achilles was a master manipulator and was able to convince Wahabi to pull the Pakistani troops from the border as well. India and Pakistan would work together to control Asia and the world. Wahabi refused unification with India, but saw the benefits of working with that country to become the dominant forces in the world.

It was all a ploy by Achilles to weaken the Indian and Pakistani armies and allow China to take over Asia with great ease. Wahabi was ignorant to this, though, and maintained his military's sights on Iran and the rest of the Muslim world.

China defeated India and Pakistan. The nations were rescued only after help from the Muslim world led by Alai. Alai wondered what Wahabi felt when it was he who had risen to power and influence and united the Muslim world—not Wahabi. The answer was simple. Wahabi became an ally to Alai, living with him in the newly established Caliphate compound in India.

Warmaker (XN)

Warmaker was a fathertree among the pequeninos, the patriarchal order of the native life on the planet Lusitania.

He captured the Catholic priest, Quim, who had traveled to preach the gospel to his family of piggies and argued doctrine with him. Warmaker starved Quim to death, exposing him to the Descolada, but was surprised to see how few of his "brother" pequeninos celebrated the death.

However, Warmaker was able to win more converts from among the pequeninos when the human citizens attacked the pequenino land, killing many piggies in the process. Warmaker taught them that humans were not worthy of the Holy Ghost, but that the pequeninos themselves were the chosen vessels.

War of Xenocide (IC)

"War of Xenocide" was the name given to the third Bugger War after Ender's victory was revealed to be the worst act in human history.

Waterjumper (CM)

Waterjumper was a pequenino, the native sentient life of the planet Lusitania. He was a scientist and worked with his fathertree, Human, and the Formic Hive Queen to reconnect a small interplanetary computer network where Jane, the sentient computer program that lived in a human body, could control faster-than-light travel.

Watersnakes (SD)

Watersnakes were one of very few life-forms that lived on the planet Lusitania. They had somehow evolved to not be killed by the plague known as the Descolada that wiped out most of the planet's life.

Wei Dun-nuan (CH)

Wei Dun-nuan was a bright young Chinese woman who taught Han Tzu the primary language of the world, Common, and refused to take Tzu out of his home to practice his reading and speaking skills.

Western Guilford Middle School (EG)

Western Guilford Middle School was the Earth-bound school (or Ground School) that Peter and Valentine Wiggin attended after Ender left Earth for Battle School.

White Lotus (SG)

White Lotus was a soldier in the Chinese Army in the aftermath of Ender's victory over the Formics. She grew disgruntled with the Chinese government when its leader, Snow Tiger, had disregarded the military advice of Battle School graduate Han Tzu.

She was ordered to present Han Tzu to Snow Tiger, presumably for execution. Han Tzu went willingly, and both he and White Lotus were witnesses to Snow Tiger's assassination. Han Tzu was crowned Emperor in his stead, which made White Lotus happy, as she was loyal to him.

White Tiger of the West ([XN])

White Tiger of the West was the name of one of the pantheon of gods on the Chinese-settled planet Path.

Wieczorek, Andrzej (English: Andrew) (PL, [TP])

Andrew Wieczorek was the sixth of Brian and Anne Wieczorek's nine children. He was tested by the International Fleet against his father's orders. He had a close relationship to John Paul, his immediately younger brother. Andrew "Ender" Wiggin, his nephew, was named for him.

Wieczorek, Anna (English: Anna) (PL)

An older sister to John Paul Wieczorek, and aunt to Ender Wiggin, Anna was one of the Wieczorek's nine children. She was number three, and as such made the family noncompliant with world government's population laws. As number three, she was the first child not allowed to attend school, though her parents homeschooled all of the children anyway to avoid the anti-Catholic rhetoric of the public schools. She was taught at home by her mother, Anne, for whom she was named. She hated learning polynomials.

Wieczorek, Anne (English: Anne) (PL, [TP])

John Paul Wieczorek's mother, Anne, was also the grandmother to Ender Wiggin. She had a favorite sister growing up, Zofia, for whom her granddaughter Valentine Wiggin received her middle name. As the mother of nine children, she and the rest of her family fell into the category "noncompliant," which referred to the population laws that allowed only two children per family. Only those two children were allowed to go to school, but Anne and her husband Brian felt the public schools were too anti-Catholic and as such Anne homeschooled her other children. She was like many in her native country of Poland, which itself was considered a noncompliant nation. Because of their strong Catholic roots, the Wieczorek family felt it wrong to use any type of birth control and that families should have as many children as possible. Consequently their family was very large.

Anne doubted her son John Paul's ability to learn faster than his older siblings until the International Fleet representatives—led by Captain Hyrum Graff—came to test the children. She was initially upset that John Paul was tested so young, but realized that she had ignored his talent and ability. It was a hard revelation for her to bear.

She moved to America with her family when Graff and John Paul made an arrangement that the family would not be poor. They changed their name to Wiggin upon entry into the United States.

Wieczorek, Arakdiusz (English: Arek) aka "Baby 2" (PL)

The second-youngest child of the Wieczoreks' nine children. This baby's name and gender are unknown in the story, but Orson Scott Card has stated he is a boy named Arakdiusz. When the Wieczorek family moved to America and changed their surname to Wiggin, it is believed this child joined them. Peter Wiggin was given his middle name, Arkady, in tribute to him.

Wieczorek, Brian (English: Brian) (PL, [TP])

Brian Wieczorek was a proud Polish man, and an equally proud Catholic. With the rise of the Hegemony and the International Fleet, Brian felt that much of his nationalism and identity were being lost. It is interesting to note that he has such an un-Polish name, yet felt such a loyalty to his country and his people. With his wife, Anne, he fathered nine children, making his family tremendously "noncompliant" with the world's population laws, which allowed for only two children in a family.

Brian worked hard to feed his family as a university professor, but lost that position and had to take a clerical job because of his family's noncompliance. The loss put great financial and emotional strain on the family.

A short time later, Brian was angry when the International Fleet sent a delegation led by Captains Helena Rudolf and Hyrum Graff to test his children. Confrontational, he initially forbade the Fleet from testing or speaking with John Paul, their seventh child. His interaction got so heated that he actually hit Hyrum Graff, a very serious offense. Graff did not arrest Brian, however. The violence, though, ended up causing John Paul to make a decision that hurt Brian even more: he agreed to move the family to America and to change their name to Wiggin.

As John Paul's father, Brian was also Ender Wiggin's grandfather.

Wieczorek, Cyryl (English: Cyril) aka "Baby 1" (PL)

The youngest of the Wieczoreks' nine children. This baby's name and gender are unknown in the story, but have been revealed by Orson Scott Card to have been a boy named Cyril. It is believed this child moved from Poland to America with the family, which changed its last name to Wiggin.

Wieczorek, Katarzyna (English: Catherine) (PL)

Catherine Wieczorek was the second oldest child of the Wieczoreks' nine kids. She was legally allowed to attend school, but because of her parents' fears that the public schools were too anti-Catholic, she was taught at home with the rest of her siblings. She was not allowed to take the Battle School screening test when the International Fleet arrived to administer it because of her gender.

Wieczorek, Mikolaj (English: Nicholas) (PL)

Nicholas is fourth of the nine children of Brian and Anne Wieczorek. He was tested by the International Fleet for Battle School screening, against his father's wishes.

Wieczorek, Piotr (English: Peter) (PL)

The oldest of Brian and Anne Wieczorek's nine children, Peter was smart. He was legally allowed to attend school as he and his sister Catherine were the only "compliant" children in the Hegemony's population laws. It is believed that Peter Wiggin, this Peter's nephew and the future Hegemon, was named for him.

When Captain Helena Rudolf arrived at the family's home to administer the International Fleet's Battle School screening test, Peter was not allowed to take it. He was considered too old at age thirteen and was jealous of his younger brothers who were required to be tested.

Wieczorek, Tomasz (English: Thomas) (PL)

Thomas is fifth of the nine children of Brian and Anne Wieczorek. He was tested by the International Fleet, against his father's wishes. His brother John Paul gave his youngest son Andrew (Ender) the middle name Thomas in tribute.

Wiggin, Andrew "Ender" Thomas (Polish Name: Andrzej Tomasz) (EGS, EG, WG, ES, [EH], GB, [YM], EE, [SH], [SP], [SG], IC, SD, XN, CM)

Andrew "Ender" Wiggin was born the third child of John Paul and Theresa Wiggin. Due to government population laws, third children were extremely rare and often mocked for their position in the family. He was named for his father's brothers, Andrew (Andrzej) and Thomas (Tomasz) Wieczorek.

Ender was often beaten physically and abused emotionally by his older brother Peter. At age three, after learning arithmetic from his sister Valentine (whom he loved deeply), Ender was given the International Fleet's monitor in the back of his neck. The device recorded Ender's actions, transmitting them to the Fleet, who used the findings to determine if a monitor carrier was eligible for Battle School.

At age six, while a student in "regular" school, Ender's monitor was removed. This was usually the sign of not making Battle School and generally led to further estrangement from one's peers. When Ender was mocked for losing his monitor, he viciously attacked a fellow student named Stilson, injuring him severely. Ender would describe the attack as an attempt to win not only that fight, but all the rest, too, so Stilson would leave him alone.

Ender had a difficult relationship with his older brother Peter. Peter often beat Ender, usually during their games of "Astronaut and Bugger," a form of "cops and robbers" based on the Formic invasions. Ender was terrified of his brother, and was sure he was a murderer at heart.

The day following his fight with Stilson, Ender met Colonel Hyrum Graff who recruited him for Battle School. Graff explained Battle School to Ender, and in spite of his parents' objections, Ender agreed to go.

On the spaceship flight to Battle School, Ender first experienced zero-gravity and found it disorienting. He laughed at Graff, seeing him in zero-G for the first time, which led to Ender being spurned by the other children as Graff insisted that only Ender was smart enough to find that funny. Graff made further efforts to alienate Ender from his peers by making him a teacher's pet. The other students were jealous and disliked Ender. This was made worse when another student attacked Ender in the spaceship, and Ender broke the boy's arm. Ender was even more upset to hear Graff say that they weren't friends, but that Graff had a job to do, and he ordered Ender to be the best of the soldiers.

At Battle School, Ender found his bunk, the only one available in his room. Following instructions given by the computer, he also discovered his locker and the jumpsuits it contained. He met Dap, his supervisor, and learned quickly the geography of Battle School.

Ender enjoyed watching the video games the older boys played and, by watching, figured out how to win the games. He beat an older boy at the video game on only his second attempt playing. Though the victory did not gain Ender any respect, it was personally gratifying to know that he could learn and win so quickly.

A short time later, Bernard (the boy whose arm Ender broke on their spaceflight) assembled a gang of fellow students. Like Peter, Bernard enjoyed picking on Ender. Bernard also mocked other students including a boy named Shen. Ender, tired of the bullying, hacked into the school's computer system and sent messages under assumed names such as "God" to the other students' computer desks. These messages mocked Bernard and resulted in Bernard bullying others further to reassert his standing among the students. The messages also served to make students like Shen grow loyal to Ender. These loyal students became the members of Ender's own gang in the school.

When Ender first entered the Battle Room at Battle School, it was an awkward experience, though by befriending Alai—Bernard's best friend—he was able to work up rudimentary skills of zero-gravity motion. The two new friends teamed up, and with Shen and Bernard, they froze the rest of the first-timers in the Battle Room.

One of Ender's most common activities during the allotted "Free Play" time each day was playing the "Giant's Drink," a video game that seemed unbeatable. Ender grew obsessed with defeating the Giant in the game, and though the process was frustrating, he eventually won. His character in the game killed the Giant, a fact that haunted the young boy. He felt that he was a murderer.

But accomplishing the impossible had a surprising consequence. Ender was promoted to be a member of the Salamander Army, commanded by

Bonzo Madrid. The promotion came over a year early, when Ender was still six. Such assignments never came before a student was eight. As he left his launch group, Ender shared a brief, tender moment with Alai, solidifying their friendship.

Bonzo resented Ender who, he felt, was too young and inexperienced to be in an army. Ignoring the harsh treatment from his commander, Ender decided to contribute all he could and learn even more during his time with Salamander. In Salamander Army, Ender also met Petra Arkanian, one of the few female students at Battle School. Both outcasts, Ender and Petra became friends. Petra took Ender to the Battle Room for an extra practice since Ender wasn't allowed to practice with his army. For further practice, Ender organized Free Play practice sessions in the Battle Room, inviting his friends from his launch group.

Ender obeyed Bonzo's orders, which included not drawing his weapon in actual battles. In a battle against Leopard Army, however, Ender finally broke from his commander and fired his weapon. As a result, Bonzo traded Ender to Rat Army. Ender was seven now. He'd been at Battle School for just over a year.

Rat Army had been commanded by the soldier known as "Rose the Nose." Like Bonzo, he tried unsuccessfully to get Ender to stop his practices with his launch group. He also ordered Ender not to use his computer desk. Ender disobeyed the orders on the advice of his toon leader, Dink Meeker.

Ender and Dink, while not friends per se, had established a positive relationship. Though Dink held a cynical view of Battle School and the Formic War with which Ender disagreed, they were supportive of one another. Dink furthered Ender's training, and after a short time slipping to number four in the Battle School rankings, Ender was back in the top position—the best soldier in the school.

Ender's launch group practices got smaller because of rumors of blacklisting. But after his unofficial team defeated several older boys, many commanders sent some of their soldiers to Ender for additional practice.

Late in the year, Dink and his fellow Dutchman, Flip, secretly exchanged holiday gifts. This infuriated Zeck Morgan, a fellow member of Rat Army and a religious zealot. Zeck complained that an apparent expression of religious devotion had gone unpunished and convinced a group of Muslim students to say their daily prayers publicly. The Muslims were arrested for the religious observance, and Zeck was ostracized from the rest of Battle School for his role in the religious uprising. It wasn't until Ender spoke with Zeck, and helped him realize the actual rights and wrongs about his religious traditions, that Zeck found any kind of acceptance among the Battle School community. It took Zeck beating Ender up, but it worked, and Ender had once again shown himself to be a remarkable person.

At this same time, Ender renewed his obsession with the Fantasy Game where he'd killed the Giant. As he played it more, Ender killed wolflike children and a snake. He realized that there was a part of him that was a killer, and it made him sad. He even saw a reflection of himself in the game's mirror, but the image was of Peter. Ender knew, deep down, that he was no different from his murderous older brother.

By the time Ender was nine, he felt like nothing much had changed at Battle School. He'd become a toon leader in Phoenix Army, with his friend Petra as his commander. He had fallen into a bit of a depression. Seeing Peter's face as his own in the mirror had been devastating. But more upsetting was the letter he received from Valentine. Although positive in tone, Valentine's letter had been forced by the International Fleet; his beloved sister had been made a pawn in the Battle School's game against him. Angry and sad, Ender threw himself into his studies more fully, fighting a war not against the Formics, but the officers at Battle School who had manipulated Valentine.

Only three years after entering Battle School, Ender was promoted to commander at age nine—unheard of in the history of the school. But it was the result of his being at the top of the rankings for years. (In the original "Ender's Game" short story, Ender was eleven at this point.) He was given a new army, Dragon Army, a stigmatized name that had not been used in four years.

Unbeknownst to Ender, six-year-old Bean had been assigned by Graff and Battle School instructor Dimak to put together a list of soldiers for a hypothetical army, but he could only use launchies and soldiers whose commanders had requested they be transferred. Bean knew this army was to be commanded by Ender and tried to create as good a list as possible. Bean believed in the soldiers he selected for Ender, including himself, even if the rest of the school felt they were too young and inexperienced.

Ender made the best of what was a seemingly bad situation. His army had been made up of new recruits, three years his junior, and lacking in experience. He asked Major Anderson for more experienced troops, but was denied.

Ender and Bean didn't get along at first in Dragon Army. Both saw the other as arrogant, without really realizing that they were actually teaching each other a great number of leadership skills. On the first day of practice as an army, Bean told Ender he wanted command of a toon. Ender said no, but Bean promised he'd earn one. Four weeks later he did—a special toon, unusual for armies at Battle School.

Following his promotion, Ender was not allowed to practice with his friends from his launch group. This put a wall up between him and the others, particularly Alai who had been told that Ender was too good to practice with the "little guys" now. Though it had been a lie put forth by the officers, Alai and the others believed it, and it motivated them to try to defeat Ender's Dragon Army.

Despite the challenges of having new, inexperienced soldiers in his army, Ender trained them well, and they went undefeated. Army after army fell to them, sometimes even two armies or more per day. But Ender's war was not with the other armies; it was with the officers of Battle School. It seemed the officers at Battle School realized this, and they returned fire. They made Ender's schedule that much more difficult, taxing his army almost to the breaking point. Yet, again thanks to Ender's strategy and leadership, the army was undefeated.

They had beaten Rabbit Army, Phoenix Army, and five other armies in the course of a week—one army a day. Ender took to watching the video footage of previous Formic battles, particularly those of Mazer Rackham and his "Strike Force." Other commanders followed suit, hoping to figure out what made Ender so dominant, but none was able to grasp what Ender did. Ender knew that all the real strategy had been edited out of the vids, but he studied them nonetheless.

Ender felt tired and on the verge of breaking. He confided in Bean that he thought the officers of the school would break him soon. Bean comforted Ender and reassured him that all would be well. He was, after all, Ender Wiggin—the best soldier in the history of Battle School.

Ender earned the ire of his former nemesis and commander, Bonzo Madrid. Bonzo was embarrassed by the shellacking he and his Salamander Army had endured at the hand of Ender's army. He made the decision to kill Ender. Dink Meeker and Petra Arkanian, both commanders and once friends of Ender's, made efforts to warn him.

Bonzo made his move when Ender was in the shower. Accompanied by Bernard and some other older boys, Bonzo moved to attack Ender. Ender used his soapy body and the bathroom's humidity to his advantage and struck back.

With vicious blows to Bonzo's face, chest, stomach, and groin, Ender unknowingly killed his attacker, saving his own life. Ender felt great guilt over beating Bonzo so severely.

Because of Ender's tremendous leadership in Dragon Army, most of his soldiers were promoted to command their own armies three years earlier than normal. His soldiers were nine, and their promotions spoke highly of the training and leadership found within Ender Wiggin. A similar tribute was given to Ender himself as he was sent to Command School, skipping over the traditional steps of first attending Tactical and Support School.

Before going to Command School, Ender was sent to Greensboro, North Carolina, where his family had moved. He saw Valentine and told her how scared he was that he couldn't defeat the Formics. He told her that he didn't understand them, and as such was sure they'd beat him. Valentine did a good job convincing her brother that he was qualified to beat the Buggers, restoring, at least momentarily, Ender's confidence.

At Command School, Ender was taught to use the communication device known as the ansible and trained in simulators. He mastered the simulators; and after a year of training on them, stated they never got any harder. Immediately after he made that comment, Ender noticed that Graff left him and he was given a new mentor to train him.

For a long period of time, Ender didn't know that his mentor was actually Mazer Rackham, the legendary hero of the early Formic invasions of Earth. Mazer and Ender fought physically when they first met. Mazer was brutal to the preteen boy, but Ender found the strength to fight back.

He was shocked to learn that many of his former toon leaders from Battle School (such as Bean, Petra Arkanian, Han Tzu, Dink Meeker, Vlad, and others) had been assigned toons under his command at Command School, though he never saw them face-to-face. Ender communicated with them over radio, giving orders as they faced the "enemy."

Ender's experience at Command School was not too different from his time at Battle School. He constantly won battles by coming up with unique strategies. Because he kept winning, Mazer Rackham and the other instructors kept making the battles more difficult. Ender described his own life as a slow nervous breakdown. He grew more and more anxious about the tests and games with the simulators. He was losing ships in the simulators and felt great levels of guilt about the lives—even if they were pretend—that were being lost because of him. He was plagued by nightmares, often waking up in tears. He even injured his own hand, gnawing on it in his sleep.

The pressure of the exams pushed Ender to his limit. In the middle of one exam, he fainted and was put to bed for three days. When he recovered, he went right back to work in the simulator/exam room.

The final game was scheduled, and a large group of observers looked on from above the simulation room. Ender sat alone in the large room, with his toon leaders communicating by radio. In this final game, Ender's army was outnumbered a thousand to one. Yet Ender pushed on, determined to defeat the enemy he was convinced was Mazer Rackham. As the small human army moved toward their simulated enemy, Bean reminded Ender, "The enemy's gate is down."

Ender and his army fought nobly, again utilizing unique strategy. Ender initialized a massive weapon, the Molecular Detachment Device, launching it at the planet below. A chain reaction burst forward from the planet's core, and suddenly the entire world Ender and his enemy were orbiting in the simulator was destroyed. The observers cheered, and Mazer Rackham hugged Ender, telling him that Ender had won. But he had not just won a simulation. Hyrum Graff and Mazer revealed to Ender that the simulations were actually real: Ender had been commanding a real army and destroyed the Formics' home world. Consequently, the Formics themselves were all killed. The war had been won by an eleven-year-old boy. And that boy had committed xenocide.

Ender felt the worst guilt he'd ever experienced over the loss of the soldiers' lives, as well as the death of an entire species. The International Fleet promoted Ender to admiral, though they did not give him a ship to command: he was only allowed simple, menial duties, which allowed him more time to think and feel guilty. All he wanted to do was sleep and return home to Greensboro and to Valentine. Unfortunately, war had broken out on Earth, and Ender's life was in jeopardy. Even after the brief conflict was resolved, Ender learned he could never return home. Essayists Locke and Demosthenes had called for Ender to stay in space. Because of these essays, and to protect his life, Ender was selected to be the governor of the first colony of human settlers on former Formic worlds.

Not yet knowing for sure that he would be kept in space, Ender watched Graff's court-martial and learned for certain that he had killed Stilson and Bonzo. More guilt over unnecessary death filled his heart and was a heavy burden. He was thirteen now, and waiting for the ship that would take him to his first new colony.

Ender became obsessed with the Formics in this period as well. He watched and rewatched the vids from the various wars over and over again, trying to understand how they could allow themselves to be so easily annihilated. This

272 THE AUTHORIZED ENDER COMPANION

obsession continued unabated, however. When Ender first toured his colony ship, he was fascinated by the Formic technology, which had been adapted for human use on spaceships. He was shocked to learn that the Molecular Detachment Device that he'd used to extinguish the Formics was also based on their own technology.

Valentine arrived at Eros and told Ender that it was she, as Demosthenes, who had seen to his assignment in the colonies and inability to return to Earth in order to keep him free from Peter and his power as the leader of Earth. She had come to Eros to join him on the first colony vessel. Graff had, moments before, told Ender that his siblings were the essayists Locke and Demosthenes. Ender loved Valentine and was glad to see her, but he had no idea that she and Peter had been so manipulative on the world stage. But their reunion was a joyous one.

As his colony ship departed from Earth, Ender posed for the requisite photos with Graff, Mazer, and other military and political leaders. Once on board the vessel, he met with the ship's commander, Admiral Quincy Morgan, and advised the officer that he would not interfere with any operations on the ship. Ender said he had no authority as governor until he arrived at Shakespeare Colony and was no longer interested in giving military orders. The conversation was a little reassuring to Admiral Quincy, who was secretly making plans to usurp Ender's position as governor when the ship reached its destination.

Ender spent his time on the ship getting to know the passengers who would be his fellow colonists. If he was to govern them, he wanted to know them all as well as possible. Among them were Dorabella and Alessandra Toscano, a mother and daughter from Italy. Dorabella wanted her daughter to marry Ender. Ender knew that was Dorabella's intent, but did not betray this knowledge. Instead, he was friendly with them, even helping them plan a reading of Shakespeare's *The Taming of the Shrew* on board the ship. The play reading earned the ire of Admiral Morgan, bringing Ender and him into another confrontation.

Admiral Morgan believed Ender was causing a mutiny by holding the play reading. He was more convinced of this when a large message from Earth interfered with ship communications. Admiral Morgan screamed at Ender, insulting him along the way. Ender listened to the insults patiently, and responded calmly to every accusation. The message, it turned out, was actually from Peter to Valentine, updating Valentine on Peter's rise to Hegemon of Earth.

Valentine arrived and showed the message to Admiral Morgan who, embarrassed, allowed the play to go on, and even ageed to attend. Ender knew that Morgan was still trying to usurp his role as leader of the people, and was now toying with him. Morgan attended the play where Ender performed opposite Alessandra Toscano. The performance increased Alessandra's affection for the future governor.

Ender fostered this affection by being kind to Alessandra, earning him the ire of his sister Valentine. She asked him to stop leading the girl on, which Ender denied ever doing. His sister's request gave him cause to think about his actions, though, and he realized that he could do more to soften Alessandra's feelings for him.

Ender also kept in contact with the governor of Shakespeare. The two knew that potential power struggles awaited Ender on the planet and were both working to prevent them. A new governor, scientist Sel Menach, would be in power when Ender arrived. He would ensure that Ender's position as leader of the colony would be maintained and respected. It was up to Ender to make sure that Admiral Morgan did not try to take over in the colony.

With the help of Hyrum Graff and the new Polemarch Bakossi Wuri, Ender created a scenario where Admiral Morgan believed he could take over the governorship, but was proved wrong. Ender interrupted Morgan's planned ceremony on the surface of Shakespeare and received a hero's welcome from the original colonists. Morgan, humiliated, was livid at Ender. Ender gave Morgan a note from Graff and Wuri warning Morgan not to interfere with Ender's position as both governor and a superior officer or he would face charges of mutiny. Morgan left Shakespeare Colony defeated, and Ender began his assignment as governor.

Ender also used his influence to give Alessandra the confidence to leave her mother on the spaceship and stay on Shakespeare, too. The two would never be lovers, but Alessandra was grateful to be free of her mother's influence forever.

Almost immediately after arriving at Shakespeare, Ender learned that a species of Formic-like creatures called Gold Bugs had been discovered. He was saddened to learn that there were no Formics on the world. Or so he thought.

More comfortable in his position as governor, Ender finally wrote a letter to his parents. It was a heartfelt communication, the first he'd sent since he left their home at six years of age. Though his parents were now very old, they cherished the letters Ender sent them.

Ender also opened communication with Peter. Although his older brother was nearing sixty, and was the Hegemon, Ender found he was able to build a relationship with him, though he would forever remember Peter as the bully of their youth.

After two years on this new planet, he learned that a new colony ship was on its way. He was instructed to find a new place on the planet for them to settle. Traveling with an eleven-year-old boy named Abra Tolo, Ender discovered a grassy hill. He recognized it as being created from the Giant's Drink game he'd played as a boy in Battle School, though that seemed impossible. Ender explored the hill, and there he found the pupa of a Formic Hive Queen. The Formics had apparently created the grassy hill from Ender's mind, and left it for him to find years later. Ender could communicate with the Hive Queen mind to mind; he promised to care for the alien creature forever.

Through the philotic communication between Ender and the Hive Queen, he was able to write the book *The Hive Queen,* which told the story of the Formic Wars from the Buggers' perspective. The book was published on Earth under Ender's new pseudonym, "Speaker for the Dead." The book was revolutionary on Earth, becoming one of the world's most-read documents.

Through the book, Ender's name was tarnished, however. He was no longer the hero of the Formic Wars, but the monster that killed billions, wiping out an entire species. Public opinion on the war, which was history now on Earth, had soured. Ender, once thought of as a hero, was now viewed as the greatest war criminal of all time—"Ender the Xenocide."

The Speaker for the Dead also wrote *The Hegemon,* a book that told the story of his brother Peter and his rise to power in world politics as well as his life with his wife, Ender's friend Petra. In writing the book, Ender spoke with Peter, and the two estranged brothers were able to make peace for the first time in their lives. Peter was an old man, while Ender was still young. But they both were grateful for the chance to reconcile before Peter's death, which occurred shortly before the Earth publication of the book.

At the request of Hyrum Graff, Ender and his sister Valentine traveled from Shakespeare to Ganges, where a former Battle School colleague of Ender's, Virlomi, was governor. Also on Ganges lived a boy named Achilles Flandres II. Achilles was actually the last missing embryo that had belonged to Bean and Petra who were married while Ender traveled to Shakespeare. Achilles II had caused some problems at the new colony. Ender sought out the boy, hoping to teach him about his true parents.

Ender discovered that it had been Achilles II who had started a religious movement from *The Hive Queen,* and destroyed Ender's reputation. Their confrontation grew violent as Ender tried to tell Achilles II his true parentage. Achilles II was disgusted at the thought that his "father's" killer was his real father. Even though Achilles nearly killed Ender, he came to accept that Ender was telling the truth. Achilles II changed his name to Arkanian Delphiki, after his real parents.

Ender soon left that colony to travel to others, with Valentine by his side, carrying the Hive Queen with him world to world. He began to hide his identity, which proved to be easy, as few believed Ender the Xenocide was still alive. He kept the Hive Queen secret for centuries as he traveled to each new world and colony. He hoped to find a planet suitable for the Hive Queen to grow and hatch new Formic eggs—relaunching the species.

Ender had been given a monetary pension by the then-grateful citizens of Earth before leaving Eros to colonize. It was a fund he lived on for decades as he traveled through space at relativistic speed, governing worlds. The fund was kept secret as public opinion changed after the war.

On what would have been his subjectively twentieth birthday, Ender arrived at the distant planet called Sorelledolce. Per the law of his home world, Ender would receive a check for the amount in the trust fund, but would also now have to pay taxes on the money. When he approached the tax collector, Benedetto, to receive his promised check for the amount in the fund, his identity was questioned, and he was accused of lying about his name. Benedetto would not allow Ender access to the funds he needed to pay taxes because he had never paid taxes. However, upon discovering Ender's assets, Benedetto was a little more helpful. Ender made an arrangement with Benedetto that would allow Ender time to take care of his taxes, but there was an apparent problem: the illegal programs used by the tax man to spy on customers' assets were gone.

Ender studied tax law on Sorelledolce, hoping to use his assets to provide life for the Hive Queen. It was a penance, in Ender's mind, for his act of xenocide with her species. If he could use his assets to give life to the Hive Queen, it would remove the blood from his hands. He was shocked to receive a computer advertisement for financial software that would answer all of his questions, particularly since interstellar travelers were supposed to be free from advertisements. He was more shocked when the advertisement spoke to him, taking the form of a young human woman, saying she was meant to help Ender specifically. She started giving him advice, addressing him as Ender. She confessed that Ender had made her, and that she evolved along the way. This was Jane, and though Ender was initially disturbed by her presence, she would become a lifelong companion to him.

On Sorelledolce, Ender also attended his first "Speaking," the funerary rite based on his books, *The Hive Queen* and *The Hegemon*.

Thanks to Jane, Ender was able to resolve his tax issues with Benedetto. When Benedetto was exposed as a crook and was killed by some of his past clients, Ender felt responsible. Jane taught him to not feel guilty about the bad things which are not his fault that happen to the people around him.

After two weeks on Sorelledolce, Ender left the planet with Valentine and Jane. He listed his occupation as "Speaker for the Dead" from that time on, taking interest in obituary columns with each new planet he and Valentine visited. At that same time, he began wearing a small receiver in his ear that looked like a jewel. It was actually his direct link to Jane. The jewel allowed Jane to speak privately and directly to Ender.

More than three thousand years by Earth's time after the victory over the Formics, Ender had traveled with Valentine to so many planets at light speed that he hadn't aged past thirty-five. He and Valentine spent many months on the Icelandic and Calvinist planet Trondheim, where they both became teachers at the university. It was here that Ender met Plikt, one of his students. Plikt challenged Ender on many of his lessons, but Ender appreciated the questions.

When Ender learned of the death of a xenologist on a planet called Lusitania, he was saddened. Jane created a simulation of the murder, graphic though it was. She also told Ender that a young girl named Novinha had called for a Speaker for the victim. Ender saw his own sorrow and premature adulthood in Novinha's face. He made the decision to travel to Lusitania and Speak this death. He was thirty-six years old now, and by the time he reached the planet, Novinha would be thirty-nine.

With Jane in command of their spaceship, he traveled to Lusitania. Though traveling to Speak for the dead, Ender also knew that Lusitania might be the best place to allow the Hive Queen to grow. The Hive Queen herself promised Ender that the species would thrive there, and they would not bother the native creatures on the planet, the pequeninos, but they sensed another life-form with whom they would be compatible.

When Ender arrived at Lusitania, he was received relatively coldly. The planet was staunchly Catholic, and the church had spoken out against Speakers. The colony's governor greeted him, but had secretly banned him access to colony maps. With Jane's help, and that of a young boy named Olhado, Ender made his way to the home of the Ribeira family—the family who had called him to Speak.

There, he was treated quite badly by most of the children. However, the longer he was in their home, waiting to meet their mother Novinha, the more they warmed up to him. Ender had the thought that he was now, like it or not, a member of the Ribeira family.

His first meeting with Novinha did not go as well, though. She was angry that he had come to Speak the death of her husband and tried to cast him from her house. Her children spoke up on Ender's behalf, though, and Novinha listened to him, albeit angrily.

Frustrated by the apparent hatred he felt from Novinha, Ender returned to his home. The next day, he investigated the life of Marcão, learning that Novinha had been unfaithful to her husband. With Jane's help, he learned it was Libo, her now-dead childhood friend, who had fathered her six children.

When Ender, hoping for more information on Marcão and Novinha, visited with the abbot of a Catholic order known as the Children of the Mind of Christ, Jane kept making comments about his conversation. Frustrated with her chatter, Ender turned off the jewel, shutting her out of his ear and mind. Jane was insulted by the act and didn't speak again to Ender for some time.

Without Jane, Ender was lost. Essentially computer illiterate, he turned to Novinha's son, Olhado, to teach him how to use the Lusitanian computer networks. He used his newfound computer access to spy on Novinha's computer files to learn about her, her family, and the deaths they'd asked him to Speak. Novinha confronted him about it, and Ender revealed to her that he'd learned all of her secrets.

Ender essentially had fallen in love with Novinha and her children. He felt that he had found a complete family for the first time in his life. Though many of the Ribeiras held him in disdain, it was his hope that he could bring love to their home and receive it in his life.

He found that he'd established a particularly close rapport with Ela, who confided in him her hopes and dreams, and how Novinha had tried to quash them to preserve Ela's life.

When Ender performed the Speaking for the late Marcão Ribeira, he exposed his wife Novinha's adultery with the man Libo. The revelation sent shock waves through the colony, but the surprise was short-lived. Immediately following the ceremony, Ender learned that the Starways Congress had stripped the Lusitanian computers of their files and revoked the planet's charter.

Ender realized it had been Jane who had exposed the violations of law that had resulted in the congressional actions. There was communication—albeit distant, but communication nonetheless—from Jane. Ender wept cathartically, realizing his friend had returned to him.

He also knew that it had been Miro and Ouanda's work with the piggies that had violated the law. The two xenologists were to be arrested and sent to Trondheim. Ender refused to let that happen, telling the now-dethroned governor, Bosquinha, to hold a meeting with the planet's religious leaders and rebel against Congress's orders.

To have a chance at successful rebellion, Ender knew he needed information on the virus that had wiped out the planet's life, the Descolada. It was information that Novinha had kept secret for decades. Ender turned to Ela to approach Novinha for the information. They knew it was the only way to save Miro and all of Lusitania.

With the information Novinha provided, Ender helped the planetary leadership decide to rebel against the Starways Congress. He also discovered that Miro had been hurt trying to climb the fence that surrounded the piggies' land. Ender and the colony leaders raced to save Miro's life.

There, Ender, along with Ela, convinced the piggie named Human to take them to the pequeninos' leaders—the female piggies known as "the wives." Using Human as a translator, Ender spoke with a wife named Shouter. With her, he wrote up a treaty that would define the relationship between humans and piggies on Lusitania and would allow the pequeninos access to the Hive Queen.

Although Ender would not make any promises for the Hive Queen's actions, he swore to turn her over to them. Humanity and the pequeninos would maintain their own lands and not kill one another. The piggies would not make war with other tribes of piggies, either.

To make the treaty a reality, Ender was forced to kill Human and plant him as a tree. It was a sacred ritual to the pequeninos, and very hard for Ender to do. But he performed the ordinance as ordered.

He also signed the treaty as "Ender Wiggin," thus revealing his true identity as "Ender the Xenocide" to Novinha and the other people of Lusitania. Novinha realized that because he'd wiped out an entire species, Ender hadn't judged her for adultery. The revelation brought Ender and Novinha close emotionally.

The morning after the treaty was signed, Ender attended mass with Novinha and her family, sitting in the place that Marcão had once sat—by Novinha's side. The two were married by Bishop Peregrino a few months later.

Prior to the wedding, however, Ender had some work to do. He found a place for the Hive Queen to be reborn from her cocoon near the pequenino land. He also helped Jane and Miro connect with each other. Miro left Lusitania in Ender's spaceship and developed a very close relationship with Jane. It saddened Ender that he and Jane were no longer as close as they once were, and he knew that that relationship with now being shared with Miro.

Nonetheless, Ender began his life on Lusitania. He was married to Novinha and had released the Hive Queen to flourish on a new planet. He knew his life work was complete. Yet a new challenge awaited him. Lusitania was set to be destroyed by the Starways Congress using the Molecular Detachment Device. Ender knew he had to work to protect his new home from the same fate he'd given the Formic home world three millennia earlier. Fortunately, Valentine, now twenty years older, had made the decision to go to Lusitania and help protect the planet alongside her brother.

In the thirty years the people of Lusitania were waiting for the fleet and, more importantly, Valentine, Ender learned that Jane had discovered a way to stop the destruction of the planet by cutting off all interstellar communication. But the move would ultimately result in her own death. Ender, growing older and still on the planet, pleaded with Jane through his ear jewel to find another way that would allow her to live. Jane agreed to try, for Ender's and his stepson Miro's sakes.

During these three decades, Ender continued to draw close to the pequeninos. He befriended a talented scientist piggie named Planter and enjoyed greatly the time he spent in the pequenino land. He often visited Human, the fully grown fathertree, and spent much time with his own family.

His stepchildren, Novinha's children, had become the top scientists on the planet. They were all working tirelessly to fight the Descolada virus. When his stepdaughter Quara theorized that the Descolada was a sentient creature and wiping it out would be xenocide, Ender offered a sympathetic position. He encouraged, as did Novinha, further study and told the family not to reveal their findings to anyone until more was known.

Quara ignored this directive and informed the fathertrees that her family hoped to annihilate the virus that the piggies needed to live. Ender chastened her for this revelation and told the fathertrees himself that more research was being done. But it was too late. The fathertrees made the determination to leave Lusitania with the Descolada still alive in them. They contacted the Hive Queen and made the decision to create a spaceship that would help them get off the planet.

Ender was present when his stepson Miro returned from space, bringing Valentine, her husband Jakt, and Plikt to Lusitania. Due to the effects of relativistic space travel, Miro hadn't aged during his nearly thirty years' spaceflight.

Ender and the rest of his family had. In fact, Ender was now seemingly older than even Valentine, though not by too much.

Ender and Valentine rejoiced in their reunion. Falling instantly back to the sarcastic banter that had defined their relationship for more than three millennia, the two were glad to be together again.

Almost immediately after their arrival, Ender took Valentine, Plikt, and Miro to see the Hive Queen in her lair. She was laying and hatching eggs, and her society was flourishing. In the visit, Ender and company learned that they were correct in their guess that the queen was building ships to take her people and the pequeninos into space.

The Hive Queen used Ender's intimately close relationships to Plikt and Valentine as a conduit to speak to the two women mind to mind, as she had Ender. It was a life-changing experience for both Valentine and Plikt.

In the course of their conversation, the Hive Queen promised Ender that she would not kill any humans and was taking the piggies into space. She also revealed the origins of her communication with him, dating back to Ender's Battle School days.

A few nights later, Jane contacted Ender, warning him that a girl on the planet Path was close to uncovering Demosthenes's true identity and her own plan of making the attacking fleet "disappear." She was panicked. Ender spoke silently to her, though Novinha knew he was talking to Jane, and it bothered her.

Ender told Jane a story of a puppet who came to life and was given a human body. The boy died in a fire, but Ender wanted that same miracle for Jane. He promised her he would try to find a way for her to leave the Philotic Web and exist on her own, but she had to truly figure out what she was first. She had to find her soul.

The next day, Ender participated in a meeting with the leaders of the planet, trying to determine how best to handle the situations with the piggies and the Descolada. He spoke his mind plainly, stating that the research to control the virus should continue, as should the research to determine its actual life status. He even supported his stepson Quim's religious mission to the piggies.

In the meeting, he also hoped to work with his fiery stepson, Grego, to determine a way for faster-than-light space travel—travel that would cross great distances instantly. It was Ender's secret desire to use the travel to save Jane, somehow.

His relationship with Novinha would not last much longer. She was angry with him for his relationship with Jane and for supporting Quim's mission to the piggies. She remained silent for days, finally exploding at him with hateful insults. It was hard for Ender to bear, as he loved Novinha deeply. He could understand her feelings, but that didn't make it easier.

Ender led the search-and-rescue party when it was discovered that Quim had been captured by the rebellious fathertrees. He and his party found Quim's body, and Ender sent word back to Novinha that her son was dead. He knew that having someone else tell his wife that Quim had been killed was the smarter choice, as she would not want to hear it from him.

A few days later, Jane contacted Ender, seeking his advice. A girl on the planet Path had uncovered Valentine's role as Demosthenes as well as Jane's existence. Jane allowed Ender to hear her conversation with Han Qing-jao, the girl on Path, as Qing-jao decided to send a message to the Starways Congress, informing them of Jane's existence and role in the disappearance of the Lusitania Fleet. Jane would have to allow the message to pass through the philotic system and wanted Ender to tell her not to.

Ender, not wanting to lose his dearest friend—for such a message would mean Jane's imminent destruction—begged and commanded her to not allow it. However, in an effort to preserve the people of Path and to find out more about who she truly was, Jane consented to the message. Ender was crushed, certain that she would now be killed by the Congress.

In the midst of this conversation, Ender sought Novinha. She had taken the news of Quim's death very hard and had joined the Children of the Mind of Christ, an abbey for married couples. When he went to the abbey to speak with her, she refused reconciliation, instead choosing to focus on her service to Christ.

Jane hoped that her impending death would allow Ender to be back by his wife's side. He was deeply saddened by Novinha's anger and longed to be with her, but not at Jane's expense.

With Miro, Ender came up with a theory on Jane's existence. He thought that if Jane had begun her existence as a philote, as he believed all life had, then finding the location of this first philote could be the key to preserving her life. Jane doubted this theory and thought pursuing it was a waste of time and resources. However, Ender, still hurting from losing Novinha, pleaded with her to help them figure it out. She agreed, realizing how important her existence was to Ender and Miro.

Jane facilitated a conversation between Ender and Ela on Lusitania and Wang-mu on the planet Path. Wang-mu had conferred with her former friend and mistress, Qing-jao, asking for her help in the tasks Jane had set before them. Qing-jao refused, but gave Wang-mu some good questions to ask about the Descolada specifically.

In asking these questions, Wang-mu led Ender and Ela down a path of discovery. They hypothesized that the Descolada virus had been created and used to control/regulate the pequeninos and all other life on Lusitania. Ender approached the piggie Planter about the hypothesis. Planter said he had come to the same hypothesis and made the choice to sacrifice himself as the lab rat to determine whether pequenino behavior was self-controlled or the result of the virus. He would be purged of the Descolada and observed to see if he still had his mind and self-will.

Ender sought out the Hive Queen to see if she could help them figure out faster-than-light travel. She had nothing to offer on that subject, but instead revealed to Ender Jane's true origin.

The Hive Queen taught Ender about the true nature of philotes. They existed in another space/time continuum, waiting to be called by the Formics (or any other life form) to inhabit and develop a biological body. Once in this body, the philotes created connections between creatures.

The Formics called upon a philote to enter Ender's body when he was in Battle School, hoping that it would create a connection between them and him. The philote's connection was with the computer program known as the Giant's Drink game. The philote used the connection with the program to build a bridge between Ender and the Hive Queen, and to expand and develop sentience. Its "body" existed among the computer networks but was not really a part of the computers or ansibles, as Jane and Ender originally thought. It was a part of Ender, since its main philote was in him.

It explained to Ender why he and Jane were so closely tied to one another. It also gave him tremendous hope that she could live even if the computers and ansibles were shut down.

The theory of calling on philotes from their home opened the door for Ender's stepsons Grego and Olhado to come up with a way to make faster-than-light travel possible. They thought that if a person could call on the philotes that made them to return home, they could then call on those to create the pattern of the location to which they wished to travel. It would require a powerful memory to maintain the traveler's original philotic pattern—and that of the ship itself—and prevent it from dispersing in the other dimension.

Jane had a memory powerful enough to remember the patterns of a few potential travelers. With Ender—since she "lived" inside of him—she, Miro, and Ela were assigned to travel into space and test this theory.

Once in Outspace, Ender and his party needed to focus on their own philotic patterns. Ender tried to do so, but was shocked to see that somehow, the philotes had created new versions of his siblings Peter and Valentine. Thanks to their philotic cores, they were real, living breathing people. Their personalities were patterned after Ender's memories of them.

He was shocked to meet his new "children," Peter II and Valentine II. They had the physical appearance of their predecessors in their teen years. But many of their memories were missing because they had been created from Ender's thoughts of them.

Ender also helped Ela test the antiviruses she had created from her thoughts in Outspace. The antiviruses were successful, and both the Descolada on Lusitania and the genetic manipulations on Path were eradicated.

On Lusitania, though, Ender had to confront the results of his journey to Outspace: his "children" Peter II and Valentine II. Each person's personality was entirely as Ender had remembered it. Val was sweet and innocent while Peter II was angry and aggressive. Ender tried to care for the young people, but found it difficult to do so. Plikt took over with Valentine II while Peter II took a journey into Outspace to deliver the virus to Path and then destroy the Starways Congress.

These two "children" of his made Ender wonder about himself. Was he the combination of Valentine's and Peter's personalities? Was that how he'd created them? Regardless, Ender refused to ever go back to Outspace, fearing that he would create more Peters and Valentines. But because they had been created from his mind and soul, they shared his philotic connection to Jane, which allowed both of them to utilize faster-than-light travel.

The trip to Outspace had a positive consequence for Ender, too. Since Miro created a new, healthy body for himself, Novinha believed it was a miracle. She reached out to Ender and visited with him at the abbey. She asked him to join her among the Children of the Mind of Christ, but he refused. He wanted desperately to be reunited with her, but not in a celibate marriage, as required by the order.

They agreed to visit each other once a month at the abbey, and both hoped the other would give up their desire for reunification and fulfill their own. It was Ender who gave in. He made the decision to join Novinha at the Children of the Mind of Christ.

He wasn't a devoted believer to the dogma being presented and taught by the order, but he missed his wife. He longed to be with her, even in the celibate circumstances of the Children of the Mind of Christ. He worked in the garden with her, and there the couple professed their love for one another.

Novinha told him she no longer blamed him for Quim's death and was glad they'd be together for the rest of their lives.

Many in Lusitania, Valentine included, believed Ender had given up on saving the colony and threw away his influence. He was trying to escape from his life, and particularly the new Valentine and Peter he'd created. They depended on him to survive, but Ender's consciousness wasn't enough to sustain Valentine II, Peter II, Jane, and himself.

Miro approached Ender at the abbey and asked for his help in protecting Lusitania from the impending invasion. Ender refused and wouldn't even communicate with Jane. He sarcastically said that Jane should have Valentine II's body. Miro and Jane thought that was a good idea and investigated the possibility while Ender returned to his work at the abbey, devoting himself not to Christ or the church, but to his beloved wife.

A few days later, Novinha found him asleep in the gardens at the abbey. He was struggling to breathe. His wife called for help, and several from the abbey came to offer assistance. Ender was unresponsive to attempts to waken him or to improve his breathing. It looked as though Ender was dying. Novinha blamed herself for Ender's state; he had only come to the abbey to be with her, and she had refused to leave. It was a heavy burden that haunted her as she sought help for her husband.

Ender lay dying in the abbey, with his one-time student Plikt watching over him. She wanted to Speak his death and had devoted her life to studying him. She was there when he spoke one word from his unconscious state: "Peter."

Why Ender called out the name of the person he most hated was unclear, but it led to a confrontation between Plikt, Novinha, and Valentine. Each woman made a claim on loving Ender the most, and each had a good reason. But they set aside their differences when Ender briefly awoke and spoke to them.

Valentine encouraged Novinha to let Ender go and promised, albeit briefly, that Plikt would not Speak Ender's death as she so desperately wanted.

Jane was forced from her computer network home shortly before Ender was to die. Jane's consciousness, her soul, or Auía, searched desperately for a new body to inhabit. She tried to live within Ender, but he still had his Auía, and the two souls fought violently within him. He thrashed around on his deathbed, injuring Novinha, Valentine, and Plikt. Jane's soul left, and Ender regained consciousness briefly.

While he was awake, Novinha told him that he could leave her. She loved him and knew he loved her, but he was okay to die. It was his time. Ender smiled and knew what to do. He closed his eyes, and his Auía left his body. The shell of Ender Wiggin that remained on the table dissolved, leaving only a few hairs from his head. Novinha, Valentine, and Plikt all kept a handful of the hair. Plikt would Speak his death, paying tribute to him as he had so many others, on so many other worlds.

Ender's Auía left his body and searched for a new place to dwell. It felt the missing pieces that had been "donated" to Valentine II and Peter II. With the help of the Formic Hive Queen, who guided the philote-based soul to its new home (just as Ender had taken the Hive Queen to her new home), it reunited with Valentine II's piece of Ender's soul and entered Peter II's body. Peter II now carried Ender's soul. He did not have all of Ender's memories, but felt a shadow of them in his new life. Ender's work was not over, though his body was gone. He would simply continue to live on as Peter II.

When Plikt Spoke Ender's death, she painted a picture of the man she idolized that showed him to be all he was: from history's greatest villain Ender the Xenocide; to the great philosopher, the Speaker for the Dead; to the loving husband and father, Andrew. He had lived to the fullest of his potential and, in his legacy, lived on in all of humanity, no matter where they lived or who they were. He had protected them from unintentionally murderous invaders and saved them from themselves. He was Ender Wiggin.

Wiggin, John Paul (Polish: Jan Pawel Wieczorek) (PL, TP, EG, SH, SP, SG)

A child prodigy, John Paul Wieczorek was able to read adult books before any of his nine siblings, though his apparent talent went relatively ignored in his early years. John Paul, named for the pope, was one of nine children. He grew up in Poland, where the Hegemony's population laws (which only allowed two children per family) were not strictly enforced. However, because his family was noncompliant with the laws, John Paul and his eight siblings were schooled at home by their mother, Anne.

John Paul knew, at the age of five, that he was smarter than his siblings, but no one else believed him. This made life particularly challenging for the boy genius. He was, like his parents, dogmatically Catholic and couldn't understand how the rest of the world could be different.

When the International Fleet sent Captain Helena Rudolf to the Wieczorek household to test the male children, John Paul insisted he be tested, too. His parents were upset that he wanted to participate, but they relented when they realized the law required he be tested three weeks later anyway on his sixth birthday. Because of his tremendous ability in logic, shapes, philosophy, and reading, Captain Rudolf felt that he might be the child the Fleet was searching for to act as their new commander in the Formic War.

A short time later, Captain Rudolf returned with her superior, a Finnish man named Colonel Sillian. He and John Paul had a contentious interaction during the first follow-up test. John Paul repeated much of his father's anti-Hegemony/Fleet rhetoric, frustrating Colonel Sillian.

When Captain Hyrum Graff arrived to make the final decision on John Paul's readiness for Battle School, John Paul took to negotiating his family's betterment in exchange for his compliance with the International Fleet. At only six years old, John Paul was a powerful leader and negotiator. He first tried to get his parents and siblings the privileges of compliant families, but that was unsuccessful. He realized he didn't want to go to Battle School, but longed to go somewhere that enabled him to study in a real school, and his family could be free of the sanctions.

He proposed moving the family to America, and then he'd go to Battle School. Graff knew that John Paul's intent was to better his familial circumstances and then refuse to go to Battle School, thus cheating the Fleet. However, Graff was a big-picture person, and agreed to John Paul's plan. The Wieczoreks would move to America and be allowed to stay there, even if John Paul didn't go to Battle School.

At age sixteen, John Paul left his family, changed his name, and renounced his religion. It was a series of acts of defiance, and they changed the course of his life.

He did not go to Battle School, and by the time he was of college age, he was confident in his intelligence to the point of cockiness. He had taken a new last name, "Wiggin," and with his family had new identities as full-blooded Americans. He'd enrolled in college in anticipation of taking a government position, secretly hoping to bring down the Hegemony from the inside and restoring sovereignty to all nations—particularly his native Poland.

He was assigned by a college computer to a particular section of Human Community, taught by Theresa Brown, a graduate student and the daughter of well-known Mormon military strategist Hinckley Brown. A front-row student, John Paul noticed his teacher had an attractive figure. John Paul was able to immediately grasp the things Theresa taught, which she found annoying. John Paul enjoyed it. And he fell in love with his teacher the moment she kicked a female student out of the class for asking a question regarding Theresa's religion affecting her teaching of science.

John Paul decided to court this teacher and he made his first move immediately after Theresa had had a bad meeting with her dissertation committee. Ever persistent, John Paul continued his advances. He made up a small picnic outside her office at the university, ordering food in intervals so that it would be hot when she came out.

During the picnic, John Paul and Theresa shared life stories and philosophies, and grew friendly. John Paul brazenly declared his love for her; they joked of marriage and found themselves kissing each other at the end of the picnic. Theresa soon fell in love with John Paul, too, and they eventually married.

Together, they lived up to their families' traditions and were noncompliant, having three children: Peter, Valentine, and Andrew "Ender." John Paul baptized all three of his children as infants, against his wife's wishes. They had hoped to secretly teach their children, but circumstances never allowed for it.

He did, however, allow the International Fleet to monitor his children, convinced that none of them would be chosen to go to Battle School. Once Peter and Valentine were rejected, he and Theresa were asked to have a third child, Ender.

When Ender was chosen to go to Battle School, John Paul was angry. He did not put up a fight when Ender made the decision to leave, though. He continued raising Peter and Valentine, which was sometimes a challenge because of Peter's aggressiveness.

During a period when Peter was failing school because the work he did was advanced far beyond the parameters of his assignments, John Paul defended Peter to the schoolteachers and administrators. Peter thanked his father for that in a letter he gave him the following Christmas.

On Earth, he and Theresa knew that their remaining children had become the political pundits Locke and Demosthenes. But in order to help them be autonomous in their endeavors, neither John Paul nor Theresa revealed their knowledge. They did, however, occasionally use this knowledge to manipulate their children's stances on world affairs. Although Ender was the hero of the Formic War, John Paul understood that his boy could never return to Earth. After receiving a letter from Hyrum Graff that subtly reiterated that fact, John Paul and Theresa manipulated their other children into writing essays calling for Ender's exile into space. Though John Paul would miss his son terribly and was heartbroken when Valentine decided to join Ender in space, he knew it was for the best.

John Paul would often share his own thoughts on the state of the world with his son Peter after reading one of Peter's "Locke" essays. This aggravated Peter, but John Paul tried his best to support his son.

When Peter finally decided to reveal his identity to the world, Theresa and John Paul told him they were proud of him and would continue to support him however they could. This support meant moving to Brazil.

Peter was made Hegemon and placed the center of his world government in Brazil. John Paul and Theresa joined their son there and were offered jobs in the new, rising government, but they refused the positions.

A few months later, Peter brought Achilles to the Hegemony compound. John Paul conferred with his son when it appeared that Theresa was betraying Peter to Achilles. John Paul theorized that Theresa was actually plotting to kill Achilles. Peter was stunned that his mother would even try such a thing.

John Paul told Peter that he always loved him, but Peter doubted his words. John Paul left Peter to figure out Theresa's actions on his own.

When John Paul confronted his wife about her plans to kill Achilles, the couple decided that it would be better for Peter if they did not kill Achilles, but instead made it appear that Achilles was trying to kill them. This led John Paul to try tracking Achilles's computer movements and discovered that Peter was already trying unsuccessfully to do likewise. John Paul and Peter's computer expert, Ferreira, worked together to figure out what Achilles was doing, but it appeared to be nothing.

The plan to have Achilles appear to be targeting the Wiggins fell apart. But John Paul received a message from Bean telling him that Achilles was actually in control of everything—he'd arranged for his own rescue at Peter's hands, and was now playing Peter.

John Paul and Theresa understood the message and informed Peter. They took their son from the compound to the United States. There, they watched proudly as Peter maintained his authority as Hegemon, giving a press conference that denounced Achilles.

Both John Paul and Theresa were committed to protecting Peter and helping him fulfill his destiny as the leader of the world. They even took to carrying firearms and serving as pseudobodyguards.

Hyrum Graff invited the Wiggin family to stay at the orbiting space-station home of the Ministry of Colonization, which was the same satellite that was once Battle School. John Paul was fascinated by the school and enjoyed seeing the layout of the space station. His time on the station was short-lived, however, as someone leaked their arrival to Earth, and it was no longer safe for the family to be there.

John Paul figured out that their return to Earth was a ruse to catch the mole. He played his part perfectly. While hiding out on the station, he asked

Dimak where Ender's quarters had been when it was Battle School. Dimak didn't take the time to show John Paul.

Theresa, who hadn't figured out the ruse as quickly as John Paul, was annoyed that he had and she hadn't. She wanted to go back to Earth but also played her role in the plan well. She disagreed with Peter and Graff on how to proceed, but knew that it was best that she go along with it.

The plan, which involved tricking Achilles into destroying a shuttle thinking he'd kill the Wiggins, came off perfectly. Peter and Bean returned to Brazil and killed Achilles, retaking the Hegemony compound.

John Paul and Theresa also went back to Earth and took up residence at the compound. Peter was again the Hegemon, and they watched proudly as he resumed his duties as the leader of the world.

They were disappointed in their son a few months later when they learned he'd been embezzling Ender's pension to fund his rise to power. Bean resolved that matter, and Peter soon was able to ratify his constitution among many nations on Earth.

John Paul and Theresa were once again proud of their son. They complimented him on unifying much of the world's population in the Hegemony, now called the Free People of Earth. Not once in their praise did they mention Ender's name, and that made it all the sweeter for Peter to hear.

Wiggin, Peter Arkady I (Polish Name: Piotr Arakdiusz) (EG, WG, EE, EH, SH, SP, SG, IC)

Born and raised in "the city," Peter Wiggin was the oldest child of John Paul and Theresa Wiggin. Named for two of John Paul's brothers, Peter (Piotr) and Arkady (Arek), he was a proud and even violent child. Peter was given the monitor device from the International Fleet. He did not qualify for Battle School, however, because of his violent nature and his inability to get people to like him—a necessity for a good leader. He lost his monitor shortly before age five.

When his little brother Ender received the monitor, Peter was jealous and took to torturing his youngest sibling with physical and emotional abuse. He often threatened to kill Ender. They played a popular game "Astronauts and Buggers," an outer space equivalent of "cops and robbers."

Thought by his siblings to be a murderer at heart, Peter actually loved his family deep down. He told Ender he loved him and how sorry he was that Ender had lost his monitor, though it was in private when Peter thought his brother was asleep.

When Ender left for Battle School, Peter was jealous; however, he told his brother to "kill a Bugger for me!" Two years later, when the family moved to Greensboro, North Carolina, Peter took to torturing and killing animals in the forest. However, this dark act was used to get his sister Valentine's attention. The sounds the lizards and squirrels made during the torture leading to death bothered Peter, but he couldn't stop. The rush of this great life-and-death control was too strong to be ignored.

He was still jealous of Ender's being chosen to go to Battle School and was envious of their mother's attention. He stole from Ender's Christmas stocking, but was caught by their mother. She showed Peter that she loved him, but also loved Ender. The conflict had a profound effect on Peter. He didn't stop being jealous of Ender, but his eyes were opening to emotions other than hate and jealousy.

In this same period, Peter encountered Mirabella, a student at his high school. Though only fourteen, Peter was a senior and was resented for his superior intellect. He offered Mirabella help on an assignment, and she rejected him. Peter couldn't figure out why people didn't rally around him. He fancied himself a great leader.

It wasn't until Valentine pointed out how cruel Peter was that he understood why he wasn't able to get followers in his school. He resolved at that moment to act in a way that made people think he liked them and was serving them. He apologized to Mirabella and thanked his family for their acts of kindness in letters he gave to them that Christmas. He even made a mosaic of Ender pictures for his mother.

It was all an act, however. He wasn't sincere in his attempts to serve or be kind. They were acts of manipulation and vengeance, trying only to increase his influence among his peers on a path to world domination.

A brilliant child, Peter had been following the movements of Russian soldiers. He realized that the world was preparing for an international conflict following the Formic wars. A clever strategist and talented writer, he came up with a plan to participate in the growing conflict on Earth. Peter convinced Valentine to create secret identities that would allow them both to write political commentary on the computer nets. The two siblings would argue political positions between each other. They used several different names at first, refining their skills, but once they perfected their writing skills, they took unchanging screen names. Peter was "Locke," a pro-Hegemony analyst who was hired to write weekly columns arguing against Valentine's "Demosthenes." The writings proved to be incredibly popular and all the while Peter kept his true identity—now a thirteen-year-old boy—hidden from the world.

The partnership with Valentine had a tempering effect on Peter. He no longer was the aggressive killer he'd once been.

By the time Peter was fourteen, the International Fleet had figured out that he was Locke and that Valentine was Demosthenes. However, they did not censor the young columnists' work. Peter still enjoyed writing as Locke, even when Valentine nearly exposed their identities in school.

As Locke, Peter was able to put an end to the conflict that plagued humanity in the immediate aftermath of Ender's victory over the Formics. Thanks to Locke's essays, the Hegemon resigned and the nations of the world found themselves at odds with one another, but no longer in full-scale war. His essays also ensured that Ender would never return to Earth following the end of the Formic War. Ostensibly to protect Ender, exiling the war hero would also protect Peter from being in his brother's shadow.

Ender and Valentine left Earth to settle colonies. They were gone, and Peter felt alone. However, he still had plans for world domination, and using his Locke name tried contacting the International Fleet. Graff and Chamrajnagar corresponded with Peter, but it was of little use to him at the time.

He'd entered the local college in Greensboro, North Carolina, at a younger-than-normal age. He had a difficult time associating with his fellow students who did not know he was Locke. But they would someday, he knew. And it would be as he rose to power.

The beginning of this exposure was when Peter received a message from an unknown individual, who he figured out was Bean, revealing the location of several of Ender's colleagues from Command School who had been kidnapped by rogue Russian soldiers under the command of Achilles Flandres.

As Locke, Peter exposed Russia's unintentional involvement in kidnapping war heroes. The Russian military mounted a secret rescue mission, freeing all of the prisoners except Petra Arkanian, who remained in Achilles's clutches.

Peter was frustrated that his parents didn't realize he was the mind behind Locke, but knew that someday they would. He would be in the history books, a much bigger presence than his brother Ender.

Having successfully helped release ten of Achilles's captives, Peter tried to arrange a meeting with Bean and Sister Carlotta. They came to see him at his university, and in the first visit, Peter and Bean sniped at each other like children.

Peter saw Bean as a sort of replacement Ender while Bean saw Peter as another Achilles. They didn't like each other, but knew that if they were to accomplish their goals (Bean wanted to save Petra, and Peter wanted world dominance) they had to rely on each other.

After enduring an annoying family dinner that included Bean and Carlotta, Peter joined his guests in a meeting where they spoke privately about him joining them in their hiding. They also determined that he should reveal his identity as Locke to the world, and crafted an intricate plan to accomplish this.

Thanks to contacts in the Vatican, and to Hyrum Graff's help in the government, Locke would be considered the public's choice for new Hegemon. Peter would say he was Locke, and as a teenager was too young to be considered for the office. He knew, as did Bean and Carlotta, that this would raise his chances of taking the office later.

He chose to announce it in Thailand, since Thailand was considered the leader of Asia. Achilles had gone to India and was apparently planning his next strikes from there. It was possible that he had aligned himself with Chamrajnagar there, making it even more important that Peter make his revelation personally rather than risk negative exposure at the hands of Achilles.

Bean would become Peter's right-hand man—his closest adviser and general. While the two didn't particularly care for one another, they knew they had to trust each other to accomplish what they each intended.

He told his parents the night before that he was Locke. They had known for years, but had kept their knowledge a secret to allow Peter and Valentine to function in their roles unimpeded. His mother told him that she was as proud of what he'd accomplished as she'd ever been of Ender. The words were what Peter had longed to hear his whole life, and affected him deeply. It took some time for him to regain control of his emotions after hearing his mother's words.

He revealed his identity and supported Carlotta and Bean as they went to Thailand to hide from Achilles. When an assassination attempt was made on Bean, Peter used his influence with the Thai government to reassure them that Bean was loyal to Thailand and would do all he could to protect that nation from Achilles's aggressive movements into Asia, using the Indian and Pakistani militaries.

With the uprising in Asia, now a year after Peter's revelation, many political observers were calling for Peter Wiggin to seek the office of Hegemon. While some doubted his ability, many others recognized his genetic brilliance, and supported his candidacy. Peter was noticeably silent on the matter, simply watching and waiting as the events in Asia and elsewhere unfolded. But he was calculating his run for office and preparing to lead the world.

Sister Carlotta sent Peter and Graff a message to forward to Bean if they didn't hear from her after a set period of time. When they learned that a plane she was on had been blown up, Peter dutifully forwarded the message.

Bean determined that Achilles's goal was not to control India, but Achilles had aligned himself with China and was spreading the Indian and Pakistani armies too thin, which would allow China to take over Asia with great ease. Peter, though taking a long time to do so, posted this plan on his Locke forum, exposing Achilles and his plot to the world.

Bean was angered at the delay and said that it sickened him that Peter would use such intelligence to forward his political career.

And forward it, it did. Peter was elected Hegemon following the crisis. Though his power was limited since much of Asia and Europe did not acknowledge his authority, he nonetheless had risen to be the figurehead of the world government.

Peter sent a message to Valentine in space, updating her on his rise to power. He also sought her advice, having grown to really miss her thoughts and comments on his courses of action. The message caused a brief problem on the colony ship because it interfered with regular communications. Peter agreed not to send so large a message again in the future.

He moved the home of the Hegemony to Brazil and reinstalled Chamrajnagar and Graff in their positions as Polemarch and Minister of Colonization respectively. He made Bean, with whom he still had a tenuous relationship, Strategos, and promised protection for all Battle School graduates and their families. He gave his parents jobs in the Hegemony and sought to govern the portions of the world where he had authority fairly.

A few months later, Peter made the questionable decision of rescuing Achilles Flandres from a Chinese prison. The move had potentially disastrous political consequences and drove Petra Arkanian, Bean, and their families into hiding. Peter was confident it was a smart move, though, and soon Achilles was in Brazil living in the Hegemony compound, working with the Hegemony's army.

Peter had brought Achilles to the compound to study him. He hoped to learn from Achilles's correspondence with his allies in Russia, China, and the rest of Asia. He promoted Achilles to the newly created position of "Assistant to the Hegemon" and spent a lot of time working closely with him.

Upon feeling that there was nothing left to learn from Achilles, Peter began the process of plotting Achilles's destruction. He was shocked to see that his mother, Theresa, was trying to break into Achilles's quarters. His initial reaction was that Theresa was betraying Peter, but after conferring with John Paul he realized she was going to assassinate Achilles.

John Paul told Peter in that conversation that he loved him, but Peter couldn't bring himself to believe it. John Paul left Peter to figure out what was really going on with Theresa and Achilles on his own.

Peter believed that everything was under control and did not heed the warnings about Achilles actually being the one in control. His parents tried to protect Peter by claiming that Achilles was going to kill them, but that plan failed. Peter grew increasingly irritated with his parents.

When Theresa and John Paul learned that Achilles had set up his own rescue, and that he was playing with Peter, they convinced their son to leave the Hegemony compound and find a safe location from where he could conduct his business. Peter was humiliated that he hadn't seen Achilles's power grabs and manipulations, but agreed to flee with his parents.

Though being discredited as an embezzler by Achilles, Peter held a press conference that reasserted his authority and position as the true Hegemon. Achilles had tried to play off Suriyawong as Acting Hegemon, but after the success of Peter's press conference, few aligned themselves with Achilles's vision.

Peter apologized to his parents for doubting them and treating them poorly over the years. He realized that his parents truly loved him. They had even taken up arms to protect him now that he was out of the compound. It was a changing point in the life perspective of Peter Wiggin. He knew he could still rise in power and influence, and his parents were assets not liabilities.

Hyrum Graff invited the Hegemon and his parents to stay in secret at the Ministry of Colonization, which was housed in the former Battle School, orbiting Earth. With the pseudonym Dick Raymond, Peter walked the halls where Ender had made a name for himself years before. There was no sentimentality there for Peter, who continued to write as Locke and to sway public opinion against China.

The Wiggins learned they were not safe for long at the Ministry as someone had secretly leaked their location to Earth. Peter created a plan with Graff that would get the Wiggins back to Earth safely and expose the mole on the station.

It was all a lie, however. The Wiggins did not return to Earth, but rather pretended to expose the mole. They discovered, thanks to Graff and the International Fleet's Digital Security Force, that Uphanad, the Ministry's security head, was leaking the information to Achilles. Achilles had blackmailed Up-hanad by threatening his family on Earth. Peter, as Hegemon, showed compassion to the officer by not having him arrested for treason. Uphanad was fired, but not arrested. Peter understood the intricacies of family.

His father figured out the ruse, but his mother did not. This made her angry with Peter and John Paul. She felt stupid for not getting it, despite Peter's assurances that she wasn't.

With the mole exposed, Peter and Graff made new plans to return the Wiggins to Earth. The plan used a decoy shuttle that Achilles shot down, hoping to kill Peter. This attack led to an authorized International Fleet attack on Achilles.

Peter led the attack, with Bean at his side. The two men stormed the Hegemony compound, accompanied by several bodyguards. Bean killed Achilles, and Peter resumed his role as Hegemon for the world. His parents joined him in Brazil as he took up his old life there. He was just a little more mature, and a little wiser, from the experiences he'd had over the last several months.

A few weeks later, Peter traveled to Damascus to meet with the Muslim Caliphate, Alai. He hoped to find an ally for the Hegemony in the Muslim world, but was unsure if it was realistic. He took Petra with him, posing as bickering lovers. It was an easy role for Petra to play since she hated Peter for putting her husband Bean's life in jeopardy for his own gain. Furthermore, she resented that he would ask her to come, taking away valuable time she had with Bean, who was slowly dying from the genetic manipulation with which he'd been cursed.

In their meeting with Alai, Peter and Petra told the Islamic leader that his people were murdering innocents in India and that he had little real authority. Alai believed them and undertook measures to reassert his true influence over the Muslim world politically and spiritually.

Alai did not promise to be an ally of the Hegemon, but was appreciative that his disloyal followers were exposed. He assured Peter it would not be forgotten.

Matters grew more complicated, however, when Virlomi in India caused an insurgency there that threatened to bring about war with both the Muslim world and China. Peter turned to Bean and Petra for counsel, and though he didn't listen much at first, they helped him develop a strategy to bring about peace once the impending war began. He would swoop in when war seemed to be the last thing anyone wanted, with offers of peace and unity in a world-wide government.

He returned to writing essays in the nets, now as "Lincoln," criticizing his own policy, along with essays of a foil named "Martel," which were written by Petra under his direction. He also realized that he needed to get as many Battle School graduates, who were the weapons in a virtual worldwide arms race, off the planet. He traveled around the world to offer a new life in space to all of Ender's colleagues. They all refused.

Undeterred, Peter drafted a constitution that would unite the world in a peaceful society. He invited many of Ender's colleagues to ratify the document and bring their nations into the ever-growing Hegemony. He was successful in gaining support from smaller countries—most of which had no connection to Ender—such as Rwanda. The leader of the African nation insisted that in exchange for ratifying the document and joining Peter's government, Rwanda would receive Bean as leader of its armies. Peter consented, and Bean was sent.

It came at a time when tensions between Peter and Bean were once again on the rise. Bean discovered that Peter had been embezzling Ender's military pension to fund the Hegemony. Thinking this was a grave injustice, Bean had Ender's money transferred to a computer program from Battle School. Peter responded by cutting the funding for Bean and Petra's worldwide search for their stolen embryos. Bean, prepared for that, had already found other funding.

Regardless, Bean and Petra agreed to go to Rwanda. With Bean leading the army there, Peter was able to gain a lot of worldwide support for his constitution. Many nations ratified it, and the Hegemony was changed to the Free People of Earth. Peter promised to resign his position as Hegemon, with no replacement, once the wars on Earth ended.

He had used the wars in Asia to ignite the world population's fear of war. This fear led to many people joining the Free People of Earth. Bean and Suriyawong defended the Free People members when they were attacked by outside nations. Their swift victories led to more people joining.

Peter had succeeded in unifying the world, at least to a point. He had a long way to go before all the world would unite—most of Asia was still divided among the Chinese, the Muslim Caliphate, and India. But he was on the correct path to victory.

His parents told him they were proud of him for all he'd accomplished. In telling him this, they did not mention Ender's name or refer to him. It made Peter cry with joy that his parents finally treated him so.

To advance his world government, Peter traveled to a neutral site where he met with Virlomi, the self-appointed goddess of India, to negotiate India's entrance into the Free People of Earth. Virlomi refused to join his government, but had designs of her own. She tried to convince Peter to marry her, which Peter also refused.

As the leader of the Free People of Earth, Peter called for his military to intervene when China, India, and Russia went to war with each other. China joined the FPE, adding to the government's ever-growing influence around the world.

Peter relied on several of the Battle Schoolers, such as Vlad and of course Bean and Petra, to help him in the wars. But during a conversation with Mazer Rackham, the hero of the Formic wars of nearly a century earlier, Peter realized it was time to send Bean and his mutated babies into space where they could wait for a cure for their life-threatening disease.

Mazer and Peter facilitated Bean's divorce from Petra, which was a crushing blow to her. He also helped fake Bean's death during a military strike in Iran.

He didn't have time to remain sentimental about his soldiers. He was still the Hegemon and revealed to the world how many countries continued to join his government. With the help of Vlad, and the eventual joining of China, Virlomi's India, and Alai's Muslim world, the FPE had become a massive organization, and his role as Hegemon had real power.

He spent much of his time helping raise Petra and Bean's children. Petra had refused to leave her responsibilities in the battlefield, and so Peter watched out for the children.

More than a year later, when Petra finally returned to Brazil, the military objectives of the FPE having been accomplished, Peter professed his love to her and for her children. Though Petra still loved Bean, she eventually married Peter and together they raised a family of her five children and five more that she had with Peter.

The Free People of Earth continually grew in influence and alliance. Soon, every nation save the United States joined the world government. Many biographers wrote Peter's story, but it wasn't until Peter read Ender's book on the Formic Hive Queen that he found the "right" biographer.

Peter asked Ender to tell his story as he had the Hive Queen's. This allowed Peter, now an old man with many grandchildren, to reconcile with Ender. The two brothers, although decades apart in age, were able to put past childhood differences mostly behind them. Ender wrote the biography of his brother, though it was not published on Earth until shortly after Peter's death.

The aggressive, unlikable boy who had been passed over for Battle School and who unified the whole world had been immortalized by the one person he had resented throughout his life. Despite the resentment of youth, both Peter and Ender did great things in the world, and neither stood in the other's shadow.

Wiggin, Peter Arkady II (XN, CM)

Peter Wiggin II was created in the home of the philotes. Called Outspace, this place allowed thoughts to become real by instilling philotes—the foundation of life—into the thoughts. Ender Wiggin unconsciously thought of his brother Peter while in Outspace, and a new, real, version of his brother appeared instantly.

Peter II looked like Ender's memory of his brother Peter at around age twenty. But this Peter was not a completely developed individual. Created from Ender's mind, he was aggressive and angry, which was how Ender remembered Peter. Also, having been created from Ender's mind and soul, Peter II had a philotic connection to Jane. This allowed Peter II the ability to travel through Outspace, instantly arriving at distant planets. But, it also meant that while he had his own thought processes and emotions, he depended on Ender's existence for his own.

Knowing that he was not wanted on Lusitania, Ender's longest home planet, Peter II chose to travel through the galaxy, planning to overthrow the Starways Congress. With Jane, he first went to the planet Path and delivered a virus that would reverse the consequences of congressional genetic manipulation on the planet.

As he left Path, he was joined by Si Wang-mu, a brilliant but shy servant girl. She was to help him in his subversive journey. They fought with each other like future lovers or even siblings. Peter II explained his creation to her as they traveled to their first destination, Divine Wind, a planet settled by Japanese colonists. Peter II was sure that it was the most important place to start their efforts of bringing down the interplanetary government.

On Divine Wind, Peter II treated Wang-mu very cruelly. They had been given a false identity as secret lovers and acted out the part, but his hatred for Ender, and his general aggression, made him unattractive to Wang-mu on the planet.

Their primary stop on Divine Wind was to the home of a well-respected philosopher named Aimaina Hikari. Hikari had done a good job easing the Starways Congress's conscience about destroying Lusitania and the Descolada by teaching that Ender's act of xenocide was not immoral but necessary.

Peter II and Wang-mu were unable to change Hikari's mind about the rightness of the Congress's actions, but they did give him cause to second-guess himself. Peter II also learned that Hikari was a believer in a religion based on the planet Pacifica, and they traveled there for the next step in their journey.

Along the way, Wang-mu could see that Peter II was developing his own personality; thinking for himself. Though he was still aggressive and angry, he was acting more out of his own volition than on Ender's will. She resented how cruel he was to her, but had hope that he would evolve.

When they arrived at Pacifica, they met with Grace Drinker, a teacher of the Ua Lava religious tradition Hikari had shown them. Grace saw through their secret identities and exposed them as the very people her friend Hikari had impossibly spoken to the day before on his world—a twenty-light-year distance away.

Grace introduced Peter II and Wang-mu to her family, but it was an awkward meeting since Peter II didn't understand the family's ominous sense of humor. However, it was not to last long. Malu, the Ua Lava followers' prophetic leader, came from his secluded, sacred island to meet specifically with Peter II and Wang-mu.

Malu told the two off-worlders the legend of a god who lived in the great web of life. Jane, they knew. Malu also reiterated the need for Jane to live. Peter II concurred, unsure of what to say to the wise man. Malu focused his energy on Peter II since he wore the jewel to communicate with Jane.

Peter II had become obsessed with saving Jane, which made Wang-mu jealous. She had fallen in love with him despite his boyish cruelty. This love saved Peter II's life in the days ahead. Jane, having been kicked out of her computer network home, was searching for a new body to house her Auía. She tried Peter II's body, but he already carried a strong portion of Ender's soul, or Auía. The two consciousnesses could not exist in the same place. Wang-mu helped free Peter II of Jane.

A short time later, though, Ender himself died on Lusitania, and his Auía reconnected with both Valentine II's and Peter II's. They had both had a portion of Ender's soul, but rejoined, they had become one person, living within Peter II. He could feel shadowlike memories of Ender's life, but could not remember specifics.

Ender's soul continued to live on in Peter II. Though Peter II was his own person, he carried Ender with him in his heart. Ender's work would continue, only in this younger, more able body. Peter II had held a deep disdain for himself, since Ender had created him, and hated the part of himself Peter represented. With his reunited soul, Peter II no longer hated himself and was at peace with who he was.

He expressed his love for Wang-mu, telling her that it was she who had saved him from the darkness of death. Together they learned that Jane had contacted the people of Pacifica before she was exorcised from the Congress's computer networks and told them to create an illegal secret computer network with a few other planets (including Lusitania) that would allow her to control faster-than-light travel.

Peter II was present when Grace and Malu started the new illegal network. They quickly discovered that with the Hive Queen and Human's help, Jane could, in fact, again control the instantaneous form of travel. There was much of Ender in Peter II. He didn't want to be tied down to one planet, and this news was a great relief to him. He knew that he would travel with his beloved Wang-mu from planet to planet. Nothing brought either of them greater joy than the idea they could be together for the rest of their lives.

Their joy would have to wait, though, as the fleet that was ordered to Lusitania deployed the Molecular Detachment Device against the planet. Jane bounced Peter II and Wang-mu, without a starship, to Lusitania. There they obtained a ship and captured the deadly missile. Using Jane's power, they returned the deadly weapon to the cargo hold on the fleet's flagship.

Peter II used his influence as a speaker to convince the fleet's commanding officer, Admiral Lands, to send a message to Starways Congress and tell them that the problems with Lusitania were solved—the Descolada had been eradicated and there was no rebellion. Furthermore, he ensured that the devastating device Ender had used on the Formics—and would have been used against Lusitania—was dismantled.

With Wang-mu he then jumped across the galaxy to the ship that housed Jane, Miro II, Quara, Ela, Firequencher, and a Formic drone. They had been attacked by ships sent from the descoladore and wanted to stop the seemingly hostile species by using the Molecular Detachment Device on them. Peter II, tapping into the part of him that was Ender's soul, convinced them to never use the device.

He exchanged verbal barbs with Quara, but was firm in his stance that communication—real communication—needed to be achieved between humans and the descoladore.

Peter II returned with Wang-mu to Lusitania. They attended Ender's funeral together, then snuck off into the pequenino woods and were married. Jane made Peter II and Wang-mu disappear, presumably on an intergalactic honeymoon. The carrier of Ender's true self was at last at peace. He'd found the true love of his life and a purpose to his existence.

Wiggin, Theresa (née Brown) (TP, EG, WG, NS, EH, EE, SH, SP, SG)

The daughter of prominent Mormon military strategist Hinckley Brown, Theresa Brown was an academic. A graduate student, she taught an undergraduate course titled Human Community. She was a stern, curt teacher who found herself particularly annoyed by the presence of one student, John Paul Wiggin. Their confrontations in the classroom amused other students, but were both engaging and frustrating to Theresa.

Theresa had essentially disavowed her Mormon beliefs, choosing to focus on science over religion. This alienated her somewhat from her father, but it made her tremendously attractive to John Paul. She expelled a student from her class for asking a question about her Mormon faith versus science, citing the questions as bigoted and troublemaking.

Theresa's research as a grad student was well respected. It was thought it would benefit the entire human race. Because of this, it came as a great shock to Theresa when she was called into a meeting with her entire dissertation committee and told that her funding was being pulled. She would receive her degree, but the government of the Hegemony had made the decision that Theresa should not be involved in her own research. It was revealed that this was the government's move against her father, in retaliation for his religion, or his war.

John Paul began flirting with her immediately after this meeting. She was frustrated and didn't wish to speak to him, but he was persistent. He set up a picnic outside her office that piqued her curiosity.

At the picnic, Theresa learned the truth about this annoying student's life and family. Like her family, his was outspokenly noncompliant. They spoke of world political philosophy and grew to be friends. John Paul declared his love for her, and she was unsure where it would lead, but she had come to admire this strange, annoying student.

As she and John Paul talked and laughed together on this most unique of days, Theresa found herself falling in love with him. They closed their first-date picnic with an unexpected kiss. Theresa Brown went on to marry John Paul Wiggin, taking his name and, in the fashion befitting their mutually noncompliant families, bearing his three children: Peter, Valentine, and Andrew "Ender." The third child, Ender, had been requested by the government, because Peter and Valentine had not lived up to the government and military's expectations for brilliance in the Wiggin household. Though not active in the religious tradition of her upbringing, she was upset that her husband baptized the three children in their infancy.

Years later, she consented to have the children monitored by the International Fleet. When it was revealed that Ender had been chosen to go to Battle School, Theresa was stunned. More so, she was angry, as the decision to recruit her youngest child had come because he had brutally beaten a boy at school. She loved Ender and was deeply saddened when he chose to go to Battle School.

She missed him terribly and continued to hang his Christmas stocking, filling it with traditional gifts like five-dollar coins. She was protective of her memories of Ender, which led to conflicts with a jealous Peter. Though Ender was not dead, Theresa acted as though he was and mourned him for years.

This experience taught Peter some lessons about cruelty. In an effort to win the hearts of those around him—though doing so only to increase his public influence—Peter made Theresa a mosaic of Ender pictures for Christmas that year. The gift brought Theresa to tears, and she expressed her love for both her sons.

Even after Ender's victory over the Formics, Teresa still missed him. She would often comment that it was remarkable to her that he would one day be in the history books as the savior of Earth.

It was with unbearable sadness that Theresa said her final good-bye to Ender. Through a letter from Hyrum Graff, she realized that her son could never return to Earth. His life would be in too much jeopardy. She and John Paul subtly manipulated Peter and Valentine, in their guises as Locke and Demosthenes, to call for Ender to remain in space. These essays worked, and the International Fleet was convinced to assign Ender to a colony on a former Formic world. What Theresa hadn't planned on, however, was Valentine's desire to go with her brother to the new colony. In the course of a few months, Theresa lost her two youngest children to space.

While on their journey into space, Valentine wrote her mother updates about Ender. Ender never wrote his parents, which broke Theresa's heart, but she was grateful to have the communication with Valentine, whom she jokingly declared was the favorite child in the family.

Not long after Ender and Valentine left Earth, Bean, Ender's confidant at Battle School, showed up on Theresa's doorstep. She recognized him and took him into her home. She knew it was dangerous to speak to him because he was being hunted by Achilles Flandres, a former Battle School student and a serial killer who was rising to power on the global scale.

Theresa shared many of her deepest feelings and thoughts with Bean. She made it clear that she loved her children, all of them, and worried about them constantly. She revealed that she knew that Peter was the political pundit Locke, and that Valentine had been Demosthenes. But she and her husband had never let the children know that they knew.

They had once wanted to raise their children religiously, in secret, but it was not to be. So they simply fostered their children's talents as best they could. She wanted Peter to have children of his own but was scared that he never would—that his ambition would get in the way of ever having a life like that. These thoughts hit Bean hard, and he felt that he would also never have kids of his own.

After their conversation, which was at times tense and condescending by both parties, Theresa greeted Peter back home. He brought Sister Carlotta, Bean's guardian, with him. The Wiggin family took Bean and Sister Carlotta to dinner that night, where the guests invited Peter to join them in their running from Achilles.

Later that night, Theresa learned that Peter would join Sister Carlotta and Bean. He told his parents that he was Locke and would be revealing that to the world. Theresa told him that she knew already, and she was as proud of him as she'd ever been of Ender. The words meant everything to Peter.

Theresa and John Paul promised to support Peter however they could, knowing that once he revealed his identity and began running from Achilles, their lives would never be the same.

They wouldn't run for long, though. As China took over Asia and Russia conquered much of Europe, Peter was made Hegemon. He moved his office to Brazil, and his parents joined him there. He offered them jobs, assisting in the rising new government, but his parents both refused.

When it was discovered that Peter had rescued Achilles Flandres, the serial killer with designs on world domination of his own, Hyrum Graff tried to convince Theresa to go into hiding to be safe from Achilles. Theresa refused, and as she and Graff spoke she realized that to protect Peter, Theresa had to assassinate Achilles. She was a little disconcerted that she had no moral qualm with killing the young man. She just started making plans for how and when to commit the murder.

She tried to break into his quarters by posing as a housekeeper, but was unsuccessful. When John Paul confronted her about her attempts to kill Achilles, the couple decided that a better route was to have Achilles appear to be planning to kill them. Though Theresa thought the plan was crazy, she went along with it to protect Peter. Even this plan was unsuccessful, however.

Theresa and John Paul received a message from Bean that told them that Achilles had actually arranged his own release from China, and Peter had played right into his hands. It was Achilles who was winning the political chess match with Peter, and Peter's parents were concerned, unsure how to protect their son.

They convinced Peter to leave the compound and go to the United States where he would continue to conduct his business as Hegemon, despite Achilles's power grabs and attempts to discredit him. Theresa and John Paul watched as proud parents when Peter, from Greensboro, North Carolina, held a press conference that was full of honesty and forthrightness about the mistakes he'd made in trusting Achilles.

Peter's parents watched out for their son. Theresa even took to carrying firearms to protect him as a pseudobodyguard.

She traveled with Peter and John Paul into space a short time later. Hyrum Graff had invited the family to stay at the Ministry of Colonization, which was housed in the refurbished Battle School satellite orbiting Earth. Theresa quietly explored the station where Ender had killed a boy but had also been an undefeated commander. She was not outwardly sentimental, but reflected on the many children she'd known who had lived at Battle School.

When it was discovered that someone had leaked the Wiggins' presence on the station to someone on Earth—presumably Achilles—Theresa and her family made a plan with Graff to escape.

It turned out to be a ruse, though. A mole on the station had been leaking information about the Wiggins to Achilles. Graff and Peter set up a plot to expose the traitor and make it appear that the family was Earthbound. John Paul guessed that it was a cover, but Theresa did not. She felt stupid that she didn't get it as fast as her husband had and was irritated with him for it.

When she finally did figure it out, she was mad at Graff, too, for not letting her in on the secret. She argued with him over how to handle the exposed mole and was angry that he and Peter had effactually gambled with her life to expose the mole.

She wanted to return to Earth. Peter and Graff set up a plan to really make that happen once the mole was discovered. The plan, which exposed Achilles's evil designs in the process, came off without a hitch. Peter and Bean stormed the Hegemony compound on Earth, with Bean killing Achilles.

Theresa and John Paul returned to Brazil to serve as counselors to Peter as he resumed his duties as the Hegemon. Theresa was pleased with the maturation that Peter had gone through during their whirlwind experiences in space and in the United States over the last several months.

She returned to her position as observer and occasional adviser to Peter and suggested that he utilize the resources of the International Fleet and Ministry of Colonization and get as many Battle School graduates off Earth as he could. Peter resented the recommendation at first, but soon saw the wisdom it contained. He made the effort, offering the Battle Schoolers a new life in space, but was refused by all of them.

Theresa was present at the christening of Bean and Petra's first child, Andrew, who was named for Ender. Ever snarky, Theresa told Peter that he should be relieved—he wouldn't have to name a child after his hated brother since Bean already had.

Both she and John Paul were disappointed to learn that Peter had been embezzling Ender's military pension to fund the Hegemony's growth. She was even more frustrated with her son when he made it clear that if Bean corrected the embezzlement problem, Peter would cut his funding to search for his stolen embryos. Theresa couldn't believe her son was so petty.

Bean resolved the embezzlement matter and led Peter's armies, which allowed many nations of the world to ratify the Hegemony constitution. The Hegemony changed its name to the Free People of Earth, and Peter promised to resign his position as Hegemon, with no replacement, once there were no more wars on Earth.

Theresa and John Paul were proud of what their son had accomplished. They told him so, never referring to Ender in the process. The moment changed Peter's life. He was finally out of his kid brother's shadow.

Wiggin, Valentine Sophia I (Polish name: Walentyna Zofia) (EG, WG, [SH], [SG], IC, SD, XN, CM)

Valentine Sophia Wiggin was born and raised in the city, but moved with her family to Greensboro, North Carolina, after Ender left for Battle School. Her middle name, Sophia (or Zofia) was given to her by her father in tribute to his mother's favorite sister. It also is the Greek word for wisdom.

The second (i.e., middle) child of John Paul and Theresa Brown, she adored her brother Andrew. It was her inability to say his name correctly in childhood that led to his nickname "Ender." Valentine had a very tender relationship with Ender and taught him arithmetic when he was three years old, which may have led to him receiving his monitor from the International Fleet that same year. Because of her family's perceived brilliance, Valentine also had a monitor, a rarity for a female child. However, her monitor was removed from her neck when she was three.

Ender left for Battle School when Valentine was eight. Two years later, she celebrated Ender's birthday all by herself in the woods around Greensboro. She missed him terribly, particularly at Christmas and on his birthdays. With Ender gone, her rivalry with Peter intensified. Valentine was scared of Peter, and fought with him even over the Christmas gifts he gave.

Not long after Ender left, Valentine discovered the bodies of the animals Peter had killed in the forest. They had been a signal from Peter, though. He had hoped to join with Valentine in what he called a game—writing political commentary on the impending world war that would follow the Formic conflict. Though initially unsure of the effectiveness of two children writing as adults, Valentine soon agreed. She wrote political analysis on the computer nets using several assumed names. Once her skills were perfected, she became the paranoid anti-Russian writer "Demosthenes."

Demosthenes became tremendously popular, earning a weekly news column. Valentine's father, John Paul, became a fan of Demosthenes, even quoting portions of the columns at the dinner table. This was a tad embarrassing for Valentine, now eleven years old. She was always nervous that Demosthenes would be exposed and she would be in trouble. It was these nerves that bothered her particularly on the day she was called to the principal's office where she met Colonel Graff.

Graff's visit to Valentine had little to do with Demosthenes, but everything to do with Ender. Graff convinced Valentine to write a letter to Ender who, he said, was not doing well at school because of what appeared to be depression. Valentine agreed, though once she wrote the letter she felt guilty for being an apparent pawn in the International Fleet's game with Ender. She loved her brother, and that love had been exploited. Her anger at the Fleet translated over to her writings as Demosthenes, which she took up with renewed vigor.

Valentine grew to love writing as Demosthenes, even though she was embarrassed that their father still quoted her writings to her. She nearly exposed her identity in a school essay and was shocked to learn that though members of the International Fleet had determined she was the real Demosthenes, they didn't interfere.

It was she who saw Ender during his brief visit to Earth between his time at Battle School and promotion to Command School. At that time, Valentine unwittingly convinced Ender to return to space and defeat the Formics. She expressed her love for her brother and reassured him that he could beat the Buggers. And she resented Graff and the International Fleet even more for tricking her into doing their bidding.

In the aftermath of Ender's victory over the Formics, Valentine, as

Demosthenes, made certain that Ender would never return to Earth. The powers of the world, including her own brother Peter, would try to make Ender their puppet. Valentine convinced Peter that Ender should not return, and the two of them wrote essays as Locke and Demosthenes, which led to his exile into space as the governor of a new human colony on a former Formic world. She joined Ender on the journey, retiring from Demosthenes at age fifteen.

Valentine watched Ender closely in the first days and weeks of their travels into space. She worried about his obsession with the Formics, as well as his seeming disinterest in becoming the governor of Shakespeare Colony upon their arrival there. She sought the advice of her parents, something she'd rarely done before, and was called the favorite child for doing so. She also wrote her parents frequent letters, describing both her experiences and her worries for Ender's welfare.

To pass the time on the journey, Valentine volunteered to teach classes in Common, the language of the International Fleet. She worked closely with an officer on the ship named Jarrko Kitunen. She also got involved in a play put on by several passengers including Ender, and Dorabella and Alessandra Toscano.

The play was briefly ordered canceled by ship's commander Admiral Quincy Morgan, who was sure that it was actually a mutiny, and not a play. His evidence for such subversion was a massive ansible message from Earth. Peter had sent Valentine an encrypted message that detailed the events on their home world since the ship's departure. Once Valentine showed Morgan that the message was not subversive, and asked Peter not to send such a large message to the ship again, the play was back on. Valentine realized through the encounter with Admiral Morgan that he was trying to usurp Ender's influence on the ship on the planet that awaited him.

Over the two years of travel to Shakespeare Colony, Valentine wrote the first of many books she would write over the years. This one, a history of Battle School, relied on interviews over ansible with Ender's childhood colleagues. It was heralded as a great success, despite Ender's minimal involvement. Valentine noticed that he avoided discussing his experiences in the war, but was still obsessed with the Formics.

Valentine also realized that Ender was, perhaps unintentionally, leading Alessandra Toscano on. The girl had a puppy-dog crush on Ender, and Ender helped foster those feelings.

Once the colonists arrived at Shakespeare Colony, Ender and Valentine had another emotional confrontation. Valentine was still concerned about how Ender treated Alessandra, though the two had no hard feelings between them. She was also frustrated with Ender's emotional distance in the early days of their arrival at the colony.

She wrote books as she traveled from colony to colony, planet to planet, at Ender's side. She used Demosthenes as her pseudonym for the books, writing the *History of the Formic Wars* while at Shakespeare, and telling the tales of each colony they visited. She particularly enjoyed writing about the colonies that failed.

With Ender, she kept in touch with their brother Peter on Earth. She last spoke to him when he was in his seventies, and she was entering her twenties—the difference due to the effects of relativistic space travel. She helped convince Ender to write Peter's biography under his own pseudonym, the "Speaker for the Dead."

She traveled with him to Ganges, their second stop. There, Ender sought out the son of his friends Bean and Petra. The boy believed he was actually Achilles Flandres's son, and wanted to kill Ender. Valentine tried to stop Ender from confronting the boy, but was unsuccessful. Though Ender survived the fight, and was able to convert Achilles II away from following in his father's footsteps, Valentine was angry with him for fighting at all.

Ender and Valentine left Ganges very shortly after their arrival there. They traveled to another planet, and Valentine continued writing her books, making Ender promise not to get himself killed.

Valentine was still traveling with Ender when they reached the planet Sorelledolce near Ender's twentieth birthday. It was there that she found out her book about the failed colony Helvetica was a smash, and she was rich from the royalties. Valentine received many fan letters on behalf of her alter-ego Demosthenes, and appreciated that people didn't realize it was she, a young woman, to whom they were writing.

She and Ender left Sorelledolce after two weeks on the planet. She was ready to write a book about crime on a criminal planet after visiting such a place in Sorelledolce. The advanced computer program known as Jane joined her and Ender on their subsequent trips throughout the galaxy. Valentine warned Ender as they left Sorelledolce that she could find herself feeling jealous of Ender's relationship to his software, though she wasn't personally familiar with Jane the individual. Ender tried to pacify his sister by reminding her that Jane was just a computer program.

For more than three thousand years of Earth time, Valentine and Ender traveled from planet to planet. They spent a longer time at the Icelandic planet Trondheim than they had other planets. There, Valentine and Ender were both given assignments as teachers at a local college. Because she answered student questions with answers and not more questions as Ender did, Valentine was the more popular teacher.

On Trondheim, Valentine met and married a fisherman named Jakt. She was pregnant with their first child, a girl named Syfte, when Ender told her that he was leaving for a not-too-distant planet called Lusitania. His departure was hard on Valentine, as she'd spent her whole life with him. But, she knew that he had to go and that her life was on Trondheim with her husband and children.

A few years after Ender left, one of his former university students confessed to Valentine that she'd uncovered Ender's true identity as the Xenocide. This student, Plikt, became a friend to Valentine, and tutored Syfte and the other children as they grew up.

Valentine continued her work at the university, but longed to be with Ender. More than twenty years later, she would be. It was revealed that Ender's new home was going to be destroyed by the same weapon Ender had used against the Formics three millennia earlier. As Demosthenes, she exposed the plan, turning public opinion against Starways Congress, but not dissuading the use of the devastating weapon.

With her husband Jakt and Plikt, a white-haired, nearly sixty-year-old Valentine left Trondheim to stand with Ender as he led a rebellion against the Congress on Lusitania. She began again the life she thought she'd given up when Ender left two decades before.

With her three children and husband, Valentine traveled for several weeks, heading toward a rendezvous with Ender's stepson, Miro Ribeira. She wrote many essays as Demosthenes, trying to keep the Starways Congress in check and hoping to keep them from destroying Lusitania. She took the opportunity to be physically close to Jakt on the journey as a reward for the sacrifices he'd had to make to accompany her on the mission.

When she finally met with Miro's ship, she and the young man argued about their views on Lusitania. Miro felt they should consider the option that the planet ought to be destroyed as the only means of protecting the hundred worlds from the deadly virus. Valentine disagreed, planning to do all she could to prevent the destruction of the planet.

At first, Valentine and Miro did not get along, but they quickly grew to respect each other, and Valentine made the decision to move from her ship to Miro's for the last leg of their journey to Lusitania.

On Miro's ship, Valentine learned about the Philotic Web—the foundation of life and communication. She also finally met Jane face-to-face. Though she had been familiar with Ender's communication with a computer program, she didn't realize the software was sentient. She had thought Jane was a code name for a group of subversive rebels. And although Valentine had first encountered Jane thousands of years earlier at Sorelledolce, she didn't realize this was the same self-aware program.

She continued to write essays trying to dissuade Starways Congress from destroying the life on Lusitania. Her essays became more impassioned now that she knew about Jane. Jane represented yet another form of new life that was at risk.

The risk grew even more serious as Jane stated that she had figured out a way to stop the congressional fleet from destroying Lusitania, but it would require Jane to sacrifice her own life in the process. Valentine watched as Miro and Ender begged Jane to find another way. She promised she'd do what she could to preserve Jane's life as well as the native life on Lusitania, the pequeninos, and the sole-surviving Formic Hive Queen, which Ender had allowed to grow and flourish on Lusitania.

When they arrived on Lusitania, both Ender and Valentine were in their sixties. But they picked up their relationship as it had been during their intergalactic travels. They relished the sarcastic banter they levied at one another.

Ender took Valentine, along with Miro and Plikt, to the Hive Queen's lair. Valentine was scared of seeing the Queen, as she had had nightmares growing up of the Bugger invasions of Earth. The Hive Queen, using Ender's close philotic connection of Valentine, spoke to her mind to mind. It was a scary and fascinating experience for the woman, who tried very hard to set aside her own prejudices against the Formics.

She learned, as did the others, that the Hive Queen was building spaceships to take her newly hatched children, as well as the pequeninos, into space.

As they left the lair, Valentine said she felt violated because of the mental communication. Ender and Plikt had never experienced such feelings but tried to be sympathetic to her plight.

Valentine learned that her role as Demosthenes had been uncovered by a young girl named Han Qing-jao on the planet Path. Qing-jao had exposed her political pundit identity to the government leaders of the Starways Congress. The congressional leaders were pleased that the fleet was on its way to destroy Lusitania, as it would also kill the hated Demosthenes in the process.

A short time later, after the murder of Ender's stepson Quim by the pequeninos, Valentine consulted with the colony's leaders on how to proceed. She warned the leaders that a riot would take place and unless strict curfews were enforced, more deaths would occur. The leaders doubted her, but another of Ender's stepsons, Grego, incited just such a riot.

Valentine confronted Grego, condemning him for his inflamatory remarks that led to a vengeful attack on the piggies' land. Grego initially refused to accept responsibility for the riot and subsequent murders, but Valentine's words convinced him to.

She was present in Ender and Ela's laboratory when they asked the piggie named Planter to confirm their hypothesis that the Descolada virus was created to use the piggies and all other life on Lusitania to maintain environmental stasis. Planter said he'd come to the same conclusion, and after speaking with Valentine about free will and genetic influence, decided to be the test subject for the hypothesis.

In an effort to help Grego figure out faster-than-light travel from his jail cell (a consequence for the riot and sharing secrets with the pequeninos), Valentine approached another of Ender's stepsons, Olhado. She hoped Olhado would be able to give Grego a different perspective on the travel methods. He, as a brick maker, wasn't confident he could help with such a scientific matter. But Valentine had faith in him.

While they talked, Olhado spoke tenderly of his relationship with Ender. Valentine saw that Olhado and Ender shared a true parent-child relationship, and it moved her to tears.

She joined Olhado at the jail when he met with Grego. They had indeed developed a theory for faster-than-light travel. Valentine was intrigued by their ideas, but didn't concern herself too much with them since she was a historian and not a scientist.

As the time grew close for Ender, Miro, Ela, and Jane to test Grego and Olhado's theories, Valentine spent time with Jakt and her family. She knew that she was not an integral part of the Lusitanian society and would really only contribute to the colony when she wrote its history. She was an integral part of her family, though, and decided to spend time with them so they knew that.

During his trip to the other dimension through which faster-than-light travel was possible and thoughts and wishes made real, Ender unintentionally thought of a young version of Valentine. This new person was created from Ender's thoughts and returned to Lusitania with him.

Valentine was wary of her younger self. Though touched that Ender had created so innocent a version of herself, Valentine struggled with being around Valentine II. Valentine found excuses to avoid this younger version, nicknamed Val. Seeing the discomfort the two Valentines felt, Plikt took responsibility for Val.

When Miro was baptized in the new body he'd also created for himself in Outspace, Valentine was a witness. She was not actively Catholic, but participated when the town gathered for penance after the murderous riots of weeks earlier.

She beseeched Miro to find Ender, who had joined his wife Novinha's religious order so that he could be with her, and convince him to return to help protect Lusitania.

Despite public opinion that she was uncomfortable around her youthful doppelgänger, Valentine spent some time with her. She learned that Valentine II was essentially dying. She'd depended on Ender for sustenance of life, but so did Peter II, Jane, and Ender himself. There was not enough of Ender to go around. Valentine was concerned about Val's life, and expressed such to Ender.

She played a bit of matchmaker with Miro II and Valentine II. Miro was hesitant to pursue a relationship with the younger Valentine, but the older Valentine encouraged him to.

A few days later, Ender lay dying in the abbey to which he'd retreated to join his beloved Novinha. Valentine went to him there and told Novinha to let him go, to give him permission to die. The request led to an angry confrontation between the two women, and also with Plikt, who had been at Ender's side all the while.

Each woman claimed to love Ender the most, and each had a valid reason. Valentine's words to Novinha stung because of their truth, and she slapped Plikt, telling her that she would never have the honor of Speaking Ender's death.

Once Ender spoke again, the three women set their differences aside, setting a goal only to support Ender as he faced his final hours. The thought of losing her brother hurt Valentine, but she knew that she had her children and husband to go home to, and that eased the burden somewhat.

She helped Novinha and Plikt comfort Ender as his body struggled with an invasion from Jane's soul, or Auía. Jane had been disconnected from her computer home, and her consciousness tried to find a new body wherein to live. She tried Ender's, but it was already full with his own essence. Jane left, and Ender regained consciousness for the last time.

Valentine watched as Novinha set Ender free of his obligations to her. As Ender passed into death, his body dissolved into nothing but a few hairs from his head. Valentine, Novinha, and Plikt each took a handful of the hairs to remember Ender by. He was gone.

For Valentine it had been three millennia of a relationship. She had explored the universe with her brother and loved him deeply. But she was also a compassionate observer of humanity and saw that throughout his life he tried to repent his act of xenocide. Though she missed him terribly, she knew that Ender was finally free of the burdens that haunted him for over three thousand years.

As the Lusitania fleet came ever nearer, Jane insisted that Valentine, Jakt, and their children leave Lusitania. Jane transported them instantly to an undisclosed location. When the planet was not destroyed, they returned to Lusitania.

Valentine attended Ender's funeral. She appreciated Plikt's Speaking for Ender's death, but found more comfort in the memories she had that no one else did. They'd been together for over three millennia, and Valentine cherished those thoughts of her younger, now deceased, brother.

Following the funeral, she joined Miro II and Jane and Wang-mu and Peter II as the two couples were married. She saw them disappear after congratulating them. She returned to Jakt and happily settled into life with the man she loved more than any other.

She would write one more book under the name Demosthenes. It would be the history of Lusitania. In it, she would write Ender's story, but only because he'd been so important in the story of that world.

She missed her brother, but looked optimistically toward her final years of life, to be spent with Jakt.

Wiggin, Valentine Sophia II (XN, CM)

Valentine Wiggin II was created in Outspace. There, the home of the life-creating philotes, thoughts and ideas can be made real as philotes combine to create them. Ender unintentionally thought of a younger version of his beloved sister, and this new person appeared instantly.

Nicknamed "Val" to avoid confusion with the older Valentine on Lusitania, Valentine II was about fourteen years old in appearance, but had Ender's wisdom. She was a kind, innocent person, as that was how Ender best remembered his sister.

The Catholic leadership on Lusitania did not believe Valentine II had a soul, and she was forbidden from taking communion or performing acts of penance. Her life was further complicated by her predecessor's discomfort around her. The older Valentine wanted to build a relationship with this genetically identical younger version of herself, but was unable to do so; she was simply too uncomfortable. Plikt, seeing the distance between the two Valentines, stepped in and took Valentine II as her quasidaughter.

Because she had been created from Ender's soul, Valentine II had a philotic connection to the sentient computer program, Jane. This allowed her to travel throughout the galaxy via Outspace. With Miro II, who had also been created in Outspace, Valentine II undertook a space journey to search for a planet that would be suitable for Lusitania's native life, the pequeninos, to inhabit.

She and Miro found several potential planets for the creatures. But upon their return to Lusitania, Valentine II felt she was slowly dying—disappearing. Her essence had been created from Ender's mind and depended on it to live. So, too, did Jane and Peter II as well as Ender himself. He could not sustain the life essence for so many living creatures, and Valentine II got the short end of the stick.

While Ender was distancing himself from Valentine II, Valentine was drawing closer to her younger self. The two slowly developed a bond, with the senior Valentine playing a bit of matchmaker for the young Valentine and Miro II.

Miro II had feelings for Valentine II, but loved Jane. Ender, sarcastically trying to rid himself of the burden of Valentine II, said that perhaps Jane could take over Val's body. Miro and Jane immediately began studying the possibility.

Miro II and Val went to the Hive Queen to ask if she could, or would, help Jane and Val unite into one persona. Valentine II said that she didn't want to be merged with Jane, because she was scared of either losing her own memories and identity entirely or having too much information in her brain—both her memories and all of Jane's knowledge—at once. Miro II saw through the fears and knew that, deep down, Val recognized that she wanted to merge with Jane because it was the only possible way for either of them to survive.

When she first met the Hive Queen, Val reacted much as her original had. She felt violated and didn't like the queen using the philotic connection she had with Ender to communicate with Val. She stuck with it, though, for Miro's sake.

In the midst of this conversation, Miro learned that his journey with Val into space was not just to search habitable worlds, but also to search for the Descolada's creators. Once Ender learned of this, he increased his support of Valentine's portion of him. She became talkative, excited. Ender felt she had a reason to live now, and devoted his energy to it.

This devotion nearly killed him, though. Meanwhile, the Hive Queen worked with the pequenino fathertree named Human to determine how to use Ender's dying philote to save both Valentine II and Jane.

Miro and Val argued like lovers as they traveled through Outspace. On this journey, they discovered the Descolada's home planet. Returning to Lusitania, they enlisted Miro's sisters Ela and Quara to return with them to the planet. That journey was essentially a suicide mission, particularly for Val, as Jane was losing strength and the ability to transport them through Outspace. Once they returned to the distant planet, Jane would not have sufficient strength to bring them back to Lusitania.

As Ender grew closer to death, Valentine II was surly and concerned. She knew that in order for Jane to take her body, her soul, or Auía, would need to leave, but because of Miro's love for her, the Auía wouldn't. She asked Miro to sincerely tell her angry, hateful things about her. It would be hard for her to hear, but was necessary.

Miro understood the importance of being cruel to Val, and though it broke his heart, he told her that she wasn't really a person, that he didn't love her, and that she didn't deserve to exist. This did the trick. Valentine II's portion of Ender's soul that gave her life left her body, reunited with the now-dead Ender's soul, and joined with their third part in Peter II. Peter II had Ender's complete soul, combining Val II and Ender into himself.

Jane, with the Hive Queen's help, was able to move her consciousness into Valentine II. In the initial phases, Jane could still sense shadows of Valentine II's memories and told Miro and the rest of their travelers to continue to call her Valentine. A few moments later, though, Val-Jane realized that she was more Jane than Valentine, and though she was in the mortal body and could no longer communicate with Peter II, Ender, or Miro's mind, she was essentially Jane. Valentine II, save for a few shadows of memories, was gone. Only her body, inhabited by Jane, remained.

Wins (EGS)

Not much is known about the boy called Wins, except that he was a soldier in Ender Wiggin's Dragon Army. He received a promotion to command his own army at the early age of nine thanks to his participation in the dominant Dragon Army. Two weeks later, he was assigned to Command School to train in the simulators with Ender and several of his fellow Dragon Army colleagues.

Wives, the/Female Piggies (SD, XN, CM)

The wives were the female pequeninos, found on the planet Lusitania. They were rarely seen, and a male pequenino needed special permission to speak to them. Ender Wiggin and his stepchildren were able to speak to the wives, but only briefly. All female pequeninos who were not "little mothers" become wives shortly after birth.

Although the male pequeninos are the most visible, the females are the most forceful. It is thought that the pequeninos are close to a matriarchy, though the male fathertrees are the public face of the race. The wives make the main decisions.

Worm (SD)

Worm was a male pequenino, the native life on the planet Lusitania. He carried ink for the signing of the treaty between humanity and the pequeninos.

Wu, King (XN)

King Wu was a character in the fairy tale *The Jade of Master Ho,* which was popular on the Chinese planet Path.

Wu "Woo-hoo" (ES)

One of the veterans at Battle School when Ender Wiggin was given command of Dragon Army, Wu (or Woo-hoo as she was known) was one of the few soldiers with any experience assigned to Dragon. She was picked for the assignment by Bean when he was assembling the army.

Wuri, Polemarch Bakossi (EE)

Bakossi Wuri was the Polemarch in the later years of Peter Wiggin's time as Hegemon. He worked closely with Minister of Colonization Hyrum Graff. The two of them sent a letter to Admiral Quincy Morgan, the commander of the first colony ship, warning him not to interfere with Ender Wiggin's installation as governor of Shakespeare Colony.

Wutan (SD)

Wutan was a citizen on the planet Trondheim. Not much is known about him except that Ender Wiggin Spoke his death and Valentine Wiggin wrote a book detailing his life titled *History of Wutan in Trondheim.*

Xingadora (SD)

The Xingadora were the only observed birds living on the planet Lusitania. They had evolved to somehow avoid extinction from the Descolada virus.

Yasunari (CM)

Yasunari was a well-respected citizen on the Japanese planet Divine Wind. He and his servant helped his friend Aimaina Hikari search for the true identities and whereabouts of Peter Wiggin II and Si Wang-mu.

Younger (EGS)

Younger, who went by his last name, was a soldier in Ender Wiggin's unbeatable Dragon Army. Because the army was so dominant, several soldiers—including Younger—were promoted to command their own armies. These promotions came three years earlier than usual, when Younger and his colleagues were only nine years old. He was later assigned to Command School where he worked in the simulators with Ender, Bean, and the rest of his Dragon Army colleagues.

Yuan Shikai (CH)

Yuan Shikai was an ancient Chinese general and ancestor to Han Tzu.

Yuan-xi, Colonel (SH)

Colonel Yuan-xi was a leader of the Chinese army and helped his military take over India after that nation had been weakened by the manipulations of Achilles Flandres. Achilles had been working with the Chinese and Russian governments to help them take over Europe and Asia respectively.

When Bean Delphiki confronted Achilles in India, trying to rescue Petra Arkanian from his clutches, Yuan-xi helped broker a deal that let Petra go free and Achilles live. The Chinese government had issued orders that Achilles was to return to China. Yuan-xi, loyal to the government, agreed to let Petra live if Bean let them take Achilles unimpeded.

Achilles wanted no part of this deal and tried to kill Yuan-xi, but Yuan-xi broke Achilles's arm before Achilles had a chance to kill him. Yuan-xi refused an offer of asylum from Bean, stating that he was loyal to China and would suffer whatever consequences Achilles had in mind for breaking his arm. Bean was certain it was death, but what actually occurred is presently unknown.

Zacatecas (SD)

Citizen of the planet Moctezuma, Zacatecas's death was Spoken by Ender Wiggin.

Zeljezo, Mayor Kovano (XN)

Mayor Kovano Zeljezo became mayor of Milagre, the colony on the planet Lusitania, replacing Bosquinha sometime during the thirty years that the colonists were waiting for the congressional fleet to arrive to destroy their planet.

He called and conducted a contentious meeting concerning how to best serve the people of Lusitania in light of the revelation that the piggies were planning to leave the planet and what to do about the Descolada.

After it was learned that the piggies had killed Ender's stepson, Quim, Mayor Zeljezo refused to enforce martial law as suggested by Valentine Wiggin. He felt that the citizens of his colony wouldn't retaliate against the piggies. He was wrong, and many pequeninos were killed in a fiery riot.

Mayor Zeljezo had another of Ender's stepsons, Grego, arrested and took responsibility for not preventing the murderous riot. As the jailer, he was present when Grego and his brother Olhado developed their theory for faster-than-light travel. He was intrigued by the idea, but focused on his role as the political and legal leader of the colony.

The colony's leader had a good relationship with Peter Wiggin II, the accidental re-creation of the beloved, albeit angry and aggressive, Hegemon. Peter II used flattery to get in Zeljezo's good graces, and the two aggressive leaders built a nice rapport with one another.

Zenador (SD, XN, CM)

"Zenador" was a term used by the people of Lusitania to refer to the xenologists on their planet.

Zofia (English: Sophia) (Does not appear in any stories)

Zofia was John Paul Wieczorek's mother's favorite sister. John Paul gave his daughter Valentine Wiggin the middle name, Sophia, in tribute to her.

The Books and Stories of the Ender Series

"The Polish Boy" (Short Story)

Year published: 2002

SIGNIFICANT CHARACTERS: John Paul Wieczorek/Wiggin, Hyrum Graff

SPECIAL NOTES: Short story published in *First Meetings in the Enderverse*.

SYNOPSIS: Representatives from the International Fleet visit the home of the Wieczorek family in Poland to test several of their nine children for possible entrance into Battle School. When one of the youngest—too young for testing—John Paul, shows the greatest aptitude, additional testing officers are sent to recruit him. Against his father's wishes, little John Paul meets with these additional officers, including a brash lieutenant named Hyrum Graff. John Paul agrees to move to America but not go to Battle School, in exchange for his family's exemption from the strict population laws. Graff agrees, knowing that John Paul would never attend Battle School. However, Graff hopes that by making this deal, the young prodigy will grow up, marry someone of equal brilliance, have a child of superior capacity, and turn him over to the Fleet and into Battle School.

"Teacher's Pest" (Short Story)
Year published: 2003
SIGNIFICANT CHARACTERS: Theresa Brown Wiggin, John Paul Wiggin, Hinckley Brown
SPECIAL NOTES: Short story published in *First Meetings in the Enderverse*
SYNOPSIS: Theresa Brown is a brilliant grad student who meets her match, an impetuous student named John Paul Wiggin. John Paul challenges Theresa on many of the topics she discusses in her university class, which John Paul is taking. After learning that the university is pulling her research funding in reaction to her famous father's politics, Theresa encounters John Paul outside of class. He has prepared a picnic lunch for her, hoping to win her affections. Though Theresa is initially irritated with the act, she soon comes around and falls for her annoying student.

"Mazer in Prison" (Short Story)
Year published: 2005
SIGNIFICANT CHARACTERS: Mazer Rackham, Hyrum Graff
SPECIAL NOTES: Story first appeared in *Orson Scott Card's InterGalactic Medicine Show* online magazine.
SYNOPSIS: Exiled to near light-speed travel, Mazer Rackham, the hero of the first two Formic invasions, has lost touch with his life on Earth. He starts receiving messages by ansible from his ex-wife and their children. He learns that he has grandchildren, too, which is a bittersweet experience. At this time Mazer is contacted by Hyrum Graff of the International Fleet and is asked to return to Earth to help train the new leader of the fleet. Rackham is mixed about returning to his home planet as several decades had passed on Earth,

though because of his relativistic speed, only a few months had passed for him. But he decides to return anyway, for the good of the planet and to protect his grandchildren by training the new military mind.

"Pretty Boy" (Short Story)

Year published: 2006

SIGNIFICANT CHARACTER: Bonzo Madrid

SPECIAL NOTES: Story first published in *Orson Scott Card's InterGalactic Medicine Show* online magazine.

SYNOPSIS: Little Bonzo Madrid loves his father and mother. His world is turned upside-down, though, when his father is exposed to having an affair. Bonzo and his mother leave his father. Bonzo's heartbreaking experience with his dad leads him to be a prime candidate for the International Fleet's Battle School.

"Cheater" (Short Story)

Year published: 2006

SIGNIFICANT CHARACTER: Han Tzu

SPECIAL NOTES: Story first appeared in *Orson Scott Card's InterGalactic Medicine Show* online magazine.

SYNOPSIS: Little Han Tzu is the hope of China—at least he is according to Han Tzu's father, who wants his son to become a great warrior and ruler of the Chinese people and their nation. He has hired tutors to prep Han Tzu on the Battle School screening tests, an act that is against the law. Han Tzu learns well and excels at the tests. However, his father's cheating is exposed. The International Fleet arrests Han Tzu's father and recruits the little boy, shown to be brilliant, to Battle School.

"Ender's Game" (Short Story)

Year published: 1977

SIGNIFICANT CHARACTERS: Ender Wiggin, Hyrum Graff

SPECIAL NOTES: Story first published in *Analog Science Fiction and Fact*; republished in *First Meetings in the Enderverse* (2002).

SYNOPSIS: In command of an undefeated combat unit, preteen Ender Wiggin is moved from Battle School to Command School, where he is trained to fight the Formics by his mysterious mentor Mazer Rackham. With the help of several of his Battle School colleagues, Ender commands squadrons of spaceships in simulated attacks on the Formics, even destroying the aliens' home planet. He is shocked and saddened to learn that the simulations were real, and he has wiped out an entire species.

Ender's Game (Novel)

Year published: 1985

SIGNIFICANT CHARACTERS: Ender Wiggin, Hyrum Graff, Mazer Rackham, Peter Wiggin, Valentine Wiggin, Bonzo Madrid, Bean Delphiki, Petra Arkanian

SPECIAL NOTES: Won the prestigious Hugo and Nebula awards. Translated into more than twenty languages. Feature film in development. Earned the Margaret A. Edwards Award, presented by the American Library Association's Young Adult Library Services Association, honoring Orson Scott Card's lifetime contribution to young adult literature.

SYNOPSIS: Little Ender Wiggin is chosen to receive a monitor from the International Fleet, which will track and record his every move. He shows a great level of intelligence and aggression (he killed a student at his elementary school) that makes him a strong candidate for the Fleet's Battle School. Leaving behind his parents, brother Peter, and sister Valentine, Ender goes to Battle School. There he is the smallest and youngest of the students to be recruited, and is bullied. He is assigned to an army, and disobeys the orders of his superior. He gets transferred around armies, but thanks to his own practice, and with help from his friend Petra, he perfects the combat strategy necessary to command an army of his own. The administrators at Battle School give Ender an impossible schedule of battles, but his army goes undefeated. When his life is threatened by his former commander Bonzo Madrid, Ender kills the older boy while trying to defend himself. With a proven track record, Ender is transferred to Command School, where he learns the strategies necessary to fight the Formics, aliens who had previously attacked Earth. Joined by some of his colleagues from Battle School, Ender leads squadrons of spaceships against Formics in simulations, even destroying the Formic home world. He is shocked and dismayed to learn that the simulations were actually real and that he caused the destruction of an entire species. He discovers one remaining Formic Hive Queen and becomes the "Speaker for the Dead," promising to find a new planet whereon the Formics can be reborn.

Ender's Game (Comic Book)

Year published: 2008–2009

SIGNIFICANT CHARACTERS: Ender Wiggin, Hyrum Graff, Mazer Rackham, Peter Wiggin, Valentine Wiggin, Bonzo Madrid, Bean Delphiki, Petra Arkanian

SPECIAL NOTES: Marvel Comics published a series of comic books based on the original *Ender's Game* novel. The adaptation was written by Christopher Yost, with art by Pasquel Ferry, who had worked with Orson Scott Card on another Marvel Comics series, *Ultimate Iron Man II.*

SYNOPSIS: See novel entry.

War of Gifts (Novella)

Year published: 2007

SIGNIFICANT CHARACTERS: Ender Wiggin, Dink Meeker, Hyrum Graff

SPECIAL NOTES: Includes small portion of short story "Ender's Stocking."

SYNOPSIS: In Battle School, religion is forbidden. But when Dink Meeker gives a traditional Dutch Christmas gift to one of his friends, another Battle School student, Zeck Morgan, causes a religious revolt. The son of an abusive evangelical preacher, Zeck incites a short-lived religious riot on the space station, encouraging Muslims to pray five times a day. Hyrum Graff is frustrated with Zeck's shenanigans, but knows things will work themselves out. After a conversation with Ender Wiggin, who exposes Zeck's father's abuses to the boy, the religious observances settle down. Zeck had once been ostracized by his colleagues, but now was slowly being welcomed as one of the Battle Schoolers because Ender reached out to him.

"Ender's Stocking" (Short Story)

Year published: 2007

SIGNIFICANT CHARACTERS: Peter Wiggin, Valentine Wiggin, Theresa Wiggin

SPECIAL NOTES: Story first appeared in *Orson Scott Card's InterGalactic Medicine Show* online magazine. Small portion of story also appears in novella *War of Gifts.*

SYNOPSIS: Peter Wiggin hates everyone. Or at least he seems to. But this Christmas, he decides to treat people nicely and see what it gets him. He is shocked to see how much respect and loyalty it gains him, particularly in light of the fact that he does not feel sincere in his attempts to befriend others. Nonetheless, he is successful in gaining trust, and promises himself to stick to appearing nice to gain the loyalty of his subjects.

Ender's Shadow (Novel)

Year published: 1999

SIGNIFICANT CHARACTERS: Bean Delphiki, Petra Arkanian, Achilles Flandres, Peter Wiggin

SPECIAL NOTES: Some story points overlap with original *Ender's Game* novel and short story, but are told from a different perspective.

SYNOPSIS: The boy named Bean is an orphan in the streets of Rotterdam in the Netherlands. He, like most of the children there, must fight for survival. He is smaller and younger than all of the other children, but he is smarter, too. He joins a gang under the direction of a girl named Poke. They are fed by a soup kitchen. A bully named Achilles joins the gang and assumes its leadership. Bean tries to have him killed. A nun named Sister Carlotta takes Bean under her wing after Achilles kills Poke, and she has Bean sent to Battle School where he would be trained to fight the Formics, aliens who had twice attacked Earth. In Battle School, Bean is rejected and mocked but befriends a boy named Nikolai Delphiki. Bean proves himself to be a talented soldier and is assigned to an army commanded by Ender Wiggin. The army goes undefeated, and Bean is given an army of his own. Soon thereafter, Achilles comes to Battle School, but is quickly dimissed when Bean and his army expose the boy as a murderer. Bean moves on to Command School where he will help Ender Wiggin in the "simulated" combat with the Formics. Bean figures out they are real battles and is the back-up man in case Ender fails. Ender does not fail, and with Bean's help he destroys the Formic home world. Sister Carlotta has learned that Bean's biological family are the Delphikis, and after the war he returns home with his friend and brother Nikolai.

Ender's Shadow (Comic Book)

Year published: 2008–2009

SIGNIFICANT CHARACTERS: Bean Delphiki, Petra Arkanian, Achilles Flandres, Peter Wiggin

SPECIAL NOTES: Marvel Comics published a series of comic books based on the original *Ender's Shadow* novel. The adaptation was written by Mike Carey with art by Sebastian Fiumara.

SYNOPSIS: See novel entry.

"Gold Bug" (Short Story)

Year published: 2007

SIGNIFICANT CHARACTERS: Sel Menach, Ender Wiggin

SPECIAL NOTES: Short story was written first, but published in *Orson Scott Card's InterGalactic Medicine Show* online magazine after the comic book adaptation of the story was published in Marvel Comics's graphic novel, *Red Prophet: The Story of Alvin Maker,* Volume One. Portions of the story are also included in the full-length novel, *Ender in Exile.*

SYNOPSIS: On a distant planet, Sel Menach, a soldier in the wars against the Formics, has become the planet's governor and its chief scientist. Learning that Ender Wiggin was set to be his replacement as governor, Sel sets out to have a scientific exploration. With the help of his young assistant, Po, Sel discovers a race of alien bug creatures working in the caverns of the planet harvesting metal by eating and absorbing the alloys until their exoskeletons are saturated. These Gold Bugs become the focus of Sel's life work as Ender arrives to take over governing the planet.

Gold Bug (Comic Book)

Year published: 2007

SIGNIFICANT CHARACTERS: Sel Menach, Ender Wiggin

SPECIAL NOTES: A comic book adaptation of the short story of the same name, this version of *Gold Bug* was scripted by Jake Black with art by Jin Han. It first appeared in the back of Marvel Comics's graphic novel, *Red Prophet: The Story of Alvin Maker,* Volume One. This first appearance was published before the story upon which it was based was featured in *Orson Scott Card's InterGalactic Medicine Show* online magazine.

SYNOPSIS: See short story entry.

"Ender's Homecoming" (Short Story)

Year published: 2008

SIGNIFICANT CHARACTERS: Hyrum Graff, John Paul Wiggin, Theresa Wiggin, Peter Wiggin, Valentine Wiggin.

SPECIAL NOTES: First appeared in *Orson Scott Card's InterGalactic Medicine Show* online magazine. Also appears as part of full-length novel, *Ender in Exile.*

SYNOPSIS: The nations of the world all hope to exploit Ender Wiggin in the aftermath of his victory over the Formics. When Ender's parents receive a letter from Hyrum Graff subtly warning them of this, they decide to manipulate their other children, Valentine and Peter, into writing political essays that will result in Ender's exile to a human colony on a distant planet.

"A Young Man with Prospects" (Short Story)

Year published: 2007

SIGNIFICANT CHARACTERS: Ender Wiggin, Alessandra Toscano, Dorabella Toscano

SPECIAL NOTES: Published in *Orson Scott Card's InterGalactic Medicine Show* online magazine. Included in full-length novel, *Ender in Exile.*

SYNOPSIS: A young girl named Alessandra learns that her mother has signed them up to leave Earth and head for a new planet and human colony. Not wanting to go, Alessandra tries reaching out, without success, to her estranged grandmother. Realizing how much her mother is sacrificing for them to have a better life, Alessandra decides it's okay to leave Earth. When she learns that the hero of humanity, Ender Wiggin—a boy her own age—is going to be on the same ship, she gets excited, thinking that she might just marry this boy.

Ender in Exile (Novel)

Year published: 2008

SIGNIFICANT CHARACTERS: Ender Wiggin, Valentine Wiggin, Admiral Quincy Morgan, Sel Menach, Alessandra Toscano, Virlomi, Achilles Flandres II, Hyrum Graff

SPECIAL NOTES: Includes short stories "Ender's Homecoming," "Young Man With Prospects," and part of "Gold Bug."

SYNOPSIS: Following his victories over the Formics, Ender Wiggin is sent into space to govern a human colony on a distant planet. He is joined by his sister, Valentine, and pursued by a young girl named Alessandra Toscano. Ender has frequent run-ins with the transport ship's commanding officer, Admiral Quincy Morgan. When the ship arrives at its destination, Ender is made governor. He discovers a Formic Hive Queen living on the planet, and takes it to preserve her life. It is a great penance for his act of xenocide. Ender and Valentine both write important books while on this planet. Hyrum Graff asks Ender to travel to another planet, Ganges, to discover the fate of the last of Bean and Petra's lost children. Ender meets this child, who believes himself to be the son of Achilles Flandres. Ender teaches the boy of his true parentage, setting Achilles II, now calling himself Arkanian Delphiki, on a better path. Ender and Valentine return to the stars and more planets.

Shadow of the Hegemon (Novel)

Year published: 2001

SIGNIFICANT CHARACTERS: Peter Wiggin, Achilles Flandres, Bean Delphiki, Petra Arkanian, Sister Carlotta, Hyrum Graff

SYNOPSIS: Ender Wiggin's colleagues are the heroes of Earth. They worked together to defeat the Formics, the aliens who twice attacked our planet and threatened humanity's very existence. Ender himself has left Earth to govern a human colony on a former Formic world, leaving Bean, Petra, and the rest of his friends alone on Earth. Achilles Flandres, a murderer and longtime enemy of Bean's, kidnaps the remaining members of Ender's army, or jeesh as it was known, except Bean. To rescue his friends, Bean turns to Ender's brother, Peter, a teenaged political pundit and a manipulator with designs of world domination. All are rescued except Petra, the secret love of Bean's life. Bean mounts a dangerous operation to save her and successfully does so, but is unable to save Sister Carlotta from Achilles's murderous hand. Petra wants to marry Bean, but he has discovered that he is growing at an incredible rate and will not live into full adulthood. He doesn't want to make Petra a young widow. Achilles is captured, and Peter furthers his path to ruling the world.

Shadow Puppets (Novel)

Year published: 2002

SIGNIFICANT CHARACTERS: Peter Wiggin, Bean Delphiki, Achilles Flandres, Petra Arkanian, Hyrum Graff, Alai, Han Tzu, Virlomi

SYNOPSIS: In the years since their victory over the Formics, the members of Ender Wiggin's army have been taken in by their respective governments and exploited for their military genius. Bean Delphiki continues to grow at an astounding rate, knowing that he will soon be dead from the genetic manipulation that gave him his superior strength and intellect. His best friend, Petra Arkanian, wants desperately to marry him, but he refuses. Meanwhile, Peter Wiggin, Ender's older brother, is getting further on the path to ruling the world. Achilles Flandres has escaped and is manipulating world politics to start wars in Asia and Europe. With Bean's help, Peter's small army and government is able to help put an end to the wars, but not without consequence. India has been taken over by the Islamic world, and is beginning small revolts. Bean ultimately marries Petra, and they set out to have children in vitro, hoping to ensure that they do not have the genetic manipulation that will kill Bean. Bean also confronts and kills Achilles, who spearheads the robbery of Bean and Petra's embryos. With Achilles dead, and the world in disarray, Bean and Petra set out to find their babies, while Peter picks up the pieces of a fractured world, hoping to unify it under his government, the Hegemony.

Shadow of the Giant (Novel)

Year published: 2005

SIGNIFICANT CHARACTERS: Peter Wiggin, Bean Delphiki, Petra Arkanian, Alai, Han Tzu, Virlomi

SYNOPSIS: Bean Delphiki has only a short time to live. He will die from the genetic manipulation that has given him superior strength and intellect, as well as accelerated his growth to giant-sized. But before he does that, he and his wife Petra must find their stolen embryos. They search throughout the world looking for them, finding all but one who had been hidden by Achilles Flandres, Bean's lifelong arch enemy. Meanwhile Peter Wiggin, the Hegemon of Earth, works to unify governments and militaries into one world government. The spiritual leader of India (a former Battle Schooler named Virlomi) and the head of the Muslim world (another Battle School grad named Alai) have united in marriage, but have set their own designs for world control in motion. With Bean's part-time help, Peter is able to cause a split between Alai and Virlomi and unify the world, bringing about an end to the wars on the planet. Peter becomes the Hegemon of the whole world except for America, which doesn't join his government. Bean, knowing that he will soon die, divorces Petra and takes a few of their children (all of whom have the same genetic manipulation he carries) into space. They plan to travel at light speed, slowing time for them and allowing scientists on Earth to figure out how to reverse the manipulation. Petra is heartbroken, but eventually marries Peter. Peter's brother, Ender, writes the story of Peter's life, and it is a book that revolutionizes the world. Decades pass, and Peter dies. Petra mourns him, but is glad that she has lived the life she did.

"Investment Counselor" (Short Story)
Year published: 1999

SIGNIFICANT CHARACTERS: Jane, Ender Wiggin, Valentine Wiggin

SPECIAL NOTES: Story first published in *Far Horizons,* an anthology of science fiction stories and novellas; republished in *First Meetings in the Enderverse.*

SYNOPSIS: Arriving at the planet Sorelledolce, Ender Wiggin, now an adult, wonders about his financial status. He tries to find his money through the bank on the planet but is denied. He discovers, however, that a sentient computer program named Jane has been managing his finances. With Jane's help, Ender is able to stump an annoying tax collector and gain access to his money. This begins a relationship between Ender and Jane that will grow deeply intimate over the next several centuries of relativisitic space travel.

Speaker for the Dead (Novel)
Year published: 1986

SIGNIFICANT CHARACTERS: Ender Wiggin, Novinha, Miro, Jane, Human, Pipo, Libo

SPECIAL NOTES: Won presitigous Hugo and Nebula awards, making Orson Scott Card the only author to ever win both awards in back-to-back years, having won the previous year for *Ender's Game*.

SYNOPSIS: Three thousand years after his defeat of the Formics, Ender Wiggin receives a call for a Speaker to the distant planet Lusitania. He travels there to Speak the death of a loved one of a little girl named Novinha. Though it feels like a matter of weeks to Ender, nearly thirty years pass for Novinha. She marries and has children by another man (her secret lover Libo), who also is killed. Her husband also died in this period. Novinha's children had become the top scientists on the planet and worked very closely with the native life-forms, the pequeninos, who had killed a few humans (including Libo) over the years. Ender's arrival sent the planet's entire culture into chaos. He Spoke the deaths he'd come to Speak and began to believe this planet might make a suitable home for the last Formic Hive Queen, whom he'd carried with him for three millennia. Though she initially hated him, Novinha fell in love with Ender and the two were married. Ender worked with her children and the pequeninos, hopeful that new relationships between species could be achieved. It was Ender's prayer that the pequeninos would stop killing humans and the Hive Queen could finally find sanctuary.

Xenocide (Novel)

Year published: 1991

SIGNIFICANT CHARACTERS: Ender Wiggin, Novinha, Miro, Jane, Han Qing-jao, Si Wang-mu

SPECIAL NOTES: Created term "xenocide," which is defined as an act of genocide toward an alien species.

SYNOPSIS: Ender Wiggin has lived on the planet Lusitania with his wife and her children for several years. The children are grown and are the top scientists on the planet, experts in the deadly virus the Descolada that threatens the world's very existence. They have continued to work with the planet's native life-forms, the pequeninos, to solve the mystery of the virus. Ender has also deposited the Formic Hive Queen, whom he carried for three millennia looking for a suitable home, with the hope that she and her race would again flourish. But when death and chaos ensue between the pequeninos and humans, the governing body of the galaxy, the Starways Congress, dispatches a fleet of ships to destroy Lusitania and to contain the virus. Ender's wise sister, Valentine, with her husband and children, travels to Lusitania to help stop the invasion. Meanwhile, half a galaxy away, a girl on the Chinese planet Path, Qing-jao, believing she is a vessel for the gods, helps the fleet in their mission. Thanks to exposure from Ender's sentient computer program, Jane, Qing-jao is stopped, and the source of her "gods" exposed. Qing-jao remains dogmatically faithful to her religious beliefs, ultimately dying and becoming a god herself.

Powered by thought, Jane and her colleagues experiment using Outspace to find a world where the people and pequeninos and Formics of Lusitania could go as the fleet approached. In Outspace, Ender creates new versions of his siblings, Peter and Valentine. They are young, and soulfully connected to Ender. They have adult wisdom, but teenaged bodies.

Ender's wife Novinha wants to leave him, jealous of his relationship with Jane. The young versions of his siblings have a difficult time becoming a part of Lusitanian society, and the fleet is still coming.

Using Jane and the travel of Outspace, young Peter Wiggin crosses the galaxy, taking with him Si Wang-mu, a slave girl from Path, desperate to stop the destruction of Lusitania.

Children of the Mind (Novel)
Year published: 1996

SIGNIFICANT CHARACTERS: Ender Wiggin, Valentine Wiggin, Novinha, Plikt, Miro, Jane, Peter Wiggin II, Valentine Wiggin II, Si Wang-mu

SPECIAL NOTES: This book is notable for Ender's death.

SYNOPSIS: Starways Congress, the galactic governing body, is going to destroy the planet Lusitania and all its inhabitants unless Ender Wiggin's "son" Peter and his friend Si Wang-mu can convince the leaders otherwise. But they have already begun disassembling Jane, the sentient computer on whom their causes depend. Ender, meanwhile, is facing a crisis of his own. His wife Novinha has left him to join a monastery. Ender joins her, but his health is failing. He soon dies, leaving parts of his soul in his "children," Peter and young Valentine. Jane is able to transfer herself into young Valentine's body, with the pieces of Ender's soul going to his son Peter entirely. Peter and Si Wang-mu are successful in changing Congress's mind and protecting Lusitania. However, the fleet commander ignores the order to stand down. With Jane's help, Peter and Si Wang-mu stop the fleet.

While this is all happening, Ender's stepchildren discover the source of the deadly virus, the Descolada, and are able to eradicate it from Lusitania. However, they also visit the virus's home planet and learn that it is actually a chemical weapon. They do not know if they will be able to free the galaxy from the Descolada, but they plan to try.

Peter and Si Wang-mu, as well as Jane/Valentine and Miro (Ender's step-son), marry. They go off on their honeymoons, leaving Ender's sister Valentine and his widow to reflect on all he gave the galaxy in his three thousand years of life.

ENDER'S TIME LINE

Time line created by Adam Spieckerman and Nathan Taylor for the Philotic Web website, www.philoticweb.net. Additional references courtesy of Philotic Web staffers Ami Chopine, David Tayman, Ethan Hurdus, and Stephen Sywak.

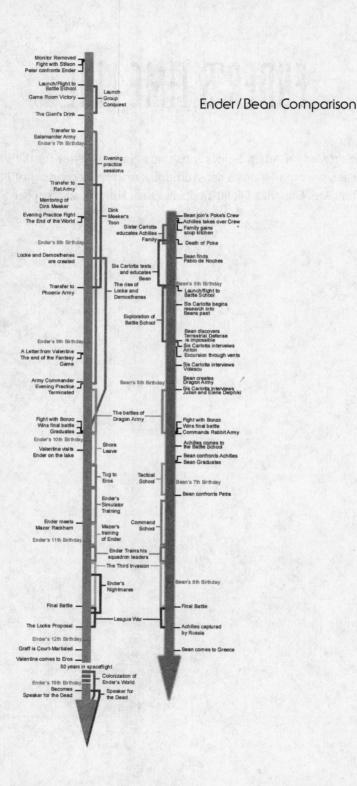

Ender/Bean Comparison

Monitor Removed
Fight with Stilson
Peter confronts Ender

Launch/Flight to
Battle School
Game Room Victory

The Giant's Drink

Launch
Group
Conquest

Transfer to
Salamander Army
Ender's 7th Birthday

Evening
practice
sessions

Transfer to
Rat Army

Mentoring of
Dink Meeker
Evening Practice Fight
The End of the World

Dink
Meeker's
Toon

Bean join's Poke's Crew
Achilles takes over Crew
Family gains
soup kitchen

Sister Carlotta
educates Achilles
Family

Death of Poke

Ender's 8th Birthday

Locke and Demosthenes
are created

Bean finds
Pablo de Noches

Sis Carlotta tests
and educates
Bean

The rise of
Locke and
Demosthenes

Transfer to
Phoenix Army

Bean's 8th Birthday
Launch/flight to
Battle School

Sis Carlotta begins
research into
Beans past

Exploration of
Battle School

Bean discovers
Terrestrial Defense
is imposible

Ender's 9th Birthday

Sis Carlotta interveiws
Anton
Excursion through vents

A Letter from Valentine
The end of the Fantasy
Game

Sis Carlotta interviews
Volescu

Bean creates
Dragon Army
Sis Carlotta interviews
Julian and Elena Delphiki

Army Commander
Evening Practice
Terminated

Bean's 6th Birthday

The battles of
Dragon Army

Fight with Bonzo
Wins final battle
Graduates

Fight with Bonzo
Wins final battle
Commands Rabbit Army

Ender's 10th Birthday

Shore
Leave

Achilles comes to
the Battle School

Valentine visits
Ender on the lake

Bean confronts Achilles
Bean Graduates

Tug to
Eros

Tactical
School

Bean's 7th Birthday

Bean confronts Petra

Ender's
Simulator
Training

Ender meets
Mazer Rackham

Command
School

Mazer's
training
of Ender

Ender's 11th Birthday

Ender Trains his
squadron leaders

The Third Invasion

Ender's
Nightmares

Bean's 8th Birthday

Final Battle

Final Battle

The Locke Proposal

League War

Achilles captured
by Russia

Ender's 12th Birthday

Graff is Court-Martialed

Bean comes to Greece

Valentine comes to Eros

50 years in spaceflight

Colonization of
Ender's World

Ender's 19th Birthday
Becomes
Speaker for the Dead

Speaker for
the Dead

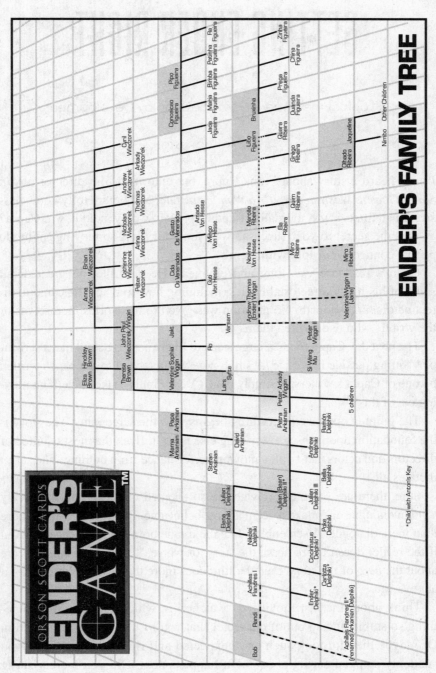

ENDER'S FAMILY TREE

DESIGN: ANDREW LINDSAY

GETTING ENDER RIGHT

A Look at the *Ender's Game* Screenplay Development

—BY AARON JOHNSTON

I once heard a story about Frank Capra, the renowned film director of *Mr. Smith Goes to Washington*, *It's a Wonderful Life*, and other Hollywood classics. In an interview, a journalist asked Capra, How do you do it, Mr. Capra? What's the secret to your success? Why are your films so moving? Why do people connect so deeply with them?

Capra's response was long and eloquent. He described in great detail some of his many directorial tactics, including how to place the camera, direct actors, and so forth. No mention was given to the stories themselves or the writers who had written them.

The next day Capra found a large stack of blank papers bound like a screenplay sitting outside his office. A small note was attached to the pages written by one of Capra's writers. It simply read: "Dear Frank, make something moving out of this!"

The point is obvious: Everything begins with the screenplay. The story is the foundation upon which everything else is built. Even the most talented of directors and actors can't pull a moving performance from nothing. The script dictates all.

Sure, there are some actors who are so talented they can pull off poorly written dialogue and make it seem almost believable. But a screenplay is more than mere dialogue. A screenplay, like the movie born from it, is a story. And if the reader doesn't care about the story, or worse, if the reader doesn't care about the *hero* of the story, then the film does more than merely bore you—it annoys you.

Think about the last movie you watched in which the hero did something so stupid and so out of character that you lost all interest in the film. Or maybe the plot took such an unexpected and ridiculous turn, that you suddenly stopped caring about what happens next. Did you merely shrug your shoulders and leave the theater indifferently? No. If you're like me, you got angry, and not solely because you just blew ten bucks on the movie ticket. No, you're angry at the characters. You're angry with the story.

And why?

Because when we go to the movies, we make a silent agreement with filmmakers. When the lights dim, we say, "Hey, I'm going to suspend disbelief for the next two hours, and I'm going to invest myself in this story. I'm going to offer up my emotions. I'm going to laugh when it's funny, and I'm going to feel hurt and possibly even cry when it's sad. I'm giving you a little bit of me, Mr. (or Mrs.) Filmmaker. And in return, I ask that you merely be true to the story, that if you establish rules, you abide by them. You don't have to follow conventions. Good doesn't always have to vanquish evil, so long as you're being true to the story."

The best filmmakers understand this. They keep their end of the bargain; they remain true to the story and don't play tricks on us or jerk us around. They tell the story they promised to tell.

Think about *The Princess Bride*. How would you have reacted to the film if at the end, after investing yourself so emotionally into the story, the dashing Wesley dumped Buttercup for some barmaid and the two rode off into the sunset?

Or what about *Rocky*? How ticked off would you have been if, right before the final bout, Rocky decides he doesn't want to box after all and would much rather study eighteenth-century Russian literature?

Extreme examples, yes, but you see my point. When we commit ourselves to a story, we expect the story and its characters to remain true to themselves.

In the case of *Ender's Game,* or any other story that has a large fan base, the filmmaker has an even greater responsibility. He need not be exact in his adaptation, of course. Some changes must be made. No novel can appear exactly onscreen as it does on the page. But there does exist this level of expectation that the story be true to itself.

How would the world have reacted if Chris Columbus (the film director, not the explorer) had cast a twenty-something-year-old hunk to play Harry Potter in the first film instead of the adorably cute young Daniel Radcliffe? Or what if Columbus had made Harry out to be a selfish brat? Or a conceited little punk?

Well, I'll tell you what would have happened: a massive global mob of preadolescents would have assembled and Chris Columbus would have been tortured into making a weepy painful apology.

No, we moviegoers expect the story to be true to itself. It need not be

identical to the novel. We're not looking for a carbon copy. But we are looking for the *same* story, the same hero, the same emotional experience we had
when we read the story.

All of us have heard it said, "The movie isn't as good as the book." And
that's probably true in many cases. But inherent in that statement is the understanding that the two tell the same story, that one established an expectation for the other.

For *Ender's Game,* the expectation is very high. Since its first publication
in 1977, *Ender's Game* has captured the imagination of millions of readers
the world over. If you're reading this book, I can only assume that you, like
me, are one of them, a fan devoted to *Ender's Game*. Which is to say you've
probably read it more than once, recommended it to countless friends and
family, and felt a touch of affection whenever you've spotted it in the bookstore, library, or hands of a stranger. In short, you love *Ender's Game*. It
holds a special place on your bookshelf as well as in your heart, and nothing
would make you happier than to see its title projected onto a movie screen.

Your excitement would wane rather quickly, however, if after the opening
credits rolled, the character of Ender appeared onscreen, not as the self-
effacing genius commander you remembered him to be, but instead as a cocky
bully who beats up Peter and Valentine for their lunch money. In fact, I'd wager
that if that *did* happen, there would be riots in the theaters and once the fires
broke out, everyone would be forced to use the emergency exits.

What was critical to the *Ender's Game* movie development, therefore,
was Ender himself. He was the story—his pain, his perseverance, his innocence, his understanding of command, his courage, his love for Valentine
and his jeesh. All of that made Ender the endearing, memorable character
he is. And it was clear to everyone involved in the initial film-development
agreement that the Ender portrayed onscreen had to be the *same* character
readers had fallen in love with in the novel. In short, the film would only
work if Ender worked. The screenwriter had to nail Ender. Everything revolved around getting Ender right.

THE INFAMOUS OUTLINE

It was early 2003, and Orson Scott Card and I were sitting in the cramped
Santa Monica offices of one of Hollywood's more successful directors. We
were there to discuss the first official draft of the *Ender's Game* screenplay,
which Scott Card had written and submitted for review. I was new to the
project—having just joined Scott Card's production company—and was

thrilled with the prospect of seeing *Ender's Game* come to life firsthand. The director, who was overseas scouting locations for his next big-budget film, had left the meeting in the hands of his young producing partner, Joe (names have been changed).

Joe had read the screenplay, but it was clear from the start of the meeting that he wasn't pleased with the draft. From behind his desk he had asked Scott Card, "Why didn't you follow the outline?"

The outline for the screen adaptation of *Ender's Game* actually included two novels: *Ender's Game* and *Ender's Shadow*. The executives at Warner Brothers, who had optioned all the Ender novels, had supposedly seen the outline and given their thumbs-up of approval. I would learn later from Scott that the producer (who we'll still call Joe) had written the outline himself, even though he called it a collaboration with Orson Scott Card.

Scott was surprised by the producer's question. He thought he *had* followed the outline—or at least as well as he thought was necessary. It was a process Scott had followed many times before as a novelist: you submit an outline to the publisher for a proposed novel; the publisher approves it; then you write the novel using the outline as a guide, not as a set-in-stone plan of action. To handcuff yourself to the outline would impede you from all the revelations and new ideas that are born during the writing process.

Take Scott Card's Alvin Maker series, for example. Arthur Stuart, arguably the second most important character in the series, was never even part of the original outline. Scott created him on a whim while writing the novel, long after the publisher had seen and approved the outline. Had Scott been a strict adherent to the outline, ideas such as Arthur Stuart—and the, no doubt, thousands of other ideas like him that are now a part of the Scott Card universe—would have been promptly ignored and left off the page.

So it was with great confusion that Scott Card sat and listened to the producer's mild reprimand. In Hollywood, Scott and I were learning, the world was a little different. When a producer asks you to follow his outline, he means to the letter.

What made this experience especially disappointing was that Joe was the gatekeeper to the studio. He was the one who, with the director's approval, would carry the script to the studio executives at Warner Brothers to get financing and the coveted green light. So if Joe didn't think the script was ready, Warner Brothers wouldn't see the draft. They would have to wait for a rewrite.

Personally, I didn't think the differences between Joe's outline and Scott's script were all that drastic. These were not huge deviations from the story or major shifts in plot or action. Scott was the original author, after all. It wasn't like he was reinventing the novels; this was *Ender's Game* as it had been originally told.

Yet from Joe's perspective, the differences *were* major shifts. Scott had taken leaps of creative license that Joe hadn't intended him to take.

When the meeting was over and Scott had agreed to do a rewrite, everyone's stress level had tripled or more. We all parted ways civilly, but the mood was somewhat tense.

I mention this experience, not to diminish your hopes that the *Ender's Game* movie will ever be made, but rather to give you a glimpse of how difficult and delicate the process of moviemaking really is, particularly in the early stages of a film's development when everyone is still trying to figure out how best to tell the story.

Too often when we think of filmmaking, we dwell on those activities that happen on set during production: managing the extras, moving the camera, coordinating a stunt, yelling "action," all the fun stuff. Those are all critical pieces of the overall puzzle, yes, but much of moviemaking—perhaps the most difficult part of moviemaking—happens in meetings such as the one just described, behind closed doors, long before a single actor is cast or a single camera rolls.

Script development is especially dicey in the case of a big-budget film because so much money is on the line. Nowadays it's not uncommon for summer or end-of-year movies to cost as much as 150 million dollars or more to produce. And in a studio's mind, every one of these films is a huge financial risk; if moviegoers don't come out in droves, studios could lose their shirts.

Take Carolco Studios, for instance. The name probably doesn't ring a bell because their big-budget pirate movie *Cutthroat Island* sank at the box office back in the nineties, losing 82 million dollars when all was said and done and taking Carolco Studios down with it.

A more positive example, one in which a studio bet big and won, is New Line, which invested hundreds of millions of dollars on an unknown director and a trilogy of novels entitled *The Lord of the Rings*. Maybe you've heard of them?

Had those movies tanked, New Line, like Carolco, would have gone the way of the dodo.

But as luck (and Peter Jackson) would have it, *Lord of the Rings* brought in bajillions of dollars and New Line was spared the joke of becoming Old Line.

In other words, the movie business is, above all things, a business. Behind every studio decision is the American dollar. Studios invest money yes, but always cautiously, always reluctantly. They're just as protective of a million dollars as you and I would be if we had it.

The old joke in Hollywood is that a movie executive's favorite word is "no." And it's true. Getting a film green-lighted is hard.

And yet movies get green-lighted all the time. It's not impossible. If studios *only* said no, no films would be made.

The trick is to assemble the perfect package. All the planets must be aligned: the right, proven director must be on board; the script must be production ready; talent must be attached; every *t* must be crossed and every *i* dotted. Get all those ducks in a row, and your chances are good. But if any of these factors seem uncertain, the studio won't finance the film.

I can only imagine Joe's anxiety, therefore, when he read a script that deviated, even if only slightly, from the outline he had shown the executives at Warner Brothers. Perhaps Joe worried that the differences between the outline and script would cause the studio to lose confidence in the project and drop it, forever ruining his chances of producing *Ender's Game*.

Who knows? What *was* clear was that Joe wanted a rewrite. He wasn't showing the script to Warner Brothers as written. Changes would have to be made.

I left the meeting feeling somewhat spent. Getting *Ender's Game* produced wasn't going to be as easy as I had hoped.

Scott left the meeting determined to write a better draft, and I didn't envy his assignment. Getting the script to a place where everyone would deem it ready was going to be very difficult indeed.

NEW WRITERS

Years ago, when Scott Card was first approached about Hollywood adapting the story, someone suggested making Ender a handsome teenager with a love interest. The story wouldn't work as written on the big screen, they said. *Ender's Game* would be better told with the addition of a few proven Hollywood conventions. Young love. A dashing young rising star.

To Orson Scott Card's great credit, and to the relief of us all, that proposal was flatly denied.

So it was with some trepidation that Scott Card had entered this agreement with Warner Brothers in 2002. Would the studio attempt to alter the character of Ender as had been proposed in the past? Would *Ender's Game* become something Scott had never intended it to be?

To protect his own and the story's interests, Scott made a stipulation in the contract with Warner Brothers that he would get a crack at the screenplay and have final say on how Ender was represented onscreen.

It was a smart move. Scott knew better than anyone why *Ender's Game* had been such a beloved novel for so long. He had lived with the character for two decades. If anyone knew how Ender should be portrayed onscreen, it was the man who had created him.

Joe the producer apparently felt differently.

After the aforementioned meeting with Joe, Scott Card submitted a second, better draft, but Joe rejected that one also. I don't remember Joe's reasoning, exactly—I'm not even sure that he gave us one. We simply found out one day that Joe was securing a new writer to bring a fresh perspective.

We were disappointed by this news of course, but hope was not lost. We reminded ourselves that scripts get new writers all the time and that this was merely part of the business. The film wouldn't be made as quickly as we had hoped and not under the conditions we had dreamed of, but the project was still alive and kicking. Hollywood was full of wonderfully talented screenwriters with plenty of proven experience. As long as the new writer understood Ender, we would be fine.

Besides, Warner was still excited about the project. The director was still gung-ho. The world was still a happy place.

As it turned out, the new writer ended up being *two* writers, a team of writers who were fresh off a very successful comic book film (their first credit).

Before they got started on the *Ender's Game* script, the two met Scott and me for lunch in Los Angeles. I was surprised when I saw them. They were young. Very young. Younger than me, and I considered myself as youthful as they come.

But they were very polite and extremely intelligent, and I liked them both immediately. It didn't hurt that one of them was a lifelong fan of *Ender's Game* and even credited the book as part of the reason why he had become a writer himself. (He may have been pandering to the author, of course, but since he was describing exactly the way *I* felt about *Ender's Game,* I took him at his word and liked him even more.)

I also happened to like the film they had just made. The movie had brought in hundreds of millions of dollars, and from the studio's perspective that was as good enough reason as any to give these boys the job. They were young, hip, and proven at the box office. What more could we ask for?

A year later, after this team had submitted two unsuccessful drafts, Scott and I were feeling rather low. The writing team had made decisions in their drafts that had created a very different version of Ender. I was never involved in their meetings with producers, but apparently I wasn't alone in my assessment. Shortly after the second script submission, both writers left the project.

The director told Scott not to lose heart. All would be well. The right screenwriter would be secured. These things happen. New writers come and go. This next one will be the one we've been waiting for.

But the next one wasn't the one we were waiting for. In fact, the draft submitted by the next writer was such a departure from the *Ender's Game* you and I have grown to love, that I had to force myself to finish reading it. Had the studio produced that draft, I daresay fans like myself would have taken to the streets and much of Warner Brothers' studios would have been leveled to the ground.

It's ironic, really. Joe's complaint to Scott in our initial meeting was that Scott hadn't closely followed the outline. And yet, the three writers Joe had hired to replace Scott so blatantly ignored the outline and took such liberties with the story, that I can't imagine what feedback Joe gave *them*.

Perhaps he asked, "Um, guys, did you even *read* the outline?"

STUDIO WOES

By December of 2005, when the option with Warner Brothers was set to expire, movie-rumor sites were saying that *Ender's Game* was in "development hell" and that fans may never see the story come to life. Too much time had been spent developing scripts that simply did not work.

Since I had read Scott's draft, I knew these rumors were not entirely accurate; there *was* a script that worked. Scott Card had written it long before any other writer had been hired. But rumors are rumors. What do you do?

Scott and his producing partners at Chartoff Pictures, along with the aforementioned director, met again with Warner Brothers to develop a plan. Fortunately, the studio agreed to extend the option for another year or so with Scott as the sole writer, writing a page-one rewrite not based on any previous script, including Scott's own.

When asked in an interview at the time why the studio hadn't given the green light, Scott said, "There was no filmable script, though in fairness to the writers so far, they may well have been following faithfully all that they were actually asked to do. *Ender's Game* is simply a very hard story to put in script form."

A year later, after Scott had submitted another draft, the studio seemed to be stalling. The director attached to *Ender's Game* had released a big-budget film that year, which had done poorly at the box office and lost Warner Brothers a great deal. No one can be certain why, but it became clear to everyone involved that Warner Brothers had decided to pass on the film and put it into turnaround.

In mid-2007, it happened. The option with Warner Brothers expired, and *Ender's Game* returned to the open market, available to any studio that might be interested in acquiring it. For legal reasons I can't go into specifics about the film's status now, but suffice it to say that *Ender's Game* is as alive as ever. Hollywood still wants to make this movie as much as we, lovers of all things Ender, want to see it made.

So believe me, it's going to happen. Despite the many disappointments since this project began, I remain resolute in my belief that *Ender's Game* will hit the big screen. This isn't the first time a film has been in development this long. Nor will this be the first time a film has gone into turnaround only to get picked up by another studio and made into a great film: *Forrest Gump, E.T., Splash, Speed, Syriana, The Last Emperor, Black Hawk Down,* to name a few.

And if that doesn't comfort you, this will: there are a lot of incredibly talented and smart people in Hollywood working on *Ender's Game* right now— producers, managers, agents, investors—all exploring new options to make this thing happen.

So, yes, there have been some hang-ups and delays and big disappointments, but keep the faith. *Ender's Game* is still in the ring.

Just ask Orson Scott Card. When he attends book signings and fans ask about the progress of the film, Scott often jokes, "The character of Ender will be played by a young actor and most likely an unknown one. I used to think that that actor, whoever he is, had in all likelihood been born by now. But now I'm pretty sure that he's at least in school."

You see? Progress. We're getting closer all the time.

Since the project left Warner Brothers, Scott has written a new draft, one that takes into accounts all the mistakes and successes of his previous drafts.

And it's great.

Fans of *Ender's Game* would not be disappointed.

What follows are my personal notes on five of the screenplay drafts that have been submitted over the years, three written by Scott and two written by others. I'll also share some of the challenges the writers faced in adapting the story and why I wholeheartedly agree with Scott's statement that *Ender's Game* is a very hard story to put in script form.

TWO NOVELS. ONE SCREENPLAY.

The biggest challenge the screenwriters had to face was deciding how best to adapt two novels into a single feature-length screenplay. I don't recall who first suggested the idea of combining the novels, but everyone, including Orson Scott Card, thought it a brilliant idea. *Ender's Shadow* added depth to the original story and gave us the origins of Bean, a character some consider the most interesting and complex of the Enderverse. Filmmakers thought fans would be thrilled to see both stories come to life simultaneously.

For the screenwriters, however, this new depth of story proved to be both a blessing and a curse. A blessing because it gave the screenwriter more story elements and subplots to work with, but a curse because the process of adaptation would now be twice as difficult.

Steven Pressfield, a novelist and screenwriter, has said that adapting a novel into a screenplay is not merely deciding what to include, it's more a task of deciding what *not* to include. That's the difficult part of adaptation, deciding what has to go. Screenwriters, therefore, must have a cruel hand, willing to cut out a beloved scene or even a whole character simply because it doesn't fit into the film.

I think it's for this reason that there persists a belief in Hollywood, among some, that a writer can't adapt his own work. He's too close to it. He holds it too precious. He can't bear the thought of losing that particular scene or character he worked so hard to craft and bring to life.

Part of me wonders if some involved in the early development of *Ender's Game* held this misconception. Sometimes I wonder if Scott Card was given the true consideration he deserved or if those involved were merely meeting Scott's stipulation of the contract and giving him a go at the script, all along intending to hire new writers once the stipulation was met.

I have no evidence of that, of course, and no one has ever suggested as much. It's incredibly unfair to those involved for me to even suggest it, but there you have it. It's completely unfounded speculation and I take full responsibility for it.

I only bring it up because in Scott Card's case nothing could be further from the truth; Scott is protective of how the character of Ender is portrayed, yes, but he isn't opposed to shifts in the story. Throughout this process Scott has listened openly to others' ideas and was always willing to change anything that was nonessential to the meaning of the story. In fact, some of Scott's producing partners from Chartoff Pictures argued in favor of sticking with the novel's way of handling various story points when Scott changed them in the screenplay.

I can speak from personal experience, too. Scott embodied this same open attitude when he and I adapted his short story "Malpractice." The screenplay and novel we wrote were very different from Scott's original creation, but it was Scott who had suggested the largest changes to the story. Were he a self-absorbed author overly protective of his work, he would have fought off any story alterations with a feverish stick instead of embracing and suggesting new ideas.

Scott, therefore, was willing to hack away at *Ender's Game* and *Ender's Shadow* to form a single cohesive story line. But the difficult question still remained: what should be cut? How best do we tell both stories in the time allotted?

The initial consensus was to cut back and forth between the two characters' origins and then unite them once they came to Battle School. Scott's first draft did this well: we see Ender on Earth with his family; we see him being re-cruited by the International Fleet; we see him hop aboard a shuttle headed for Battle School; and then we cut to the dirty, crime-filled streets of Rotterdam, where Bean is a tiny street urchin using his smarts to stave off starvation. Sister Carlotta tests him, recognizes his genius, and informs Battle School of her find. Bean and Ender then meet up at Battle School, and we're off to the races.

In a later draft, the Rotterdam scenes occur as flashbacks late in the film as Bean recounts to Ender the horror of witnessing Achilles killing Poke.

In another writer's draft, the sequence in Rotterdam is even briefer. We see the children coming into the soup kitchen. Sister Carlotta inquires to know who was smart enough to think up a way to get them in. And the children point to Bean. We don't meet Poke. We don't see Bean's genius at work, thinking up the plan. Nor do we see Bean's brutal survival instincts or his willingness to kill Achilles once he recognizes that Achilles is a threat. In short, we don't see much of what makes Bean . . . well, Bean.

In the draft written by the writing team, we don't see Rotterdam at all. They chose to ignore Bean's origins altogether, and therefore ignore Sister Carlotta, Poke, and Achilles as well. All we know of Bean is what we see him say and do at Battle School, making their draft 95 percent *Ender's Game* and 5 percent *Ender's Shadow*.

These decisions made by the screenwriters on what *not* to include in the screenplay resulted in very different adaptations of the two novels. What one screenwriter considered important, another writer considered immaterial and left out completely. Here are a few more examples.

1. THE MONITOR

The monitor, that little device implanted on the back of children's necks used to monitor their intelligence and determine their candidacy for Battle School, is missing from most drafts. Of Scott's drafts, only his most recent includes a scene in which Ender's monitor is removed.

The writing team that followed Scott also included a monitor-removal scene, although, unlike the scene in the novel, in their version, a member of the I.F. is present to witness the removal and to confiscate the monitor.

The third writer changed the monitor completely. In his version, the monitor is a bracelet. Why he made this change is unclear. In fact, I'm not sure that the audience would have known that the bracelet Ender wears in the beginning of the film *is* a monitor since it's only referred to later in the script and very briefly at that. Were I in the audience and ignorant of the screenplay, I would think the bracelet a mere wardrobe accessory and not a critical tool of the I.F.

The screenwriter does however make an effort to demonstrate Ender's readiness for Battle School by adding a scene in which Graff gives Ender an exam. In the exam, Ender is asked to build various shapes using holographic blocks. The shapes become more complex as Ender successfully makes them, and his little hands move so quickly that we the audience can only conclude that this is one bright kid.

The flaw with this exam, however, is that it doesn't test the right things. It doesn't measure those characteristics of a military leader that the I.F. would find so appealing. It merely shows us that Ender is great with Legos® and can solve a puzzle. It doesn't show us what the real monitor showed the I.F. in the novel: that Ender is equal parts Valentine and Peter, that he won't hesitate to use violence when no other option is available, that he understands what motivates people and drives their behavior, that he is humble, that he is capable of love, that he is decisive and quick on his feet, and on and on and on.

2. STILSON

An early scene in the novel that clearly illustrates why Ender is a wise candidate for the I.F. is the scene in which a bully named Stilson and some of his cronies confront Ender after school. Now that Ender's monitor has been removed, the boys think they can push Ender around without any adults knowing. Rather than stand there and get pulverized, however, Ender defends himself and knocks Stilson down. Fearing that the other bullies will seek vengeance later, Ender puts fear in their hearts by ruthlessly kicking Stilson three times while he's down, in the ribs, the groin, and the face. That last kick, we learn later in the novel, kills Stilson.

The problem with the Stilson scene is that it would be hard to watch in the theater. In the novel, the scene works wonderfully because we know why Ender is doing what he's doing. We can read his thoughts. We know he hates being violent. We know it pains him to do this.

But in a film, as said before, we don't have that luxury. We can't get inside Ender's head. All we know is what we see characters do and say. So when Ender kicks a man who's down and then makes angry threats to the bullies still standing, we assume he's expressing his true feelings. Our interpretation of the scene would be exactly what the bullies would assume: that Ender is a violent, dangerous kid.

Rather than endear us to Ender by teaching us how averse he is to violence, the Stilson scene in the film could potentially lead the audience to dislike Ender. For this reason Scott Card chose to exclude the Stilson scene from all of his drafts.

The writing team that followed Scott, however, thought the Stilson scene a necessary plot point. Their execution of it complicated the matter further, however, because for them, it wasn't enough for Ender to merely kick Stilson while he was down. In their draft, Ender does a little karate move and shatters Stilson's nose. Then Ender proceeds to beat Stilson to a bloody pulp, kicking his head, hitting him as hard as he can, beating him viciously in the chest and stomach, and slamming his fists repeatedly into Stilson's already broken nose.

It's an extremely violent scene, possibly even violent enough to earn the film an R rating. It surprised me. It painted Ender, right from the beginning, as a vicious kid driven by bloodlust and went beyond what was necessary to scare off the other bullies. To be fair to the writers, the scene that follows the Stilson scene shows Ender running off and crying, visibly shaken for what he has just done. But I don't think it compensated for what we would have just seen Ender do. When I read it, I despised Ender for it. And I presume audiences would have had the same reaction.

3. THE FANTASY GAME

Scott Card's first draft incorporated the Fantasy Game a great deal. It was a clear way of showing that the Formics were trying to communicate with Ender and keep him from committing xenocide. At certain points throughout the draft, Ender picks up his laptop and plays the game. His game character, Ender Mouse, beats the Giant's Drink, the supposed dead end of the game, and proceeds to explore Fairy Land and find the castle tower where the Formic queen is waiting.

In Scott's later drafts, the game appears less, though he does use other devices to incorporate the game into the story. In one scene, for example, we're inside Fairy Land, and we think Ender is playing the game. Then Ender Mouse finds the Hive Queen, she pounces on him, and Ender wakes up, revealing that it was only a dream. The scene is significant because it proves that the Formics don't even need the laptop anymore to get inside Ender's head.

The other writers, however, chose to exclude the Fantasy Game—with one exception. In one scene of one draft, as Ender is walking in the arcade-like game room, he passes a kid playing the Fantasy Game. There's no dialogue exchanged or emphasis given to the game. It's merely mentioned in the screenplay as part of the landscape. If you blink you miss it.

4. GRAFF

For die-hard fans of the novels, it might sound like blasphemy to suggest that *Ender's Game* be made without Hyrum Graff. But the suggestion was made. Someone in the script-development process asked, Could the film work without Graff? And more specifically, what if Graff and Mazer Rackham were the same character? What if it were *Mazer* who comes to the Wiggin home at the beginning of the film to recruit Ender? And *Mazer* who follows Ender through Battle School?

The screenwriters after Scott explored this idea. In one draft, everyone knows and recognizes Mazer when they see him. But in another draft, neither the audience nor the other characters know he's Mazer. We think he's simply a commander in the I.F. No one recognizes him because the International Fleet has kept the vids from the invasion classified. It's not until late in the film that the big Aha! twist is revealed: that this Graff-like character is in fact Mazer Rackham.

Scott Card explored a similar idea, but rather than ditching the character of Graff altogether, he merely gave Mazer some of Graff's duties and therefore beefed up the character of Mazer. In Scott's draft, Mazer—not Graff—comes to the Wiggin home in the beginning of the film to recruit Ender without identifying himself or being recognized. After Ender agrees to accompany him, Mazer escorts Ender to Battle School and places him under Graff's care. Mazer reappears later in the film when Ender's training on Eros begins and there reveals his true identity, just as he does in the novel.

Personally, I thought this a smart move. It introduces the audience to Mazer's face early in the film and establishes him as a character of great importance. That way, when we see him later in the film, he's not a total stranger. We're not introducing a character at the beginning of the Third Act. It's also smart because Mazer Rackham is one of the few characters in the film who could be given to a name adult actor, someone who would have some pull at the box office. Beefing up that part by giving Mazer more to do at the beginning of the film makes the role more attractive to name actors.

5. BATTLE SCHOOL JARGON

Battle School soldiers have their own vernacular. When two soldiers greet each other in the corridor, for example, they'll say "Ho" instead of "Hello."

"Ho, Ender."

"Ho, Bean."

Or rather than call someone a four-letter word, a Battle School kid would use the term *eemo.* "Hold you fire, you stupid eemo!"

In the novels, these unique words and phrases added another dimension to the Battle School experience and gave it a feeling of authenticity. Kids make up words all the time. As do soldiers in war. Language evolves that way.

The words were never overused. They weren't distracting. And if they appeared, the reader needed no translation. Their meaning could easily be surmised from context alone.

Scott Card used Battle School jargon in his drafts of the screenplay, but the writing team that followed him did not. The screenwriter who followed them *did* use Battle School jargon, but it was jargon of his own creation, not words lifted from the novel. I found it interesting that I could immediately identify his words as unauthentic even though it had been a few years since I had last read *Ender's Game.*

6. THE TWIST

Another complication of adapting both stories was deciding how best to reveal the big twist. In *Ender's Game,* the reader learns that the simulation on Eros is the real war at the same time Ender does: after the battle is over.

If you were lucky enough not to know this twist when you first read the book, it was a humdinger of a reveal. It came out of nowhere. "NO WAY! He was fighting the *real* war?"

But in *Ender's Shadow,* the reader knows this already. Even before we crack the book open, we know the big twist at the end. Scott Card solved this in the novel by wisely giving us another twist, something that *wasn't* revealed in *Ender's Game* but arguably just as surprising: Bean knew the truth. Bean figured it out. Bean knew he was sending men to their deaths during the final simulation. And because Bean understood Ender, because he knew how the truth would affect him and how it could jeopardize the entire mission, he kept his mouth shut and simply did his job.

So what should the film do? Should the final twist be saved until the end? Should the audience learn the twist when Ender does, as in the first novel? Or should we learn from Bean as he does in *Ender's Shadow,* long before the final simulation?

Since film is a visual medium, Scott Card and the filmmakers agreed that the final battle would be more engaging and exciting if we cut back and forth between the Ender's simulation and the real battle, showing the pilots in their starships as they bravely followed the orders that would lead them to their deaths. It made for a very exciting sequence, and all agreed that fans and the uninitiated alike would enjoy watching the I.F. battle it out with the Formics in space.

With that direction in mind, it was clear that the reveal had to happen *before* the battle, with Bean discovering the truth as he does in *Ender's Shadow*. The great difference among the various screenplay drafts, however, was deciding when and how to reveal that information.

In the writing team's draft, Bean figures out the truth by watching the vids of the Second Invasion. He notices that I.F. communication had a time lag and that the Formic communication did not. From that simple fact he makes the amazing, yet accurate, leap in logic that the I.F. has learned how to communicate instantaneously, has launched a fleet to attack, and will direct that fleet from Earth.

In Scott Card's drafts, Bean learns the truth just as he did in the novel: while eavesdropping on the teachers from inside the air vents at Battle School. This occurs at the end of Act II, just before Ender leaves for Eros, with about twenty minutes or so left in the film.

In the third screenwriter's draft, Bean also discovers the truth by eavesdropping, but he does so on Eros, immediately before the final battle and just as the fleet is arriving at the Formic planet. In this version, the audience is kept in the dark for the longest time possible, learning the truth just before the fleet and the Formics duke it out in space.

THE BIG DIFFERENCES

So far I've mentioned a few story elements that were included in some drafts and left out in others. These differences, while significant in some respect, are minor compared to the following story changes, which greatly influenced my overall perception of the drafts.

I. BONZO'S DEATH

Go on, admit it. Bonzo is one of your favorite characters. You simply love to hate him. Well, believe me when I say that you wouldn't be disappointed by the Bonzo portrayed in the film. In all drafts I read, Bonzo is as bad as they come, clearly the villain. When he's not bullying Ender, he's demeaning other members of his army or plotting dastardly deeds.

Bonzo's critical scene in the film is the final showdown with Ender. In both the novel and in Scott Card's drafts of the screenplay, this scene takes place in the showers. Bonzo and a group of his cronies have come to the shower to beat Ender to a bloody pulp, if not kill him. Ender, being the genius he is, lathers himself in soap, turns all the shower nozzles to the hottest water setting, and proceeds to taunt Bonzo in the hope that Bonzo will be so angered that he'll insist on fighting Ender alone. The taunting works, of course, and Ender turns what could have been a lynching into a one-on-one confrontation.

And we all know what happens next.

The concern some of the filmmakers had with this scene was the nudity. Ender isn't wearing any clothes. He's taking a shower. How could the scene be shot without exposing him? Or from another perspective, what young child actor would do this? What child would agree to wrestle with another actor without wearing his Fruit of the Looms?

Scott Card was confident the scene could go as originally written. The camera could avoid exposing Ender and yet give the *impression* that he was nude. Scott thought it important to preserve the scene because Ender is so incredibly helpless. He has no layer of protection, and his only weapons are soap lather and hot water. You can't get more defenseless than that. Bonzo would clearly have the upper hand. That way, when Ender defeats him, Ender's victory is all the greater.

The producer disagreed. The scene couldn't be in the shower. And subsequent drafts of the screenplay written by others had a very different climatic final scene with Bonzo.

It's also worth pointing out that in Scott Card's drafts, Bonzo dies as he does in the novel: by accident. Ender doesn't intend to kill him. When Ender delivers his single blow and hits Bonzo with the back of his head, it's not meant to be fatal. He's merely trying to hurt Bonzo enough to make him stop. He despises violence, loathes it. Killing Bonzo is the furthest thing from his mind.

This isn't the case in the draft written by the other screenwriters. In those drafts, Bonzo suffers a much more violent death at Ender's hand. In one draft, the fight occurs in the Dragon Army barracks. Ender enters the barracks, thinking he's alone, and Bonzo steps out of the shadows wielding a lead pipe. Bonzo then pushes Ender onto a glass table, shattering it. As Ender tries to crawl away, Bonzo slams the pipe into Ender's back. Then he pushes the pipe across Ender's throat, trying to choke him to death. Ender retaliates by grabbing a large shard of glass from the broken table and slashing Bonzo across the chest. The cut isn't deep, though, and Bonzo smacks Ender around some more, toying with him. Then Ender gets behind Bonzo and wraps his arms around Bonzo's neck. Bonzo tries to free himself by repeatedly slamming Ender into the wall, but Ender's grip is too strong. Finally, with all his exertion, Bonzo slams Ender into the wall one more time. This time, however, the force of the blow results in Ender snapping Bonzo's neck, killing him.

In the other draft, Bonzo and two of his cronies jump Ender in the corridor and throw him into the Battle Room—and zero gravity—where they hope to beat him senseless. The cronies smack Ender around a few times and easily avoid his attempts to fight back. Then Bonzo steps in and slams Ender into a few of the Battle Room obstacles like a cat toying with a captured mouse. Ender then uses their tactics against them and incapacitates the two cronies, leaving only Bonzo.

Now the real fight begins. Bonzo punches Ender in the head. And then, by the screenplay's own admission, Ender loses all control, becoming completely feral and savagely attacking Bonzo. He head butts Bonzo in the nose, sending globules of blood floating into the air, then punches Bonzo repeatedly in the face, showing no mercy and releasing all his pent-up aggression. The screenplay describes it as a brutal attack, with Ender's face twisted with blind rage, his fists furiously striking Bonzo again and again.

The beating doesn't stop until military policemen storm in. But by then, it's too late. When Ender releases his attacker, Bonzo's lifeless and bloody body floats away like a drowned man at sea.

Both of these different adaptations of Bonzo's death are violent, but the latter, like the Stilson scene already mentioned, borders on warranting an R rating. I dare say fans, and sensitive parents alike, would be troubled by such an aggressive attack from Ender.

Besides the violence, however, the scenes also failed to show Ender's genius and understanding of military command. In the original scene, Ender uses all of the resources, however small, in his environment to his advantage. He also displays a bit of psychological warfare to even the odds and remove Bonzo's cronies from the battlefield without throwing a single punch.

But in the other versions, Ender merely resorts to brutal violence. He doesn't demonstrate spur-of-the-moment strategic thinking. He doesn't use tactics of hand-to-hand combat. He simply swings and slashes and punches where he can, a strategy that even the lowest of privates might resort to. In these scenes, it's not brains, but brawn that wins Ender victory. And considering that Ender, compared to Bonzo, is much smaller and physically weaker, Bonzo's death seems all the more unbelievable. It's hard to kill someone by merely hitting him in the head, especially if you're a nine-year-old.

What's also troubling about these scenes is that in them both, Ender cries out for help. Rather than use his own skills and quick thinking to save himself when Bonzo first attacks, Ender looks into the nearest surveillance camera, which he knows the teachers are watching, and screams for someone to come save him. It's only when help doesn't come, when Ender realizes that he's in this fight alone, that he fights Bonzo to the death.

This bothered me. Ender isn't fearless, of course. But the Ender I grew to love in the novel always solved his own problems. When challenges arose, he quietly faced them. He didn't run to the nearest adult and seek refuge. He took Peter and Stilson and Bonzo head-on. Alone.

Equally troubling is how the teachers handle the situation. In the original story, Graff allows the fight to begin but does not expect it to end so tragically. And as soon as it's obvious that someone is hurt, the teachers rush in. In these new versions, however, the teachers watch the brutal fight between Ender and Bonzo without interfering, even when it's obvious that Bonzo is very close to killing Ender. As Bonzo pushes the pipe into Ender's throat and Ender's eyes roll back and his face turns blue, the teachers merely watch from the surveillance room, without reacting. I found that incredibly hard to believe. If you thought the fate of all mankind rested on the shoulders of a nine-year-old boy, and that boy was slowly being murdered in the room a few doors down, wouldn't you do something about it? If not for the boy's sake, then at least for your own?

My last complaint with these scenes is that they demean Bonzo. No one gets to Battle School without being incredibly intelligent. Bonzo is one of the smartest kids on Earth. He's a bully, yes, but he's a very smart bully. He also greatly values his own standing in the school. So he's not going to do something that will ruin his chances of advancement or threaten his graduation from Battle School—at least, not if he thinks he'll get caught.

In the novel, it's no coincidence that Bonzo attacks Ender in the shower, the one place at Battle School you might assume the teachers aren't watching. But in these new versions of events, the surveillance cameras are all in plain sight. They're positioned on the wall in the barracks and the Battle Room for all the world to see. So Bonzo *knows* the teachers are watching. He *knows* they can see him strangling Ender to death. He even makes a comment to the effect, that he doesn't care that the teachers can see him. This sort of reckless behavior and total disregard for the consequences of his actions makes Bonzo look like quite the idiot. Is he really so driven by hate that he'll try to kill Ender in front of the teachers? That seems completely self-defeating. How could he know the teachers wouldn't interfere? If he knew they were watching, wouldn't he assume they would try to stop him? And once they did, what would his actions have accomplished beyond his own expulsion from Battle School and court-martial for attempted murder?

No, I think Bonzo is smarter than that. Heck, even murderers are smarter than that. They kill people in private because they don't want to get caught and be held accountable for their crimes. Bonzo is at least that smart. He wouldn't have knowingly sacrificed his military career—and long-term prison time—just to get in a few punches.

2. COMIC BOOKS

As mentioned before, the writing team that followed Scott Card had just finished a successful comic book film when they signed on to do *Ender's Game*. Months later, while working on *Ender's Game,* the team agreed to write another comic book film as soon as their contract with *Ender's Game* ended. Comic books, it seemed, was quickly becoming their niche.

Perhaps that's why the team added comic books into their draft of *Ender's Game*. Comics were their thing. Slipping a comic book into the *Ender's Game* screenplay would be like an inside joke to themselves.

Whatever their reason, their version of Ender loves comic books. He reads them all the time—especially Superman. He's so obsessed with the man in tights, in fact, that when packing his one suitcase for Battle School, Ender tosses in a few comics because he apparently can't live without them.

In the later draft written by the other screenwriter, comic books again reappeared. Ender sneaks his comics into Battle School, and he and Petra learn that they share a mutual interest in superheroes. One evening, while sitting in their adjacent bunks, they debate about who's the better superhero, Spider-Man or Superman.

For me, this scene was the comic book that broke the camel's back, so to speak. I couldn't see the significance of using comic books as a story element in the film. Comics do nothing but deviate Ender from the task at hand and make it appear as if he's obsessed with grandiose heroics, which he clearly is not.

In fact, in the novels, comic-book heroics are the farthest things from Ender Wiggin's mind. The only reason he assumes the responsibility given him and does heroic things is because he has to, because he knows there's no one else who can. He's not trying to emulate a fictional demigod. He's not seeking the praise and respect showered upon superheroes. That's what people like Bonzo do. No, Ender is simply doing his job. His motivations are purely selfless. Comic books are simply not his style.

Besides, the International Fleet would never allow comics in Battle School anyway. Comics, like anything else that might remind a soldier of his previous life, would be forbidden. Isolation is part of a soldier's training. He must be cut off completely from the world. If these children aren't allowed to contact their parents, why would they be permitted to read comic books?

This isn't to say I'm opposed to comics. I happen to subscribe to a title right now, thank you very much, and I have nothing but the utmost respect for the medium. But to have comics *in* the story feels wrong. It gives a false impression of Ender and introduces an element to the story that has no clear justification. For me, it felt as if the writers were inserting themselves into the story, like a painter who signs his name so large on the canvas that it fights the art for attention.

3. THE BATTLE ROOM

For many of us, when we say we want to see *Ender's Game* come to life on the big screen, what we really mean is that we want to see the Battle Room— just as we saw it in our minds when we read the novels.

The screenwriters differed to some extent on how best to execute the Bat-

tle Room, but the overall idea was the same: small armies of children soldiers battle it out in zero gravity, armed with weapons that shoot tight beams
of light that "freeze" their enemies. In some versions, the weapons were hand-
guns the soldiers carry into battle. But in at least one version, one of Scott's
versions, the weapon was part of the flash suit, tucked into the glove at the
end of the index finger.

The environment of the Battle Room differed as well. Each of the writers
added new elements, like obstacles that rotated instead of remaining stationary, mist that clouded visibility, or small asteroid fields that made movement
dangerous and difficult for soldiers. In one version, the walls of the Battle
Room actually projected an image of space, making it appear as if the soldiers were floating and soaring through the galaxy. The one possible flaw with
that idea is that a projected, realistic image of space would remove a soldier's
depth perception. He wouldn't see a wall. He would see only space, and
therefore he wouldn't know when to stop or where to push off. He'd simply
smack into the wall the way people walk into big panes of glass.

Size was another difference. Some described the Battle Room to be as big
as an indoor pro football stadium, while other versions described a much
smaller, contained environment.

How the game was won also differed among scripts. In the novels, five
soldiers are needed to complete the ritual that wins the game. Each soldier
places his or her helmet on one of the four corners of the enemy's gate, and
the fifth person passes through the gate.

But in the final screenwriter's version, only a single soldier is needed to
win the game. As soon as anyone passes through an enemy gate, the game
is over. This occurs in one scene when Ender, still a lowly member of Bonzo's
army, slowly floats unnoticed past the enemy army and through the enemy's
gate, winning Salamander Army the game and astonishing everyone.

The flaw with this idea is that were this the rule, armies would vehe-
mently defend their gates. No one would leave their gate accessible to soldiers casually floating by. Whole toons would be responsible for blocking
passage to the gate and preventing the other team from winning. The incident with Ender as described in the screenplay simply wouldn't occur.

Such a rule would also greatly change how a team battled offensively. If
all that was needed to win the game were to pass one soldier through the
enemy's gate, there would be tactics to achieve just that. Commanders
would create maneuvers that rushed the gate or incapacitated its defenders,
and battles would be fought mostly around the gates. It would be a very different game indeed.

The biggest difference in that script, however, as far as the Battle Room is concerned, was the addition of jet propulsion packs. Rather than have the soldiers use the walls and obstacles to propel themselves through space, the screenwriter outfitted them each with a jet propulsion pack that enabled them to change direction midflight and maneuver around at will.

In the novel, Ender and Bean demonstrate their intelligence and inventiveness by creating new ways to maneuver in zero gravity. Ender trains his armies to push off each other, for example, in order to propel themselves in opposite directions. And Bean utilizes a cable attached to his waist in one instance to win a crucial battle. These demonstrations of ingenuity are lost however as soon as all soldiers are equipped with jet propulsion packs. Movement in the Battle Room is not inhibited at all.

Another addition to the room from this script only appeared during practice sessions and not during actual battles. I call them training balls, which are hard, softball-sized balls that emit from the wall upon request and are used for target practice. You can also program the balls to attack the soldier. If you don't shoot them in time, they'll strike you at high speed and knock you silly. I couldn't help but be reminded of the quaffle from the Harry Potter series.

4. THE ANSIBLE

In the screenplays written by Scott Card, the ansible is the Formic technology adopted and used by the International Fleet to communicate instantaneously across vast reaches of space. Without it, there would be huge time lags in communication.

But in one screenplay *not* written by Scott Card, the ansible is more than that. It's also a weapon. Somehow the I.F. has figured out a way to send a transmission via the ansible that kills all Formics instantly.

They even tell Ender this. Toward the end of the film Mazer instructs Ender that he should "fire" the ansible in the final simulation.

In other words, the I.F. knows exactly how to win the war. To defeat the Formics all Ender must do is push a button and send a fatal transmission.

This of course begs the question: Why go to all the trouble of finding genius children to train as commanders if you know how to win the war? If all that is needed to defeat the enemy is to push a button, why train commanders at all? Any buck private can push a button. Wouldn't the current leaders of the I.F. consider themselves capable of such a task?

Secondly, if all one must do to defeat the Formics is send a transmission, why send a fleet? Why not send the transmission from Eros? Why not kill every Formic in the universe from the comfort of I.F. Headquarters?

In the novel, Graff explains to Ender how the previous war with the Formics was won: "The only thing that saved us was that we had the most brilliant military commander we ever found."

Shouldn't *Ender's Game* the movie be the same? Isn't that what fans want to see? A child who's a brilliant commander? A child who can pull off a victory when adults see only defeat?

5. ENDER'S FAMILY

In the beginning of the novel, Ender is six years old, Peter is ten, and Valentine is somewhere in age between them. That's young. Finding a talented cast at that age—not to mention all the other children needed for Battle School—was a concern of the filmmakers from the beginning. Everyone agreed that Ender needed to be young, but the role would require so much maturity, intelligence, and stamina, that Scott Card and others thought it best to make Ender a little older.

In Scott's first draft submitted in 2003, Ender is eight years old, Valentine is eleven, and Peter is thirteen. In terms of casting, this would make all the difference in the world. Ender could safely be played by a ten-year-old and still appear young enough to be considered a child.

In a later draft not written by Scott, the screenwriter took even greater liberties. In his draft, Ender is eleven years old, Peter is fifteen, and Valentine is twenty, the oldest of the three.

Choosing to make Valentine so much older greatly alters the relationship that Ender has with his sister. In the novel, this relationship is a crucial one. Ender decides to go to Battle School partially because of his love for Valentine and his desire to protect her from the Formics. That love stems, at least in part, from Ender and Valentine's shared experience. They're both victims of Peter's bullying. They've both relied on the strength of the other to survive Peter's abuse. And they both recognize what no adult can: that Peter is evil. Put another way, they share a common mind-set and cling to one another for both safety and mutual understanding.

But if Valentine is twenty years old, the sibling dynamic is changed drastically. To Valentine, Ender is a child, not her equal. He's someone whose hair she can tousle, someone she looks down upon, not someone she'd feel comfortable sharing her feelings with, not someone she can run to whenever she feels threatened by Peter. In fact, she never *would* feel threatened by Peter. That experience is no longer something they share. Ender is now simply a cute kid brother.

And the same goes from Ender's perspective. In his eyes, Valentine is simply an older sister. The only thing they have in common is their parentage and an elevated intellect.

It becomes clear late in the screenplay why the writer chose to make Valentine so much older, though some will argue that the rationale doesn't justify the change.

Valentine is a college student studying exobiology. Apparently she shows great promise in that field, because the International Fleet asks that Valentine work as a laboratory assistant in their Top Secret Exobiology Program. The I.F., it turns out, has a Formic "specimen" they want to vivisect, and Valentine finds herself at the operating table, assisting the I.F. scientists perform the most important autopsy in recorded history.

Why the I.F. feels that a civilian—and an inexperienced one at that—is qualified for such a monumental task is not made clear. One would think that the I.F. would keep such a discovery within the military, and turn to their own scientists, who have no doubt studied the Formics ever since the Second Invasion, to perform the operation.

Perhaps the biggest question, however, is if the International Fleet does have a specimen, why have they waited so long to inspect it? The Second Invasion was eighty years previous. Why wait so long to take a look at the enemy? Wouldn't the I.F. have done so before sending a fleet? Wouldn't they want to know the physiology of their enemy?

And lastly, why do they have only one? When Mazer Rackham destroyed the queen in the Second Invasion, all her minions died instantly along with her, right where they sat. Millions of Formic corpses were left over from the war.

The writer evades this question by stating in the script that the other Formics destroyed themselves. When the Hive Queen died, the remaining Formics disintegrated and crumbled away into space.

In this same script, Ender's father is also different. Or perhaps it's more accurate to say that Ender's father is absent. We learn early in the screenplay that Ender's father died at some point in the past as a soldier in the I.F.'s Engineering Corps. The significance of his father's involvement in the I.F. and subsequent death are never explained. Perhaps this change was made so that Ender would have respect for the I.F. before he joins it. Or perhaps this was a way of lessening the minor characters in the film and lowering the casting budget. I can't be sure. In any event, John Paul Wiggin is a no-show in that draft.

6. THE FORMICS

In his novels and screenplays, Scott Card describes the Formics as antlike. Their exoskeleton so closely resembles insects, in fact, that children have given them the vulgar name Buggers.

Their minds, however, are far more advanced than those of lowly insects. Their technology is proof of that. It's far superior than our own, and were it not for Mazer Rackham, their advanced weaponry and starships would have annihilated Earth.

But in one draft written by another screenwriter, the Formics are a very different kind of creature. The queen is described as a perfectly round, eyeless, limbless shape with intricate geometric designs. We know she's the queen because a white spherical egg emerges from her center when she gives birth.

The male Formics are no less bizarre. Rather than fly in starships of their own design, the Formics *are* the starships. They can live and breathe and apparently propel themselves unaided in open space, swarming and attacking the I.F. fighters like a hive of angry bees.

The conclusion one would naturally make from this idea is that the Formics have no technology. They are their own weapons. They can fly across the galaxy just as easily we can walk across a room.

This idea, while interesting, pokes a few holes in the *Ender's Game* storyline. If the Formics have no ships, what did Mazer Rackham blow up with his carefully aimed missile during the Second Invasion? Was it merely the queen, floating in open space? If so, Mazer Rackham was given far more credit than he deserved. Since the queen looks completely different from the males and was floating there exposed for everyone to see, anyone would recognize her as a unique target. You would not need to be a military genius to fire a missile in her direction.

Secondly, if the Formics don't have ships, why do they have an ansible? If they can communicate in open space without technology, why would they have developed a device that does just that?

7. BEAN

In one draft, Bean is not a young, starving orphan in the streets of Rotterdam, but instead an eleven-year-old computer hacker in London. When we first see Bean, he's hacking his way into an ATM to steal a few food credits. Once he secures the credits, he promptly uses them to buy an armful of chocolate bars.

Bean is then tasered from behind, and a gang of street urchins led by Achilles steals Bean's chocolates as Bean writhes in agony on the pavement. Achilles then sets off an alarm that alerts the police and leaves Bean to be arrested. The police show up, apprehend Bean, and carry him to the hospital, where Sister Carlotta is waiting. She's so impressed with his hacking skills that she wants to offer him a place at the prestigious Battle School. Bean is reluctant to go until he learns that he'll be given all the food he can eat.

My first question upon reading this sequence was: If Bean can so easily hack into a computer and get food credits, why does he find the offer of food at Battle School so attractive? He has all the food he wants in London. And secondly, if Bean is so easily overpowered by a gang of street urchins, why does the I.F. think him so capable of command? Wouldn't they be more interested in Achilles, who at least leads a group of other teens and was smart enough to overpower Bean and notify the police? Were I the I.F., I'd see much more potential in Achilles's ability to command than in Bean's ability to hack.

Once he gets to Battle School, Bean does nothing that would lead the teachers to believe that he has any potential of command. Upon arriving, he slips away into the air vents and lives there for much of the film, sneaking out only long enough to grab food from the cafeteria. He doesn't go with his launch group. He doesn't go to class. He lives only in the air vents. He does nothing that would draw the attention of the I.F. leadership or make them consider him as an alternative to Ender in their search for the next great commander. And through it all, Bean maintains a snarky, know-it-all attitude that is neither endearing nor remotely like the character of Bean in the novels.

Quite frankly, this interpretation of Bean is so far distant and opposite to the original Bean that it can hardly be called an adaptation of *Ender's Shadow*.

8. THE ENDING

Ender regrets having committed xenocide and is committed to saving the Formic cocoon placed in his care. In Scott Card's screenplays, Ender finds the cocoon on Eros, the asteroid used by the Formics as a base of operations during the Second Invasion. The Formics dug an intricate system of tunnels in the asteroid, and Ender crawls into one of those tunnels and discovers the cocoon.

We then cut to one of the Formic worlds, now being scouted by I.F. soldiers. A marine walks among the Formic corpses, grabs a handful of dirt, and states that the world is safe for human habitation, a nod to the human colonization that will follow. And the film ends.

In another of Scott's drafts, the scene with the I.F. marine is cut, and the film ends with Ender being put onto a starship headed toward a colony planet. Mazer wishes him well, and Ender says his good-byes. No one knows he is secretly carrying a cocoon and hopes to rectify the damage he has done.

In the screenplays not written by Card, the endings are very different from the novels. In one version, the I.F. is holding a banquet in Ender's honor after the war. Mazer steps to a podium and introduces Ender as their guest of honor. To everyone's surprise, Bean comes to the pulpit instead and Ender is nowhere to be found. Bean then proceeds to read a statement written by Ender in which Ender details his intent to carry the Formic cocoon to a safe planet and reintroduce the Formic species. At that moment, Ender takes off alone in a ship and flies overhead. Bean and everyone at the banquet look heavenward and watch Ender fly away.

The problem with this idea is that if the I.F. knew that Ender had a Formic cocoon and intended on reintroducing the species, wouldn't they try to stop him? Wouldn't they shoot his ship out of the sky? They just sacrificed thousands, if not millions, of I.F. soldiers to defeat the Formics once and for all. Why would they allow Ender to get away with a cocoon? That would negate everything they had just done and sacrificed. No, for Ender to reveal his intentions to the I.F. would be suicide.

In the other screenplay, the writer goes even further. In his version, Ender himself tells Mazer his intentions. He shows Mazer the Formic cocoon and divulges his plan to fly to a planet where the queen and her people can be reintroduced. Inexplicably, Mazer gives his blessing and even supplies Ender with the ship he'll need to make the journey.

This defied all logic to me.

Why would Mazer do that? Wouldn't he seize the queen and destroy her instantly? Wasn't that the purpose of the fleet, to find and destroy all remnants of the Formics? Why would Mazer have such a sudden change of heart? Wouldn't that go against everything he had stood for? Wouldn't that be the most un-Mazer-like decision he could make?

9. ENDER

I've discussed many of the story changes among the various screenplays, but as I mentioned earlier, the success of the film depends largely on the filmmakers' ability to capture the true character of Ender. Changes in story can be forgiven, even applauded, as long as Ender is Ender on the big screen.

Scott Card's screenplays achieve that. Though they differ in many ways, the Ender on paper in each version is the Ender I remember from the novels. He's determined, but never cocky, compassionate, but never soft with his soldiers; brave, but never reckless, inventive, but never demeaning. He demonstrates an understanding of command and proves through his actions that he's deserving of the confidence the I.F. places in him.

The writing team and the screenwriter that followed, however, created two other versions of the character. In their scripts there are instances in which Ender glares, scowls, storms out of a room, tells adults to piss off, tells Mazer to screw himself, smashes Battle School property in a show of defiance, yells at teachers, makes demands of the teachers that inexplicably they comply with, deceives Mazer, and even threatens other students with vengeance.

In one scene Ender gloats to Peter for having his monitor longer. Then Ender threatens to give back to Peter every abuse that Peter gave him—in essence saying, "When I'm older, Peter, I'll have my revenge and give you a taste of your own medicine."

Hmm. Not exactly the Ender I remember.

And there's more.

In another scene, Ender calls Peter a loser, boasting that he made it to Battle School and belittling Peter because he didn't.

When Ender reaches Battle School, this new behavior doesn't change. He mocks Bonzo in the cafeteria. He gloats to the teachers, telling them he beat them. He complains to Graff that Battle School is too hard and whines that he can't shoot or play the game well.

When Bonzo is rough on him, Ender hurries to Graff to beg to be transferred.

When Ender goes to the arcade, he insists on playing several strategy games at once, systematically defeating all of the soldiers who oppose him and humiliating them all in the process.

There were of course many instances in which Ender behaved like any fan of the novels would expect him to—showing courage, showing that he loves his family, being inventive in his approach to the game, and demonstrating true genius.

That said, fans would have a hard time looking past the instances in which Ender acts more like Peter or Bonzo. Those moments stand out like bright red stains on an otherwise stark white garment. They're hard to forget and forgive. And even though much of the scripts played out exactly as I had hoped they would, I couldn't see past those moments in which Ender was simply not himself.

GETTING ENDER RIGHT

I haven't told you everything about the existing screenplays or their develop-ment. Not even close. There are countless plot points, story changes, and other surprises still unmentioned. A full analysis of them all would require a much thicker book than this one and possibly spoil some of the fun of see-ing the film.

Some of you may think me a harsh critic and that I've been too unforgiv-ing with the screenwriters' deviations from the original material. If so, I wouldn't blame you. *Ender's Game* had a profound effect on me when I was younger, so I'm naturally more protective of the story and more critical of those who alter it for reasons I can't understand.

Die-hard Ender fans would likely side with me. And since you bought this book, you're probably one of them. Like me, you have very high expecta-tions indeed. You want the film to be just as moving, engaging, and memo-rable as the novels are.

I'm convinced it can happen. People in the industry with the means to bring it to life are showing great interest. A very good script exists.

Anything could go wrong, of course, and Orson Scott Card isn't the only man capable of writing a great script. Other screenwriters could be brought in, and the process could begin again. Who knows? If I've learned anything in my limited experience, it's that Hollywood is as predictable as lightning strikes. And sometimes just as painful.

But take heart, fellow Ender fan. *Ender's Game* will come. Of that I am sure. How and when is anyone's guess. But when it does, you can bet your flash suit that Orson Scott Card will make sure it's the same Ender he cre-ated thirty years ago, the same Ender all of us remember and expect.

THE
TECHNOLOGY OF *ENDER'S GAME*

Some Thoughts on How the Battle School and
the Battle Room Might Function

—BY STEPHEN SYWAK

Orson Scott Card was aware of Stephen Sywak's early work on the Battle School technology, and it informed his thinking as he worked on the Shadow books and Ender in Exile, *though it is not authoritative, since the final look of Battle School and the Battle Room will be worked out in conjunction with artists working on the comic book series for Marvel and designers working on the movie.*

THE CREATION OF THE INTERNATIONAL FLEET

After the first invasion of the Formics against the Earth, the independent national governments (led by the three economic giants of China, the United Arab Emirates, and the United States of North America) created an international consortium dedicated to creating a war machine capable of defeating the Formics in any and all subsequent invasions.

Earth heavy industry was redirected toward the production of a massive defensive and offensive infrastructure. The U.S. and Chinese space programs were redirected from their mission plans of landing men and women on Saturn's icy moon, Enceladus, and focused on creating an interstellar wartime fleet capable of interstellar travel, close-in fighting, and deep-mission support.

The fleet was modeled on the successful organization of the naval fleets of Japan, Germany, and the United States during World War II, and included interstellar surrogates for aircraft carriers, battleships, cruisers, destroyers, corvettes, minesweepers, patrol boats, and various amphibious assault ships. In addition to the surrogates (analogues) for the naval vessels, surrogates for bombers, reconnaissance aircraft, and long- and short-range fighters were also produced.

Aircraft carriers became immense interstellar hives, carrying everything from small one-person fighters up to twelve-person minesweepers, support ships, and most everything in between. Battleships became heavily armored cities, bristling with energy-based and kinetic-kill weaponry. Corvettes became high-speed attack craft, capable of "orbiting" the larger, high-mass, slow-moving vessels such as the carriers and battleships as they protected them.

STAR DRIVES

At the time of the First Invasion, physicists were already in the early stages of what would eventually become the "Alcubierre drive," based on the work of physicist Miguel Alcubierre in the late twentieth century. The Alcubierre drive was an attempt to create a controlled volume (a Cleaver/Obousy space-time sphere), within which a vehicle could be made to move at relativistic velocities with respect to its surroundings. Complications in the propagation speeds of the space-time wave front at the leading edge of a moving vessel had stalled the research until the Formic drive systems were retrieved from captured starships. The discovery of the crystalline "Eggs" within the drive bays of the Formic ships and the eventual realization that they were the basis of a field-based star drive generator was the breakthrough required to move the Alcubierre drive research forward. Lessons learned from the Formic drives (primarily, the ability to create and manipulate vectors of the subatomic strong-force), coupled with the knowledge gained from the separate development of the Alcubierre system, brought about the creation of highly controllable relativistic drive technology to power Earth's interstellar fleets.

The Formic Eggs develop a spherical force field (an analogue to the Cleaver/Obousy sphere, as mentioned previously), whose diameter is configured to extend beyond the major dimension of the ship within which the drive is situated. Interstellar dust, molecules, atoms, photons, free electrons, and—as was eventually learned—dark matter are attracted to the sphere's surface like dust is attracted to a static-charged balloon. However, these interstellar particles are not the only material attracted to the surface of the sphere. Space-time itself is attracted to and becomes wrapped around the sphere— the sphere injects itself into a fissure it creates within space/time. The Alcubierre drive then draws the space-time geodesics around it through the application of directed atomic strong-force vectors. The space-time draws away from the front of the sphere, wraps around it, and closes up behind it, drawing the sphere (and the spaceship within it) through space-time. The particles present on the surface are broken down into their constituent subatomic constituents, and the energy from the breaking of those bonds is supported in the force field—held on the surface of the field as potential energy, used to continue and strengthen the cycle. The subatomic remnants of the particles also flow around the surface of the sphere and are ejected off the trailing end. Research is continuing as to exactly what happens to the dark matter that is entrained and ejected by the sphere.

A common analogy used to explain this mechanism is to compare it to modifying the surface tension on the forward end of a flat disk placed on the surface of a body of water. The disk is drawn forward toward the disruption in the surface tension. Obviously, the Alcubierre drive is far more complicated in that it involves nine additional spatial dimensions and the breaking of molecular, atomic, and subatomic bonds.

One of the great benefits to the fact that the Cleaver/Obousy sphere slides along a self-made fissure in the multiple dimensions of space-time is that the ship itself and the crew and equipment onboard do not experience any acceleration as the ship changes speed from Newtonian to sublight Einsteinian speeds. The ship and its contents remain in a zero-G ("free fall") condition as they travel along the slip-plane in the fabric of space/time. Without the Alcubierre drive, the "normal" acceleration required to make the distance between the stars achievable would crush or disable the crew onboard any ship. Countering that acceleration with artificial means would be difficult if not outright impossible. As an example, centripetal force (such as is provided by rotating habitation wheels or rings; commonly used to simulate gravitational acceleration), cannot be used to reduce an imposed acceleration. Electrically driven electro-synthetic planar gravity fields, often used where centripetal wheels are not an option, were explored in early pre-Alcubierre drive experiments. Unfortunately, the slightest dropout of one of these generated gravity fields would subject the ship's payload to sudden, high imposed accelerations, leading to the loss of both the payload and the test vehicle.

The Cleaver/Obousy spheres have the advantage of being self-sustaining—to a degree, based on the density of the matter surrounding the drive sphere. Upon the loss of the central Alcubierre drive (such as from a power loss or the failure of one of the inner generating fields), the energy stored from the dissociation of the particles on the surface of the sphere maintain the integrity of the sphere and allow a steady, stable collapse of the field, eventually bringing the ship to a safe stop.

ARTIFICIAL GRAVITY

Studies in the late twentieth and early twenty-first centuries had already shown the critical need to maintain near-Earth gravity onboard spaceships for the long-term health of their occupants. Trips to Mars in the first quarter of the twenty-first century relied on large, rotating habitation wheels to provide 85 percent Earth-normal gravity for the duration of the voyage. Around that same time, the first electro-synthetic planar gravity generators were being developed. Early efforts with Bose-Einstein condensates, running at subfractional 0K temperatures, proved successful, but highly impractical. The ability to fabricate nanotechnology-engineered superconducting materials eventually led to the creation of Bose-Einstein resins, and resulted in reliable, moderate-power, room-temperature planar gravity generators. Furthermore, the discovery of similar Formic technology on ships captured during the First Invasion allowed important increases in efficiency and control of the generated fields, including the addition of three-dimensional volumetric (or "shaping") control.

Reliability issues and the need to provide single-point-failure-proof artificial gravitational systems led to the choice of building dual-mode systems into all starships and similar long-term space assets, such as the Battle School. These dual-mode systems rely on both large, rotating habitation wheels to create gravity through centripetal acceleration, and electro-synthetic planar gravity generators. The failure of one system does not cascade into the failure of the secondary system, providing a safe haven for the crew until the failed system can be repaired.

Normal production electro-synthetic artificial planar gravity generators have a short effective range and only effective over 5 to 10 meters (at which point they exhibit a rapid falloff). The specialized focusing generators used by the "Hooks" within the Battle Rooms have an effective range of 45 meters.

MOLECULAR DETACHMENT DEVICE/MOLECULAR DISRUPTION DEVICE

As mentioned previously, the Cleaver/Obousy (C/O) spheres are self-sustaining, to a degree, in the relative vacuum of deep space. The subatomic dissociation of trace amounts of interstellar gasses, dust, molecules, and atoms, along with sparse amounts of dark matter, allow the creation and storage of potential energy in higher-dimensional waves along the surface of the sphere.

In a denser environment, however, the amount of energy created and stored by the C/O spheres is immense. In the presence of dense solids, such as another spaceship or a planetary body, the energy created cannot be long contained. The C/O sphere may rapidly grow in size in an attempt to provide the necessary surface area to store the energy. The sphere acts in a manner similar to electron orbitals surrounding a hydrogen atom. Intentionally imposing certain harmonic frequencies in the field energy can cause the C/O spheres to jump to higher and higher macro-orbital energies at an increasingly rapid rate. The growth in the size of the macro-orbitals increases the rate of energy creation, and the system heterodynes (exhibits runaway feedback) to the point where it becomes unstable. Cleaver/Obousy spheres, when manipulated into instability in the manner described, will expand until the material density surrounding them exhibits a sudden dropoff, at which point they continue to destroy the subatomic bonds of the denser material and eventually collapse onto themselves and dissipate.

As one might expect, a controlled force field with the ability to disrupt every molecule and to disassociate every atom that touches it makes a nearly irresistible weapon. None of the Formic ships was found to contain the modifications that Earth's scientists and engineers made to weaponize the Alcubierre drive system. It has therefore been assumed that this weapon was not in the Formic arsenal.

The weapon that was developed from modifications to the Alcubierre drive was initially named after the molecular disruption effect of its operation, and was called—quite simply—the "Molecular Detachment Device" or "Molecular Disruption Device." This name was changed, with colloquial use, to "MD Device," subsequently "Dr. Device" (MD equaling "Medical Doctor" in the English language), and eventually the "Little Doctor." This device was of course used, as history recounts, by the fleets controlled by Andrew (Ender) Wiggin in the final battle of the Third Invasion against the Formic home world. The chain reaction set up in the planetary material by the Cleaver/Obousy sphere caused the complete destruction of that planet.

Early designs of the MDD required that the field generator equipment be relatively near the center of the Cleaver/Obousy sphere, leading to the need to place the devices in physical projectiles or missiles. Later designs were able to form and project the sphere away from the central generator, actually separating it from the generator completely. This allowed the weapon to be used remotely, more akin to a high-powered beam weapon such as a laser or proton beam device. An additional advantage of projecting the C/O sphere is that due to its self-sustaining nature and its origins as an interstellar-drive, once created it accelerates forward toward its target at a high rate. Upon striking its target, the field generators adjust the frequency supporting the C/O sphere, in order to halt the acceleration and lock the sphere to its target.

If not carefully controlled in this manner, a weaponized C/O sphere may still behave as if it is a star-drive and accelerate away from its target without warning, and with an unpredictable acceleration vector. While this error typically still results in the destruction of the intended target, the collateral damage created by such an uncontrolled runaway is often equally devastating.

ECSTATIC SHIELDS

Modifications to the strength and field orientation of the Cleaver/Obousy sphere (its ability to shift the disassociated particles on its surface rapidly to a "trailing edge") allow it to be used as a protective shield, without the creation of movement for itself and the ship that contains its generator and—more importantly—without the runaway energy conversion, storage, and feedback that makes it an aggressively destructive offensive weapon. This defensive application is typically referred to as an "Ecstatic Shield," which is believed to be a colloquial derivative of the etymologically more correct "Static Shield." Paralleling the development life cycle of the Molecular Detachment Device, the Ecstatic Shields were originally generated in a purely symmetrical sphere about a central generator. Eventual improvements in technology allowed them to be projected asymmetrically from their generators. Current state of the art still requires the generators to be within the Ecstatic field, though they are no longer required to be at the geometric center of the sphere. Some experiments have been able to project the field away from the generator, but critical issues regarding field stability cause the fields to collapse rapidly.

BATTLE ROOMS

After the first invasion of Earth by the Formics, and before the establishment of the International Fleet, the political and military minds of the Earth's leading nations realized that they needed a way to train a new type of military mind. They realized that all of their Earth-centric training regimens were, in one way or another, simply two-dimensional strategic games. Even aircraft and submarine battles at most extended into "2-1/2" dimensional strategies. There would be a primarily flat playing field, with the slight addition of limited vertical motion. They realized that in deep space battles—even in battles surrounding planetary systems—a new way of thinking and fighting would be required. A true three-dimensional approach was required.

This need led to the development of the Battle Rooms—large, zero-gravity environments that were free of the up/down "vertical" orientations imposed by operations on or near the surface of the Earth. The first Battle Rooms were freestanding buildings built on the surface of the Earth. They relied on the use of the recently improved planar gravity generators to locally nullify Earth's constant gravity. Due to what was considered the entrenched 2D mind-set of the current military at the time, the decision was made to train students who were of pre-secondary-school age.

These first Battle Rooms were built as fully functioning prototypes. They allowed a trial-and-error approach to the development of three-dimensional strategies for use in large-scale planetary and deep-space military operations, as well as the design and implementation of the practical aspects necessary to achieve those training goals.

The initial designs of the Battle Rooms modeled the wall dimensions at 100 meters (m) to a side (roughly 330 feet). Due to Earth-bound construction limitations at the time, these early Battle Rooms were instead built with their interior walls at 75m on a side (just under 250 feet). After extensive use, it was determined that 75m cubes provided more than sufficient room for the proper training of the young strategists. The larger design had almost twice the airflow requirement and would have required huge structural trusses to support the longer spans of the walls. Once the 75m walls "proved themselves" (in essence, were "battle tested"), the design settled in.

The "Stars" were first developed with these land-based systems. The early models were approximately ¼m to 1m per side, and were built in various geometric shapes such as spheres, tetrahedra, etc. As the realization that the best way to utilize the Battle Rooms grew from hand-to-hand training to the larger planetary and deep-space theaters, the Stars changed from their original, "personal" sized units to the large, gravity-suspended, padded cubes currently used. The majority of the Stars are approximately 3m on a side, and all possess recessed handholds on all six of their faces. These handholds allow soldiers to hold on to, push off from, and reorient themselves as they pass by or lock on to a Star.

The Stars are held in position by local volumetric modifications to the electronically generated gravity fields. Because the positions of the Stars are maintained by these pseudogravitational forces (as opposed to rigid structural connections), the force of a student/soldier landing on or bouncing off a Star—if unopposed—could cause it to change position within the Battle Room. Radio-linked position sensors within the Stars report their positions back to the room control computers fifty times/second, and the projected gravity field adjusts itself though servo-control electronics to maintain each Star's position and orientation to within a highly accurate 5 millimeters (<0.1°). The Star's large mass (nominally 500 to 1,000 kilograms) allows sufficient resistive forces to be generated by the electro-synthetic gravity to keep the Stars in position against the impact loads of multiple students.

Stars are stored within the walls of the Battle Rooms. Large padded panels unlock and swing into the Battle Room to provide access to sizeable storage regions behind.

The "Hook" was developed as a means of modifying the generated gravity fields to allow for safe, controlled movement of the players within the volume of the Battle Rooms. Typically, a Hook is provided to the captain of each army during a skirmish, and "enabled" only at the close of the battle. It permits the captains to retrieve soldiers from free-floating positions at the center of the volume, and direct them with a controlled force vector toward a nearby wall, gate, or handhold.

The Hook does not manipulate the generated gravity fields directly. It sends commands to the room control computer, which controls the generator/focus system, which in turn relaxes or increases volumetric gravity gradients. This modification of the gravity gradients causes tightly controlled force vectors to accelerate the target masses in the desired directions. A laser-targeting system built into the Hook allows the user to "paint" his target, and the control computer for the room's gravity generator system calculates the location in space of the targeted origin and destination points, and directs the field modifications to those volumetric regions. Programmed buttons on the Hook's control screen permit large-scale behaviors to be easily triggered (such as moving all players to an adjacent wall, all players to adjacent gates, etc.).

The Hook also controls the thawing of the flash suits in a similar manner. It broadcasts a request to the room control computer, which in turn drops the active broadcast of the suit immobilization signals. This is detailed further in the flash suit section.

The Stars are also moved through the use of focused gravity gradients, controlled by the Hooks or similar administrator-level tools.

The material of the interior walls of the Battle Rooms also advanced from hard plastic and metal in the original designs to softer padding. As the technology became available, interior lighting progressed from harsh, recessed, intermittently placed strip lighting to a flexible, self-luminescent skin over the entire inner padded surface of the Battle Rooms.

The reliance on planar gravity generation for the prototypical Earth-based

Battle Rooms also permitted early experimentation with the orientation of the entry corridors to the Rooms. After a few weeks of experimentation, however, this variation was rejected and the entry corridors were left with a uniform "up" direction, aligned with Earth's natural gravity vector. The logistics of handling the variations in corridor orientation turned out to be highly complicated, and the small benefits of obscuring the Earth's gravity "bias" was deemed to be unnecessary. This "up" bias in the access hallways to the Battle Rooms is still represented in the final designs of the Battle School.

The locations of the Gates, the Student's Gates, and the Teacher's Gate were also established during this initial design phase. The Gates, the entry points for the competing armies during strategy training sessions (games), are located at the center of the faces of opposing walls. The Student's Gates, critical for the students' initial introduction to the Battle Rooms and used for early training exercises, are located at the "bottom" edge of those walls (the same walls as the Battle Gates). The Teacher's Gate is located at the center of the "south" face of the Battle Room to provide an isolated entrance point for the officers in charge of training. It is unclear why no additional Battle Gates were placed in the east and west walls; it is thought that perhaps the typical two-team elimination approach common to many sports and military training methods at the time prejudiced the original designers toward this implementation.

Orientations within the Battle Room environment are very important, and need to be mentioned. Andrew (Ender) Wiggin illustrated how important understanding one's orientation within the Room environment could be toward winning a battle, and established what are now considered to be the standard references for orientation within the Battle Rooms. In the Wiggin nomenclature, the Battle Gate used to enter the Battle Room is considered to be the "up" gate. The far Battle Gate (the "Enemy's Gate") is down. To the left is east; to the right, west. Above is north, and below is south. Though any one of the four surrounding walls could be considered "north," and the remaining walls being assigned the remaining directions, typical use has been to consider the Teacher's Gate as being located on the south wall, with the other orientations falling into place. This also places the Student's Gates, previously mentioned, along the southern edges of the "up" and "down" walls.

As discussed, there are five doorways for each Battle Room. The doors to the Student's Gates and the Teacher's Gate are designed as "sloats"—they pull slightly away from the center of the Battle Room, and then slide sideways into a recessed slot (pocket) in the adjacent wall. The action of these

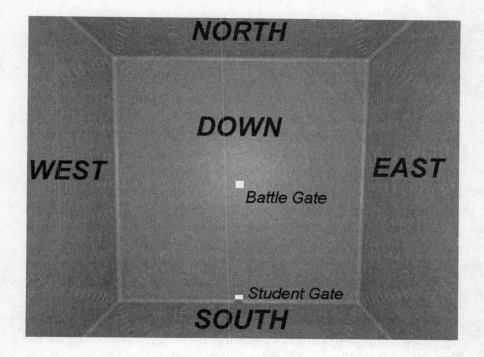

three doors is not speed-critical, and therefore this simple, robust approach is warranted. The two doors of the Battle Gates, however, must move out of position far too quickly at the onset of the "Victory Ritual" (when four remaining soldiers from a given team each press the large, lit panels at the corners of their "Enemy's Gate") for the slower sloat doors to be practical. Therefore, the Battle Gates are one of the few applications of "force field" technology on the Battle School.

These are not the force fields used by the Formic-derived star drives, or the Ecstatic shields derived from the Molecular Detachment Device. The force fields used to block the Battle Gates represent a purely Earth-based development for repulsive force fields. They function much as a solid wall would: strike the surface of the force field, and one feels an equal and opposite reaction. These force fields can be adjusted to provide anything from a purely elastic reaction (an object will bounce off the field with fully conserved, though reversed, momentum) to a purely inelastic reaction (an object will dump all of its momentum into the field, striking it like a dead blow hammer). These fields are not self-sustaining and in fact require a large expenditure of energy to maintain. Therefore, the Battle Gate openings are provided with mechanically sloated doors for general use, and force fields for use during training sessions. The force fields are translucent (transmit light but not images), but can be made nearly—but never fully—opaque. They do not emit any light of their own.

The construction of the Earth-based Battle Rooms filled a very important need in the early development of zero-G strategic training. Unfortunately, prototype testing is not without its failures. For example, the initial implementation of the Battle Rooms incorporated hard-surfaced handholds on the interior faces of the Battle Rooms, extending out from the walls into the playing volume. This design caused numerous injuries during practice and gaming sessions, including broken fingers, wrists, and ankles, as well as sprained lower backs from striking or snagging these extended handrails during newly developing zero-G maneuvers (such as "sliding the walls"). This led to a rapid redesign and reimplementation of the handholds as recessed elements with a slightly compliant surface material. Handholds for climbing (movement) are placed at the standard 0.3m (1 foot) apart; handholds for reorientation and related wall maneuvers are spaced nominally at 1m.

The most notable failure of all, however, occurred well after the initial test-and-adjust period and the two-month-long Site Acceptance Test for the Earth-based Battle Rooms. Five months into the initial trials of these Battle Rooms, a full bank of artificially generated planar gravity fields failed and the affected Battle Room was thrown, without warning, into its natural full-Earth-Gravity condition during a fully attended training session. Eighty children—two armies of forty children each—were either killed or badly injured when they fell from heights as far up as 75 meters. The horror of losing the zero-G field with young students suspended 75 meters in the air has been impossible to forget. This disaster led to a near-immediate acceptance of the existing proposal to create an orbiting Battle School—a low Earth-orbiting space station designed to provide a series of nine Battle Rooms (with "natural" zero-G), plus living quarters, classrooms, support logistics, and a permanent outwardly-facing military presence in space.

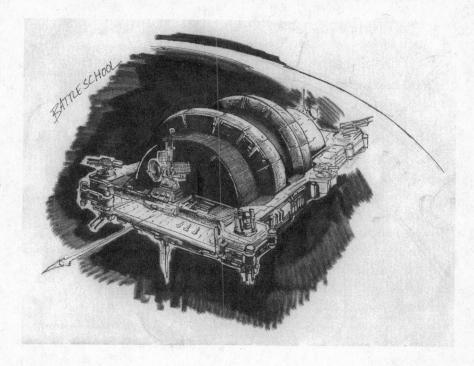

BATTLE SCHOOL

THE BATTLE SCHOOL

The Battle School is a special purpose space station, built with the cooperation of the Earth's major political and economic powers, and larger international corporations, designed to provide a unique training environment for the next generation of military minds.

The School is approximately 550 meters long and 500 meters wide. It consists of a nonrotating central core, and two 350-meter diameter rotating habitation rings. The volume is approximately 26 million cubic meters, and the mass is roughly 30 million metric tons (30 billion kg).

The stable orbital attitude (orientation) of the Battle School in orbit is maintained through the use of large magnetic torque bars built into the stationary core, as well as Hydrazine-II fired attitude control thrusters.

The nonrotating central core houses the nine Battle Rooms, the main docking bays, fighter bays and other weapon emplacements. The majority of the station's infrastructure is also located in the central core—power generation, heating/ventilation/air-conditioning systems (HVAC), air purification systems, water purification systems, recycling systems, refrigeration, cryogenics, oxygen generation, storage, etc. Quarters for the International Fleet's

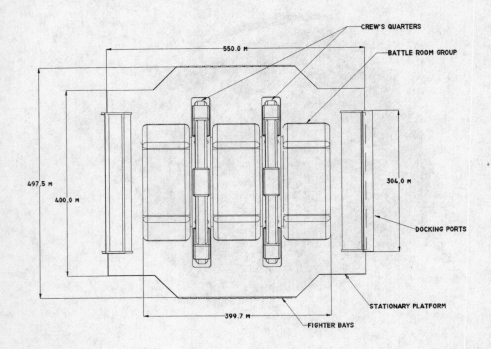

CREW'S QUARTERS
BATTLE ROOM GROUP
DOCKING PORTS
STATIONARY PLATFORM
FIGHTER BAYS

550.0 M
497.5 M
400.0 M
304.0 M
399.7 M

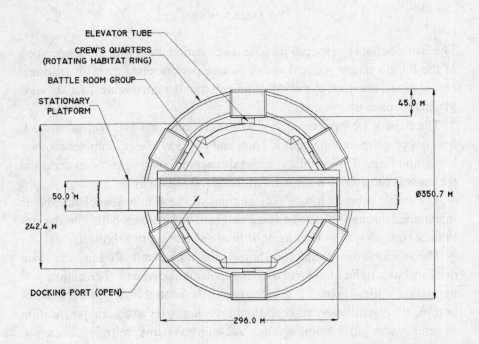

ELEVATOR TUBE
CREW'S QUARTERS
(ROTATING HABITAT RING)
BATTLE ROOM GROUP
STATIONARY
PLATFORM
DOCKING PORT (OPEN)

45.0 M
50.0 M
242.4 M
Ø350.7 M
296.0 M

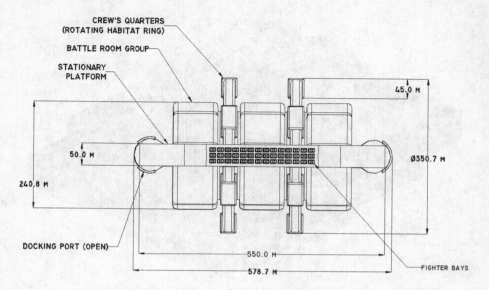

military defense crew are also located in the central core, as are many of the administrative offices, the larger lecture halls, and many of the regular classrooms.

The central core is also home to many of the station's scientific laboratories and micro-G fabrication facilities, ranging from pharmaceuticals to structural and electrical materials fabrication.

The electro-synthetic planar gravity generators are distributed throughout the stationary central core to create an even gravity field. Typically, they are placed in the structures below and supporting the floors, where they require the least amount of focusing to create a uniform field. They are placed in the curved corridors that provide access to the various levels of the Battle Rooms, where their short effective range can be used to advantage.

The Battle School was designed and assembled under an accelerated schedule. The finished state of the Battle School reflects this fast-tracked approach. Overhead piping and wiring runs remain exposed in some sections of the station. Manual overrides for valves were placed, late in the design process, where space allowed (sometimes tens of meters away from the equipment rooms they control). Critical areas such as the Battle Rooms, where the designs began and sufficient time was available to refine the designs, show a high degree of finish. Other areas such as barracks, classrooms, and the command and control center show the rough edges: last-minute piping runs, hand-run power and data lines, excessive splices and joints, and other evidence of insufficient time to review and clean up the designs.

Regardless of its use as a specialized training facility, the Battle School

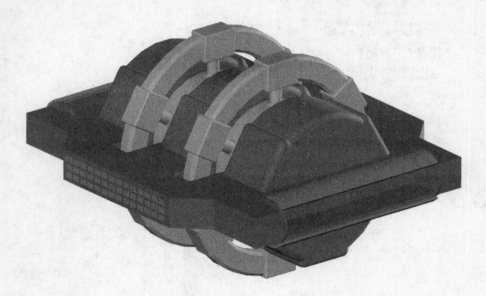

shares a lot in common with naval battleships and aircraft carriers from Earth's own wars. The four corners of the stationary central core are fitted out with energy weapons on the top and bottom surfaces for a total of eight emplacements. The sides of the central region are also populated with launching tubes for short-range fighters, considered primarily for emergency defense of the Battle School.

Within the Battle School, a series of airtight bulkhead doors are provided to allow the isolation of sections of the ship in the event of a breach in the hull or a loss of internal air pressure.

The heart of the Battle School is, without question, the Battle Rooms. The Battle Rooms are divided up into three groups of three rooms each. The two rotating habitation rings serve to separate the three groups of Battle Rooms. This permits people on any one ring to access the nearest two groups of Battle Rooms directly. Central passages connect all three groups to each other along the central axis, and allow for general movement from one end of the central core to the other.

Docking of all ships is also handled at the central, stationary core. It was realized as early as 1929 (Hermann Noordung/Potočnik in an article titled "Designing the Space Station") that space stations not only need a means of creating artificial gravity—typically through spinning habitation rings—but also a means of docking at a stationary, stabilized platform. The problems of docking at a fully rotating station—in terms of the level of control required, the dynamics of moving, rotating and orienting an object the mass of a

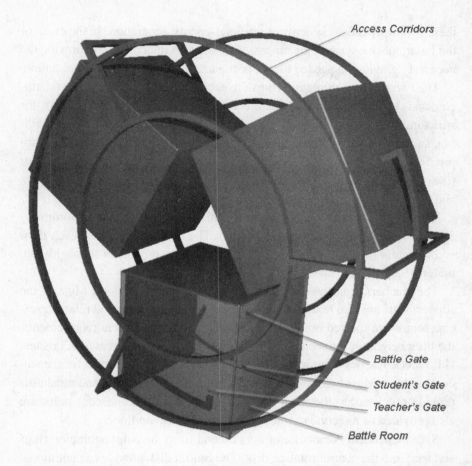

Access Corridors

Battle Gate

Student's Gate

Teacher's Gate

Battle Room

shuttle (or larger), the amount of propellant expended in doing so, and the subsequent problems of off-center masses once the vehicles were docked—were found to be insurmountable. Noordung, showing his early insight, also realized that finding a method of moving effectively from the nonrotating core to the rotating rings was critical to the success of such a station.

The design of the Battle School represents a mixed-approach to the creation of artificial gravity. Normal living quarters and general use areas were designed to provide nominally 1G (Earth-normal) gravity. The Battle Rooms were placed in the stationary central core to provide a reliable zero-gravity environment. The gravitational acceleration on board the Battle School is produced in one of two ways: either through the use of centripetal acceleration from large, revolving habitation rings, or through the use of electro-synthetic planar gravity generators in the central core. For reasons touched upon earlier, all large-scale, long-duration mission space assets (such as interstellar ships, and the Battle School) were intentionally designed to rely on these two independent systems of artificial-gravity generation. In the event of the failure of one system, the other system remains intact, and can provide the necessary gravitation needed for the occupants of the ship or the space station.

The two rotating habitation rings are each nominally 350 meters in diameter and 33 meters wide. These are exterior dimensions, and account for structural wall thickness, plumbing, piping, power and data, radiation shielding, and the like. The interior, usable dimensions are therefore smaller by approximately 3 meters per exterior wall and 5 meters for the exterior perimeter (the outer hoop). Interior walls and floors are of a more standard construction, and typically take up 0.5 meter and 1.5 meters respectively.

These dimensions place the first level in the habitation ring at nominally 340 meters diameter (170 meters radius). The nominal height of each floor is 2.5 meters (8 feet). Allowing for floor thickness provides for roughly 3.0 meters (9.8 feet) per floor.

The teachers' quarters are placed along the outermost floor. Most of the support staff are also housed on this deck. The gymnasiums and related exercise rooms are located on the second level. Due to equipment requirements, the floor height for the second deck is increased from 2.5 meters to 3.5 meters (11.5 feet). The next four levels (A through D decks) are reserved for the student soldiers. Mess halls are also located on A Deck. Elevators and escalators provide quick access between decks. Ship's ladders and descent poles are also provided as a secondary means of moving between floors.

Six independent banks of elevators ascend from the outer habitation rings and feed into the central rotating disk. The central disk provides an additional series of concentric circular deck corridors that serve as station platforms for the shuttle cars that run between the rotating portions of the Battle School and the stationary central core. The outermost such deck is also the location of the "Game Rooms," a collection of strategy-based video and holographic electronic games that are made available to the students of the Battle School.

Because of the varying radii of all these decks, the centripetal gravitational acceleration is different on each one. The rotational speed of the habitation rings has been selected such that Student Deck D experiences 1G (Earth-normal) gravity. The gymnasiums see 104 percent Earth-normal gravity, and the Teacher's Deck sees 109 percent Earth-normal gravity. The Game Room Deck, the outermost deck available for accessing the shuttle cars, has a nominal radius of 79 meters, and therefore sees approximately 51 percent (just over half) Earth-normal gravity. The mechanical requirements of the subway cars force the radial spacing between these more central decks to be on the order of 5.5 meters.

The rings rotate at approximately 2.4 rpm (25 seconds per revolution), and have a tangential speed of 44 meters per second (m/s) (98 miles per hour, or 144 ft./sec.) at their circumference.

The rings revolve against a pair of physical bearings set into the central core. The bearings present friction into the system, and therefore require additional energy to keep the rings spinning. However, the alternate— electromagnetic "floating" bearings—would have required more energy to maintain, and presented an unacceptable failure mode (loss of energy results in the rings binding up against the central core, causing a sudden and catastrophic deceleration). Because of the large size (nominally 180 meters diameter) of these physical roller bearings, the radial loads caused by the subtle eccentricities in the dynamic weight distribution of the rings results in minimal stresses in the bearing. Estimated bearing life for each of the four main bearings in the Battle School is greater than a hundred years' continuous duty, with proper maintenance and lubrication. The bearings are sealed to assist in maintaining a proper pressure differential across them to contain the 80 percent atmospheric pressure within the Battle School. Additional rotating seals are provided adjacent to the bearing interface in order to maintain this pressure differential and provide redundancy.

In order to maintain the proper speed and synchronization of the two rings, large direct-drive torque motors are built into the interface between the rings and the stationary core. High-energy permanent magnets are arrayed in a circle around the rotating rings, adjacent to the support bearings. The wound motor coils are encapsulated in a heat conducting compound, and set into a recessed ring on the central core, adjacent to the ring magnets, with a constant 5-millimeter gap between the two. Because of the large diameter of the torque motor, only a small amount of power (on the order of 200 kW) is required to maintain the speed of each ring. Hall effect magnetic sensors in the stationary core sense the position and speed of the rings, and feed this information back to a servo control system that keeps the rings in synchronization and at proper speed. Because each coil is independently wound and terminated, the failure of a number of coils can be compensated for in the controlling software.

In the unlikely event of a complete motor failure (such as might happen in the case of a large scale power loss), calculations show that it would take three days for a ring to despin, thereby providing sufficient time to relocate personnel to the central core and the adjacent ring. Should a ring lose motorization, the friction of the bearings and seals is sufficient to cause a dynamic counterrotation in the body of the Battle School. Automatic control systems are programmed to respond using the attitude control thrusters and

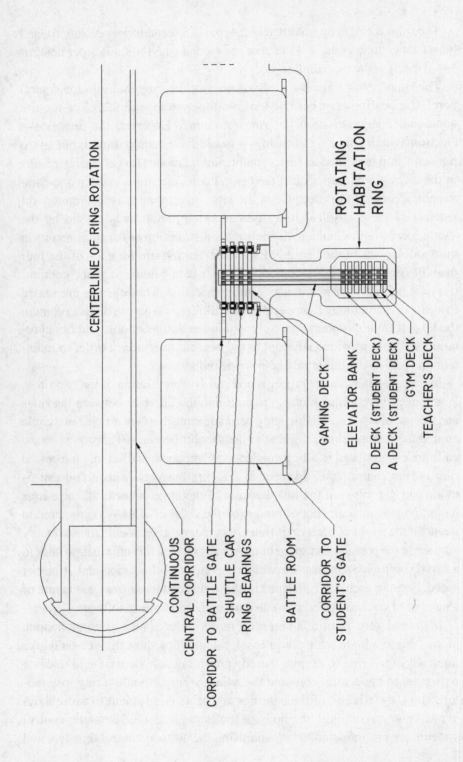

CENTERLINE OF RING ROTATION

ROTATING
HABITATION
RING

TEACHER'S DECK
GYM DECK
A DECK (STUDENT DECK)
D DECK (STUDENT DECK)
ELEVATOR BANK
GAMING DECK
BATTLE ROOM
RING BEARINGS
SHUTTLE CAR
CORRIDOR TO BATTLE GATE
CONTINUOUS
CENTRAL CORRIDOR
CORRIDOR TO
STUDENT'S GATE

the magnetic torque bars to maintain the School's orbital orientation if such an event should occur. Enough fuel is stored onboard to react against despin forces in the event that *both* ring motor systems should fail simultaneously.

The Battle Rooms, as previously described, are cubes with an interior dimension of 75 meters to a side. They are built in three arrays of three Battle Rooms each. Each array has a series of circular corridors connecting, at one level all the Battle Gates, and at a lower level all the Student's Gates. Secondary corridors coming from the Student's Gate corridors feed to the Teacher's Gates on the south face of the cubes. For orientation purposes, the south faces of the Battle Rooms are all located at the radially outermost points. As an example, if the central core were to rotate with the habitation rings, the Teacher's Gates would be "down." However, by placing the Battle Rooms in the stationary central core, they experience no gravitational acceleration, and provide the ideal zero-G training environment.

The spacing and orientation of three Battle Rooms in their "array" allows for large otherwise empty volumes between them. These volumes are taken up by storage spaces for the "Stars" and ancillary support equipment, and by the specialized electro-synthetic gravity generators and focusing apparatus needed to fix the stars in place and permit the Hooks to work in their intended way.

BATTLE SCHOOL: SHUTTLE CARS (SUBWAY CARS)

As mentioned previously, the method of moving between a rotating habitation ring and a stationary central core is of utmost importance for the effective functioning of a large space station such as the Battle School. The immense size of the Battle School both creates the problem and provides a means for its solution.

Given a rotational speed of 2.4 rpm, the outermost point of the habitation rings moves at a tangential speed of 48 m/s (98 mph). Further in, closer to the center, the tangential velocity is proportionally reduced. At the radius of the Game Room Deck (roughly 89 meters from the center axis of the Battle School), the tangential velocity is 22.3 m/s (50 mph). This Deck is also the first access level to what are called the "shuttle cars" that allow movement between the rotating habitation rings and the stationary central core.

The shuttle cars are similar in concept to subway cars. They run independently of each other, as single car units, on concentric pairs of linear tracks. There are a series of four such tracks, arranged at each interface between the rotating habitation wheel and the fixed core, for eight tracks per wheel, sixteen tracks overall. The innermost ("uppermost") of these tracks is allocated to service cars that allow equipment and supplies to be moved between fixed and moving elements. The remaining three outer tracks per location are dedicated to personnel. The tracks and the track beds are part of the fixed central core. The shuttle cars run on the tracks, and either remain at zero velocity on the tracks (aligned with marks on the central core), or are brought up to speed and synchronized with the central disk area of the rotating habitation rings.

For reference and orientation, the sense of gravity in the Battle School is always directed outward. Moving higher in the station brings one closer to the central axis, and results in a reduction of the effective centripetal gravity.

For the purposes of this illustration, the shuttle car system shall be described as viewed from the Battle Room Access Deck. This deck is located three levels above the Gaming Area, and is therefore aligned with the access corridors to the Battle Gates of the adjacent Battle Rooms. For reference, its radius from center is approximately 72.4 meters.

The Battle Room Access Deck is a part of the rotating habitation rings. It is accessed by taking an elevator from one of the six available elevator banks in each ring. The Access Deck is above the living quarters, closer in to the central axis of the Battle School. These floors have a more severe upward curvature to them, and the centripetal-gravity effect is lower (very roughly half of normal Earth gravity). The Access Deck is approximately 30 meters (100 feet) wide, interrupted by regular support columns and the elevator banks, and runs the full circumference of the central disk. Facing the long axis of the open deck area (along the circumference), with the floor curving up in front of and behind the viewer, one views walls to the left and right. The upper portions of the walls are clear Plexiglas, and the lower portions are opaque. Automatic, electrically operated doors are set into these walls at regular intervals. A call button is provided to the left and right of each door.

Looking through the Plexiglas and down, the viewer sees two polished tracks, raised on short supports above the track bed. These are the tracks for the subway car. There is a third track, a wide, flat black ribbon that runs parallel to the polished tracks. This central ribbon carries signal and power to the subway car (transmitted via induction), and houses the coils for the linear electric motor that drives the car along the track. The tracks are moving relative to the viewer at 18 m/s (41 mph).

On the far side of the tracks, and sharing a common support structure with them, is another wall: Plexiglas on top and opaque below. Automatic doors are set into those far walls at the same intervals as the near wall.

The far wall, however, is not fixed with relation to the Access Deck. The far wall, as described, is part of the central, stationary core. Because of the constant relative motion between the habitation ring and the stationary core, the far wall also moves with a relative velocity of 18 m/s as compared to the near wall and the Access Deck. Even though the Access Deck is a part of the rotating habitation rings, a viewer standing on the Access Deck will perceive himself (herself) as stationary, with the opposite wall moving past.

Visible beyond this far wall is another hallway. This is the access corridor for the Gates. Since there are three Battle Rooms along this corridor, these three Battle Gate entrances will pass by a viewer on the Access Deck every twenty-five seconds.

Every concentric track has a single shuttle car (subway car) mounted to it. The wheels of the car are more like roller-coaster wheels—in that they grab onto the track top and bottom—than they are like actual subway or rail cars. When one of these cars is at rest, it is aligned with a default doorway on the side of the stationary core, and does not move on the track. Being stored on the tracks on the stationary core, there is no centripetal force (artificial gravity) to maintain the car's position on the tracks or keep it from floating off, hence the wraparound wheels and the captured track.

When one of the call buttons is pressed on the Access Deck side, it activates a sequence of events to bring a shuttle car to that doorway:

1) The shot pins holding the shuttle car locked against the platform on the stationary side release.
2) The shuttle car's electric linear motor is activated, and the car is accelerated up to the speed of the rotating platform (in this case, 18 m/s). Typical acceleration does not exceed 10 percent G, and it therefore takes approximately twenty seconds for the car to come up to speed.
3) The shuttle car aligns (synchronizes) its door system with the door system adjacent to the call button.
4) The shot pins on the moving platform engage the shuttle car. This makes sure that the car remains aligned to the doorway even in the event of power loss. The car, now synchronized with the ring, experiences the same centripetal gravity appropriate to that deck.
5) The corridor doors and then the shuttle's doors open, allowing access. Passengers enter (or exit) the car.
6) Doors close, and the pattern is reversed.
7) As the car decelerates to match the speed of the stationary central core, it slowly loses the effect of centripetal gravity. Electro-synthetic

planar gravity generators built into the floor of the car activate and carefully blend the gravity of the Access Deck to that of the central core (typically kept at 100 percent Earth-normal gravity).

The shuttle cars, whether full or empty, represent a large rotating eccentric mass which might otherwise cause an imbalance on the fixed central core. The Battle School's central computer uses the other cars in a given concentric group as moving counterweights to overcome this dynamic imbalance on the core.

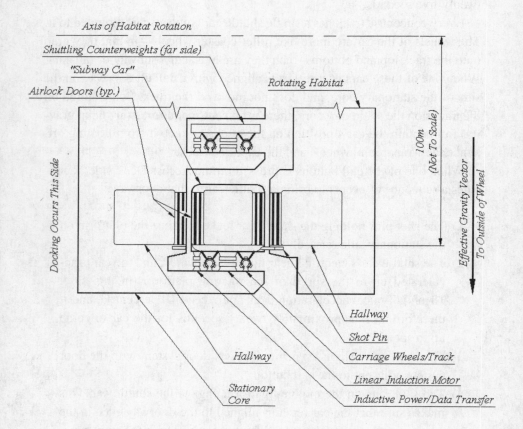

FABRICATION OF THE BATTLE SCHOOL

Due to the sheer size of the Battle School—28 billion kilograms, or roughly 100,000 times the mass of the original International Space Station—it was by necessity constructed entirely in orbit. The volume of material required mandated that mining and smelting operations be established on the surface of Earth's moon. Due to the practical difficulties of manufacturing components in a zero-G (or micro-G) environment, much of the manufacturing for the elements of the Battle School and the ships of the International Fleet was also relegated to these lunar facilities. The amount of material required to build not only the Battle School, but the ships of the International Fleet, would have depleted Earth's resources to the point of worldwide economic collapse. Further economic analyses showed that the cost of launching this material from Earth to orbit was on the order of ten times the cost to set up this lunar mining and manufacturing infrastructure. These lunar manufacturing stations were later employed in the fabrication of the large colony ships, intersystem commercial, corporate, satellites and exploratory vehicles, and similar space-based assets, leading to further amortization of the initial costs.

The facilities established on Earth's moon were used to manufacture more than 92 percent of the structural components required for the Battle School, and a large percentage of the infrastructure and incidentals. After the discovery of copper deposits over 300 feet below the surface regolith, fully 97 percent of all ships' electrical wiring was produced at these plants. The regolith itself was used to create the over 600 miles of optical fiber, used for signal transmission throughout the Battle School, as well as the thousands of miles of optical fiber used in the I.F.'s ships.

Linear accelerators constructed on the moon were used to throw these prefabricated components to the low-Earth orbit assembly site for the Battle School, where they saw final assembly. Due to the low gravity on the moon—and therefore the low escape velocity—items as large as 50 meters on a side (if properly supported) could be launched from the surface of the moon to low Earth orbit for final assembly.

FLASH SUITS

The term "flash suit" describes the collection of gear worn by a student at the Battle School when he or she is to be involved in a training session in one of the Battle Rooms. The flash suit consists of a helmet, a gauntlet-style flash gun, and the suit proper (the garment).

The flash suits—the garments worn by the students during their training in the Battle Rooms—are composed of interwoven fabric and third generation "Shape Memory Alloy" wires. These Nickel-Titanium-Tungsten wires—derived from a material known as "Nitonol" first developed in the 1960s—are able to remain highly flexible under normal conditions, but stiffen and hold whatever position they were in when a high-frequency voltage is applied across them. This feature enables the flash suits to be "Frozen," preventing further movement of the student wearing the suit when he suffers a simulated laser "hit." The suits are divided into zones, so that a student may be partially frozen (legs only, arms only, one arm only, etc.) prior to becoming fully immobilized.

The suits are padded to protect the students against injury.

Long-range RFID (Radio Frequency Identification) chips are also woven into the suit material at multiple locations. These chips allow the suits' position and orientation to be tracked while it is within the confines of the Battle Room, as part of the overall tracking and targeting program used to identify which suit has been hit by which flash gun's simulated laser burst. These RFID chips are also secreted in other items of clothing, and all may be tracked by sensors scattered around the Battle School itself.

The insignia of the various armies are permanently imprinted onto the fabric of the suits. These insignia and related decorative treatments wrap fully around the suits on the front, back, and sides. Typical use places the insignia centered on the student's back, but other approaches have relied upon elaborate designs distributed across the overall suit, gauntlet, and helmet.

A lightweight helmet and visor are included in the flash suit configuration. The helmet provides for simple protection against collision with the walls of the Battle Room and with other students. A visor, described below, provides a controlled amount of tactical feedback deemed necessary to perform a particular training exercise. A small microphone and speaker are also provided in the helmet for two-way radio communication. Two small, high-powered speakers flanking the student's mouth utilize destructive audio interference methods to block or muffle the speech of a student as penalty for being frozen. This is coupled with the temporary disabling of the student's intercom system, thereby knocking a frozen student out of the communication loop with his army.

Each suit is equipped with a gauntlet-style flash gun that wraps around the student's wrist, and provides a means to identify a target and simulate a shot fired against that target. The gauntlets are provided with multiple RFID chips to allow the sensor arrays built into the Battle Rooms to track position and orientation of the gauntlets accurately during gaming sessions. This motion-capture information is fed into the Battle Room's control computers, cross-referenced with position and orientation information of the other students' flash suits, and appropriate hits are logged when a simulated shot is fired. Secondary infrared LEDs built into the gauntlet allow the room computer to verify the strike through the use of infrared cameras mounted throughout the rooms.

The flash guns are also provided with a tightly focused, full-color Light Emitting Diode (LED), which allows a student to see what target he or she has "painted" prior to taking a simulated shot. The beams of these bright LEDs are not normally visible by the students in Battle Room sessions. This minimal information is supplemented by the virtual tactical display presented in the visors. The color of the LED is controlled by the room computer at the onset of a given game to provide different targeting colors for opposing teams. The four lights surrounding an army's entrance gate are also coordinated with these colors.

The Gauntlets house the electronics required to communicate with the Battle Room control computer, to feed the visor display, and to freeze the suit itself. It also contains the rechargeable batteries needed for pistol, suit, and helmet operation. A palm switch attached to the gauntlet controls the firing trigger.

Each flash gun Gauntlet is a dedicated right- or left-handed unit, custom fit to the student through the use of simple low-temperature thermoforming methods.

When a flash suit is "struck" by a virtual laser shot, the Battle Room control computer logs the hit, and also responds by broadcasting a coded command to that suit's specific unit address to freeze the struck portion of the suit. As more portions of the suit are stuck, additional commands are broadcast. The Hook may be used to initiate a "thaw" command to all flash suits, to flash suits from a particular army, or to individual suits. The Battle Room control computer can also be programmed at the administrator level to automatically thaw suits after a predetermined period of time, or follow some other programmed thawing protocol.

The helmet visors are made from a clear polycarbonate plastic embedded with transparent organic LED material to provide a stereoscopic heads-up display. Minimal tactical info (primarily simulated laser paths and hits) is provided to the soldiers within an army. Platoon leaders are provided with more tactical detail, and the commander of an army is provided with the greatest amount of tactical display data.

The displays embedded in the visors provide simulated "laser beans" to permit proper targeting by the students. However, the translucency of these virtual beams can be modified, and the beam images and their target images can also be disabled at the will of the observing officers or game administrator, based on the training needs of a particular session.

ANSIBLE

The ansible is the means of communication used by the International Fleet (I.F.) to communicate with its interplanetary and interstellar ships, the Command School, planetary colonies, and other space assets. It allows for instantaneous communication between transmitter and receiver, regardless of the distance between them. As such, it is considered to be a "faster-than-light" communication tool.

The ansible works by imposing a stream of digital information into a stream of "entangled photons." The photons on the ansible transmitter are "entangled" (in a quantum sense) with a sister stream of photons housed within the receiver. A change in the spin-state of a photon in the first stream is indirectly read as a change in the spin-state of the entangled photon in the second stream.

The rate of transfer is the frequency, or "bandwidth" of the transmission. Low-bandwidth transmissions are suitable for simple texts. Higher bandwidths can provide radio and still-image communication. Transmission frequencies in the megahertz and greater ranges are capable of carrying both audio and video signals, or simply greater amounts of lower bandwidth data.

Two references to faster-than light communications that bear on the science of the ansible. The first reference, by John G. Cramer, was published in the December 1995 issue of *Analog Science Fiction & Fact Magazine,* and was titled "Tunneling through the Lightspeed Barrier." In that article, Cramer describes tests performed in 1993 through 1994, where quantum tunneling of microwave radiation across an insulating gap led to calculated propagation speeds in excess of the speed of light. According to Cramer, a number of scientists took advantage of the quantum effect called "tunneling" to have a microwave signal jump across an insulator, which normally (assuming Newtonian mechanics) would have blocked the signal. When they measured the distance across the gap, and divided that distance by the time it took for the signal to jump the gap, they came up with speeds almost five times the speed of light.

The second article comes a lot closer to the functioning of the ansible. The article is from *The New York Times,* Tuesday, December 16, 1997, and is by Malcolm W. Browne. Titled "Physicists Report the 'Impossible': Teleporting a Particle's Properties," it is about a phenomenon first described in the mid-1930s by Einstein, Podolsky, and Rosen. This phenomenon is called the Einstein-Podolsky-Rosen correlation, and is more commonly known as "photon entanglement." It is possible to create a pair of photons from a single action (such as firing a pulse of ultraviolet light at a nonlinear crystal, as was done in 1997 in Innsbruck), and the pair of photons thus created are "entangled."

When that one high-energy photon of ultraviolet light bombards the "nonlinear" crystal, two lower energy photons are emitted from the crystal. Because of the nature of the crystal, one of the emitted photons will be polarized in one direction (let's say "vertically," just to continue the discussion), and the second photon will be polarized in the other direction (horizontally, for instance). Because of the Heisenberg uncertainty principle, if you were to measure the state of one of the photons, you would lose other information about that photon.

You would cause its "state" (the condition of the information—the energy—about that photon) to collapse from a *probabilistic* condition to a *measured* condition. This is also called the "waveform collapse" of the photon.

By measuring the object, you affect the object. But, more importantly, since the two photons we are discussing are "entangled" based on how they were created, when you cause the collapse of the information state of the first photon, you also cause a collapse in the information state of the second photon. This mutual collapse occurs simultaneously, regardless of the distance between the photons.

The creators of the ansible were able to develop a method of measuring the states of photons in two entangled streams. By measuring the state of photons in the first stream, they caused a collapse in the informational state of those photons. By indirectly measuring the states of the second photon stream (by measuring its effect on another nonlinear crystal), they were able to determine the pattern of waveform collapse of the first stream. By modulating the measurements performed on the first stream in a controlled pattern (think of Morse code as a simple form of information modulation), they were able to send information from one entangled stream to the other. Because of the nature of entanglement, the transfer of information is immediate, regardless of the distance between the streams.

The earliest ansibles were limited in the amount of information they could transmit. The two entangled photon streams were of a limited length (duration), and once the end of such an entangled stream was reached, transmissions ceased. Further development efforts led to the creation of a method for creating entangled streams of high-frequency photons in entirely independent transceivers, on demand. Once that milestone was reached, the era of truly instantaneous high-bandwidth communication had begun.

DESKS

The term "Desk" refers to the personal, rugged, wireless, solid-state tablet-style computers used in classrooms, both on Earth and on the Battle School.

These computers are equipped with ultra-wide-angle auto-stereoscopic displays (three-dimensional images capable of being viewed without the use of special glasses from up to a 60-degree off-angle from the face of the screen), solid-state terabyte flash-drive memories (encompassing both RAM and storage), advanced wireless connectivity, an instant-on operating system, and touch screens with pen and finger interfaces. The Desks are ruggedized against dropping, water, scratching, etc. The units are smooth on all sides, with no openings. They are recharged through the use of noncontact induction technology, and audio is made available either through focused planar speakers behind the screen, or wireless earbuds. Data is transferred through the wireless connection to wireless memory keys, thereby doing away with the need to physically insert a memory key into the unit. The omnidirectional antennas for the Desks are embedded within the body of the computer.

Applications are specific to the operating environment. New applications are loaded wirelessly to the Desks.

FRIENDS OF ENDER

It was the first time I had stayed up all night with a book. The red numbers of the clock passed 4:00 A.M., then 5:00 A.M., and then my mother was coming down to find me eating breakfast at the table, still fondling the pages of the book I found in her closet. I couldn't stop reading, because every word screamed to a young, twelve-year-old girl who didn't care about fashion, boys, MTV, and who did too well in math: *There are more of you. There is a place where you can be loved and respected.* Which is ironic, of course, since love wasn't something Ender ever felt accustomed to.

And the next time a bully gripped me to throw me onto the sidewalk, I grabbed his hands and pulled him down too. As he lost his balance, I kicked him hard in the groin and pushed him over my head. When he was on the ground with a girl standing over him with fire in her eyes, he crawled away from me on all fours and he never lived it down. They didn't pick on me physically after that. Ender taught me that sometimes, even if you don't want to, you have to fight. You fight dirty and you win.

As the years pass, I read the book over and over again. Every time, I see myself as a new character. It was Valentine who inspired me to become a journalist, because there is so much power for good in words. Not the talking heads like you see on TV who blather on about nothing. I sit down and speak with alcoholics and mothers of murder victims and try to actually find the truth rather than impose it. I pull out Peter for the meetings with the money-crazed executives, smoothly cynical and unemotional. I network. I schmooze. I wrap myself in a core of arrogance so strong no one could ever accuse me of being vulnerable. Peter's strength protected me after I was raped, because even with all his dark impulses, he was never ashamed of what he did, or what happened to him. He only tried to learn, control, move forward. Everything was calculated, and when you're rebuilding who you are, a little calculation doesn't hurt.

Now I am Ender again. The games that once mattered to me so much now seem unimportant compared with the friends I love. I am redeemed by my ability to stare truth in the face and speak it, if I can. There is a certain power in being willing to look at both the good and the bad side of yourself with objectivity and honesty, and not hiding either.

If Ender could be whole, so could I. And I wove myself back together with pieces of him.

Jennifer McBride, journalist
Polson, Montana

There are three books that I can't remember not having read: *The Lord of the Rings, The Chronicles of Narnia,* and *Ender's Game.* I therefore don't have a story about the first time I read *Ender's Game,* because I simply don't recall a time when Ender (like Frodo and Lucy) wasn't a part of my life. These are also the three books I've read to pieces; I surrendered my original copy of *Ender's Game* to the trashcan only when a couple of the pages, having separated themselves from the three chunks the book fell into, went missing entirely. Of course, it didn't really matter at that point as I could probably have recited them from memory—but that didn't stop me from pestering my mother to take me to the bookstore immediately to buy another copy. There are some books one simply must own.

Jessica Sheffield, graduate student
State College, Pennsylvania

In my first year of teaching, I taught basic Senior English. After muddling through *Pride and Prejudice* with my predominately male classes (what was I thinking?!), I decided to have them read *Ender's Game* the following quarter. My classes were completely different than they had been just a few weeks before. Kids who had never finished a book in their lives suddenly came to class with intelligent questions and comments. Discussions were amazing, and both boys and girls really got into the book. One student in particular made a total change in his attitude in class and, consequently, in his grade. By the end of the book, students wanted to know what happens next to Ender and Valentine and what happened on Earth. I told them about later books in the series and other books they might also be interested in.

I had always hoped that I could recommend some of my favorite books to kids, but had never really had the chance yet. I also had students choose their own final projects to create to show me they understood the book, and I had some fantastic book covers, sound tracks, displays, and presentations. And because more of them actually read the book, they did better, on average, on the test than they had with previous books. More than anything else, *Ender's Game* got students genuinely excited about reading. Many who had never willingly picked up a book in their lives now realize that there are books out there that they can not only learn something from, but also truly enjoy.

Ashley R. Miller, high school English teacher
Midvale, Utah

I was an aimless, wandering eighteen-year-old, freshly booted from the military (medical discharge USN—bad cartilage in left knee), living with an oppressive stepdad and in need of *something* when my big brother Mike invited me to stay with him in Brooklyn for a few weeks.

Mike, sensing my ennui, told me to read three books: *The Princess Bride* by William Goldman, *A Prayer for Owen Meany* by John Irving, and *Ender's Game* by some cat named Orson Scott Card. The first two I'd at least heard of, the last one just sounded, well, weird. But, trusting my brother, I pored through them.

Today, at thirty-seven (almost thirty-eight), there are three books I read once a year then pass along to any of my friends and family who haven't yet had the pleasure: *Princess Bride, Owen Meany,* and *Ender's Game*. And while I adore the first two and recommend them to everybody, it is *Ender's Game* that to this day still resonates with me.

Ender showed me something I dearly needed to see: Don't trust the grown-ups. He taught me something I dearly needed to learn: Look out for yourself because no one else will. And, most important, he gave me the road map I needed to deal with a crippling childhood loss, that of my father.

I have tried (and just as often failed) to be like Ender in real life, or at least as much as you can if you don't live on an orbiting military space station. I've tried to be as much Speaker as Xenocide, tried my best to love even those I wanted to introduce to Dr. Device.

And I have missed Ender dearly in my adult life. If you're ever in a rest room in South Jersey and see scrawled next to all the "For a good time call" messages a little, scrawled "Ender Lives!" you know who to blame.

Terry O'Brien, entertainer/columnist
Cape May, New Jersey

I have known how to read since the age of two and this talent never was a popular trait among my peers. While reading has been a life passion, it's never been something that I could share with others.

I hated that. Even when I was among readers, few were convinced that I had good books to recommend; they were always the ones doing the recommending. And while I'd take their advice (and enjoyed a great variety of tales), they were far less inclined to take mine, or if they did, less likely to be as impressed with the stories as I had been.

After the birth of Harry Potter, a greater number of kids my age began to see the joys of books. I decided not to let this opportunity go to waste and found books to share after they put down their wizard school fantasies. They told me about T. A. Barron's Merlin series.

I wished for a genie who could grant me wishes. One of my first would be that folks would take me seriously when I told them what works of entertainment would be worth their time. No such luck.

In eighth grade, my best friend recommended a novel about a boy in an outer-space military school. I liked sci-fi and this premise appealed to me. Despite the fact that he told me the ending (like he did with *The Sixth Sense*—jerk), a year later, I read *Ender's Game*. It didn't matter that he told me the ending because the story itself was great. I finished it in two days; a rare occasion even for a speed reader like me.

Best of all, I didn't need that stupid genie. I had what I needed: a chance to prove to people that I have Good Taste. A month later, I got my next-door neighbor a copy to read, and to my credit, I didn't blab the ending. My neighbor loved it. He told others about it. I told more.

To this day, *Ender's Game* is my most loaned-out novel in my sizable library. I've shared it with the majority of my family members (it took three years, but I did it), friends from school, friends from church, and folks who would never open a book in their lives before then. Reviews have been favorable.

I've forgiven my friend for telling me the ending; he's now married, serving in the U.S. Army, and still an active reader. I'm grateful that he shared a story that I can pass along to others, and in that spirit, I have one thing left to say:

Ender's Game is worth your time. Read it.

Raymond L. Gifford, Jr., fast-food cook
Anderson, CA

Some people enjoy a nice time in a pool, or maybe a kickin' party. For myself, I love reading and writing. I try to write at least every other night, and I read every night. Books aren't just stories or novels, they are life-changing tools.

Well, my father has read almost the entire Ender series, and he was the one who first introduced me to the book. I wasn't expecting much, just a good book that I could read for reading points. To my surprise, it completely changed my life.

Ender is my all-time favorite character in the world. I can never get enough of him. He made me want to succeed at everything I did. So I started really stepping up in my schoolwork, slowly becoming a perfectionist. As odd as it is to look to a fictional character for a life model, I would try to make my actions as if it would be what he would do. I am now an A+ student, a cheerleader captain, and a great volleyball player. As crazy as it is, this phenomenal book is the reason this all happened to me.

Ender is such a great role model for any person. He is strong, brilliant, and amazing. I wished over and over that he was real, and not fictional. He is perfection in my eyes, and I oddly began to idolize every little thing about him. I just can't get enough of him. I am thirteen and I honestly don't know that much, but I do understand and know for a fact that the book *Ender's Game* is the best thing that has ever happened to me. I have told almost everyone I know about it and have offered it to them. I have gotten six people to read it, and not one of them did anything less than love it. I probably sound like just another obsessive fan, and maybe I am, but at least I got the joy of finding such a breathtaking book.

I can't say in words how much I love the book *Ender's Game* or all the ways it changed my life. I am just thirteen in eighth grade, I don't know much at all, but I do know that the book is a masterpiece.

Makenna Quigley, attending school
Carmel, Idaho

My first encounter with *Ender's Game* came from my sophomore-year English teacher in high school. After getting inducted into the National Honor Society, he gave me the book as a present. On the inside it said:

Rich,

Be proud of this NHS induction. It is a testament as much to your warm and amiable personality as to your intelligence. Something about you always reminded me of the greatness within Ender Wiggin. Trust me!

Regards, Mr. D

When he handed me this, my first reaction was that it would probably end up sitting on my shelf because I was never big into reading books except those for school. So I looked up who Ender Wiggin was, and laughed a little bit because the first thing I read was that Ender Wiggin destroyed an entire alien race. I made a comment to my teacher about relating me to a guy who killed things, but he told me it had nothing to do with that part of the story. The book ended up sitting in my room for almost a year when I finally read it on a cross-country trip. I finally understood what Mr. D was saying about it. It made me feel very proud to know he looked at me as that kind of leader and someone who is always able to come up with new ways of thinking even if they do not always coincide with the rules.

After reading *Ender's Game,* I went out and picked up the rest of the series that was out at the time as well as other books that looked like they might be interesting in the same genre. This book started me on a track to read anything and everything I could get my hands on, including going to book sales and buying books by the dozen even if I have not heard of some of the titles. It helped me start a new chapter of my life and learning as I entered college that I have come to truly appreciate. I have been opened up to a whole new world of thought that comes with science fiction books that I never would have seen if I did not take the advice of my teacher and sit down to enjoy a book for once.

Richard Scibetti, student
Freehold, New Jersey

I hate reading. That is, I used to hate reading. I first read *Ender's Game* on a three-day weekend trip with my family in Colorado. My friend let me borrow it and I figured it might be a good way to pass the time. I couldn't put it down. I read the entire book in three days, which is amazing considering that up to this point I hadn't read more than eight or so novels all the way through in my entire life (I was eighteen at the time).

Now I know you're thinking what comes next is I fell in love with books and I read all the time now. Sadly though I lost interest after that weekend and didn't get around to reading any of the other books in the series. It wasn't until the spring of 2007, when I purchased *Ender's Game* along with *Ender's Shadow* and *Shadow of the Hegemon*, that I was able to rekindle my fascination with the Ender universe. I read *Ender's Game* again (and it was even better the second time). I continued reading on in the Shadow series until about thirty minutes ago when I finally finished *Shadow of the Giant*.

The point I'm trying to make here is in the past year I've read almost the same amount of novels that I did in my whole life prior. And I love the moments when I can find time to tackle a few more pages. I read a few pages in between classes, or if I'm really lucky, I get time to sit and read a whole chapter (I actually couldn't stand it anymore and read the last seventy pages of *Shadow of the Giant* tonight). But my view toward reading has changed. It's a tremendously fun experience reading what other people can imagine and I'm very honored to have had the privilege of reading *Ender's Game* . . . twice! It makes me sad thinking about what I've been missing out on all this time. I can't change that, but what I can change (or shape, I should say) is the future. I already have *Speaker for the Dead* sitting on my shelf waiting for me, but not before I read *Ender's Game* a third time, of course!

David Collin Copeland, Waco, Texas

I was fifteen the first time I read *Ender's Game*. It was my parents' copy. I took up residence on the couch and followed Ender on his journey.

He was just like me—alone among his peers when all the adults gave him special treatment. Except that he was something great and I wasn't. But the victory of the book turned out to be not his military success, but that he had come to understand his enemy and love them. In the end, he saved his enemy, too.

I could be at peace with others not understanding me, not even bothering to get to know me. I might be different, but I wasn't messed up. I didn't have to change myself to be like them. I didn't have to regard them as less to be able to regard myself as okay. I could try to learn their language. See them for who they thought they were, make them feel comfortable. That was the real power that mattered in this world. I'm not sure how well I succeed, but that is a goal worth devoting a lifetime to. It might not be surprising that *Speaker for the Dead* turned out to be my favorite book of the series.

Fifteen years after I read *Ender's Game,* I gave it to my daughter to read. The story has now touched three generations of readers.

Ami Chopine, writer
South Jordan, Utah

Growing up I was an avid reader but never much liked science fiction or fantasy literature. I was instead an avid reader of historical fiction. I did not start reading science fiction until after I graduated from college and it was all because of the Ender stories. In fact, I did not read *Ender's Game* first. I was given a copy of *Speaker for the Dead* by my college anthropology professor with whom I was working on an archaeological excavation at the time.

The year after I graduated it was assigned as required reading for the comprehensive exams in anthropology because of its excellent treatment of interactions between cultures and the effects of that interaction. My professor thought I would enjoy it and brought a copy along on the dig for me. So, once I finished reading all I had brought with me, I tried it. I was hooked. It was not just anthropologically interesting, it was just a good read with characters I wanted to know more about. I couldn't wait to get back to "civilization" and buy *Ender's Game* and fill in the blanks. Though *Ender's Game* was a bit different in style and nature I enjoyed it, too, and couldn't wait for more.

Ender's Game and the books that followed it showed me that science fiction could be as compelling, "real," and full of interesting cultures, characters, and dilemmas as historical fiction. As a result of my encounter with it, I have gone on to try reading other science fiction/fantasy and expand my reading horizons.

Sylvia S. Duggan, homeschooling mom and ex-archaeologist
Philadelphia, Pennsylvania

Two of my friends convinced me to read *Ender's Game* when I was in seventh grade. I was against it at first because I really didn't like science fiction—or so I thought. By the time I reached the climax of the story I was literally pacing around the house. My mother kept calling me for dinner, but my attention was locked in the story.

I was always an avid reader, but *Ender's Game* opened a whole new universe of stories for me. I became fascinated by science fiction and fantasy stories. It opened my mind in a lot of ways, not only with regards to what books I like to read. The characters taught me a lot about what it means to be human. I learned about my own character as I related to the characters in the book.

To this day I consider *Ender's Game* to be my favorite book, and I have recommended it to countless people. I'm not often successful in convincing people I know to read books that I love, so it means a lot that I have actually convinced so many people to read *Ender's Game*. Every time a friend reads it, they thank me for telling them about it.

Jennifer Peterson, homemaker
Provo, Utah

I read *Ender's Game* in sixth grade, and finally felt as though there was fiction about young people that had characters like myself.

Four years later, I joined one of the two authorized online role-playing games based on the book. Two years after that, I met the man I would one day marry, and six and a half years after that we were, indeed, married.

Anne Davis, student
San Antonio, Texas

Ender's Game played an important role in my adolescent life and continues to do so in my adult one. I was fourteen when I was given a copy of it by my math teacher who thought it would do me good. Boy, was he right. Before I read it, school was always a hassle to me. I honestly didn't care about what I was learning and I never read a book unless I was forced to. *Ender's Game,* in a way, woke up an intellectual side of me that I never knew existed. It taught me to try and be the best that I could in anything that I did. I learned to be patient, strong, and above all I learned how to be a student. My grades got better and I began to explore the wide-open and enchanting world of reading.

Ender's loneliness and his inner struggle is something I identified with as a freshman in high school. It's tough to enter a new place and meet new people but *Ender's Game* gave me the strength to rise to the challenge. It also made me push myself beyond my limits in order to grow.

I am currently in college and I have to read *Ender's Game* before every school year. It's now become a ritual to me. It builds me up and gives me the strength to get through the grind of college life. Without *Ender's Game*

I honestly don't know if I'd even be in college. I don't know if I would enjoy literature as much as I do now. *Ender's Game* has had a profound impact in my life and it's the first book I recommend to people who are looking for a captivating and interesting novel. Without it, I would be a very different person from who I am today.

Daniel Dolocheck, student
Nutley, New Jersey

My childhood before *Ender's Game* could be described as . . . brutal.

My father had a job with the government, which called for relocating occasionally, but no matter what school I went to I always ended up getting into fistfights with the other students. I came home with more bloody noses than runny ones.

It wasn't until my freshman year of high school that I came across *Ender's Game*. I had heard of it before. A kid was telling me how great it was, but all I can remember thinking was, "Little kids are sent to outer space to fight aliens called Buggers? Give me a break."

I was a fool for fate though, so when I came across the book lying on the ground in an empty classroom I couldn't help but read the first couple of pages—and by then I was hooked.

I learned more about life from that book than I had in any of my classes. Human behavior and the utilization of everyday variables were things I had never even thought about before, but all of a sudden I understood. I understood that I could manipulate the way people perceived things. I understood that people only knew what they thought they knew, and I could take advantage of that. Life became a mind game.

At the beginning of my sophomore year, a group of older kids were verbally harassing the incoming freshman girls with a megaphone from across the street. Bellowing such things as "Freshman girls! Please report to my pants!"

The vice principal, along with security, came out and started walking in their direction, but the kids scattered. They weren't going to get in trouble; they were just going to come back and do it again, and it made me angry. No young girl should ever be subjected to that kind of crude hazing.

I remember thinking, exactly, "What would Ender do in this situation?"

I know, cheesy, but it's true.

I wasn't sure what to expect, but I hopped on my bike and rode into the neighborhood the kids had retreated to, from a different direction. I saw the kids walking along laughing, and I said, "Hey! They're still coming, guys!" So they started running again to get deeper into the neighborhood. I went with them and once we were all "safe" we just walked around talking about how stupid the vice principal was.

I didn't really have an opinion about the vice principal, but I knew I didn't like these guys, and I wasn't sure what I was going to do, but now I had their trust. Eventually the group whittled down to just me and a few of the kids including the big shot with the megaphone. We talked about random things forever, until I finally saw an opportunity.

The big shot mentioned something about his glasses. So I asked him, casually, if he was nearsighted or farsighted. He said he wasn't sure. I told him to give me his glasses because "I could figure it out by looking through them." Once I had them in my hands, I held them up to my eyes and said, "It looks like you're going to have to talk to the vice principal if you want these back." And I pedaled off as fast as I could back in the direction of the school.

Sure, it was silly. But it worked. The big shot, along with some of the others, eventually came back to the school and got in trouble. Sure, I was harassed by them for the next couple of years, but it didn't bother me at all. I won a fight against a bunch of big kids without throwing a single punch. I was proud.

Thanks to *Ender's Game,* I've never been in a fistfight since, I studied psychology at Southern Oregon University, and I approach life with an open mind.

Jack Montague, freelance production assistant
Portland, Oregon

I found *Ender's Game* on a shelf in my middle school's library when I was in seventh grade. It was an old beat-up paperback copy and when I read the back I immediately identified with the story. You see, I had a lot of problems in school and to tell the truth I was continually thinking of suicide. I just wanted everything over with, but then I found this book with a character in a similar situation to me. But unlike me he was strong, he fought no matter what, he didn't just accept his lot in life. He actively did everything he could to improve it, he fought back against his tormentors. I can honestly say that

Ender's Game saved my life and gave me the strength to go on no matter what. To this day I feel a debt of gratitude to this story and the author because without them I truly believe I would not be here to write this.

Cody Dobbs, student
Norman, Oklahoma

Ender's Game was a gateway book for me. Before my freshman high school English class, I had never even picked up a science fiction novel. I couldn't believe that our teacher was going to make us read a novel about boys in space! Much to my surprise, I was instantly fascinated by the story and couldn't put it down. Although it sounds hokey, *Ender's Game* did, in fact, change my life. I read every speculative fiction book I could get my hands on in high school, and went on to major in English literature in college.

I completed my M.Phil in Popular Literature at Trinity College Dublin (Ireland), where most people had never heard of *Ender's Game,* even though there is a strong science fiction following. When the subject of my dissertation came up, I didn't have a doubt in my mind. When I first told my (very Irish) adviser that I wanted to write about *Ender's Game,* he was skeptical. Once he had read the book, though, I've never seen him so excited. I can tell you that there is now a local following there as well! I just started a career in writing based on the magic that I felt when I first read about Ender.

Holliann Russell, writer
Frederick, Maryland

When I was fourteen years old, one of my good friends recommended *Ender's Game* to me. I took one look at the cover and decided that it wasn't my kind of story. A fourteen-year-old doesn't read about spaceships and aliens! I was way too mature for that!

But a couple of months later I ran out of interesting books to read and ended up taking it from the school library. And when I say "taking" it, I mean "stealing" it. I was immediately hooked and ended up hiding the book in my backpack and taking it home, an act of thievery that still haunts me to this day.

I read that copy over and over until it fell apart. And to make up for my klepto-cism, I made it a mission in life to purchase the book and give it away to as many people as possible. I don't know how many copies I have purchased, but it is probably around twenty—I know I sent four copies to soldiers in Iraq this past Christmas.

What I couldn't tell from the cover is this: *Ender's Game* is about bigger issues than spaceships and aliens. It is about Truth and Duty and Perseverance. The story is a success because the characters—from Ender to Graff to Valentine—stay true to their own selves, their own moral consciences.

Ender realizes a Truth early on: If you want to stop a ruthless enemy, you have to go for the win. If you try to reason with someone who wants to hurt you, it will just make them hurt you worse. The only way to "defuse" someone with evil intentions is to beat them to the punch. Or to put it another way, when a situation is kill-or-be-killed, always go for the throat.

That was a harsh truth to digest when I was fourteen, but it was important. And now that I have a wife and three kids, I identify even better with the idea. If someone messes with my family, I'll hurt them so bad their life will never be the same.

Thanks for the life lesson, Ender.

Dustin Dopps, marketing
Portland, Oregon

The most profound concepts provided by the Ender novels are the racial undertones. I have had conversations with fellow readers and was surprised to hear most had never considered the novels from that angle. While reading *Xenocide,* I began to reflect on the interactions the different races had with each other. Consider the humans assuming murder by the piggies when in fact the intent was to glorify. Think about the Queen's interaction with Ender and the ignorance that was shown on both sides. These novels offer invaluable lessons and the humans of planet Earth would do well to learn from them.

Roman Pierantozzi, computers
Endicott, New York

Christmas morning 1987 was a normal one with plenty of gifts and surprises. One gift though was very strange. It was a set of paperback books with one called *Ender's Game* and the other called *Speaker for the Dead.* My father had picked these up for me since he knew I was reading books for my freshman high school English class and was tackling books that were probably way over my current reading ability as someone new to the whole idea of reading for fun.

At first I was a little stunned. Dad hadn't read these books and had no clue if they were any good. He said the guy at the bookstore recommended them and how it was the first time the Hugo and Nebula Awards had gone to sequels. To me as a young teenager, it seemed like a lame gift that required little thought and I quickly set them aside for more exciting gifts.

Eventually it came time to start another book for my class and I began looking around for something to read. I saw the "lame" book on the shelf and thought about it with the still bitter memory of what seemed to me at the time as a "I'll just get the brat something" gift, but somehow decided to open it up and see what all the hooey was about.

Needless to say, after I started *Ender's Game* I wasn't able to put it down. This was a first in my life since before this I really didn't like reading. Of course I was a slow reader, but there were a number of sleepless nights where before I knew it, it was early in the morning. I was totally caught unaware of the twist at the end since I knew there was a sequel and didn't think much that the book might end suddenly. When I gave my report to my class, it was a very exciting and upbeat report.

After that I was a book reader. I continued on in the series and picked up other books with eagerness. Once I saw in *Ender's Game* that you could connect with characters and care about them like they were real, it made reading for enjoyment a passion.

I have reread *Ender's Game* more times then I can count. I always recommend it to people and challenge them to read the first twenty pages with the bet that they won't be able to stop after that. No one has yet.

Jay Taylor, computer engineer
Grafton, West Virginia

My name is Lars Doucet and I have a brain disease. I was diagnosed at the age of fifteen with a fairly severe case of Tourette's Syndrome.

Tourette's patients suffer from uncontrollable, random bodily movements and vocal outbursts, sometimes violent, sometimes obscene, always embarrassing. Most people consider us to be "freaks" or "spazzers." The silver lining is that we tend to make up for this strange behavior with above-normal intellectual and creative faculties.

Long, long before I was diagnosed, I'd been showing what we now know to be symptoms of TS. Throughout those dark years I was disciplined by teachers and principals, harassed by my fellow schoolmates, and excluded from almost every social activity.

Ender's Game has always been my favorite book since I read it in sixth grade. That year I endured not only the worst teasing at the hands of other children, but the unrelenting scorn of one of the worst ultradisciplinarian middle-school math teachers I've ever had the displeasure of knowing.

I always related to Ender; I think a lot of kids like me probably did. Even more so, I related to Bean. Being alone in a world where you were a freak to not only your peers, but also the teachers who were supposed to protect you, was a story that spoke to me.

All those years I was in the dark, not realizing that I even had a disease. I just believed everyone when they called me a freak. As far as I knew, I *could* control my symptoms if I tried hard enough, but I just had bad habits, like biting my fingernails.

The best part though, was that Ender and Bean seemed like real kids to me.

You see—most adults who write stories "for children" do not understand children. When I read *Ender's Game* the first thing that came to mind was, "Wow! These kids actually act like me!"

A lot of other people who write those kinds of books—or try to—just treat children like imbeciles or babies. You'd be surprised the level of conversation you can carry on with a ten-year-old!

So, thanks for providing a bright spot in the worst year of my life, and reminding me that sometimes it's up to the freaks and the spazzers to save the world.

Lars A. Doucet, video game developer
College Station, Texas

Prior to *Ender's Game,* I had never read sci-fi/fantasy; just not my genre, I'd thought. I'd heard much good from many people about *Ender's Game,* but only after my wife read it, did I—just to see what all the fuss was about. Turns out it is everything I heard it was and more, because for me it was a gateway novel.

Had I not read Ender, I never would have read the scores of other amazing novels in the sci-fi/fantasy world and I certainly would have never attempted writing my own contributions to the genre. My sci-fi/fantasy writing led to workshops and writer's groups, from which I have dear friends who I never would have known and I suspect will be around for a long time to come.

My life would not be nearly as enriched, nor would I be the reader and writer that I am today were it not for a Third.

Christopher Miller, trainer
North Salt Lake, Utah

I first encountered *Ender's Game* as an adult in my thirties. I loved the story and the surprise ending. I knew when I first read it that it would be *great* for eighth graders. I collaborated with two other English teachers, and in 1993, I convinced them to let me write a unit on this book for all the eighth graders. I knew the book was a success when the students kept reading ahead. The students thought that they were reading just an exciting adventure story, but I knew what was coming. I could sneak in lessons on tolerance and fairness. We had wonderful discussions on, "Does the end justify the means?" This is my thirtieth year of teaching. Every year I teach different books, but the only book that stays on my syllabus from year to year is *Ender's Game*. It reaches students at every level economically, academically, and socially.

Many students go on to read *Speaker for the Dead* and *Xenocide*. The themes in *Ender's Game* make a great lead in to our study of the Holocaust. At twenty-five students a year for almost sixteen years, hundreds of lives have been touched by *Ender's Game*.

Sandra Wilson, teacher
Marietta, Georgia

At the age of eleven, it took me a little over a week to finish the book. This was only because I eagerly absorbed every word. I had read some sci-fi before. My grandmother had a wall full. I had been to "The Red Hills of Mars" and I knew the first rule of robotics, but I had never been to battle school. I had no idea a young boy could save the world . . . and he was a boy just like me.

My ability to relate with Ender and his conflicts got my attention. I have been seeking that feeling every since. Alvin Maker was another character I soon found. As I get older the magical reads seem fewer and farther between, but I still read and my children now go to my wall of books much as I did to my grandmother's. When I see that spark in their eyes, I can understand it. This is, after all, why we read.

Scott Robert Dantzler, chef/writer
Crawfordville, Florida

When I was in the seventh grade in 2001, my older brother Marko, who was in college at that time, introduced me to *Ender's Game*. He had the book since he was in fifth grade. After finishing it, I couldn't stop myself from reading it for the second time . . . then the third, then the fourth and so on. I must have read it at least ten times.

Now I'm twenty years old and I'm still in love with the story. Each time I read it, there's always a new personal realization that comes to mind. I realized that humans can be capable of so many things: love, hate, and survival. This book means so much to me because in a way, I saw myself in some of the characters but most especially in Ender. Though I am not a genius like Ender is, I could relate to him because he was a child who had to act strong despite his own personal fears.

In a way, Ender's story helped me realize that I, too, am capable of triumphing over challenges and it doesn't matter whether I'm seven or thirty years old. *Ender's Game* will forever be a part of who I am.

Rossanna V. Fojas, college junior
Metro Manila, Philippines

I was something like thirteen years old when my mother brought *Ender's Game* back from the library. And there, I fell in love. The whole universe was in my room. Of all the books that I had read and loved, laying on my bed, my fingers wrapped around the book's cover and the shivering pages, none was ever as good as that one. But most of all it was the opening of a huge dream too big for my head: the universe. And the start of a big frustration: WHY don't I live in those kinds of worlds, me, hmm?

Today I'm twenty years old and I still dream of living adventures like those in the science fiction books.

To live like Ender, with lots of technologies so hallucinating, the conquest of space and the infinity everywhere, everywhere, to travel at light speed, communication by ansible, to go and see in a black hole if the physicists are right, what is going to happen and how to react when facing the unknown.

To visit the infinity of the universe! To never stay anywhere, to be everywhere, to know many lives, to write about new living forms and about the wars that we've won, the healed wounds and the scars as trophies, to live for so long thanks to the effects of relativity and to have the possibility of seeing everything, breathless, to cry the departures, the inexorable, to search for the edge. The edge of infinity.

Ender made me discover galaxies that I could touch with my fingertips, astrophysics, dreams out of the atmosphere.

Seeing that I'm just an ordinary girl and that I don't have the destiny of an astronaut (but without abandoning the hope of an extraordinary and memorable destiny to discover in the weeks to come, or to, one day, be part of an experimental program). I continue to read science fiction and I say to myself that surely, one day, I will write some to live it from the inside as much as possible.

PS : I'm French and I'm very sorry if my English is, hm, not very good. I've so many things to say. It's easier in French.

Emmylou Haffner, student
Bruxelles, France

Sixteen years ago I was a senior in college. It had been a rough year. I had been diagnosed with a rare form of cancer and had dropped out of school so I could live at home. My life changed in unexpected ways. I had always been the link between my two best friends, but while I was gone they forged their own bonds of friendship, and I felt left out. And although it was true that I liked to flirt with almost anyone who would flirt back, it still hurt to find out that while I was gone another friend was spreading rumors about how I liked to steal other girls' boyfriends. Not only was this untrue, but it was embarrassing, because my friend was beautiful. It would have been humiliating to even imagine stealing a boyfriend from her. Ironically, at about the same time, her roommate started dating one of my best friends, and he never spoke to me again. While I had cancer I also figured out what I wanted to do with my life, and it wasn't what I was majoring in.

After Christmas, I was plunked back into my college life with nothing more than a huge scar on my leg to show that I had ever been gone. Somehow, everything was different though. I had a huge class load. I was determined to graduate on schedule, so I could start graduate school in the fall. Although I thought of myself as smarter than average, I had never applied myself before. Everything that had seemed important about college seemed vaguely asinine now. I was having unexpected difficulties fitting back in, but these were my friends, and I loved them. Leaving college without healing my friendships would have left a bigger scar on my heart than the one on my leg.

Then someone handed me *Ender's Game*. After I read it I started over and read it again and again. *Ender's Game* became my manual for life. Ender's struggle to forge a place for himself in Battle School helped me reshape my college experience. I read it when I was stressed about finishing my master's thesis, the night before I got married, while I was pregnant, and again after my children were born. I held on to *Ender's Game* like a lifeline when my husband and I moved across the country to Maine—my own personal transfer to Command School. I have it on my computer table right now as I struggle to edit my first novel.

I am amazed at the way that Ender has helped to define and shape my life. When I first read *Ender's Game,* I was not much like Ender. I was too afraid to find my own limits. Ender was the missing balance in my life. I'm a natural born follower, but Ender has taught me not to fear my own uniqueness, because there is no excellence in merely doing what everyone else is doing.

Melanie Crouse, mother/author
South China, Maine

My dad was a very intelligent and quiet man. He provided a wonderful life and education for three, sometimes rowdy, girls. He loved the three of us in his own quiet way, but we never really had too much in common with him.

In high school, I was going through his two eight-feet-by-six-feet book-shelves each stacked three deep of sci-fi and fantasy books, when I asked him, "Would I like any of these books?" With a smile on his face he handed me *Ender's Game*. It was like he was waiting for at least one of his children to love what he loved. When I finished, he asked what I thought about the story. That was the first time he ever asked what I thought about anything. We talked about the story and he recommended other books I could read.

We had finally found a common bond. It showed me we could talk about everything, not just books. The bond continued until the day he died. My mom gave me those books after he passed, and I treasure them. They are my link to the world my dad loved.

Paige Wurtsbaugh, data auditor
Marion, Ohio

In graduate school, Eduardo, a friend from Argentina, gave me *Ender's Game* as a gift with the inscription: "When I first read this book and Ender's moral decisions, I thought about you." Eduardo and I had had a number of important conversations about ethics and culture, so I valued his recommendation and eagerly approached the book, though I had read nothing written by this author before. When I started reading, I was hooked and found myself trying to squeeze in reading the novel while at work at my campus job in the library.

Since then I have read a host of other works by Card, attended his writing workshop in Virginia, and used his books (*Ender's Game, Speaker for the Dead, Pastwatch,* and *Red Prophet*) in the classroom. I am in the process of writing a book that relates his work to that of C. S. Lewis, J. R. R. Tolkien, Gene Wolfe, and the TV show *Lost*. I hope that one day Eduardo will be able to read this so that I can again thank him for his gift.

Brett Patterson, professor of Theology and Ethics
Anderson, South Carolina

In December of 2005, I was sitting around my brother-in-law's house waiting to enjoy Christmas dinner when I noticed this book sitting by the chair. I asked about it and discovered that it belonged to my teenaged nephew. He hadn't read much of it but had picked it up at a bookstore a few weeks earlier.

I remember sitting there reading the first page, caught up in the chapter title "Third," wondering at the abuse this little kid in the book was taking. I had never heard of Card, much less Ender. I finished the book in twenty-four hours (excluding Christmas dinner).

I've often reminded my nephew of this story because of the impact it had on me. I must have read a dozen different Card books since then. However, my nephew never finished *Ender's Game*! I did give him *War of Gifts* for Christmas.

Cliff Thompson, University Theater professor
Henderson, Tennessee

At the time I read *Ender's Game,* my life was the flip side of normal. Taking care of grandparents in my stepparents' home, waking my brothers up for school because Dad was at work, and trying to develop some semblance of a relationship had taken over my sanity and was giving me little, if any, normal hold on my life. At best, I was a disillusioned teen trying to make sense of a mad world. My mother was an alcoholic and I tried to make the best of it by being the "good boy." At best, I identified myself as a young adult, because who else my age would be dealing with this stuff? What I had done then, was to begin forming an identity of myself, but it had to be secret, something that gave me strength.

I don't know exactly when, but my little brother brought home *Ender's Game* because his history teacher recommended it. Since I was and still am an avid reader, I didn't mind picking it up, because if I knew it was a good book, I would have it finished by tomorrow anyway. I was wrong—I finished it the night I picked it up. So profoundly had the tale of Ender gripped me, that I needed the companionship the book gave me. No one else could give it to me until then.

What *Ender's Game* has given me is a moral compass so to speak. I don't use the logic in it to make my decisions, but I do use the technique of thinking things out thoroughly and definitely, as Ender did, to make my decisions. I've learned that when you eventually are self-aware enough to develop your own beliefs, it's okay that they be challenged or even dismissed if they have no moral value. I learned that responsibility is not just saying you'll do something, but that you'll do something and be the best at it that you can possibly be.

DJ Bookout, Special Ed paraprofessional
Newton, Kansas

I was twelve when I read *Ender's Game* and stayed home sick to finish the book in one day. I loved the characters, and was fascinated by the games in the book. I knew very little programming at the time, but decided I wanted to make a video-game version of the Battle Room. I wrote to the author requesting further details, and treasured the reply greatly. At the time, almost all games were two-dimensional, but I wanted a fully three-dimensional simulation of the Battle Room. I taught myself trigonometry, projecting coordinate systems, sprite graphics, collision detection, all so I could relive that game.

I ended up getting my master's degree in computer graphics, and today work for the Air Force, building a touch-table interfaced battlefield visualization system. Over the years my tastes have changed a little, and I am not so interested in playing the Battle Room as I once was. But I'm thinking about starting on something like the Fantasy Game . . .

Douglas Summers-Stay, computer research scientist
Bellbrook, Ohio

I first read *Ender's Game* when I was in third grade, and immediately felt an extraordinary bond with Ender's character. Like Ender, I was considered the smartest and most talented kid in the community and, also like Ender, I was under constant and considerable pressure from my teachers to achieve increasingly difficult goals, to the point of impossibility. Ender's dual yet contradictory qualities of ruthless determination and empathetic gentleness are qualities that I always strove to balance in my own day-to-day life.

This has served me well later in life, both as a musician and a pilot. I recently finished writing an opera based around Ender Wiggin, chronicling his life from the time his monitor is removed to his final destruction of the Buggers. Now, an opera is a huge undertaking, even for a full-time professional composer. For me it was even more daunting, and yet once the seed of the idea sprouted in my imagination there was no turning back. Ender had inspired me to such great heights, and I needed to pay him back.

I had already written a few pieces either based on or dedicated to Ender, but this was a different animal altogether. I needed to do Ender proud, to give his story the power and energy that it so richly deserves. I spent more than a year studying every musical technique available to me and picking and choosing what felt right for Ender. Now I have over two hours of no-holds-barred emotional music ranging from Ender's cautiously introspective reflection on his love for Valentine to the bombastic frenetic fury of the Battle School to Bean's achingly poignant lament for the soldiers in the far-flung human fleet. Only now, finally, two decades after I first read about Ender, can I finally say that I have created something worthy of the impact that he has had on my life.

Every moment of the music touches on the connection that Ender and I share, that bond that develops between a person and their most revered hero, even if he is an imaginary hero. Ender has shaped all aspects of my life, not so much by instilling certain qualities in me but by showing me that the qualities I possess are worth having. He has helped me pursue and achieve my life's ambition to fly for the Navy and he has helped me live as any decent person should: with grace, compassion, and honesty. More important than anything else, though, he has provided me a muse.

Music is my language, and Ender is my reason for speaking.

Joe Stephens, Navy pilot and composer
Pensacola, Florida

I gained a love of science fiction very early, thanks to my stepfather. Although I only saw him and my mother once or twice a year, it was a great enough impact that I began to seek out new works to satisfy my growing need for good stories.

When I visited one summer, he handed me a copy of *Ender's Game* with a smile on his face. I had it read (twice-over) in a matter of days. When I finally had my fill, he and I sat in the living room for hours discussing all the intricacies of the young protagonist and his journey. The depth of that discussion, and the love of Ender and his companions, have propelled me into my adult life with a sense of wonder regarding the unknown. Do I walk through with the obvious paths at hand, or do I find an unusual, unexpected approach? And though my stepfather is long since gone, *Ender's Game* will always represent in my heart a bond of understanding between parent and child, two followers of such an enduring story.

Katherine Stafford, college student
Hot Springs, Arkansas

Mom read sci-fi. We were merely her children, and we didn't really care about sci-fi. That was before we encountered *Ender's Game,* published in the August 1977 issue of *Analog.* I remember reading it, rapt, in my attic bedroom by the light of oil candles.

I really cared about Ender Wiggin, more than I cared about Luke Skywalker, to whom I was also introduced that summer of '77. By the time Ender saved the world, he was about my age (I was a rising high school freshman). Ender was me like no individual I'd ever read in fiction. He was smart, he was an outcast, he was being manipulated by a system he didn't understand. I gloried when he successfully carried the fate of the world on his shoulders.

I'm old now. But I can look back and see that I was changed by that story. I began to believe that my life could matter. I began to understand the terrible sacrifices that sometimes accompany meaningful success. I began to look at my siblings as people for whom I wanted to feel the loyalty Ender felt for Valentine, rather than merely the fear or disgust Ender felt for Peter.

I can't go back and live a life where I didn't read *Ender's Game* to objectively measure the difference the story made in my life. But I do know the example of Ender Wiggin—boy, soldier, priest, man—made me a better person.

I count myself blessed that Mom read sci-fi.

Meg Stout, program manager
Annandale, Virginia

Ender's Game came home with me from the public library because it had cool spaceships on the cover and because the back promised a young boy rising up to lead an army of the future. My kind of material. I read it while on a family vacation to the North Carolina coast. It was the summer that spanned the gap between the watercolor cocoon of elementary school and the social minefield of middle school. I was eleven.

As we started out on our way to the ocean, I tackled the first page. I didn't like it. There was no way to tell who was talking! When I pressed on I was startled by the brutality of the first chapter. This kid was the hero? My sympathy for Ender grew over the passing miles with the introduction of his siblings. I never forgave Peter Wiggin for that game of buggers and astronauts, even if Ender did. And then there was Valentine. In the beginning, I loved Ender because Valentine loved Ender.

My memories of that beach trip are inseparable from my memories of the book. When I was swallowed by an ocean wave, I was Dink Meeker spinning in zero gravity. While floating, I would pull my legs up to my chest, fire between my knees and think, "The enemy's gate is down." I read every moment I was not engaged in a family activity. When I would finally turn off the light to sleep, the images played on inside my head. I tried to double numbers like Ender, but I never made it very far.

I finished the book on the way back home. When Graff and Ender returned to space, I read the name of a place that sounded familiar and asked my dad, "Where's the Pamlico Sound?"

"It's right outside the window," he replied. I looked out, imagining towers of concrete and steel. When Ender learned that he had not been playing a game, I put down the book, bent forward, and placed my hands on the side of my head while taking deep breaths. My family thought I was carsick. And when I finished the book, just a few miles from home, I cried. My dad asked me if it had a sad ending, but that wasn't it at all. The ending was pure hope. It was the simple fact that the book was over. My journey with these characters, these friends, was over. Ender had drifted off into the universe like the smoke from the birthday fire.

Now I teach eleven-year-olds, some already weary of the lives they lead, and I hope they find a book that teaches them what *Ender's Game* taught me: People do not like it when you stand out, but sometimes that is what it takes to be great. No matter how many battles you face, you can survive. Childhood is a treasure, to be valued and protected at any cost.

And, of course, the enemy's gate is down.

William Tobey Mitchell, teacher
Dobson, North Carolina

I have always been an intelligent child, maybe a genius, maybe not, the definition of genius is far too variable to apply to yourself, but I was definitely smarter than a lot of my classmates, and they knew it. And they hated me for it. It may sound like arrogance to say such things, but it was simple fact. I tried not flaunt it, but I knew answers, and wasn't patient enough for the teacher to give up asking and tell us. I wanted to learn and I wanted to keep learning. This, of course, led to abuse.

All throughout middle school and into high school they teased me and taunted me, and it hurt me, and depressed me, and probably worst of all made me angry. When I lost control it just looked weak, because I was small and didn't know much fighting.

Then I picked up *Ender's Game* on a recommendation from my cousin. I started reading it on the way to a family vacation in Key West, and that first day I stayed in my hotel room until I had finished it.

I just kept going and couldn't stop. I was so easily able to immerse myself into Ender's character, to understand his point of view. It made sense to me, it was like Ender was me only, of course, better. I was stunned at the accuracy and depth of the portrayal of the mind-set of a child like Ender, and I was stunned because all of a sudden it wasn't a character in a book, it was me.

After reading the book, I was able to draw strength from Ender's ability to endure, and I was able to draw confidence from the strength. When one carries themselves with confidence, people start treating you differently. Without any hyperbole, I can say my life changed for the better the moment I read that book—to the point that whenever I go to a new, strange place I bring it with me, and whenever I feel weak I read it. It gives me the courage to smile and do what I have to do. I am going to college soon, and when I arrive, the first thing I will do is open *Ender's Game* and read it again.

Nicholas Gilbert, student
Griswold, Connecticut

When *Ender's Game* was introduced as required classroom reading in high school English, I initially regarded it as I did most such literature: with a resigned annoyance at yet another in a long line of books that teachers gush about and that I can look forward to wasting hours of my life trying to figure out what the author "meant" or "felt" when they wrote the book in the first place.

I soon found that *Ender's Game,* and many of the books that followed it, were different altogether. As an adolescent who had been quickly advanced through earlier grades and was present in a class of peers several years my senior, I found a literary mirror that offered an examination of many of the same feelings and challenges that I was going through. The difficulty of bully magnetism to a younger kid (in my case, my rotund physique did not exactly help). The feeling of isolation; each success driving a further social wedge between myself and my peers. The congruency of finding comfort in a group of similarly ostracized freethinkers.

While I certainly could not claim any real experience of mortal danger or having somehow saved the fate of humanity by my own story's end, I can definitely say that *Ender's Game* provided a comfort in a difficult situation. Here was a story of a fictional youth enduring many of the same sorts of challenges that I had endured. He framed that intellect into executing each task put before him despite his personal struggles and constructed a life of excellence around his gifts, using a backdrop of friends to complement his weaknesses and provide the grounding necessary to succeed.

In *Ender's Game,* I found support for my own journey through adolescence and the message that excellence is not only acceptable but is not a unique condition. Silent observation. Calculation. Hope. A drive to be the best. These are themes that I wish every teenager could have the same opportunity to internalize through literature.

Wayne Anderson, systems engineer
Brighton, Colorado

I used to not be a science fiction fan, or a fan of any fiction for that matter. I read *Ender's Game* for the first time last summer after a friend brought it to work. He gave me a summary of the story and I spent the next few hours reading it over his shoulder. Since then I've read every book in the Ender series, and passed it on to several friends. Having just finished *Children of the Mind,* it feels like I've lost a close friend since there aren't any more books to read.

Ender's Game has fueled my interest in politics, history, and literature. It has inspired me to go deeper in my education and create a new class at my university. My philosophy professor and I will be launching a Concepts of Rights and Justice class next semester that will deal with the founding of new government laws and ethics. After reading *Ender's Game* I began to see a lot of things differently. Ender has a knack for seeing past what people are saying and finding what it is that they really want and need. I've tried to implement that into my own life as much as possible and the outcome has been amazing. *Ender's Game* is more than mere fiction. It has the ability to teach people new things and inspire them to greatness.

Garrett Stevenson, college student
Elk City, Oklahoma

I have always been into science fiction and was reading a lot of Robert Heinlein in those days, and a buddy of mine asked if I had ever read a book called *Ender's Game,* and I hadn't.

We were in the library (this was back in high school and since I didn't have a car like the cool kids, I pretty much hung out in the library with all the other geeks) so my buddy Boaz went and grabbed it off the shelf and put it in my hands. He had never steered me wrong with literature before, but I was skeptical when he told me it was about a bunch of kids in space. But he was/is my friend, so I cracked it open and began to read. Nothing could have prepared me for the journey I underwent.

I would like to tell you that this book changed my life, but I think that would be overstating things just a little and might sound faintly corny. What I can tell you is that it did change my mind about how much of an impact the written word can have on an individual. Because the ending is so unbelievable, I was completely unprepared for it, and it hit me like the proverbial ton of bricks. I literally read those words in awe.

That story made me want to be a better writer. They say when you are in the presence of greatness you're either embarrassed or you're inspired and I would definitely say this book inspired me and still does to this day. It's a story that I keep coming back to in my mind and I don't make the mistake of trying to write a story like *Ender's Game* but I want to do to a reader what was done to me—when the truth of that moment opened my eyes to an entire world of possibilities I hadn't previously considered. This is the kind of story I have passed on to friends and family and one day if I ever have children I will share it with them. I carry Ender and his courage in my heart. And in my heart he will live forever.

James S. Wirfs, Jr., Wal-Mart
Oak Harbor, Washington

In my freshman year of high school, my English teacher required that we read one book per semester. So of course, as most students would, I waited until that last minute to find one and get the grade. I had never been interested in reading books, as there were girls to swoon and baseballs to be thrown around. My best friend had picked up *Ender's Game* randomly from our school library because, he had said, that the cover was cool. Upon reading it, he hurriedly told me that I didn't have to worry and that he had found the book that I was to read for the class project. Something like, "Yeah dude, it's a cool book. The main character gets in space battles and stuff—you'll like it."

Needless to say, I had my work cut out for me. I didn't care what I read, as long as it was relatively easy and at least mildly entertaining. It took me two school nights to read it. My mind was blown—never had I believed that a story told in print could grip my imagination so completely. From that point on, reading became one of my most important activities. Simply put, through *Ender's Game* I learned to love stories; through stories, I've learned to love life. For me, *Ender's Game* was a life changer.

Jonmark Ragsdale, college student
Tampa, Florida

My brother had to read *Ender's Game* in high school. He loved it and raved about it. The next year, I had to read it as well and fell in love with it and read *Speaker for the Dead, Xenocide,* and *Children of the Mind* and it really opened up my mind and opened me up to a lot more of OSC's books.

At this point in my life I was still living as a male . . . I am a postoperative male to female transgender. At the age of twenty I confronted my long hidden secret and exposed my true self to the world, risking everything for the chance at a happier life. After nearly being shot in the face, I decided I loved life, but if I would have died, no one would have known who I was inside. So at the age of twenty, I confronted the skeletons in my closet.

With the right education and the right approach, I was able to share my struggle with my loved ones and friends, and what I received in return was absolute acceptance and respect.

I didn't want to be dead, I love life, but living in the wrong body and living the lie made me feel like I would rather be dead, but I knew I loved life and loved living. So the only way I could do that would be to make the full transition, which I have done quite successfully.

How this applies to OSC is that my name Jane was taken from the self-aware supercomputer in *Speaker, Xeno,* and *Children.*

I always connected greatly to that character and I loved the name. Having freshly reread the series around the time I was making these most pivotal life decisions, I was greatly influenced by the work.

My deceased grandmother's name was Joyce. I didn't want to use it for my first name. Jane, in my mind, represents the ultimate feminine, and power (because of these books), and it is a common name but I never once had met a Jane.

It was already written in the destiny of my life, but *Ender's Game* opened me up to *Speaker, Xeno,* and *Children,* which have been omens for the path that I walk.

Jane Joyce B, graphic designer, musician
Phoenix, Arizona

Ender's Game quite literally saved me from insanity, from myself. I'd just been kicked out of one of the U.S. Military's most academically challenging programs—a place I feel is as close to Battle School as anything today—for medical problems out of my control. I was spiraling downward, struggling with depression, with suicide, to the point where I had to be hospitalized.

My bonding over the Ender books with a friend I discovered there saved me. It felt as if we *were* Battle School students. It was nice to revitalize my mind, stretch my thinking, and mentally click with a friend who shared my love of *Ender's Game* and, incidentally, my view on many things in life.

Feeling like you are part Ender or part Bean gives you a sense of belonging, a sense of purpose, when all other means have failed you. Somewhere, somehow, the stories explain, there was someone who thought like you, who did the things you'd do, and they accomplished great things.

Michael Heath, Starbucks barrista
Ogden, Utah

I was introduced to *Ender's Game* by my school's librarian. She praised it as being a book she loved, even though she hated science fiction. I already loved science fiction, so that was enough to sell me. That year, my freshman year in high school, I found myself totally absorbed in the stories of young Ender at Battle School and in the stories that followed in *Speaker* and *Xenocide*. I became something of an *Ender's Game* missionary, recommending the novel to everyone until there was something of a cult following at my school.

The book spoke to all of us on such a profound and spiritual level. For me, I found solace in Ender's story, insofar as he had to find the strength to persevere through utter isolation and almost complete mental breakdown. I drew strength from knowing my own story was not entirely unique to me. I decided I was pushing myself too hard, with Ender serving as an example to me of what to avoid, and I think I may have thus avoided a similar breakdown or worse.

Ender also helped reaffirm for me the truth and honesty of some of the values I had taken from my Christian faith. I already knew that killing was a sin, and that war was a moral wrong, but Ender gave me words to articulate why. The amazing message of the novel on the importance of empathizing with your enemy, of the dangers of engaging in total war, and the heavy toll such an approach to conflict takes on those who wage it all came together to give voice to my beliefs.

After high school I continued being a missionary of Ender's message. I've lost track at this point of how many times I've given out the book as a gift, but it happens at least a few times a year.

After the horrific terrorist attacks of September 11, 2001, my work to spread this message seemed even more vital. In those dark and trying months after the attack, Americans were filled with hate and anger and prejudice. We sought retribution. When it came it was swift and terrible. We rained "shock and awe" on those we felt had wronged us with our superior destructive technology. At first our hate was aimed at those who may have deserved it. But then, led by liars and demagogues and opportunists and warmongers, and informed by our bigotry and fear, we extended our wrath to others who had done nothing at all to deserve it. Innocents died. Our allies disappeared. Our nation lost face. We started doing far more harm than "good." We were making the same mistakes as the IF, repeating Ender's tragedy, all for the same inability to empathize at all with our enemy, understand the nature of the conflict, or realistically evaluate its costs.

My fervor in spreading the word of Ender grew. I started sharing the book with as many people as I could. Often it worked. After reading and discussing the book, I convinced many of errors in their thinking. People who had supported this unjust war and the liars who argued for it, thanks to Ender's story, were now campaigning to vote those very liars out of power. Of course I don't have any hard figures, but I'd like to think that some of my little movement may have had an impact during the last midterm election. I further hope that it might have an impact in this presidential election cycle. If that happens, then *Ender's Game* would not have merely had a profound impact on me personally; it will have helped save the world against insanity, bloodlust, misguided moral conceitedness, and abhorrent egocentrism. Forces every bit as terrifying as the buggers.

Ryan Nay, teacher
Centreville, Virginia

I've read *Ender's Game* many times, but two times were the most significant. The first time I read the book, I was barely a teenager. Like most teenagers, I felt manipulated by adults, and powerless against them. I saw everything from Ender's eyes and cheered him on when he defied the teachers. The ending was an absolute shock to me at that first reading and I remember feeling hurt, that they would use my good friend, Ender, that way. I didn't understand the love of the game, the desire to win at all costs, and the necessity of what he did. I just wondered, "Why did he stay? Why didn't he just refuse to play?"

The second time *Ender's Game* had more significance to me, I was a parent.

I cried when he was taken from his mother and sister, with him so vulnerable and not knowing what was ahead. I cursed them for making him grow up so fast, taking away all shreds of innocence. I marveled that he survived in such an environment and finally, I understood why the teachers did what they did. They had a higher purpose in mind and he was the way to succeed. His innocence was a necessary sacrifice. I wondered if I could do the same, if my child was the hope of humanity.

Someday my daughters will want to read the copy of *Ender's Game* on my bookshelf and I'm anxious to discuss these ideas with them. They will come up with their own feelings and conclusions about this book and I just hope that I can see it from their perspective.

Jennifer Hahn, mother, musician, and writer
Parker, Colorado

Through the series of novels beginning with *Ender's Game* and ending with *Shadow of the Giant,* I have come to have a much deeper understanding of things that most of my life I have known intellectually to be true but could not find it in my heart to feel in earnest.

Speaker for the Dead taught me that every man, no matter what wrongs he has committed over the course of his life, has done at least something that redeems him of his transgressions, if only a little.

A novel much later in the series built upon this idea. God gives his love freely to all. Card's *Shadow Puppets* taught me that no greater evidence than this is necessary to prove that each man is worthy of the love of his fellow man.

Lance Dodson, IT professional
Oklahoma City, Oklahoma

I'm not sure how my aversion to reading fiction developed. My mother used to devour science fiction novels, and I may have been jealous of her time. Perhaps I felt the enjoyment of fiction was a silly female trait that I didn't wish to be defined by. But by the time I was eighteen, I was an intractable fiction snob. There is not much hope for most of us.

I was a college freshman in 1988, and for reasons that seemed good to them at the time, my parents made me the guardian of my sixteen-year-old brother. We lived in a small Victorian cottage down the hill from the University of Utah, and I made sure he had enough cheese and chocolate milk to survive. We had relatives in the vicinity. Still, I worried about him as I felt it was my duty to. He didn't talk much, particularly about things that I felt were at the center of life.

One autumn day we got an emergency disconnect notice from the gas company. Not having a vehicle and being reticent to venture downtown alone, I recruited my brother to go with me. As we walked, I tried involving him in conversation about school, college plans, and career aspirations, but he didn't have much to say on any of that. Finally I asked him to tell me the story of the book he was reading at the time, which was *Ender's Game*. He asked if I really wanted the story spoiled in case I ever decided to read it. I assured him there was no danger of my ever reading it.

As he explained the plot to me, his reticent manner gave way to an animated intensity. It was like a gossip session about old friends, to hear him recount the adventures of Ender, Bean, Peter, Valentine, and the unfortunate Bonzo. Those things I had feared were not at the center of his life existed, they just didn't revolve around the particular points mine did, such as my parents and their reasons for things seeming good to them. I suppose I got drawn into this center; I was curious to see, as the saying goes, what made him tick. And so I read *Ender's Game* and I found it very lively, and I became a devoted reader of Card and tried other forays into fiction. But *Ender's Game* is there at the center of my literary universe.

When I meet people who don't read much fiction, especially science fiction, I feel sad for them, but hopeful that someday they may trick themselves into trying just a little taste.

Tricia Voss, bookkeeper
Baltimore, Maryland

My dad gave me *Ender's Game* to read when I was in sixth grade. I was skeptical, never having read anything like it before. He guaranteed I'd like it, so I read it, and I am eternally grateful that he showed it to me. *Ender's Game* opened up new worlds. I now knew there were genres other than fantasy and realistic fiction.

I lived in Ender's universe for three years after that, almost until I started high school. I greeted everyone I knew by saying "Ho" and fantasized about Battle School. But more than that, *Ender's Game* opened up my mind. I began wondering about sentient beings on other planets, about space travel, about intelligent viruses that evolved. Things that would never have crossed my mind before now controlled my every thought. *Ender's Game* is the book that changed the way I thought. I began thinking in terms of the universe, and became convinced we were not the only sentient creatures around. But I no longer had the childish notion that "aliens" were green with giant black eyes and a largish head. In fact, I did not even think of them as "aliens" anymore. While they may not be human, they were no longer strange, at least to me.

I was, and I still am, completely comfortable with the thought of other sentient beings and habitable planets. I know Earth cannot be the only one. It has been five years since I first read *Ender's Game,* and I have strayed little from the path it has set me on. While I no longer obsessively quote the book in conversation, I still make references every once in a while when they're relevant. *Ender's Game* is the book that taught me to believe, the book that taught me to question. It changed the way I looked at the world, at the universe. It changed my life, for the better.

Nicole Friedman, student
Trumbull, Connecticut

When I was in high school, I was given the choice of two books to read for an English assignment. I chose *Ender's Game* over *Fahrenheit 451,* mainly because it looked more interesting and was longer (I was a bookworm). I read the book over a weekend, and went on to read it at least a dozen more times over the years. When I met my husband-to-be, I shared it with him and he, too, was fascinated by it. When it came time to name our second child, a little boy, we immediately hit upon "Ender," as we felt that the hero from our favorite book had all of the qualities that we would like our son to have. So, on May 20, 2002, Ender Scott (his daddy's name is Scott) was born into this world. Small for his age, and very intelligent, he "flies" through our house, bouncing off walls, and flipping through space. If I close my eyes, I can almost see his namesake soaring through the battleroom.

Stacy Fluegge, homemaker
West Palm Beach, Florida

I first read *Ender's Game* when I found it on my brother's bookshelf—it must have been shortly after it was published in paperback—and it was a great reading experience that raised the bar for sci-fi for me forever. I didn't think about it too often after that until about fifteen years later while I was deployed with the Army to Kosovo.

We had a rough time on that deployment; I was working in MEDEVAC and wasn't prepared to find that most of our patients were kids and old people, folks like that who are true noncombatants. One day our platoon received a care package from a Boy Scout troop, and in it was a dog-eared copy of *Ender's Game*. I think I actually whooped in delight and took it to the on-call tent and plopped down to read it.

I can't explain why, but *Ender's Game* saved my sanity on that deployment. It was a rough time, and of the many books that I read, only this one really took me away in time and space from the place I was (and didn't want to be). Perhaps it was Ender's plight, being smaller and brighter than everyone around him. Perhaps it was the writing. In any case, I still have that copy of the book (more dog-eared than ever), and reread it every year or two.

S. Corrie Blackshear, military
Fort Leonard Wood, Missouri

I had good reason to be skeptical, I thought, considering that I had never had someone insist that I read a book simply for its quality. A more pressing reason for my doubts was the nagging feeling that I was getting in over my head with the girl who lent it to me, and that that kind of complication was the last thing that my sixteen-year-old self needed.

Still, I read *Ender's Game* with a devouring interest, at first because of its science fiction elements, but later for a much more personal reason. In its covers I found, to my horror and shame, who I really was, and why I was. But unlike many others, who so closely identified with the genius children of space or the kind sister who always loved her younger brother, I found that I was the monster of the beginning of the novel: Ender's terrifying older brother. Though I tried to shake the feeling, I was Peter in all his bristling arrogance, fierce cunning, ambivalence, and rage. I was also Peter in his insecurities, in his dashed hopes and ambitions, in his insatiable hunger for control.

Peter's family felt like my family writ large; for a boy of sixteen who had lost his tender sister to suicide, and had lost his brother to the other house of a broken home, the relationships between the children of the Wiggin household were the terrifyingly familiar beginnings of my own life. I was able to explain for myself how easy it is for the oldest boy to lash out when he had never been taught what to do with a younger brother who was better at most things, and better liked, or to blame others when he had never been taught how to recover from the inevitable failures and losses in life.

The painful and liberating aspect of this story was not that it excused me from what I had done, but it showed me that the pain I caused was real, and that its very reality was itself a source of hope. For the novel's end was in all ways hopeful, but that possibility of redemption was only realized through truth. It is only when Peter tells his story with unvarnished honesty that Ender can understand and forgive him; it would only be possible to find the reconciliation I craved if my brother could fully understand my acts and my motives, my former cruelty with my abiding love for him. It was in just that way that fiction became true, and gave a teenaged boy, reading alone in the near darkness in the spring of the year, hope—hope that personal evils could be purged and cherished relationships reborn. I wanted so desperately for the truth to do for me what it had done for Peter.

And it did.

Jason Wutzke, teacher
Calgary, Alberta, Canada

By the time I was eight years old, the speed at which I could devour books was legend in my family. One day after school my stepfather pulled me aside excitedly to hand me a book he'd just finished and said, "I don't care what you're reading now, I want you to read this." I glanced at the cover, unsure if I would like something that looked so . . . mechanical. Then I opened the book, read the first page, and wandered off to my room without speaking to him.

Two days later I had finished *Ender's Game* and was halfway through rereading it again. Here was a book that spoke to me; it didn't just offer respite, like the books I had read before. In Ender's world, children were flexible and brilliant and fallible and adults were firm within their mistakes—what struck me then (as it does today, twenty years later) was the underlying message of empathy. Be unafraid to think, to speak the way you speak, but never stop loving. Love your enemies, so that you may understand them. At an age when my own emotions confused me only slightly less than those of the adults around me, it was a lesson that would carry me through the turbulent reconstruction of self that adolescence thrust on me, safe to the other side.

Ender's Game first introduced me to the idea that the big people around me had no more knowledge of how to navigate these waters than I did—and that was alright. I could think for myself, discover my own path, and allow us each our own mistakes. After a spectacularly pitiful high school career, it surprised everyone but myself when I began working as a professional programmer at age seventeen. Why not? My first lessons in empathy were from a little boy who grew up inside a machine. Having spent my elementary childhood learning to speak the language of each person I met, to understand them so that I could communicate with them, it seemed like a natural step to learning the language the computer used, that I may understand it.

My mother died two years ago—I am twenty years older than I was when I first took my stepfather's copy of *Ender's Game* from his hands. One of the side effects of the grief of losing her, the most tenacious and limiting, has been my anger at her for leaving. A cold distance from my real memories of her, replaced with questioning blame. Another side effect: this year has been the first since I learned to read in which I did not sit down at some point and lose myself in page after page of enveloping text. I have lost my mother, books have offered me no relief.

So Friday night I dug through boxes and boxes, not looking for anything in particular, just attending to the chore of sifting through another person's lifetime of artifacts, until I found a tattered copy of *Ender's Game* in with toys and clothes my mother packed away years ago. I've had other copies of *Ender's Game* since then, loaned to friends, left on airplanes—I didn't realize the first copy was so near me. I sat down in front of my computer and opened to the first page. Four hours later I was finished and I wept, because something inside me had unclenched and some silvery thread had linked me to the sensitive little girl I once was, linked me to my earliest sensations of my mother who I understood best when my love for her was a child's: unstinting, unanalyzed, unafraid of all the places in which my mother's mistakes have become my own mistakes. I love us both for it.

Brianna Privett, programmer
Crestline, California

ACKNOWLEDGMENTS

This portion of any book seems an awful lot like an acceptance speech at an awards show. However, the people listed here are deserving of my most sincere thanks as they each helped bring this book to pass.

First and foremost, thank you to my wife, Michelle, for giving me the space, time, and ability to research and write the encyclopedia of the Ender Universe. During this time, our son, Jonas, was born, cut his first teeth, and even started walking. Without Michelle's support for me and her care for our son, this book would never have happened.

Kathleen Bellamy deserves as much credit as anyone. She consulted with me on points in the manuscript and has been a patient colleague and aide as I brought the manuscript to its finished form. She must also be thanked for securing the graphics that augment the entries.

Kristine Card was also incredibly sweet and unwaveringly positive as we put the *Companion* together.

Aaron Johnston was a terrific resource when it came to questions about Hyrum Graff, about whom he is cowriting a novel, as well as the *Ender's Game* movie.

Ami Chopine and Andy Wahr provided invaluable clarifications on items from the Ender Universe I didn't catch, making the encyclopedia as accurate as possible.

Nick Lowe, Jordan White, and Lauren Sankovitch at Marvel Comics were the first real tests of the *Companion*'s usefulness as they edited the *Ender's Game* comics. They helped me make sure I knew what I was talking about.

Thank you to Beth Meacham at Tor for believing in this project, and getting it launched at the San Diego Comic-Con in 2007.

Brad Meltzer reinforced my sometimes-shaky confidence in heroic fashion. I will be forever in his debt.

Thanks to Chris Cerasi, a friend always and a championing force in my life and career. And also to Jordan Hamessley for her commitment to all things Ender.

Finally, thank you to Orson Scott Card for inviting me over to play with his toys.

—J.B.